Daughters *of* War

Dinah Jefferies began her career with *The Separation*, followed by the No.1 *Sunday Times* and Richard and Judy bestseller, *The Tea-Planter's Wife*. Born in Malaysia, she moved to England at the age of nine, and went on to study fashion design, work in Tuscany as an *au pair* for an Italian countess, and live with a rock band in a commune in Suffolk.

In 1985, a family tragedy changed everything, and she now draws on the experience of loss in her writing, infusing love, loss and danger with the seductive beauty of her locations. She is now published in 29 languages in over 30 countries and lives close to her family in Gloucestershire.

To find out more about Dinah Jefferies:

www.dinahjefferies.com
www.facebook.com/dinahjefferiesbooks
@DinahJefferies

Also by Dinah Jefferies

The Separation
The Tea Planter's Wife
The Silk Merchant's Daughter
Before the Rains
The Sapphire Widow
The Missing Sister
The Tuscan Contessa

DINAH JEFFERIES

Daughters *of* War

HarperCollins*Publishers*

HarperCollins*Publishers*
1 London Bridge Street
London SE1 9GF

www.harpercollins.co.uk

HarperCollins*Publishers*
1st Floor, Watermarque Building, Ringsend Road
Dublin 4, Ireland

Published by HarperCollins*Publishers* 2021
1

A catalogue record for this book is available from the British Library

ISBN: 978-0-00-842702-3 (PB)
ISBN: 978-0-00-845870-6 (TPB, AU, NZ, CA-only)
ISBN: 978-0-00-848787-4 (HB, US, CA-only)
ISBN: 978-0-00-847941-1 (PB, US-only)

Typeset in Dante MT by Palimpsest Book Production Ltd, Falkirk, Stirlingshire

Printed and Bound in the UK using 100% Renewable Electricity at
CPI Group (UK) Ltd

MIX
Paper from
responsible sources
FSC C007454

This book is produced from independently certified FSC™ paper to ensure responsible forest management.

For more information visit: www.harpercollins.co.uk/green

For my sister, the sisters in my own family,
and all the sisters in my extended family.

CHAPTER 1

THE PÉRIGORD NOIR, FRANCE

SPRING 1944

Hélène

If only it was late summer, and she could smell the sun-soaked scent of fir and spruce and be able to stand and watch the finches and starlings flitting between the branches. Her optimism might have outweighed the claustrophobic sensation of life leaning in, of ancient lichen-covered stone houses enclosing her as she walked through the village and the light began to fail. And maybe then she would remember they were all just ordinary people trying to make the best of impossible circumstances. Ordinary people longing for the return of a normal life.

Hélène craved daylight, to see more than what lay before her. She needed it to see into the distance, into the future, into her own heart. She needed it like others needed air. But she told herself, when all of this was over, she would still have her whole life before her. Why worry about the worst thing when it might never happen? And surely there would be better news from the Allies soon?

As she left the edge of the village, she glanced up at the indigo sky and heard the early night birds shuffling in the trees. She thought of her sisters, here in France, and her mother in England. Once, when she'd asked her mother if she was pretty like her sister Élise, her mother had said, 'Darling, you have a comfortable face. People like comfortable faces. They don't feel threatened by faces like yours.'

Hélène was only eleven at the time and her mother's comment had hurt her. She had gazed into the mirror for half an hour after that and hadn't known what to make of her face. She had prodded and poked at it, pulled different expressions, pouted, smiled, grimaced, and then told herself it didn't matter. But it had been a lie. It *had* mattered. And now? Her face had matured. She was tall, athletic, with a strong constitution just as her father used to have, but she also had his straight, light brown hair. Ordinary hair. It rankled, but her mother had been right, her features *were* too strong to be pretty, although people admired her kind nut-brown eyes and warm smile. She was the most pragmatic of the three sisters, the eldest, the most responsible. Was it terribly shallow to long for someone to tell her she was beautiful?

The war was a fight between good and evil, people said – although it wasn't always certain which was which. And now her job had become more challenging than she'd ever dreamt. She had enormous respect for her boss, Hugo

Marchand, the town doctor and mayor, and she adored his warm-hearted wife, Marie, a generous soul who always saw the best in people and had been a mother figure to the sisters. But the things Hélène witnessed, the things she heard – the lies, the little deceits, the deeds she could never mention – all of them she'd rather not have known.

After crossing a small field edged by wild poppies, she headed through a walnut grove, picking her way to avoid the waddling geese, until she eventually reached the track and her own gate. She frowned to see the worn wooden gate had been left open.

They never did that.

Their higgledy-piggledy farmhouse seemed to have grown out of the land naturally, its hand-hewn limestone walls soaking up the sunlight so by early evening they glowed, golden and honeyed. She passed the chestnut tree in the garden and glanced up at the foliage-draped façade. The vines remained undisturbed, cascading around the front door just as she'd left them, too early yet for the violet passion flowers she loved. Two medium-sized shuttered windows painted dusky blue flanked the oak door and as the wind got up and the creaky wooden shutters moaned in complaint, she shivered.

She burst through the door, hurrying into the kitchen to drop her bag on the table. From the huge roughhewn beams above her, herbs hung to dry: rosemary, lavender, bay, mint, sage, thyme and more. Hélène raised her head and breathed in their familiar scent, before unlacing her shoes and abandoning them on the flagstone floor hollowed in well-worn patches from centuries of passing feet. Hélène liked to imagine who had been there before her, and on dark nights it wasn't difficult to imagine their shadows still collecting in the gloomier corners of the house along with the cobwebs. But most people were living in the shadows, one way or another, and not just the dead. She shivered again and glanced at the huge fireplace with its carved stone surround; even in spring the house could be chilly in the evening, but the wood burner hadn't been lit.

Back in the hall she thought she heard someone at the top of the house.

'Hello,' she called out. 'Florence. Is that you?'

No reply.

'Élise, are you home?'

CHAPTER 2

Hélène paused for a moment and looked around, feeling uncertain. She was about to go into the sitting room – just in case – when she spotted Élise struggling down the stairs with a bulky bundle, her body tipping back slightly to counterbalance its weight. As usual she was wearing dark, wide-legged trousers, along with a faded blue jumper and brown lace-up boots. With long dark wavy hair and huge expressive eyes, the colour of cognac, she looked just like their mother. Relieved now to see her, Hélène let out her breath.

'You're back early,' Élise said, but then glanced down at her wristwatch. 'Oh, not so early.'

'You left the gate open.'

'I think it might have been Florence.'

'It gave me a scare . . .'

Despite her huge bundle, Élise managed a shrug.

'So, what's that you've got?'

'Just some bits and pieces for a new safe house.' Élise tilted her head to one side and narrowed her eyes at Hélène. 'Do you know you have paint in your hair? Rather a lot, actually.'

'Oh God, really?' Hélène stepped back to glance in the hall mirror and saw the tell-tale white streaks running through her hair and a delicate splatter on her left cheek.

In their hallway, oil paintings and posters peppered the walls, and framed pictures the girls had drawn as children were displayed together. The large mirror, into which Hélène was now frowning, with its ornate carving of grapes and trailing vine leaves, had reflected their faces most of their lives. They were either held up by their mother, Claudette, when they were small, to grin and laugh at their own expressions or, as now, they glanced at it for a quick check of their hair. There was also an older, yellowing photograph pinned there; a shot of their mother with her sister Rosalie not long before she had run away. All three sisters felt the history of the house, the sense of family, and of roots, and nowhere more so than here.

'So how was work?' Élise asked.

'Hugo had me painting the walls of the cottage hospital this afternoon. It hasn't been done for years and, as there are no patients checked in at the moment, it seemed the right time to tackle it.'

'Well, your *extensive* nursing training at the Sarlat Hospital has clearly gone to good use! Umm . . .' She scratched the side of her head in mock contemplation. 'How long was it now?'

Hélène laughed. 'Three long years. And you know it.

Anyway, I actually enjoyed the painting today.' She paused then picked up on what her sister had said. 'Why a new safe house?'

'The Germans are getting edgy. And an edgy Nazi is an even more dangerous Nazi. The Resistance is making sure there are enough places to hide out.'

'I wish you would just lie low like the rest of us. Honestly, Élise, you're putting us all in danger of Nazi reprisals.'

Her sister did not reply.

Hélène gazed at her but, knowing nothing was going to change Élise, she gave up and glanced around. 'So, where *is* Florence? I'm assuming she's not out playing daredevil too.'

Élise pulled a dismissive face. 'Hardly. She's still in the garden. Watering now, I think. Oh, I nearly forgot, there's a letter on the table.'

'You forgot?' Hélène said with an incredulous look as she glanced down. Receiving any kind of mail was so rare she hadn't even thought to look.

'It's addressed to you.'

Hélène picked it up. 'Geneva postmark.'

'Open it then.'

'Let's wait for Florence. We can read it together.'

Hélène knew it would be from their mother, Claudette. The only way they could receive post from England was if their mother sent it to her friend Yvonne, in neutral Geneva, who would then slip it into another envelope and post it on to them. She heard the back door opening and made her way to the kitchen with Élise.

Florence stood by the door. Petite with a heart-shaped

face, alabaster skin and gunmetal grey-blue eyes, her skirts were muddy, her golden blonde hair floated wildly around her head and her cheeks were pink with the exertion of a day spent in the garden. More delicately feminine than her sisters, she had insisted on stitching herself dresses and skirts, which she wore even when digging.

Hélène held up the letter.

'Ooh, finally! From Maman?'

'Probably.'

Hélène slit open the envelope and glanced at the letter. After a few moments, she spread her hands and let the letter flutter onto the table.

'Well,' Florence said eagerly, 'What does she say?'

'Almost nothing. Read it yourself.'

Florence picked it up but looked a little disappointed as she read, then handed it to Élise.

'Well,' Élise said, after a moment. 'How utterly enthralling!'

'Don't be sarcastic about Maman,' Florence said.

Hélène sighed, but understood how Élise felt. Their mother had written only a few lines commenting on how busy she was being kept with the war effort. How she had joined the WI and was mainly knitting and making jam. She had barely asked how the girls were coping, had not mentioned how difficult it must be for them living under occupation, and had mainly complained about her noisy neighbours and how hard life in England was, what with rationing and all.

'At least she wrote,' Florence said.

Élise just turned away and, shrugging, left the room.

CHAPTER 3

Hélène was pensive as she threw open her bedroom window the next morning to listen to the church bells. Thank goodness it was Sunday and she didn't have to go to work. She loved gazing at the magical view over their part of the Dordogne or, as their mother always called it, the *Périgord Noir*. It was a land of oak and pine trees, rocky gorges and clifftop castles and the prettiest villages you'd ever see, their limestone buildings soft and buttery. She watched as the sun broke through the early-morning mist to reveal the silvery shine on the river and golden sunlight bathing the rooftops of the village. Spring was well and truly here, and the air was as fresh and clear as crystal.

'We will have fun here, won't we, Hélène?' Florence had asked seven years before, when they'd first moved to their mother's old family summer home down a winding track, just outside the village of Sainte-Cécile.

Poor Florence had only been fifteen back then and

Hélène had needed to keep reminding herself her sister was still a child as she found herself in *loco parentis*.

'We will visit the castles and the caves?' the girl had added.

'We will. Of course we will,' Hélène had replied, desperate to try to protect her sister's innocent world view.

All of their lives had changed irrevocably following the sudden and unexpected death of their father, Charles Baudin.

As a child, their mother had spent many of her holidays in Sainte-Cécile, as well as summer breaks during the earlier years of her marriage when their father had been at home, working. He was half-English and half-French and before his death had worked as a civil servant in the Foreign Office in London. Everyone here in the village knew 'Maman' of old, which had made it easier for the sisters to slot into the community, although there were still a few who didn't approve and continued to tut and fuss about three girls living alone.

Élise popped her head through the door of Hélène's room. 'Just off to the café.'

Hélène looked right into her eyes. 'On a Sunday?'

'I'm only going for a few minutes.'

'Aren't you afraid?'

'Of course. From the moment I wake up until I go to sleep. Anyone who says they aren't afraid is lying.'

'Oh Élise, you will be careful.'

Élise laughed. 'You are an old worryguts.'

Hélène tilted her head to one side. 'It's the glamour, isn't it? Gives you a kick.'

'Course not. Resistance is dangerous, not glamorous. If you knew the men and women, you'd see.'

'I'm sorry, I didn't mean—'

Frowning in exasperation, Élise interrupted her. 'They have to hide out in horrible places. Hungry. Cold. Remember the freezing temperatures we had in the winter?'

'Élise, please.'

'And when I deliver weapons hidden beneath potatoes in my shopping bag, I'm in more danger than if I was bearing those arms against the enemy.'

Hélène sighed. 'That's exactly my worry.'

Élise stalked over to the door and then twisted back to glare at her sister.

'I said I was sorry.'

Élise ignored her. 'And people think we're bandits. Terrorists. No, Hélène, it is not glamorous.'

As Élise slammed the front door behind her, Hélène's mood darkened. She hated falling out with Élise and hadn't meant to make light of her work, but her sister in a querulous mood was hard to handle. As she stood there, feeling rather at a loss, she heard a wail coming from Florence's room. She sighed at the total disintegration of her peaceful morning, threw on her robe and went to her sister's aid. Florence was hunched up in the corner of the room, her face even paler than usual. The window was open and the light muslin curtains were blowing slightly in the breeze.

Florence looked dazed as she turned towards Hélène. 'Did you hear it?'

'Sorry. Didn't hear a thing.'

'I think it was a *demoiselle.*'

Hélène only just stopped herself from rolling her eyes. She had little time for her sister's dreams and fantasies.

'Florence,' she said firmly. 'Wake up. There's no such thing. Those forest fairies of yours aren't real. They're damselflies. You heard a noise outside, nothing more.'

'Did I? I thought I saw her. Dressed in white. She sat at the bottom of my bed.'

'If they were real, which they are not, they'd only live in caves and grottos.' She laughed, not unkindly, and held out her hand to her sister. 'They wouldn't come and sit on an ordinary person's bed.'

The muscles around Florence's eyes constricted but then relaxed. She took Hélène's hand and rose to her feet. 'You're right, of course. But I thought I heard her whispering.'

'Whispering what?'

'Horrible things,' Florence muttered.

'It was only a dream. You know?'

Florence hung her head. 'Yes. Sorry.'

Her youngest sister had matured these past few years, but could still be fragile and sensitive, retaining the naiveté that characterised her as a child.

'Just forget it,' Hélène added and gave Florence a hug. 'Get dressed and perhaps we can make some crêpes. We've still got lemons and honey.'

'They make the wind, you know?'

'Who do?'

'Oh, Hélène, the *demoiselles*, of course. And they can calm it too . . . Well, that's what I read anyway.'

Hélène bit back her irritation, but then it flared up

anyway. 'For heaven's sake, Florence. It's an old wives' tale from Lourdes. Now come on, buck up.'

'Where's Élise gone?' Florence asked. 'I heard the front door.'

'Opening her damn 'letter box' of course. I wish she'd stop.'

'She won't. She believes in what she's doing, like you. You believe in nursing.' Florence gave her a curious look. 'You do, don't you?'

Hélène walked to the door and thought about it. Did she?

'Hélène?'

She glanced over her shoulder. 'Sometimes, I think you're the only one doing what you believe in.'

'Gardening and cooking aren't things you believe in. They're just something to do.'

'But you *are* doing what you love.'

'I suppose . . .'

Now Hélène was luxuriating in a rare half hour to herself, reading *The Hour Before the Dawn*, a novel by Somerset Maugham. She had no sooner reached the conclusion that Dora had to be a Nazi spy, which was far too close for comfort, and was thinking about trying an Agatha Christie instead, when she heard Florence calling. Oh, blow it! Reluctantly relinquishing her book, Hélène stood up.

Just beyond the back door, the acacia tree had blossomed, its delicate jasmine-like scent floating on the breeze. Hélène took a leisurely breath of mild spring air, then moved across the little terrace which was surrounded by a low stone wall. She continued down the stone steps and along the snaking path Florence had marked when she first designed the garden.

Her sister, looking red-faced, was jiggling up and down next to a cluster of pink and purple wild orchids at the bottom of the garden, clutching a spade. Her blonde curls dusted her shoulders and were pinned back at either side of her temples, yet despite that she still looked wild.

'What now?' Hélène asked. 'I *was* reading.'

With a perplexed expression on her face, Florence fastened her eyes on Hélène. 'There's something here.'

'You're always digging up old stuff.'

'This is different. It looks meant. Hidden, I mean. I wasn't intending to dig so deeply, but the ground was already loose.' She dug the spade in again to demonstrate.

'Crikey. Is it a grave?'

'God, I hope not. I wondered why the earth had already been turned over, so I carried on. It looked recent, as if the visible ground had just been covered with stones, so once I started it was easy to go deeper.'

Hélène peered into the hole and saw the edge of a large metal container or cannister.

'Let's get it out.'

'I tried. It's too heavy.'

'Give me the spade.'

Florence passed the spade over and Hélène began to dig around the box, so they'd be able to get a better grasp of it. After a few minutes, heart pumping from the effort, she stood back and pushed the damp hair from her eyes. 'There. That should do it.'

Together they pulled at the box, which was heavier and bigger than they'd first thought, and eventually managed to lift it out of the ground and pull it up onto the grassy bank.

'Let's drag it up to the house.' Florence said. 'But can you hang on a minute? I want to cut some of the acacia flowers first. Lucille is coming later today, and I thought we'd have them then. She's going to do my hair. And the strawberries are ready too. The *Gariguettes*. I'll make a strawberry tart.'

Hélène's mouth watered, though pastry made with hardly any wheat flour was rather like cardboard. Florence also grew Charlotte strawberries, wonderful with thick cream. Hélène stared into the distance imagining it. They had no thick cream.

Lucille Dubois was Florence's red-haired friend who, with her mother, ran a small hairdressing salon in Sarlat. Lucille and Florence were as thick as thieves, but the girl's mother, Sandrine, had long been a supporter of the Vichy regime and believed collaboration was the only way through this war. '*There is no better way to show patriotism to our beloved France than to support Vichy*,' she was fond of proclaiming. Hélène and Élise were contemptuous of the Vichy supporters who would happily kiss the collective German arse. She was unsure of Lucille's views. At nineteen she was pretty and curvaceous like her mother, with rosebud lips and the creamiest complexion with just a light dusting of freckles across her nose and on her cheeks. Perhaps a little silly and empty-headed, she giggled a lot and loved a good gossip, but Florence adored her, so they painted each other's nails and Lucille trimmed Florence's hair.

'Chérie, because of what Élise is doing, Lucille can't come at the moment,' Hélène said, in a voice that brooked no argument.

'She wouldn't say anything.'

'Listen, instead of Lucille coming, why don't you and I try on some of Maman's hats?'

'Where are they? I haven't seen them for ages.'

'In the attic somewhere.'

Florence picked her acacia blossom and then they turned back to the metal box. It was too heavy to drag easily over the bumpy ground, but Hélène had no difficulty lifting the lid. She frowned when she saw the contents.

'What is it?' Florence asked. 'Looks just like a row of wrapped up sausages.'

Hélène cautiously unwrapped the calico covering of one of the 'sausages'. 'Oh, for God's sake,' she said, grimacing.

Florence peered at it. 'Is it plasticine? Weird grey colour.'

They stared at the assortment of pens and wires and other paraphernalia.

'So, what's it all for?' Florence asked.

'Explosives. This is what they use to make explosives.'

CHAPTER 4

Hélène was taking her anger out on the garlic and herbs she was pounding with a pestle. The three of them were sitting at the kitchen table helping Florence prepare a rabbit stew. They rarely ate, if at all, their favourite *cassoulet, noisettes de' agneau* or *coq au vin* these days. Élise was rubbing mustard all over the jointed rabbit, which would then be left for a few hours before slow-cooking the next day. Florence was peeling potatoes.

Finishing her task, Élise leant back on her chair and put her feet up on the table.

Hélène exploded. 'Honestly, Élise! How many times? Do you want to break another chair? And we *are* preparing food here.'

'Sorry,' Élise muttered, not looking a bit sorry, but she removed her feet from the table and straightened up, all the same.

'So?' Hélène asked as she glanced up from her job, still

annoyed by her sister's insouciant attitude. 'Are you still in contact with Victor? I'm assuming it was he who asked you to bury the explosives.'

'Of course. He saved my life.'

'You don't know that.'

'Well he saved me from being held at knifepoint.'

Hélène gazed down at the table to hide the dampness in her eyes. She reached out to squeeze Élise's hand. 'And the Maquis are properly active again, even after what's happened?'

'Especially after what's happened.'

The Resistance was known locally as the Maquis. They'd fought back against the German occupiers, but many had died and there had been dreadful Nazi reprisals. After the shock of those weeks when the German Brehmer division and the BNA or *Brigade Nord Africain* had rained terror across the Dordogne, Hélène and her sisters were at last regaining some emotional stability. Hélène had first seen the paramilitary BNA in Sarlat's main square, a bragging, strutting mercenary group. Violent thugs, they later found out, formed from the Paris underworld. Some had come from Morocco, but most were native Frenchmen born and bred. They wore wide belts with genuine Waffen SS buckles, navy-blue berets, dark boiler suits and sheepskin jackets. Heavily armed with machine guns, they carried pockets full of grenades which they scattered like confetti. They were evil men, who raped, killed, and tortured, indifferent to the suffering of others. They arrested civilians and Maquis alike, executed whoever they wanted, burnt homes and farmsteads, stole everything they fancied, and were hated by almost everyone. But not the collaborators, she reminded herself. Oh no. These BNA men had been let loose in the Dordogne because the Gestapo and police had been unable to control the activities of the Resistance. The Maquis had exploded bridges, blocked tunnels, attacked German military units and blown up storage depots. The BNA and the Brehmer division was the Nazi revenge.

'I heard they're back,' Élise said, her voice unnaturally flat.

As Hélène recalled the day Victor had brought Élise home, her face bruised and her eyes wild with rage. Florence shivered then put her fingers in her ears. 'La la la,' she intoned, and Hélène gave Élise a look that implied *we need to change the subject*.

For as long as she reasonably could, Hélène had hoped to create a world where the war would not encroach too heavily on the lives of the sisters. She had mainly kept them safe, but ever since the day that Élise's life had been threatened, her sister had no longer been willing to stay out of the Resistance effort.

Élise held up her hands. 'All right. I'll get rid of the explosives, but now let's do the acacia fritter thing, the oil should be hot enough.'

Florence brightened instantly. 'Call a good thing by its proper name. It's called *beignets de fleurs d'acacia*.' She had already washed the clusters of flowers and put them in a bowl with sugar and a few drops of what was left of their Armagnac. Now she prepared the batter, mixing a little of their precious flour, egg, milk and some water, and then she dipped the blossoms into the mix. After deep-frying them, she sprinkled them with sugar and the sisters happily devoured the lot.

Their house had always been a house of happiness, though a little damp when they'd first arrived, and the garden had been a wilderness. Now, especially when Florence concocted these treats for them, these wartime evenings meant so much. Being cloistered like this after curfew brought them closer and it helped push back the now endemic fear. Back at the beginning, they'd known nothing of waiting and praying, of fearing the worst, and lying awake at night with no idea what the morning would bring. And even after July 1940, when their country had been invaded and defeated by Nazi Germany, and France had been split into two regions, they had still not suffered an Axis military presence. Not until the Nazis also occupied their so-called free zone in November 1942. Then that was it; Vichy France was occupied too. And then the invasion and demoralisation of their world had become complete. It had been a devastating blow.

'Hélène and I are going to try on Maman's hats,' Florence said, glancing at Élise as she was wiping a trace of crispy batter from her lips. 'You want to join in?'

While Hélène and Élise went up to the attic to find the hats, Florence remained in the kitchen to take care of the washing up. With an attached pantry and laundry, painted blue cupboards, and ancient pine table with a mismatch of wooden chairs, the kitchen had always been the heart of the house and Florence loved it.

On the ground floor was the main hallway from which

rose the impressive staircase, the 'drawing room' which their mother always insisted was the correct term, though for the sisters it was usually just a 'sitting room'. Hélène rarely played their upright piano as the piano tuner had gone to war in 1939, so it was now completely out of tune. There was also a small study, and another room the girls used as their sewing room and office, which led to what had once been the servant's staircase.

When they first arrived, the sisters had made striped blue-and-white curtains and pretty lampshades and scatter cushions of every colour. Nothing matched. Classic, richly coloured Persian rugs, most of which their mother had bought years before, lay on the uneven oak floorboards of their bedrooms, and paler flat-woven French Aubusson rugs with elegant, flowing, floral patterns belonged in the sitting room.

Now, at the top of the stairs, Hélène shoved and pushed and eventually managed to release the ladder up into the dusty attic to look for their mother's hats. Then she and Élise climbed up. Prior to their arrival, so much junk had already been stored in the attic that – save for looking for any important paperwork – they'd never felt the urge to sort it out properly. They decided to make a start by looking inside a couple of large trunks in case the hats were there. As Hélène lifted the lid, she saw the first trunk seemed to contain mainly kitchenware and no hats at all. All the same, she dug out a yellow enamelled jug, rusting at the edges, a set of blue-and-yellow striped *café au lait* bowls, two ancient decorative charcuterie platters, a set of six light blue enamel canisters, a typical French butter dish or crock and some hand-thrown stoneware. Then Hélène lifted out a porcelain chamber pot decorated with pink roses around its rim.

'Roses. How nice. Pity they can't mask the smell.'

They both laughed.

Élise bent over the trunk. 'Look. There's heaps of copper stuff in here too.'

She handed Hélène a copper coffee pot, then an old cafetière, a large jam pot, and a kettle. 'Florence will love these once they're cleaned up.'

'Florence loves anything old,' Hélène said as she worked, although she valued Florence's work in the kitchen and in their garden. Florence grew most of their food, cooked their meals, made their gorgeous strawberry jam and their scented soap too. Meat, pasta, sugar and bread were all rationed, but as long as the Nazis didn't requisition their produce – or know what they had hidden – the girls were relatively well fed. Florence hid their seed potatoes under a water barrel in the laundry and had created more hiding places for their eggs and other precious foods outside, a crime for which she could be arrested. Men were allowed cigarette coupons and four litres of wine a month, but chocolate was like gold dust. Hélène would have given anything for chocolate. Butter was highly prized, and Florence made rather thin – but pure – white butter from their goats' milk, cheese too, and concocted remedies from herbs she grew, which was why Hélène and Élise affectionately referred to her as their 'little witch'.

Élise picked out an ancient cooking basin and a

ceramic wine jug. 'And I could use these in the café,' she added.

Hélène sighed. 'You're opening properly again? I didn't realise. Isn't that a bit mad?'

'Be mad not to,' Élise said, meeting her gaze but then changing the touchy subject. 'Shall we lower all this in baskets? I'll nip down and get a couple.'

As Hélène watched her sister go, anxiety lodged inside her. She had prayed her sister would not go down this route again, or at least just let it be a café and nothing more. She distracted herself by opening the top drawer of an old chest. Some fraying linens, a blue woollen blanket and some worn towels were neatly folded inside it. The second drawer contained more of the same, but in the third she spotted swathes of discoloured tissue paper and, wrapped inside, something red and shiny. She pulled gently and when it revealed itself, she whistled. A crimson dress, silky to the touch. She ran her fingers over it, caressing the fabric as she held it up. Too small for her. The strapless bodice was still intact and beautifully boned, but as she lifted it, the long skirt fell into dozens of ribbons, lifting and floating as she held it against her body. The skirt had been sliced and sliced, over and over.

Élise's head appeared at the top of the ladder. 'Gracious, where did you find that?'

Hélène pointed at the chest of drawers as her sister fully entered the attic, then she held the dress out. 'It's been cut. Destroyed.' She shook her head. 'Try it up against you.'

Élise took it and held it against herself, then she smiled. 'My size.'

'Yes.'

'Let's get these two baskets filled and show the stuff to Florence.'

'We haven't found the hats.'

'Maybe later. I'll take the dress downstairs . . .' Her voice trailed off and she paused for a moment. 'Hélène, are you all right?'

Hélène was standing motionless and staring into the distance, feeling bewildered and a bit dazed.

'Hélène?'

Hélène blinked. 'I . . .'

'What happened? You looked weird.'

'I felt scared suddenly.'

'Why?'

'Not sure. Something came back to me.'

'From when?'

'A long time ago. I was on my own in the dark. I think I may have seen the dress before.'

'Here, in France?'

'I don't know.'

CHAPTER 5

Florence

The next couple of days were stunningly beautiful and warm, too. Florence had decided she would dig up a new patch of the garden currently overrun by brambles. She loved the garden, especially with summer on its way, when it would be overflowing with fruit: apples, pears, figs and plums, although she had to promptly bottle everything and hide it from German patrols in search of food. Once she had closed the door, she pruned a little of the honeysuckle climbing the back wall of the house. Nothing evoked summer as much as the intoxicating scent of honeysuckle, and soon the wall would be swathed in clusters of golden flowers.

She walked down the path, the sound of a chirping house sparrow following her, then slid down a sharp slope leading to stony ground at the bottom of the garden – an area hidden from the house and largely left to go wild. They could always do with more vegetables and the Nazis would never notice anything she grew down there, so would be unlikely to seize it. The starlings were singing, and a soft breeze blew the long grasses about. She filled her lungs with gorgeous fresh air and felt energised as she watched a buzzard flying overhead as it headed towards the whistling call of another. A pair of brown and white butterflies hovered over the wild red poppies, the candytuft too, now a beautiful deep lilac, and the subtler looking, but more pungent, spike lavender. Nothing made her happier than looking forward to when the meadows would be full of lavender and heather.

She felt grateful to be alive, watching the butterflies, enchanted at feeling the true spirit of the place unspoilt by war. She never wanted to leave. Of course, she was sick of the war like everyone else, but she relished every moment of peace that came her way. She threw her arms up in the air and whirled around and didn't mind her sisters thinking her whimsical. Bewitched by the sounds of a phantom orchestra, she danced as if she were Titania, in a pale flowing gown, surrounded by Peaseblossom, Cobweb, Moth and Mustardseed. *A Midsummer Night's Dream* had always been her favourite Shakespeare play and the Queen of the Fairies her favourite character.

But she could be dogged too, so after a few moments of glorying in her dream world, she put on her most robust gardening gloves and began pulling back the brambles and removing stones. Before long, feeling boiling hot, she glanced about to ensure nobody was in sight, peeled off her blouse, then stripped down to her underskirt.

Once the brambles and most of the stones were gone, she began to dig. She had covered only about a metre of the patch when she heard someone cough. She straightened up and froze when she spotted a young clean-cut, blonde man looking at her from the track running along the bottom of the garden, a blackbird hopping around a rucksack at his feet. This was the track the hunters, with their sights on wild boar and deer, used before the war, their tall hunting platforms now sometimes hijacked by the Maquis as lookout posts. From the look of his immaculate clothes, she was certain he was neither a hunter, nor a maquisard. Feeling the heat of the sun on the back of her neck, she grabbed the blouse and skirt she had cast off so recklessly, then lifted her hair and retied her ponytail.

He turned away while she dressed.

When she was ready, he smiled and held out a bottle. 'Lemonade. Do have some.'

She stared at him in confusion.

'I won't bite,' he said, and she saw he had beautiful blue eyes the colour of a summer sky.

When he could see she was not responding, he backed away. 'I'm so sorry. Forgive me. I am disturbing you. You just looked so hot.' Fluent as his French was, Florence heard something in his accent and frowned.

'Are you German?' she asked.

He seemed to gulp before he spoke. 'I'm afraid so.'

'Your French—'

He interrupted. 'I know. I'm a translator. It's in my interest to speak good French . . . my love for the language is now the only way I manage to keep away from the front lines.' He looked around them. 'Your garden?'

She hesitated before speaking. Was this wise? Could he be after information or something? But then she saw the candid expression in his eyes. There was nothing wrong in talking to him, surely? 'Me and my sisters live here,' she eventually said. 'I'm the gardener though. And thank you. I would love some lemonade.'

He passed her the bottle and they both sat on a fallen tree trunk. She drank deeply then passed it back to him.

He sniffed the air. 'Lemon verbena, I think.'

'Yes.' She pointed at the lime-green leaves of the plant just a few feet from where they sat. 'You know your plants?' she asked.

'I am a keen gardener. It runs in the family. I could help you,' he said, pointing at the spade. 'If you have another one.'

'Really? I do have a digging fork.'

'Excellent. Together we will break the back.'

She laughed. 'I hope not literally.'

Then she rose to her feet, nipped up to the shed and within a couple of minutes was handing him the fork.

He took off his jacket, rolled up his shirtsleeves and, as they began working together, Florence examined her feelings. Here he was, a stranger *and* a German, offering to help and she had accepted. People would think she was mad. She paused mid-dig and glanced at his well-scrubbed hands. His hands, with long, elegant fingers and neatly cut nails, didn't look as if they were accustomed to manual work.

He noticed. 'Anything wrong?'

'I'm just trying to decide if you're going to murder me and chop me up into little pieces with my spade.'

He laughed. 'How did you guess?'

She shook her head. 'Let's get this finished.'

For another hour they carried on in what felt like companionable silence.

When he straightened up, he took a long slow breath and rubbed his shoulder muscles, his face red now from the physical exertion.

'Shall we sit in the shade?' he asked.

'Let's. Any more lemonade?' They may not be able to enjoy everything they'd once had, she thought, but she was going to make the best of things.

He dug in his rucksack and came up with another bottle. 'I have sandwiches too.'

'You came prepared.'

'I like to walk in the countryside, and I have a few days off.'

'Lucky for me. Shall we go into the woods? It'll be much cooler.'

They meandered through the dappled sunshine, passing scatterings of periwinkles and wood anemones until they reached Florence's favourite picnic place. The girls had found the clearing long ago and had constructed a roughly hewn table and bench. The beauty of it was that at any time of day, it remained cool.

'It's beautiful here all year round,' she said. 'But I think my favourite might be autumn when you find swathes of tiny pink cyclamen carpeting the woods.'

He smiled then glanced back into the trees and, hearing something, put a finger to his lips.

'A roe deer, I think,' he said after a moment, and then unpacked the picnic from his rucksack.

'I've been looking out for a civet cat. Some people claim to have seen them, but I haven't. Plenty of foxes, badgers and rabbits. Weasels and stoats too.'

Florence felt an affinity with the woodland animals, sometimes even imagining that their wild energy coursed through her own veins. As a child in Richmond, she'd tried to save an injured fox, but sadly it had died and she'd been inconsolable.

'Do you fish in the river?' he asked, interrupting her thoughts.

'Yes, although I'm not too good at it. My sister is better.'

He tilted his head as he looked at her. 'I like to fish.'

'So,' she said, between mouthfuls of a rather good cheese baguette. 'Where do you come from in Germany? Do you live in the countryside?'

'We are from Munich, but my favourite place in Germany is Lichtenstein Castle in Baden-Württemberg. People call it the fairy-tale castle of Württemberg. It's built on the edge of a cliff and overlooks the Echaz valley.'

She smiled at his choice. 'You must be a romantic, I think.'

He inclined his head as if to say *perhaps*.

'Where else is beautiful in Germany? I've never been and I'm afraid most of us French think it must be a very ugly country.'

His eyes looked sad. 'I understand,' he said quietly.

'Do you?'

'I think I do. Not every German is a Nazi.'

She thought about it. Of course, there had to be Germans who weren't fascists and who didn't agree with what Hitler was doing.

'So why aren't you?' she asked. 'A Nazi, I mean.'

He looked up at the sky as if in search of an answer.

'Looking for castles in the air?' she said. 'Or avoiding the question?'

His blue eyes sparked in response and she felt so drawn to him. Despite everything she knew about the Nazis, she felt sure he was different. He was gentle, sensitive, *and* he loved animals and gardens. Her sisters would not approve, and she had to question herself too, but a man like that couldn't be vicious and cruel like the rest of them.

'Well,' he continued. 'I love my country just as you must love yours, but I cannot condone what is happening.'

She understood. It must be hard to tread such an uncomfortable line. She changed the subject. 'Have you been to Beynac castle? It's one of the most famous of the Périgord and was the stronghold of us French during the Hundred Years war.'

He shook his head. 'Maybe you could show Beynac to me?' he suggested.

She hesitated.

'Sorry, I am, of course, being too forward. Anyway, it

has been so lovely to meet you. By the way, I'm Anton,' he said, extending his hand and rising to his feet.

She stood and shook his hand. 'Very pleased to meet you.'

'And you?'

'Ah yes, of course, I'm Florence Baudin.'

See, she said to herself, as he picked up his rucksack and turned to leave, and she walked back up to the house. *Good things can still happen.*

CHAPTER 6

Hélène

Hélène walked home from work wearily, feeling extremely hungry, looking forward to a bath and then a quiet night by the fire. But when she arrived, she saw the back gate had been left wide open again. It was annoying. You couldn't be too careful these days. She went inside the house and glanced around for Florence who would normally be in the kitchen at this time preparing their supper. Maybe she had already made it? She spotted a pot left beside the cooker and lifted the lid to sniff the contents. Still warm, it smelt delicious. She picked up the wooden spoon lying nearby, dipped it in and licked. Florence's garlicky lentil soup with her own secret herb combination was a firm favourite. It was all Hélène could do to stop herself grabbing a bowl and helping herself, but she felt it only right they should all eat together whenever possible. Sticking to the family traditions as best they could helped preserve the illusion of normality in their increasingly difficult lives.

She rolled her shoulders to relieve the stiffness from hours spent hunched over Hugo's desk sorting out the patients' files, went through to the hall to hang up her jacket and then glanced into the sitting room. Florence had painted the dark old-fashioned furniture Claudette had inherited in pale shades of blue, green and cream, including a nineteenth-century French *bibliothèque*, or library. There was a chic bureau, their mother's favourite, and she'd re-covered a sweet little *repose-pied* in floral fabric. She had also painted the beams a rustic red, an idea Hélène had fought but, in the end, she had to admit it added to the charm. Neither of her sisters were in there, so she went back through the hall, glancing in the mirror as she did. Goodness, she looked a mess. She raised a hand to smooth down her hair but stopped when she heard whispering coming from upstairs.

Feeling a momentary unease, she ran up the winding staircase. At the top she found the trapdoor to the *grenier*, or attic, hanging open and Florence doing her best to conceal someone who was crouching on the floor behind her skirt. The attic ladder had been pulled halfway down.

'What on earth?' Hélène said.

'It's stuck,' her youngest sister replied, as if that was the point, which it clearly was not.

Incensed, Hélène glared at her sister. 'Who the hell is he? And what is he doing here?'

'Well,' Florence puffed out her cheeks, her expression

defiant. 'I found him trying to hide in our shed and I wanted to put him in the attic.'

The person behind Florence rose to his feet and Hélène saw a thin young man, looking no more than about seventeen and wearing a German soldier's uniform. He was trembling, his cheeks smeared with mud, his dirty short blonde hair sticking up on end and his blue eyes wild with terror.

'Oh my good God, is he a German soldier?' Hélène demanded, blinking rapidly at the sight of him. 'Is he armed?'

'I checked. He's not. His says his name is Tomas. He doesn't speak much French or English. I think he's delirious.'

'I just can't believe this.' Hélène folded her arms over her stomach.

'We have to help him.'

'Florence, don't be an idiot, we can't keep him here.'

'We have to. He'll be shot if we don't. He's run away from Toulouse.'

Hélène heard a noise and turned to see Élise climbing the stairs. This morning Élise had plaited her thick chestnut hair, then coiled and pinned it at the back of her head but now strands of it were flying loosely around her face. When she reached the small landing, her eyes widened. 'What the hell is a German soldier doing in our house?' she hissed.

The cowering boy immediately raised his hands in surrender and Hélène saw a wet patch spreading between his legs.

Oh Lord, she thought.

'He ran away,' Florence muttered, as she stepped forward to defend him.

'You mean he's a deserter.' To take a proper look at the boy, Élise nudged her sister back a step or two.

Florence stuck out her lower lip. 'I didn't want to use that word. It sounds bad.'

'Sounds bad. Is bad. Bad for him, bad for us,' Élise replied. 'Time to turn him over to the Maquis.'

Hélène intervened, attempting a tone of calm assurance she didn't feel. 'No. We must simply inform the authorities.'

Both girls turned on her and spoke in unison. 'No!' and, 'Over my dead body!'

Florence shook her head and added. 'Not the military police.'

Hélène sighed in exasperation. Was it always to be like this? When their mother had first proposed the idea of the three sisters coming to live here, Hélène had been excited by the idea of doing as she wished, painting when she wanted, eating when she wanted. Instead, very quickly, she'd had to earn a living as a nurse, working for Hugo, their village doctor, while trying to keep the younger two girls under control. And, of course, back then nobody had believed there would be another war so soon.

'Take him to the Maquis,' Élise insisted, while Florence began tugging at the ladder again.

Spots of colour appeared on Florence's cheeks. 'They'll kill him,' she said, turning on her sister, her eyes beginning to dampen with tears.

There were a few moments of strained silence.

'Right,' Hélène said, finally reaching a decision. 'We *will* put him in the attic. I can't see what else we can humanely do.'

'Oh, thank you.' Florence flung her arms around Hélène.

Élise threw her hands up in the air. 'Why is she always the one to say?'

'Shut up, Élise. She decides because—'

'Only tonight,' Hélène interjected. 'While we work out what to do. Florence, you get him something to eat. Can we spare some lentil soup? He looks famished.'

'So now we're voluntarily feeding the damn Germans,' Élise muttered. 'And how do we know he hasn't got a gun? He might be a spy.'

'He's hardly more than a child. Look at him. And Florence already checked. No gun.'

'He stinks.'

'May have been sleeping rough for days.'

'He's properly starving. Look at the hollows under his eyes,' Florence added.

The boy's frightened eyes were darting from sister to sister, understanding a disagreement was taking place but with no idea what they were saying.

Just then they heard a car arriving and the sisters exchanged anxious glances. It was almost time for the curfew so this could not be good.

'Should we turn off the lamps?' Florence whispered.

'Too late. Get him into the attic quickly. I'll go down.'

As Florence began to speak again, Hélène put a finger to her lips and edged down the stairs.

In the kitchen the shutters were closed but a tiny sliver of light from the kitchen could usually be detected outside. Unless there was a full moon. Was there? Hélène didn't think so. For a few moments she heard nothing but then came the sound of footsteps on the cobblestone path leading to the back door. More than one person, she thought. German soldiers come for their deserter? Something even worse? She stood listening at the door. Please God not those BNA devils back again.

CHAPTER 7

Once Hélène heard the familiar knock, two taps, a pause, then three more taps she knew it was a friend and breathed more easily. She allowed a few more minutes to pass, but when she finally opened the door, she was surprised to see not only the doctor's wife, Marie, looking a little flustered, but with her, an unknown man. A fair-haired, rugged-looking man with a sandy moustache, wearing civilian clothing and shouldering a rucksack.

'He's SOE, I'm afraid,' Marie said, pushing back pins into her loosening bun of greying dark hair and nodding at Élise and Florence as they entered the kitchen. 'I'm sorry, Hélène, I know bringing him here is risky for you, but I have no choice.'

Hélène felt sick, but she shot Élise an enquiring look, and with the slightest of nods her sister narrowed her eyes to let her know the German deserter was now safely hidden in the attic. Better hope he keeps quiet, she thought.

'Special Operations,' the stranger added.

Hélène focused on the man. She would have to quiz him about England. She'd had to do this before, but had vowed never to do it again. And yet here he was. 'British, then?' she said.

'English. And you sound English as well. Surely you're not?'

The sisters all shook their heads, but only Florence answered. 'We're French,' she said.

He raised his brow and whistled. 'So, you young ladies are all bilingual?'

'None of us are *ladies*,' Hélène said.

'Speak for yourself,' Florence said with a laugh.

'Anyway,' Élise spoke over them. 'When we lived in England, we spoke French at home with our parents and English at school.'

'Could be useful.'

Hélène pulled out a chair. 'Would you care to sit?'

He grinned. 'Damn right I would. Any chance of a beer?'

'What about home-made wine?' Florence smiled sweetly and picked up an already opened bottle to show him. 'Plum *digestif*.'

He gave her the thumbs up. 'Anything. Just as long as it's alcohol.'

'Marie, won't you sit down?' Hélène said and put an arm around the older woman's shoulders.

Marie shook her head and kissed Hélène on the cheek. 'It's fine, I can stand.'

'So why are you here?' Hélène asked, looking at the Englishman.

'Two nights ago, I was dropped into the area by parachute. Made a bad landing, but Bill, my partner, is missing. Been searching for him but with the place crawling with Nazis, well . . .' He shrugged. 'I spent all night in a tree right under the noses of the German search party. Took a bit of a tumble climbing down, but luckily Marie here picked me up and I've been at the doctor's surgery since last night.'

Hélène noticed his wrist was bandaged. 'Doctor Hugo?'

'Yep. But it's nothing,' he said. 'Just a scratch.'

'A scratch that needed stitches,' Marie added.

Hélène observed him as he talked. Clearly physically and mentally robust, there was an ease about him. He had an open, honest-looking face too and his green eyes seemed candid. There was no way this man was a German spy.

'So, for security, I need to ask you a few questions,' she said. 'Can you tell me what the Seven Years' War was?'

'French and British fighting over North American land rights.'

'And who won?'

'We did, of course, although I suppose I should say *you* did not, since you say you're French. Are you?'

Hélène narrowed her eyes. 'If you don't mind, I'm asking the questions. Tell me, what's the largest lake in England?'

He gave her a mock chastised look. 'In England? That's Windermere, in the Lake District.'

She asked a few more questions, all of which he answered impeccably.

'And where do you come from?'

'Cirencester in Gloucestershire.'

'And your school?'

'I was a boarder at Cheltenham College.'

'What road is it on?'

'Bath Road. Is that it? Do I pass?'

She smiled. 'You pass.'

The sisters already knew of SOE who'd been dropped by parachute, both in their area and further north and east. And if the talk they heard was true, he, like the others, would be there to prepare the Resistance for direct action.

'What do we call you?'

'Jack. You can call me Jack.'

Marie had been leaning against the wall and watching with half-closed eyes. Now she spoke. 'The thing is, Hélène . . .' She paused as if preparing herself. 'Can you keep him here for a few days, until it's safe for him to move on?'

Hélène felt as if a cord had suddenly tightened around her throat. She sucked in her breath then let out the air slowly.

'Well?' Marie said.

Hélène couldn't speak. She just stood there chewing the inside of her cheek and staring at the floor. Why was Marie asking her to do this? It was impossible.

'No,' she eventually said, glancing up. 'It's too much of a risk. We can't. Marie, you know we can't.'

She felt her sisters growing increasingly tense too. Dangerous enough to house an SOE at any time and she'd always resisted anything like this before. But it was totally impossible with a German deserter currently hiding in their attic. When Florence began to speak, Hélène shushed her, then she glanced at Élise, who shrugged. Hélène knew she would have to be the one to decide.

'Can't he stay with you? Or in one of the safe houses?' she asked, not expecting a positive response.

'That was the plan, but as there are more Gestapo around at the moment, we can't safely move him. Normally I wouldn't ask you, but the surgery and clinic are too central. Hugo thinks his injury needs to heal a little before he moves on.'

Hélène thought of the doctor's beautiful eighteenth-century townhouse overlooking the main square in the medieval part of the village of Sainte-Cécile, with its pretty fountain and ancient church nearby. The house had the same golden stone walls as their own house and the same breathtaking view of the Dordogne river that ran through the heart of the Périgord Noir. Inside, the old fireplaces and wood-beamed ceilings, along with the original parquet flooring, made the house feel like a home from home for Hélène. And she had spent many lunch breaks sitting in the pretty, walled rose garden with Marie, nursing an aperitif and chatting about life. But it really *was* in the heart of the village and quite likely would be watched.

'What about his missing partner?' she asked Marie.

'Could be already captured. Maybe it's why the Gestapo have arrived.'

Jack gave her an affronted look. 'Bill would never spill

the beans. We've both been active in France before. This is our second trip.'

Hélène closed her eyes for a moment wishing the German boy in the attic would have vanished by the time she opened them again.

Hélène beckoned Élise to follow her and they went out into the hall and exchanged worried looks. 'What the hell?' Élise whispered.

'I know. What are we going to do?'

'I think we'll have to let him stay.'

'He will hear us going up and down to the attic. What shall we do about Tomas?'

'I can still hand Tomas over to the Maquis.'

'Élise. He's only a kid,' Hélène pleaded.

'A German kid.'

'Think about if it was one of ours lost and alone in Germany.'

'Well he can hardly remain here, can he? Not now.'

'Maybe we should just tell Jack the truth.'

Élise gave her an exasperated look. 'You're mad.'

'He seems a decent sort.' Hélène felt herself redden.

'Hélène Rosemarie Baudin, I do believe you've taken a shine to him.'

'Don't be ridiculous.'

'So, where are we going to put him?'

'For now? In your room at the back.'

Élise frowned. 'Why mine?'

'It's obvious and you know it. Yours has its own staircase and he's less likely to hear us going up to the attic from there.'

'And what about me?'

'Come in with me.'

'Share a bed with you? No way. You snore and wriggle. And I need my beauty sleep.' She stuck out her lips in an exaggerated pout.

Hélène laughed. 'That'll be the day. Anyway, there's the camp bed.'

Élise sighed grumpily.

'Thank you, darling.'

They returned to the kitchen.

'Very well,' Hélène said and could see how closely Jack was observing her. 'He can stay for a day or two.'

He winked at her. 'Thank you, ma'am.'

'I must get back to Hugo,' Marie said and kissed each of the sisters on the cheeks before making for the door.

'Be careful,' they all chorused.

'You too, *mes chéries*,' she said, then took her leave.

CHAPTER 8

Florence

After the others went up, Florence knew she wouldn't settle to sleep, couldn't imagine being able to rest while her mind was racing. She felt disturbed at having two unknown men in the house, and the dreadful scenarios she kept imagining would only keep her awake because there wasn't a lock on her door. Everyone had always said she was too highly strung and too impulsive. Florence didn't agree. It was true that sometimes she could be a little more wistful than her sisters, but in her view Élise was equally impulsive, only in a different way. But Jack seemed trustworthy, didn't he? And although the trapdoor to the attic usually just clicked in place, tonight they had bolted it on the landing side, so Tomas couldn't get out even if he wanted to. She comforted herself with that.

In the kitchen, she pulled out one of her mother's old,

dog-eared recipe books. She didn't need recipes; knew all her favourites by heart and, since the war, had invented some of her own too, but right now she couldn't decide what to bake.

She flicked through the pages, her mouth watering at the delicious possibilities: *baba au rhum*, *gâteau Basque*, *petit fours*. Most demanded flour, sadly in short supply, but eventually she came across a recipe for Périgordian walnut cake. She tied on her apron, checked which ingredients she could lay her hands on, and wondered why she'd never thought to bake this one before.

Walnuts grew locally, butter she made from their goats' milk, and she had eggs, although not much sugar. A little honey left in a jar one of the old boys in the village had given Hélène as a thank you. Hélène's work often resulted in handy little gifts: fruits, cheese, duck eggs, even the occasional rabbit or pheasant. Florence collected the ingredients and the tools then began by grinding the walnuts into the consistency of breadcrumbs. As she imagined the delicious aroma of a freshly baked cake, she was soothed by the thought of her sisters finding it in the morning.

She knew it had been rash to bring the German soldier boy into the house, but she couldn't have just left him outside to starve to death or tried to shoo him away, could she? He was so young, even younger than her, and she'd always been unable to stop herself rescuing hurt animals or mice and birds from the cats. It didn't mean she wasn't scared though. Her mind flitted to the other German, Anton, the one she'd met when she'd been digging in the garden. She had to admit she'd found him sympathetic.

Well, she'd probably never see him again, so she turned her attention once more to the cake. In a separate bowl she whisked the honey and butter, then stirred in the ground walnuts. She cracked the eggs, separated the white from the yolks and added the yolks to the mixture, beat the whites until super stiff and then folded them in. Once the mixture was in the tin, she slid it into the oven and sat down to wait.

She glanced at the kitchen bookshelf, where most of her mother's recipe books leant against each other like drunken dominoes, and her mind skidded off in a different direction for, in amongst them, she spotted a book of fairy tales by the Brothers Grimm. It didn't belong there, but everything appeared to be shifting these days – rules, people, lives. Sometimes she felt as if she had shifted so much, she didn't fit her own skin any more.

Enchanted by the dark, disturbing tales, she pulled out the book. Grimms' tales hovered between the macabre and the comic, but it was the psychology she loved and, finding Rapunzel, she began to read about the poor girl sold by her dreadful parents. Bought by a wicked witch for a handful of plants, she was imprisoned in a tower, only to find the witch climbing up her long golden hair. As a child Florence had empathised with the weak, the downtrodden, the poor, but in this story, the mother's failure to control her longing for the plants fascinated her. Such overwhelming desire for something scared Florence and, in this case, it led to her daughter's imprisonment.

In the dim electric light, she held the book close. Her practical sisters mocked her for her enduring love of these stories, but to Florence, fairy tales offered hope. Élise and Hélène believed she sailed through life without a thought, expecting everything to be lovely, no matter what. It annoyed her because she was not an idiot. She knew about the brutality of the occupation, the cold-blooded sadism of the Gestapo and the SS, their hatred of the Jews, and the tragedies unfolding daily. But what could she do about any of that? She wasn't brave like Élise, or an important nurse like Hélène. Instead, she had put her heart and soul into keeping everyone's spirits up by feeding them, nurturing them, making a home.

And, from an early age, fairy tales had helped her cope with feelings that were too big and unsettling to understand. Like shame, anger, and jealousy. And another strange feeling she couldn't even name. Memories fluttered about in her mind whenever she thought of her childhood in Richmond. She could never catch hold of them and, when she tried, they flew off. Her thoughts bent and twisted around the images as she tried to dig out the truth, but eventually she sucked in her breath and let it out in a puff.

She glanced down at the book. The scariest fairy stories were the most satisfying because even these usually resulted in a turnaround of fortune and a happy ending, no matter what. Good and evil were separate with no confusing blurred edges. You were either one or the other. You couldn't be both. Not like now.

She put the book back on the shelf, leant back in the chair and closed her eyes, beginning to feel sleepy and wanting her bed, but then became aware of the gorgeous aroma of baking filling the room. She leapt up, worried the cake might be burning, grabbed a protective glove, then opened the oven and pulled out the tray. She held it up to the light, but it looked gorgeously golden with just a few crunchy bits around the edges. Then, after waiting for a couple of minutes, she gently eased the cake out on to a wire mesh tray to cool. Phew! She'd got it out in the nick of time. She left it on the table, turned off the light and went upstairs.

CHAPTER 9

Élise

As she had expected, Élise had a restless night. She was a light sleeper, the camp bed had been particularly uncomfortable, and Hélène really did snore like trooper. In any case, it had been impossible to fall into a deep sleep with two fugitives hidden in the house. Yes, they were tucked away down a track away from the village, but still . . . Deciding to dress in the kitchen, she clutched her clothes to her chest and went down.

A couple of years before, Violette Courtois – a seamstress and Hélène's best friend – had made them both a paper pattern they had then used to alter the men's clothes they'd found in the house when they first moved in. Both she and Hélène usually wore the comfy trousers they'd made themselves. A tweedy navy-blue pair and a pale blue shirt was what she would wear today.

In the kitchen she spotted a cake, smelling delicious, and sitting bang in the middle of the table as if had been magicked there. 'The little witch must have been up half the night,' she thought as she draped her clothes over the back of a chair and cut herself a slice of cake to eat on the way.

Once dressed, and with her hair tied up, she picked up her bundle of blankets from the hall and was out of the house in minutes, wanting to see if Victor was already at the café. Today three of them were due to discuss the viability of the new safe house. There were dozens of these places dotted about the Périgord. Old unused barns, abandoned farmhouses, even huts and sheds. Occasionally safe houses were situated in villages right under the noses of the Nazis, although these were rare. And now, more urgently, she needed to ask for Victor's help. Only he would know what to do with Tomas.

She left the house, then headed up the track, passing through the walnut grove and along the small field edged by wild poppies. She took a bite of the cake and thought of last night's events, the German deserter, and Jack, the SOE man. The boy was her main concern. Jack would be well able to look after himself once Dr Hugo had removed his stiches. But all the same, Marie had taken a risk bringing him to them.

She recalled the initial visit Marie had paid them when they first arrived in Sainte-Cécile. A small bustling woman carrying a little too much weight and with her dark hair, even then turning grey at the front, kept in an unruly bun, she'd looked the perfect example of a country doctor's wife. She had sailed in wearing a pale green and white sprigged cotton dress, with a basket under her arm.

'Thought you could do with some help,' she said and placed it firmly on the table. 'I am Marie Marchand, Doctor Hugo's wife.'

'How kind,' Hélène replied. 'But—'

'But nothing,' the woman interjected with a smile. 'It's only a few bits and pieces. I heard your mother would only be here for a week or two.'

All three sisters had been in the kitchen, but then Claudette entered looking as elegant as ever, though with eyes as hard as marbles. Élise watched her mother give Marie a cursory incline of her head as she took in what was happening, then turned away.

Marie, in contrast, greeted her warmly. 'Claudette. Good to see you.'

Claudette shot her a sideways look. 'Most kind, Madame Marchand, but my girls do not need your charity.'

Marie frowned. 'Come now. It's not charity, just a few neighbourly preserves to set your girls up after you've gone.'

Florence had begun looking in the basket and was excitedly holding up jars. 'Maman look! *Foie Gras*, damson jelly, preserved lemons, apple and cinnamon conserve, and prunes, whole prunes.' She dug deeper, uncovered a cardboard box, and opened the lid.

Claudette folded her arms. 'No, chérie, we absolutely cannot accept all this.'

Florence gave her a pleading look. 'But Maman, they

are little strawberry tarts with vanilla cream. You know I love those.'

'No, Florence,' Claudette began in a sterner tone of voice.

'Ooh, Madame Marchand,' Florence said, ignoring Claudette. 'There is a chocolate cake. Please will you show me how to make it?'

Marie chuckled. 'Of course, I will.'

Claudette drew in her breath and relented. 'Well maybe just this once. But I am leaving you girls my recipe books, so you certainly won't need any further help. I hope that is understood.'

Élise felt so embarrassed and angry at her mother's lack of generosity that she went to shake Marie's hand. 'You are very kind, madame, and we are most grateful. Thank you.'

Claudette remained icy and, as soon Marie Marchand left the house, she shot Élise a furious look then marched back upstairs without another word.

Élise had been expecting something worse.

While they were growing up, Claudette had reserved her most scathing attacks for Élise, the daughter who most resembled her. As Élise grew older she had become more recalcitrant in response, storming out, staying away for hours. Claudette hadn't even noticed she was missing. As a rebellion it proved most unsatisfactory. At the very least Élise had hoped for a heated explosion. When none was forthcoming, she decided she might as well do whatever she wanted, for real consequences – beyond sour verbal attacks – never materialised.

Despite Claudette's insistence, Élise remembered just how much they had needed Marie's help after their mother had returned to England. Marie had been there to show them where to buy the best quality, but also best value, provisions. She'd told them which farmers to trust for vegetables until they could grow their own. She'd introduced them to the villagers and arranged for deliveries of wood and coal and she had persuaded Hugo to arrange training so that Hélène could work as his nurse. How young they'd been to be left alone. Élise, herself, had only been seventeen and Florence two years younger. Hélène at twenty-two had had a great deal to contend with.

But without Marie, their lives would have been so much tougher, and it still rankled that Claudette had been so mean-spirited with her. Élise glanced across at the doctor's house, shutters still closed in the early-morning light. A few moments passed and then she shrugged. She'd spent too long being angry with her mother. It was all too far away in the past to feel upset about now, and she had other things to worry about. She walked on and arrived at the café, unlocked the door, and slipped inside to find Victor already there.

CHAPTER 10

Hélène

Tomas had been asleep when she had gone to check, so she'd left water and a piece of cake beside him. She'd thought of just leaving him some bread but had felt mean, as these days it was hard and chewy, made from cornflour and ground rice. The Nazis had seized much of the wheat to feed their troops. She gazed at Tomas, let out a long slow breath, and prayed he'd be gone very soon.

When she knocked on Jack's door and then pushed it open, she found him sitting up in bed, bare-chested and gazing out of the window overlooking the strip of grass beside their sheds. He had a good profile, strong nose, well-shaped jawline and was clearly a muscular, vigorous sort of a man.

Her breath quickened a tiny bit, but she managed to mask it with a cough. He turned, scratched the top of his head, and left his fair hair standing up in a spiky peak. His face in repose looked almost grave, perhaps rather sad, but when he smiled at her, it changed completely. His eyes became animated and warm. He did not seem the least bit bothered by his state of semi-undress, but when she tilted her head in a gesture of mild censure, he pulled the sheet up over his chest.

'Sorry.'

'Doesn't matter. I'm a nurse. There isn't anything I haven't seen.'

He raised one eyebrow and she smiled.

'You look different,' he remarked after a moment.

She had pinned back her hair in a tight bun at the nape of her neck and had already slapped a beret on top. She touched her hair.

'Nurse's uniform,' he said.

'Ah.'

'I heard some odd noises in the night.' He glanced up at the ceiling and raked his fingers through his untidy hair. 'Mighty big rats, I'd say.'

She avoided eye contact.

'Any fool could see your unease last night when Marie asked you to let me stay here.'

Hélène considered this, then came over to him, placing his drink and cake on the bedside table. He clearly had a sharp mind. Close up, something stirred in her and she gazed at him. What was it she wanted to say?

'Sit,' he commanded.

'On your bed?'

'I don't see a chair. Look, I promise not to ravish you,'

he said with half-closed eyes and a broad smile. 'Although I must say, a fine-looking woman like you . . .'

'Now you're making fun of me.'

'Why would you say that? I don't think I've ever seen more soulful eyes.'

She planted herself at the bottom of his bed. 'Really, Jack, can we just be serious. I'm too worried for this.'

'Sure,' he said, chastened. 'Sorry. Why don't you come clean about what's going on?'

She took a slow breath, realising he hadn't been teasing her, then began speaking. 'The thing is . . . yesterday we found – well, it was Florence who actually found him.'

His face perked up. 'Bill. You found Bill?'

She shook her head. 'No. Sorry. Florence found a young German deserter hiding in one of our sheds.'

'Good Lord. And he's in your attic now?'

She wrinkled her face. 'Yes. He can't get out and he isn't armed, but he's in a dreadful state, shaking and stuttering. I gave him a strong sedative last night to help keep him quiet, but I'm worried about what to do next.'

'I knew something was up. I can talk to him if you like.'

'You speak German?'

'Somewhat. But for your sake, you'll need to move him as soon as you can.'

'I know. I wish I hadn't agreed to have him here. But he was in a terrible state, completely bedraggled and starving. I don't know . . .' She sighed. 'It's so hard to make the right decision when things are this uncertain. But if they come looking for him and find him here, well

. . . you can imagine. The consequences for us don't bear thinking about.'

He gazed at her and she could see he understood.

'I have to go to work now, but Florence will look after you. You'll need to stay in here, but if the worst were to happen, just jump down out of this window onto the tin roof of the shed below. Then you'd have to make for the woods.'

'Don't worry,' he said. 'I'm a trained survivor. If I can survive the mayhem earlier this year, I can survive anything.'

She didn't doubt it. If you needed someone on your side, it was he.

'So, what exactly are you here to do?' she asked.

'Exactly?' He smiled. 'I can't *exactly* say. I guess you already heard about the Allied bombing of ammunition factories, warehouses, railways, ports, other industries, and especially electricity generating plants?'

'Of course.'

'And you'll also know it has inflicted massive damage on the German war machine.'

'So, you're the reason why our electricity supply has been playing up.'

''Fraid so,' he agreed. 'Now I'm here for the next phase.'

'Which means?'

He raised his brows and gave her a knowing look. 'I'll leave it to your imagination.'

Ah, she thought but didn't say, he means blowing up railways and roads.

'You wouldn't know of someone who'd know of a nice flat meadow, would you?'

She frowned, but then twigged there would need to be Allied parachute drops of armaments and maybe even small plane landings. 'I'll pass it on,' she said.

'Your sister, Élise,' he said. 'Is she here?'

Hélène responded slowly, gazing up at the ceiling before looking back at him. 'I think she's left for her café. She runs it as a central letter box.'

'I see.'

'It worries me. Men desperate to dodge two years forced labour – we call them *refractaires* – turn up at the café wanting to know how to join the Resistance. She passes their messages to the camps. The leaders send back details of meeting places where they'll decide which of the *refractaires* are trustworthy. As you can imagine, sometimes the men who turn up are really spies.'

He whistled his admiration. 'Good girl. Plucky. She'll be useful to us.'

'Reckless girl. Anyway, she'll be able to put you in touch with an SOE agent who is already here.'

'You must be proud of her, though.'

'I suppose I am, but I'm also scared for her. She's resilient and courageous. But she is taking a huge risk of the Nazis finding out whenever she allows the café to be used in this way. And she's especially close to one of the Maquis, a man called Victor, and that endangers her too.'

'Her boyfriend?'

Hélène shrugged and made for the door.

'Nice cake, by the way,' he said, taking a bite.

'You can thank Florence.'

He chewed, swallowed his mouthful, then said, 'Before you go. I'm curious.'

'About?'

'How you three ended up here.'

She wavered, unwilling to go into it. 'It's a long story.'

'Give me the short version then.'

'Well,' she said, deciding to tell him something. 'After our father's sudden death, our mother sold our family home and bought a small place in Gloucestershire where she now lives, and we moved here.'

'That's it?'

'Yes. Now you need to rest. I'll see you later.'

She didn't say how shocked they'd felt when Claudette told them their lovely Richmond home was up for sale and, as the Sainte-Cécile house was too small for them all, the family was to be split up. The sisters would be sent to France with just a small allowance which Hélène would control, and for the present their mother preferred to live in the little cottage she'd bought in England. When the time came, Claudette had travelled with them to settle things but soon went home. It was meant to have been a temporary arrangement, but the war got in the way, Claudette had stayed put and so had they.

For most of the seven years they had lived here, they'd looked after themselves. Yes, they'd received that recent short letter from her, but any post coming directly from England had been stopped long ago. And without a phone either, they had little contact with their mother.

As Hélène left the house and made her way to the

village centre along its well-worn streets and warren of houses and gardens, she knew Jack's presence had awoken buried feelings. Or maybe it was having Tomas in the house that had left her feeling so unsettled. Either way, she had trained herself not to think of Julien, trained herself not to think of what she couldn't have, yet now memories flooded her mind. Jules had been her only real romance in seven years, but had gone to war and now nobody knew where he was. She remembered the heat of his hands on her body the night before he left when she finally gave in to him, quickly calculating she was at the safest time of the month. Soon after they made love that night, he left, but she stayed in the barn listening to the comforting sounds of the night. The owls, the night birds, the creatures snuffling in the undergrowth. She still loved the feeling of stillness once the sun was going down; the time when the oaks and chestnuts turned dark and heat rose from the land and everything was quietly breathing. Sometimes she'd hear the brief interlude of a nightingale's song. And now the space between the days was her only chance of peace. She would sit in the darkness of the garden after her sisters were in bed and she would take a long slow breath and ground herself in her life.

CHAPTER 11

As she neared the surgery, Hélène passed the usual old women who liked to be out and about early, their knitted woollen shawls wrapped round their shoulders despite the fact it was now spring, with only a soft and gentle breeze. She heard the whistle of a passing train, a noisy cock crowing in somebody's backyard and several dogs barking in a village on the opposite side of the river, its red roofs and ochre houses glowing in the morning sunlight.

The usual shops clustered around their own village square – *boulangerie, patisserie, épicerie, boucherie* – plus, just off the square, Maurice Fabron's smithy and the town's *auberge* around the corner, owned by crazy Madame Deschamps, who still dyed her frizzy white hair a startling red. Her curvaceous, bosomy daughter, Amelie, whose dresses were always too tight, ran the place in a determinedly efficient way. Most of the shops were more than half empty, offering not much more than a few vegetables, carrots, swedes and so on, plus eggs, although, if you had the money, there was always the black market. Despite the curfew, farmers still came at night delivering vegetables by horse and cart.

The pale blue van from the local garage crawled up the street, she assumed being driven by Victor, whose father owned the garage. She thought of all the fighters in the shadows; some clinging to the cover of maintaining their ordinary jobs, while others hid out in lone barns or in the deep dark forests. And now she and her sisters needed Victor to help them.

Hugo came into the hallway. 'Morning, Hélène. Goodness, are you all right? You do look pale.'

'I'm fine. A bit tired, that's all.'

'Very well. Would you mind helping old Madame Deschamps undress?'

'I was just thinking about her. How is she?'

He pulled a face. 'Getting worse, I fear. She's in the waiting room.'

'Her memory?'

'Yes, but she has been experiencing an irregular heartbeat too. I want to give her a thorough examination.'

'Carrying so much weight won't help her heart.'

'No.'

Hélène donned her nurse's apron then went to Hugo's waiting room to escort Madame through to Hugo's office, where a blue screen closed off a small section that served as a changing room. But the woman was in an agitated state and resisted leaving the waiting room, tenaciously gripping the edges of her chair, and shaking her head.

When Hélène finally persuaded her into the office, cajoling her with the promise of biscuits – the woman was a demon for anything sweet – she then refused to go behind the screen, insisting she sit in Hugo's leather chair at his desk to eat her biscuits there.

'Biscuits after your examination,' Hélène said and forced a smile.

Eventually, when Hélène finally manoeuvred the woman behind the screen, she plonked herself down on the wooden stool in there and stubbornly folded her arms across her body.

'Let's just get your woolly cardigan off,' Hélène said as soothingly as she could. Her patience was wearing thin and the old lady was picking up on it, making matters even worse.

'Bugger off,' the woman said.

'Come now, madame, be nice.'

But every time Hélène attempted to remove her cardigan, the old lady continued to pull it back on and Hélène, usually so calm and considered, felt tense and frustrated. At one point a strand of the woman's hair got caught up around a button and she shrieked like a banshee. It was then Marie came in, obviously having heard the commotion.

'Can I help?' she said, with a glance at the old lady who was now pulling at her hair and muttering about young people these days.

'Please do,' Hélène said with a deep sigh. 'I'm so sorry. I don't know what's the matter with me.'

'Look, why don't you go and make us all a tisane and I'll get Madame Deschamps ready for Hugo.'

Relieved to be out of there, Hélène went straight to the kitchen. Usually so efficient, she hated letting Hugo down. Women before the war had been politically non-existent, unable until 1938 to even take a job without a father or husband's permission. As Hélène's father had died, Hugo was able to employ her and arrange her training

She opened the cupboard above the sink, thinking of making peppermint tisanes but discovering they were out of dried mint leaves. She lifted the glass jar to wash it but, clumsy with tiredness, it slid from her hands on to the tiled floor where it shattered.

She could have cried, but instead she groaned, fetched the dustpan and brush, and cleared up the mess. When she checked the cupboard for other herbs, she found only chamomile, which Hugo hated. Feeling increasingly desperate to leave the surgery, she decided to see if Élise might spare her some mint from the café.

She removed her apron and slipped out, striding across the square to the café where a couple of old guys sitting at one of the three pavement tables wished her a cheery good morning. When Élise had first opened the café, she had painted the chairs in bright colours with walls to match and people had been suspicious. Many folk hereabouts were old-fashioned, liked only what they were accustomed to and frowned at anything new. But Élise had persisted and the combination of her good-natured laughter and Florence's cooking had won them round. Their mother had sent money for Élise to start the café, but with the proviso it must become self-sufficient quickly.

Now Élise was a valued part of the village and they could no longer remember a time when she hadn't been there.

These days the café, apart from serving as a letter box, was also the meeting place for old boys who huddled together, gossiping about the past, while enjoying a bit of stew. The coffee was never real now, but a revolting mixture of chicory, barley, malt and acorns known as *ersatz* coffee. Hélène preferred to stick with tisanes. In the summer, ninety-year-old Clément, a stooped and whiskery fellow, would carry his chair and accordion out to the pavement and play the classic street music of Paris, where he'd lived in his youth. It was known as *bal-musette* music and the sound of it tended to leave everyone misty-eyed.

Inside, Hélène found Élise sitting at one of the tables surreptitiously glancing at a map hidden inside a novel. In the corner, a young mother was preparing to leave with her toddler. Hélène smiled to acknowledge her and, once the woman had left, she pointed at Élise's map.

'What?' she asked.

'Just checking things out.'

'You're not becoming more involved?'

'More than the letter box? No. I'm only checking out where the new safe house is.'

Hélène sat down at the table and picked at the skin around her nails.

'You feeling jumpy?' asked Élise.

'Terribly.'

'Me too.' Then she lowered her voice. 'I've spoken to Victor.'

'About moving you-know-who?'

Élise nodded.

'He'll be round tomorrow night.'

'Tomorrow? We need him to come tonight!'

'He can't, not tonight.'

Back in the surgery, Hélène's next patient was a young lad who had cut his finger badly while using a saw. Hélène wondered if it had been a ploy to get out of being called up to work for the Nazis. Doctor Hugo had seen him, stitched him up and now Hélène had to dress the wound.

'I heard the Nazis are searching all the villages around here,' the boy said, just as she was finishing.

'Oh? Do you know why?

'Not sure. People say they are looking for stashes of armaments.'

'They say that, do they?' she said, thinking of the explosives Élise had buried in their garden and feeling relieved they were gone.

'But it could be anything, couldn't it?' he said. 'All sorts of rumours are flying around.'

She swallowed and kept her voice controlled. 'Are there?'

'I heard it from my uncle that they're looking for a deserter from the German army. Can you imagine that?'

She didn't reply, but her mind was moving faster than before. Tomas had to go. And if it couldn't be tonight it had to be tomorrow without fail.

Back home she went straight up to see him. The boy was sitting up and eating some bread Florence must have brought for him. His eyes widened in fear at the sight of Hélène.

'It's all right,' she said and tried to smile, but he did not understand her, and of course it wasn't all right at all, but ridiculous to allow him to stay another night.

They had given him the chamber pot with the roses circling the rim and she saw it was gone from the attic. Florence must have taken it down to empty it. She watched him for a few minutes more, but as she couldn't speak any German, and he could speak neither French nor English, they had little to say.

When he held out his arm to show her a deep graze, she narrowed her eyes.

'I'll get something to clean and disinfect it,' she said and left the attic for her medical bag.

Once she had finished cleaning his graze, she dressed it and afterwards went to see Jack, who she found asleep. She didn't wake him, but enlisted Florence's help to clear out anything in the house that might cause a problem should there be a search. God, she hoped there wasn't.

'What's going to happen about Tomas?' Florence asked. 'I've been feeling worried sick all day. Is he going tonight?'

'No. I'm afraid not. But don't worry. Victor is going to help us to move him.'

'Soon?'

'Yes. Tomorrow. Come on, let's do this. Just in case.'

'You mean in case they come to look for Tomas.'

'Yes.'

Everyone in the village thought they were French. Their

father had seldom visited the summer house, and no one had any idea he was half-English. If the Nazis came to look for Tomas, she wanted to be sure they wouldn't also find anything that might lead the SS to discover and then probe into their English heritage and ancestry. Plenty of people knew they'd had an English upbringing, but not that their grandmother was English. The last thing they needed was to be transported to a camp because of it.

The attic still needed finishing, but their shuffle through when they first arrived, and then more recently, had revealed nothing of significance. Just clothes, small pieces of furniture, an old rocking horse, and other such items and, of course, the kitchen items and the red dress. But in the winter Hélène had found a wooden box stuffed up the chimney breast in the small office at the back of the house beneath Élise's room. To conserve wood they had never lit a fire in there and when she decided to try, smoke billowed into the room, and she discovered the blocked chimney and the box. It had remained unseen for the seven years they'd lived in the house and perhaps for a great deal longer. It was black and sticky from congealed soot and dust, so Hélène had wiped the muck off and, after a cursory look, had put it aside to deal with later.

Now, it was time to open it, and Hélène, sitting cross-legged on the floor, lifted the lid then separated the contents into two piles, one for her and one for Florence on the top of which was a photograph.

'Is that Maman?' Florence said, squatting beside her and picking up the photo.

Hélène glanced at it and sniffed. 'I'm not sure. It might be her sister.'

As they rummaged, they found yellowing bank statements, an old credit note, some faded postcards sent by their father from England to their mother when she'd been staying here, and a few bills. Hélène spotted one of the postcards which, judging by the stamp, had not been sent from England. Most of the writing, obscured by mould and damp, was indecipherable except for the words *'My beloved'*. She folded it up into her pocket and remembered the only time she'd received a letter from Julien. It had been a farewell letter and he had not called her his beloved.

'What was that?'

'Nothing,' she lied. 'Just a picture of a forest. Have you found anything?'

'Only some old bills from our Richmond house. Shall I burn them?'

'Is the boiler lit?'

Florence told her it was and, taking the paperwork, left the room.

Hélène drew out the postcard from her pocket and tried to work out what the blurred words might mean. Still nothing. Except, clear as day, the words, *My Beloved*. Who was the beloved? And beloved by whom? She couldn't imagine her mother writing so amorously. Her father then? Or was this somehow connected to the ruined red silk dress? As it came back to her, she screwed up her eyes as if to will the memory to surface. Something was tapping at her mind. Maybe if they could mend the dress, it might become clear but, for now, only an image of the dark attic reared up before her.

When Hélène and Élise were young, they became aware of a shadow in their parents' marriage. In Richmond, Élise had found a note saying *Please. I'm sorry. Don't do this,* written in their mother's hand but torn in two and tossed in a bin. It made no sense and then, after they overheard the tail end of a parental argument, the venom was something they couldn't unhear.

Hélène shook her head. It was all in the past and now she needed to concentrate.

As they were finishing their task, they heard Élise arriving home and a few moments later she came to stand in the doorway.

'We've been sorting through stuff,' Florence said, glancing up.

'I can smell the burning. Anything interesting?'

'No. Mainly postcards Papa sent Maman.'

'And bills,' Hélène added.

'How is Tomas?'

Hélène filled her cheeks and blew the air out in a puff. 'Sleepy. Tired. Scared.'

Élise laughed. 'Just like us then.'

'You know,' Florence said, rising to her feet. 'From the look of the postcards we found, Father really did love Maman.'

Élise stared at her. 'I never said he didn't.'

'And they loved each other so much too. She was so brave at his funeral, wasn't she?'

Élise raised her brows. 'Brave? Are you crazy?'

'No. Why?'

'She was as cold as ice, Florence.' Élise darted a look at Hélène, who shrugged.

'You've always been against her, Élise. Can't you try harder?' Florence's bottom lip began to wobble.

Élise frowned. 'Try to do what harder?'

'Like her. Love her. After the funeral I asked her how she would get on alone without Papa and she said she would put one foot in front of the other. That was brave.'

Hélène was becoming sick of this conversation. She'd heard these arguments too many times before and tried to change the subject. 'Do you remember how we went carol singing to raise money for the Battersea Dogs Home? Maman didn't want us to go alone, but Father thought we should.'

Élise laughed. 'Yes, and we made a fortune.'

Hélène smiled wryly. 'That you said we should spend on sweets and only give a fraction of it to charity.'

'And you wouldn't let me.'

But Florence was having none of it and turned for a moment to glare at Hélène. 'What's Battersea Dogs Home got to do with anything?'

Hélène puffed out her cheeks and saw the distress on her youngest sister's face and that she was edging dangerously close to tears.

'Maman did her best,' Florence said doggedly, returning to the topic that was bothering her. 'You must see.'

'Her best?' Élise snorted.

'Oh, come on. Why are you so mean? At least she tried.'

'Not hard enough.'

'Right,' Hélène finally said. 'Enough. I think we have more pressing matters to worry about than getting tangled up in whether Maman was brave or not. Or whether she deserved to be loved. Like . . .' And she emphasised the word as she repeated it. '*Like* how to get rid of a German deserter.'

'And Jack,' Élise said.

'Jack can take care of himself.'

CHAPTER 12

The next day the sun was shining and, as Hélène walked along the tree-lined track, the scent of pine hung in the air. She passed plane trees, cedars, holm oaks and, of course, walnut trees and glanced up at the leaves, so fresh and green while the unforgiving heat of summer was yet to come. The village itself looked beautiful, with dark blue irises and lilac bushes blossoming in the gardens and crab-apple trees in bloom. There was a harmonious and timeless simplicity about it and yet Hélène was feeling even more anxious than before. Burning everything had been the right thing to do and had helped a little to put her mind at rest, but for now, all she could do was try to put Tomas – and Jack – out of her mind and focus on her work.

And yet it was so hard. Up until now she had managed to keep away from trouble. But now trouble was in her own home. Of course, she understood why people joined the Resistance, faced danger every day, but she couldn't do that. Her way was to carry on working, stay alive, keep her sisters safe – while all the time praying that soon there would be good news from the Allies and that life would return to normal.

She stopped to speak to Clément, who was slowly heading for the café, tapping his walking stick on the cobbles as he went, a pack of Gauloises peeping from his white shirt pocket. She even caught a hint of the pungent cigarette smoke hanging in the air between them.

'Good morning,' he hollered, raising his voice in the way slightly deaf older people often did. 'Off to work?'

'Yes. I'll be coming by later this morning to see to Gabrielle.'

'Right you are then.'

He was a lovely old boy who always had a smile for everyone and lived with Gabrielle, his equally ancient wife, whose sciatica and arthritis often kept her bedridden and whom Hélène had to treat for bedsores on a weekly basis.

As she said goodbye and walked on, the morning sun washed the buildings with amber light. Theirs was a village of light but also shade, wonderful when the blinding summer sun grew so hot you felt your bones were melting. The spirit of the place had not been broken yet, although it had been damaged. In the main square an eighteenth-century market hall, its roof held up by stone pillars, stood just a step away from the town hall or *mairie*. Not far from the surgery, the *mairie* was where you registered births, deaths and marriages and on the steps there she spotted their parish priest, Father Bernard Charrier, who simply gave her a wave and went on by.

The sweet shop was closed but Angela, the middle-aged woman with brassy blonde hair who owned it, was an effervescent soul who loved to gossip. Now she sat on a cane chair in her doorway both to see and be seen. Her husband had died from a stroke some years before, so now the shop with its original tiled floor, polished mahogany counters, and pendant lights was her world, along with her fat marmalade cat, Beau. From the other side of the street Hélène gave her a little wave and moved on.

Thank goodness today everything in the village appeared peaceful enough and there were no SS in the square or the surrounding streets. But as soon as Hélène reached the surgery, her heart lurched when she saw Marie rushing out of the side entrance still in her dressing gown and with curlers in her hair.

'Oh, thank God you're here,' Marie said with a look of anguish on her face and twisting her hands together over and over. 'The bastards have taken Hugo. They came in a Nazi staff car at dawn. It wasn't soldiers.'

'Gestapo?'

'Maybe.'

Hélène blinked, scrambling to make sense of this, but a shrill ringing in her head went on and on. Struggling now to inhale, her chest tightened as this terrible news undermined everything that she had held dear. Doctor Hugo. How could it be? She glanced at ashen-faced Marie, her lips almost blue, but couldn't find the words. Oh God. She had to be strong to help Marie.

She swallowed, managed a deep breath, and held out her arms.

The two women hugged, holding each other up.

Hugo Marchand was the town's only doctor and a kinder, more generous man you could not find. The fact that he was also mayor had been of benefit to the Resistance because, while he had to maintain the appearance of loyalty to Vichy, behind the scenes he was actually cooperating as little as possible by dragging his heels whenever he could. But now the Germans had drafted in a tall, thin man called Pascale Giraud to be Hugo's new clerk, whose primary role was not clear.

'What do they know?'

Marie shook her head. 'They took his mimeograph machine. He only uses it to it provide information for patients. That Pascale might have told them he had one. Although Hugo says he is trustworthy.'

The mimeograph was a low-cost duplicating machine which forced ink through a stencil onto paper and was often used by the Resistance to print material for distribution.

'And his radio?' Hugo's radio had been their only source of information and the Nazis had done everything they could to track down radio sets and punish their owners.

Marie shook her head. 'Well-hidden. We can still get news from Radio Londres.'

'So, do you think this could be something to do with Jack appearing out of the blue?'

'Do you trust him?'

'Yes, Marie, I do. And he couldn't have known about the machine.' She paused. Had she been taken in by Jack's obvious charm? Could she trust anyone after such a short time? There *were* British working for the Germans, after all, and perhaps his story of the missing partner, Bill, was just that – a story.

'Maybe Pascale saw me bundling him into the car after curfew.'

Hélène forced herself to think, stay calm, concentrate on the facts. 'It could be a coincidence. I'll speak to Élise.'

'What about the surgery?'

'Many waiting?'

'Not yet, but I think we'll be packed out. Bad news travels fast.'

'Tell everyone to wait. When I get back, I'll take the surgery. If anyone prefers to see the doctor, they can come back another time.'

Marie accepted that and Hélène reached out to pat her on the shoulder. 'Come on. Don't lose hope. Get dressed, have something to eat, and then we'll see where we are.'

As Hélène hurried across to Élise's café to wait for her sister, she would have given anything for this not to be happening. She had tried not to give in to panic in front of Marie, but could now feel the fear beginning to rise again. She longed to scoop Hugo up from wherever he had been taken and keep him safe forever.

But she had no way of doing that.

There was a room at the back of the café with a side entrance and Hélène had a key. She reached the door, unlocked it, then sat on the only comfortable chair to wait. Her heart ached for Doctor Hugo, with his intelligent grey eyes and his traditional Périgordian moustache which curled up to a point on either side of his cheeks. He was always beautifully turned out in a smart suit and with the usual grey fedora on his head, and in the winter a navy woollen overcoat with a fur collar.

Feeling overwhelmed by a sense of helplessness, she forced herself to think about the way women like Élise, like Marie, and like her friend Violette, had come so far since the early days of the Resistance. It had been a struggle, but they'd had the audacity to prove their abilities, despite ridicule, and had battled the stereotype of feminine weakness. Some women were now fully involved as *résistantes*, gathering intelligence and even taking part in sabotage attacks – unthinkable back in 1940. These women had taken up arms not only against Hitler's Nazis, but also against the prejudice towards their sex – the norm at the start of the war and worsened by Pétain's repressive measures. Chief of the collaborating Vichy administration, he was an ageing soldier with penetrating blue eyes, and lived in luxury at the Hotel du Parc. He had banned women from taking jobs in the public sector, abolished divorce, and abortion now carried the death penalty.

As for the Resistance, in other areas of France it was more organised with recognised leaders, but here the Maquis were wild. The terrain of the Dordogne was the perfect area for guerrilla warfare. They had been strong before the dreadful reign of terror meted out by the BNA and were growing strong again now, but would they be able to find a way to help Hugo?

CHAPTER 13

Hélène watched as Élise swung open the door, wheeled in her bicycle, leant it against the wall and then dumped her satchel on the table. She took the food basket from the bicycle and only then, as she glanced up, did she see her sister sitting in the gloom.

'Jesus, Mary and Joseph! You gave me a fright. What's wrong? You look awful.'

'Oh Élise. It's terrible. We really need your help.'

'What's happened?'

Hélène pressed a palm against her chest. 'Hugo . . . has been taken,' she said, and her voice broke.

'When?'

'Today. Early.'

Élise paled, her eyes wide with shock. 'Jesus. I'd better get hold of Victor quickly. He's not long gone.'

'Leo might know something.'

Leonard Delacroix, their local policeman and a

Resistance sympathiser, listened in on the central telephone lines to try to find out about German plans and the movement of troops. He was affectionately referred to as Leo and was unusual among the French *gendarmes* who usually took the side of Marshall Pétain. These days most of the police had become German puppets and did the dirty work of the SS.

'And Victor?'

'They've got a job on this morning. The less you know . . .'

'I'll ask if Violette has heard anything. She may have seen Suzanne.'

While Élise was a maverick and resistant by nature, Hélène was far more likely to want to adapt to current circumstances and work behind the scenes. Suzanne, meanwhile, a good friend of both Hélène and Violette, was a sinewy blonde upper class idealist, who lived with her husband Henri, a crack shot French officer. He had been imprisoned and then released by the SS, only to find his chateau had been converted into a German command centre and temporary prison. Whilst he appeared to cooperate with the enemy – he and Suzanne were forced to work at the chateau – Suzanne supported the Resistance by passing on intelligence about the whereabouts of missing persons or any German plans they may have overheard.

Once Violette had let Hélène in, they went straight into the garden where nobody could hear them, and Hélène rapidly told her about Hugo. It was terrible news on such a lovely day; there was not a cloud in the sky and the honeyed vanilla scent of Spanish broom floated up from the lower terrace. Close by it mingled with the aroma of thyme – pungent, warming, spicy – and the perfumed sweetness of blue violets. Tubs of daffodils and primroses grew next to even more herbs: clary sage, tarragon, dill, chives.

'Sit,' Violette said. 'Just for a moment. Now, what are we going to do?'

Hélène took in her friend's neat chignon, her finely pencilled eyebrows and her high cheekbones. She had worked for a couturier in Paris and still looked as if she belonged there rather than in the rural backwater of Sainte-Cécile.

'I don't know. I'm hoping Leo has heard something. We need to find out where they've taken Hugo.'

'But he hasn't done anything, has he?'

Hélène shrugged. 'I don't know. Are you expecting Suzanne today?'

'I hope.'

As a person of consequence, despite her current situation, Suzanne was freely allowed into the village to shop and to consult the seamstress and other merchants. At times she was accompanied by an SS officer or two, which caused raised eyebrows, but as she had to maintain her cover, few in the village knew what she was really up to. The Germans at the castle liked her because of her typically Aryan looks and her perfect manners. She often gave Violette the news about what was happening at the chateau and adjoining castle, and Violette passed it on to Élise at the café. She, in turn, handed it to the Resistance.

This little network of three – Violette the seamstress, Suzanne the grand lady of the chateau, and Élise the Resistance worker – had recently asked Hélène to join them to make a fourth. There was always a chance she might overhear useful intelligence concerning injured German officers who'd been treated by the doctor. Hélène had previously declined, solidly insisting she couldn't run the risk.

Now, though, things were different and she gazed at her friend, feeling morose and worried. 'Violette, I will let you know about anything I hear in the surgery. But maybe not just yet.'

'You're thinking they might come after you next?'

'Since they've got Hugo, they might. I don't want to endanger Florence or Élise.'

'Élise is already endangering herself. And they won't come after you. Why would they?'

Then Hélène, keeping her breathing calm, went on to tell her about Jack and Tomas.

Violette gasped. 'Good heavens, you're properly up to your neck in it, aren't you?'

Hélène scratched her neck. 'Yes. I never intended to be.'

'They might search your house, I suppose. Do you think they arrested Hugo because they knew he'd treated Jack?'

Hélène shrugged. 'It's possible.'

'So, what's first?'

'Well, Victor has a plan for the German boy.'

'Where will he go?'

'I have no idea.'

'And your Special Operations man?'

'That's different.'

Violette raised her brows suggestively, but Hélène ignored her.

'Speak to Suzanne if she comes. See if they've taken Hugo to the castle.'

The chateau owned by Suzanne and Henri Dumas was set back from a cliff not far from Sainte-Cécile. On one side it was attached to a much older castle, parts of which were still in dire need of restoration. Before the war, the couple had drawn up plans to improve their home and the chateau itself was now finished with a long drive lined with walnut trees, far-reaching views and a landscaped garden overlooking the ramparts. When the Nazis requisitioned it they had found what remained of the older castle useful too, especially the two historic dungeons dating from the eleventh and twelfth centuries. The castle's two conical-roofed towers were used for surveillance, but the chapel decorated with sculptures was ignored, with its concealed stone staircase extending underground and into a hidden room beneath the chateau.

The chateau roofs were steeply pitched and inside, a massive oak-beamed hall set the tone for the rest of the place. Suzanne and Henri had transformed it from a crumbling, fire-destroyed ruin with burst pipes and water damage, into a sumptuous palace. With its high ceilings and large windows overlooking the land, it was no wonder the Nazis had decided to take it over. Now, with silk cushions and velvet curtains, antique chimneypieces, walnut antiques, exposed timber and restored stone floors and stairs, it was stunning. But only Suzanne and Henri knew all the secrets of castle and chateau, and they had taken care to destroy their original plans so the Nazis would never find out. As the couple now worked as housekeepers for the Germans, they had been allocated a small room behind the kitchen to use as a bedroom; it was extremely galling. But the castle had survived attacks by Richard the Lionheart, among others, and both buildings offered a warren of tunnels, wells, large drains providing escape channels, concealed rooms, stairways and cellars which Suzanne and Henri made good use of, and which their occupiers knew nothing about.

'How is little Jean-Louis getting on at school?' Hélène asked, standing and gathering up her bag, conscious of the patients waiting at the surgery.

'Well, you know, he's five, full of beans when he's well and up to mischief.'

'It must be hard.'

'You mean bringing him up alone?'

'Yes.'

Violette shrugged. 'Not so hard. Pierre has been gone for a while. I've got used to it.'

'How is his chest? Any better?'

'Yes. Always better with the warmer weather. Ah, look. Here he is now.'

A little boy with enormous brown eyes, curly blonde hair and freckles ran into the room and threw his arms round Hélène's legs.

'Hello, little curly top,' she said, smiling at him and roughing up his hair. 'And how is my favourite little boy?'

Jean-Louis giggled. 'I am naughty today.'

'Are you indeed?'

'Oui! Oui! Oui!'

'But you're never naughty. Your maman told me.'

He ran to his mother, who swooped him up and covered his face with kisses.

Hélène moved towards the door. They all knew Alexandre Lacroix, the schoolteacher, was a Vichy collaborator and they had to be careful what they said in front of the child.

'I'm off,' Hélène said, and bent to kiss her friend's cheeks. 'I have to see to Hugo's patients. Send a message via Élise if Suzanne has news of Hugo.'

By the evening there had been no news and Hélène was exhausted from a long stream of curious patients. To them all she simply relayed the information that the doctor had been called away on urgent business. Doubtless they saw through the charade, but she had remained tight-lipped and tried to hide her worry.

On her way back home, a German staff car – one of those converted to wood gas – crawled through the town, slowing even further as it drew level with Hélène just as she crossed the square. She held her breath, expecting to be stopped and ordered to present her identity card, ration book, work permit and documents proving her Aryan descent, but this time they went on by. In the distance a shot rang out. She felt jumpy and prayed the car was not headed towards her house.

At home Hélène half-filled the tin bath in the vaulted

laundry room from a faucet in the corner, while Florence carried through pitchers of boiling water from the kitchen.

'Here,' Florence said and handed Hélène the soap before throwing some dried rose petals into the water. Their luxuries were few, but without Florence there would be none at all. It was Florence who'd hidden the chicken run and the pen for their two remaining goats, Florence who kept the animals fed, called them *mes jolies petites chèvres,* and Florence who remained endlessly cheerful in the face of disaster. And Hélène felt she had to protect her.

'I'll leave you to it,' she added. 'Towel's on the chair. I've seen to Tomas. And Jack's been asleep most of the day. I think he went out last night.'

'How is the boy?'

'Less shaky.'

'I'm hoping we'll get him out of the house tonight.'

'How?'

'I don't know yet, but Jack will need to go too.'

'Well, have your bath and try to relax. There's no reason to think because they took Hugo, they'll come for you. After all, they've left Marie alone, haven't they?'

Hélène conceded that was true.

The laundry was the only place to bathe in the house. Icy in the winter, but in the warmer weather not so bad and, as well as the faucet in the corner, there was a large ceramic sink. They had an outdoor lavatory and, luckily, a second one accessed from the laundry. The house needed modernising, but since the war began there had been neither money nor inclination.

Hélène sat in her bath, thinking. Hugo was not their

only problem. How could she relax with the German boy in the house, and an SOE operative too? Hopefully, both would be gone by morning. And if there was no news about Hugo by then, perhaps Élise could try her luck at the chateau. It was heavily guarded so it would be tricky, but she knew her way through the 100 hectares of farmland, pastures and meadows and over 400 hectares of walnut, chestnut, oak and poplar trees to a track that wound close to the house.

The door was opened cautiously, and Hélène turned her head towards it expecting Florence. But Jack was standing there staring at her and blinking. Why had he even come downstairs? She slid down into the bath to try to hide her breasts, but he had already seen everything. He held up both palms towards her in a gesture of apology and turned his head to one side. 'So sorry,' he said, and quickly backed out, but she had felt something flow between them.

She could tell she'd turned scarlet, but still she ran her hand over her breasts under the water. The nipples were firm and prominent. She felt a tingle between her legs too, but climbed out quickly before she could embarrass herself any further. Then she grabbed her towel and dried herself vigorously, unable to process, for those few seconds when his eyes had been on her, that she'd felt an overwhelming need to be touched.

She dressed and went through to the kitchen where Jack was now sitting at the table, peeling carrots. He glanced up and gave her a warm smile, his teeth whiter than ever. She felt torn between wanting to back out and wanting to stay. And now Élise was coming into the kitchen through the back door. Hélène pulled herself together. Stop it. Just stop it.

'Any news?' she asked, keeping her voice flat to cover how hot and bothered she felt.

Élise leant her back against the wall and glanced at Jack.

He pushed back his chair and began to rise.

'No,' Élise said. 'Stay. You might be able to help us.'

'Hugo?' Hélène asked.

'Yes. Hugo is at the castle. Suzanne saw them bringing him in.'

'In the dungeon?'

'She doesn't know.'

Hélène's heart sank. What were they doing to him? The idea of anyone hurting mild, gentle Hugo made her feel sick.

'Maybe they needed a doctor,' Élise added. 'Perhaps he hasn't been arrested. Anyway, Hélène, you'll be glad to know Victor and another English agent are on their way here.'

Hélène sighed in relief.

'Victor is going to help us move the German boy tonight.'

'And Jack?'

'Yet to be decided.'

'You do realise now they've taken Hugo they may come after me? To find out what I know. Especially if they get a whisper about Tomas or Jack.'

There was the usual double tap on the door and Élise opened up to let Victor in, along with a short wiry man with black eyebrows and a serious look. Victor introduced him as Claude, another SOE operative. Jack and Claude shook hands as Victor glanced at each of them, as if assessing their capabilities. He was a passionate advocate of resistance, the fire of idealism burning in his dark eyes, but he had no time for those who held back, and Hélène had always felt a little judged by him. His brown hair was cut short, his olive skin shone, and his body looked powerful in his black clothes. She could see Élise light up as she gazed at him.

'I know you understand this,' he said, and glanced around the kitchen. 'But I want to remind you of our objective, which is to create widespread psychological fear in the Germans.'

Everyone murmured their agreement.

'We do this by cutting their communication lines and destroying their supplies, their vehicles, their armament stores, but remember our goal is not to kill one or two here and there, but to derail their entire operation.'

'Although we can kill one or two in the process,' Élise said rather too eagerly.

'You're either with us or against us,' he continued, with a glance at Hélène. 'No middle ground.'

She chewed the inside of her cheek nervously.

'So,' Victor said. 'I will take your deserter to a safe house tonight. Something big is going to happen and the Germans will be distracted.'

'You won't hurt him?' Florence asked.

Victor shook his head. 'He may be able to help us with information. At the very least he can help us compose some leaflets in German to convince the soldiers they are losing the war.'

'And Jack?' Hélène asked.

Victor shook his head. 'For now, he stays here. Just one more thing . . .'

'Oh?'

'I need Élise to come with me.'

'Élise. Why?'

'It needs two of us. Claude has to remain undercover and my men are engaged on another operation.'

CHAPTER 14

Élise

Élise marched up the stairs feeling excited to be taking on a more operational role than simply running her letter box. She'd been secretly hoping for this for some time, although she hadn't mentioned it to Hélène. She slipped into khaki trousers, a grey shirt and a dark green man's jacket Florence had altered to fit her. Then she tucked her hair inside a cap. 'Ready,' she whispered to herself with a smile.

When she returned to the kitchen, Florence had already slipped up to the attic to bring Tomas down and Hélène was busying herself putting together some provisions for the journey – water, dried fruit and some biscuits Florence had baked. And the men were talking quietly among themselves.

As soon as Tomas entered the kitchen, blindfolded and

recoiling in terror, Jack spoke to him in German. Florence patted his shoulder soothingly and told him not to worry, but he clearly did not understand, and crouched, trembling, in the corner. Jack told him what they were going to do and then repeated it in French for the rest of them.

'Maybe I should come too,' he added and glanced at Victor, who had now put on a balaclava.

'You speak German. All good. But three of us with him is too many and you don't know the lie of the land. If we end up getting separated, well . . .' He shrugged and turned down the corners of his mouth as if to suggest he couldn't be responsible for what might happen.

Jack yielded. 'Fair enough. It was just a thought.'

'What happens afterwards?' Florence asked. 'To Tomas, I mean.'

'Good question,' Victor said. 'If we move him successfully, he'll remain in one safe house or another for the duration.'

Florence frowned. 'But it may be for months and months. And what will happen when the war is over?'

'He'll have to take his chances. Deserters are not generally treated kindly.'

Élise twisted round, and with her hair pinned up inside a cap, could be taken for a man. 'Okay. I've got everything we need. Come on, let's go.'

'Please be careful,' Hélène said as she kissed Élise on both cheeks. 'And stay safe.'

Élise tilted her head and looked up at the ceiling to avoid her sister's searching eyes because Victor had already told her of the plan. What Hélène didn't know wouldn't hurt her, and she didn't know their plan was even more dangerous and involved than simply delivering Tomas to safety. Hélène didn't know that first they were going to go to a forger in La Roque-Gageac, to collect some fake identification cards. After that that they would turn back on themselves and take a five-kilometre track to the fortified town of Domme. There was a German outpost there, but it was where they would hand Tomas over to a guide who would take him to the safe house, *and* where they would pick up Victor's motorbike which had been repaired there following an accident nearby.

The three of them then slipped out quietly.

They passed through the village heading in a westerly direction, keeping to the road as far as possible, and checking nobody was on their tail. Tomas wouldn't have a clue where he'd come from, or even where he was now, so once they were away from the village, they removed the blindfold. Luckily, the sky was cloudy with little moonlight, and the night was not cold, though nor was it warm. Élise thought more clearly when she was calm, but could be driven by sudden urges when she was anxious. Right now, she was surprised by how calm she felt, bringing up the rear as they walked in single file with Victor taking the lead. The quiet of night helped too and for much of the time the only sound was their own footsteps.

Suddenly Tomas came to a halt, his face rigid with terror and his eyes darting about as if he wanted to make a run for it. Élise felt exasperated. Didn't the stupid boy realise they were risking their lives trying to help him? Perhaps, if Jack had come instead of her, he'd have been able to explain things to the increasingly agitated boy. Did Tomas think they were going to kill him? She poked him in the back roughly, and they moved on.

While they walked silently through the night, Élise tried not to think.

And, after walking for some time, they arrived at La Roque-Gageac, a small medieval village nestled beneath limestone cliffs overlooking the river Dordogne. All was quiet. The village lay between the cliffs and the river and they had no choice but to pass through it. They had started along the silent main street, keeping to the shadows, when she spotted the swaying silhouettes of three men coming their way.

'Backs against the wall,' Victor hissed. 'German soldiers.'

The three men had been laughing amongst themselves, but then Élise made out one of them scratching his head and looking as if he was peering into the darkness. The curfew had long since started although, of course, it didn't apply to soldiers.

'Hello. Who goes there?' the man shouted, and, from the tone of his voice, Élise could tell he was drunk. All they needed to do was get off the narrow road bordering the river as quickly as possible and then run. But as there was only the river on one side and the village on the other, they'd have no alternative but to head up through the houses.

Tomas began to whimper, no doubt terrified they would shoot him on the spot.

'Quiet,' Élise hissed. Then she backed away, pointing to one of the little streets they had just passed.

'Halt!' they heard. '*Nicht bewegen*! Halt!'

They edged along the wall and, as Victor grabbed her hand, she pulled Tomas in behind her. They darted into the dark cobbled street where houses huddled beneath the overhanging cliffs. They needed to ascend through the village quickly, but the men weren't far behind. Almost immediately a shot rang out and they began to race up the hill, Tomas following them. Élise didn't know the way, but halfway up, Victor slipped into labyrinthine side streets and she ran after him as he turned left and right through the darkness. Then, panting heavily, he stopped to take a breath and pulled her into the recess of a stone wall.

'Damn it, where's Tomas?' she said, looking round frantically.

'Right behind us, wasn't he?'

They heard a second shot. A cry, more like a scream. Then another shot.

'Oh God,' she hissed, 'Oh *God*. Did he try to give himself up?' Her heart couldn't beat any faster. 'Was that . . . do you think he's dead?'

'Almost certainly,' Victor said grimly. 'He isn't in uniform. The soldiers wouldn't have realised he was German. All they'd expect to see would be a maquisard, illegally out after curfew. Anyone running is assumed to be Maquis.'

'What if he isn't dead? What if he tells them about us?'

'Keep your voice down. He's dead, Élise.'

'He might not be. What if he shouted out in German and the shots were just a warning?'

'From here we'd have heard. But all we *did* hear was a

cry, a scream in fact, in between two shots. Which tells me he *is* dead. Now stop thinking.'

'Do you think they saw there were three of us?'

At that moment they heard boots pounding one of the lower streets.

'Come on,' he whispered. 'I know where to go. Let's hope *they* don't.'

He pushed her ahead of him along a narrow alley leading to the foot of the cliff. At the top she slipped and fell onto her knees as some loose stones clattered down the alley. Her heart pounded in alarm.

'Shit! Do you think they heard?'

They listened to shouting lower down in the village.

'They heard,' he said, and put a finger to his lips.

This time he took the lead and they scrambled up a perilous series of notches carved into the rock, leading to what had been a troglodyte fort, where cave dwellings carved out of the overhanging cliffs still existed.

'Built in the twelfth century to withstand the invaders from the north of France,' he said in a low voice. 'Hurry up.'

She bristled. 'I know my history. Let's hope we can get away from the current invaders.'

They carried on climbing past the nests of swallows, swifts and sand martins.

'Up here,' he said, after he'd gone on a little further.

Unable to find a foothold and clinging to the side of a cliff with armed and drunken Nazis heading their way, she felt suddenly terrified. 'I can't see the way,' she hissed.

He edged back to help her, holding out this hand. 'Shhh. It's not far now. They'll never find it in the dark.'

'How come you know this place?'

'Sign of a misspent youth,' he said and chuckled quietly.

The cave dwelling was dry but smelt of dead animals, and yet Élise still felt a burst of elation to have avoided the soldiers. 'Close shave,' she said, not trusting her voice.

'But fun,' he added.

She felt excited, enjoying the adrenalin of the moment, even though poor Tomas may well have died. Besides, he was a German at the end of the day, and they had done their best to help him. Both she and Victor believed fighting back was their duty, the right thing to do, but she had to admit they also loved the thrill. She dug around for a level area where she sat with her knees drawn up to her chest, then she drew out the bottle of water from her satchel. She drank and passed it up to him. He hunkered down beside her, wrapping an arm around her shoulders, and pulling her close to him.

'Seriously, what did you used to do up here?'

'Just kids' stuff. You know what boys get up to. Things weren't too great at home, so I used to camp up here to get away.'

'No girl stuff going on up here?'

'The girls I knew would never have deigned to dirty their pretty white dresses or graze their hands climbing up the cliff. That's what I like about you. You're game.'

She smiled. 'I was always the tomboy of the family, getting into scrapes and scuffles. *A young lady does not have scabs on her knees*, my mother used to say. *A young lady does not brawl in the street like a guttersnipe.*'

He laughed then kissed her on the cheek. 'I'm fond of this guttersnipe. Now try to get some sleep.'

'What about going to Domme?'

'We'll go straight to the safe house in the morning and maybe a day or two later go to Domme on our way back home.'

Suddenly they heard distant explosions and stared at each other. 'Tonight's ambushes are happening all right,' he said.

A few minutes passed.

'Maybe I should get back home to warn my sisters.'

'Warn them of what?'

'If Tomas isn't dead, he'll tell them about our house, about us hiding him in the attic, about Jack and everything else.'

'I didn't have you down as a worrier.'

'No. I'm not a worrier. It's my sisters I'm frightened for. But . . . if Tomas is dead, well that's a bit unsettling too, isn't it, shocking even?'

'You need to stop thinking about him *and* about your sisters. You can't leave here now in any case. The German soldiers may still be close by.'

But the potentially unthinkable consequences for her sisters played on her mind. If Tomas was still alive, then what?

'You're still thinking,' he said. 'You must rest.'

'Sorry.'

She nuzzled his neck, loving the closeness and the smell

of him. So male, she thought, smoky and sweaty, but not at all unpleasant, and after a while the village below grew silent, and the night grew darker and her heart went back to its steady rhythm.

'They've given up?' she asked.

'I think so.'

She gazed out into the starless ink-black sky then rested her tired gritty eyes.

CHAPTER 15

Hélène

The same night, Hélène woke with a start, her stomach muscles instantly tightening. She listened in the darkness and heard a muffled rumble. Thunder? No. Something exploding. Then came another blast. Louder. Booming. Hades, the angry God of the underworld, roaring, she thought. And Cerberus, the three-headed dog, growling and snarling as he guarded the entrance to Hell. The world was cracking and splintering deep in its bowels. And people were falling through the cracks, never knowing which of them was going to meet their fate. Hurt, killed, or captured, it all turned on the throw of the dice.

As her thoughts spun and tumbled, all she could do was pray they would survive. She reached out to switch on the bedside light then glanced around her room. Light. Thank God for it. And the sight of her familiar things and everything in its rightful place, brought her back from the hellish thoughts. Her books, her toiletries, her silver hairbrush and matching hand mirror, her pictures on the wall. She sat up, held a pillow to her chest, and hugged it.

After a moment, Florence, looking pale, came running in to climb into bed with her, her hair fluffy and flying around her face.

'Is Élise back?' Hélène asked.

'I looked. She's not here. But she wouldn't be, would she?'

'You're right,' she replied and bit down on her lip to hold back tears.

'What?'

Hélène blinked the tears away and shook her head. 'I'm fine. It's too soon for Élise to be back.'

Florence shivered. 'I'm scared.'

Hélène wrapped an arm around her sister and pulled her close. 'Me too, darling.'

There was a tap on the door and, their nerves already strained, they both jolted in surprise.

Neither of them spoke, but then Jack popped his head round the door carrying his oil lamp. 'Are you two okay?'

Hélène gazed at his long shadow stretching across the floor as if reaching towards her. 'Better go back to the attic,' she said. 'It's not safe for any of us if you're down here.'

He sighed. They'd moved him up there as soon as Victor, Élise and Tomas had left, and you could tell he wasn't enjoying it.

'Another blanket?' she suggested. 'If you're cold.'

He pulled a face of mock distress then gave her a cheeky wink. 'Cold and lonely. No room for a little one in with you?'

'Very funny.'

Hélène got out of bed and hurried out onto the landing where they kept spare blankets in a tall linen cupboard. As she reached for the handle, she felt Jack's hand on her shoulder. The heat from his palm spread through her whole body and she could feel his warm breath on her neck too. She longed to lean into him, have him wrap his arms around her, feel the comfort of a man, just as she had felt with Julien all those years ago, but instead she pulled away.

'Here,' she said, quickly opening the cupboard and pulling out an old eiderdown and bundling it into his arms while trying to conceal the fact she was trembling.

'What's wrong?' he asked.

She shook her head, eyes downcast. 'My nerves are all over the place,' she said and escaped back to her bedroom.

As she lay in her bed, she thought about Jack and then about what Victor, Élise, and the other maquisards were doing. What brave adversaries they had become. But still she chewed her nails, the worry for Élise gnawing deep in her belly. Once the Jews had either escaped or been carted off, the Milice in particular turned their attention to hunting out Maquis communists, interrogating suspected family members, dragging acquaintances off to be tortured, constantly keeping watch, and infiltrating the Resistance groups.

And the Milice were everywhere. Originally a paramilitary

arm of the Vichy government, by the end of 1943 they had become the national paramilitary force, specialising in the capture and torture of *résistants*. With their local knowledge and wearing sinister uniforms – black jackets and trousers, black berets and long black boots – they were ruthless opponents and greatly feared. Fortunately, the Maquis were gaining strength again, operating from valleys and forests they knew intimately, and able to melt away at a moment's notice. And these days, many in the village were on the side of the Resistance. Much of the Périgord was too, but there were always those who were not. And then there were the different factions of the Resistance. The FTP – communist resistance fighters – was the largest in their area, then the maquisards, in which Victor was a leader. But there were other groups too, including those who supported Charles de Gaulle, leader of the Free French Forces in London. All were united in their fight against fascism, if not united with one another.

Through the bleak remaining hours of the night, she lay awake listening to further explosions followed by gunfire. Florence's breath had slowed, and Hélène was glad she slept.

She thought about how the war had changed their lives and prayed Hugo was all right. In the beginning, collaboration with the French government at the inland spa town of Vichy in the middle of the Massif Central, had had many converts. '*Our duty is to stand beside our Marshall Pétain*,' was what you heard in the streets and cafés. Hélène herself had thought it made sense, at first.

When she grasped that the Vichy government did not support the British in fighting back, and just wanted out of the war, it troubled her deeply. She saw they did not care about England, did not believe England could succeed where France had failed, and so completely changed her mind about supporting Vichy and Pétain.

From then, when she was cleaning the house, she would always sing a patriotic English song to herself. 'There'll Always Be an England' had become enormously popular back home since the summer of 1939, and singing it kept her spirits up. But it had been awful when anti-Semitism and Anglophobia had been so easily stirred up here, and it left her in no doubt the Vichy approach was wrong. Even if the racial prejudice against the Jews had previously been stifled or suppressed, the hatred buried in people's hearts still lingered.

The French and German propaganda was powerful and all it took was one incident here, another there, for it to remerge. The Jews were branded 'evil' people to be feared and denounced. And denounced they were, even by their French neighbours and so-called friends. It had brought out the worst in human nature and Hélène felt ashamed of her country. But, gradually, some began to open their eyes and then, as the Resistance grew, the mood changed. The young were the first. More sincere, more dynamic, less cautious, less scared, many joined the Maquis. Many now led the Maquis.

Hélène twisted and fidgeted in bed, longing for sleep but unable to stop her mind finally turning back to the issue of Jack again. He hadn't been able to reveal the details himself, but Élise believed he would be kept busy liaising with the Maquis and other SOE to ensure the destruction of the communications infrastructure, particularly the railways. In other words, they would be rendering the Dordogne impassable for the German army when the Allies arrived.

Hélène wanted him to stay for a while. She wanted him in her bed. She wanted him every way a woman might want a man. But it couldn't be. He'd leave soon, and she'd most likely never see him again. She had to hold back her attraction. No good could come of a wartime liaison.

CHAPTER 16

When it was light, only moments after Hélène had finally drifted into a troubled sleep, she was woken by hammering on the front door. Oh God, had Élise been caught? Heart juddering in fear for her sister, she ran onto the landing, grabbing her dressing gown on her way, before glancing up at the attic hatch. It opened a fraction and she hissed at Jack to get back and climb into one of the trunks and cover himself with blankets.

Florence came out of the bedroom, bleary-eyed. 'What's going on? Has something happened to Élise?'

'I'm going to find out. Stay here.'

Then she ran down the stairs and found Marie at the door.

'We have injured men at the clinic,' Marie said, her voice urgent and afraid. 'Please can you come now? And hurry.'

'I heard the explosions in the night.' Hélène reached

out to squeeze her hand. 'Let me get dressed. Wait here.' And she raced back upstairs, told Florence what was happening and threw on her uniform.

All the way to the little surgery, the acrid smell of smoke lingered in the air. Marie whispered that the Maquis had blown up a bridge over one of the tributaries in the Ceou Valley, but before that they'd loosened the buttresses at one end. When two truckloads of German soldiers tried to cross, the bridge gave way and they had plunged into the river. Even before the explosion happened, they had jumped out of the trucks.

'But I heard lots of explosions,' Hélène said.

'Yes, the others were at a weapons store. They did that to force the convoy to cross the bridge as they headed towards it.'

A small crowd had gathered outside the surgery door, which had been left wide open. Hélène rushed inside and then through to the adjoining building Hugo used as a small clinic or cottage hospital. At first, she couldn't tell if the injured were German or French, but gradually she understood all the voices she heard were German. She checked each man, six of them, all soaking wet. It was a miracle none had been killed. She asked Marie to get blankets for them and then turned her attention to their captain who, by the look of things, needed a doctor urgently.

She called out to Marie to order one of the German soldiers she'd seen outside to get up to the chateau and bring Hugo back double quick. 'Tell them the captain is losing blood. If he doesn't see a doctor soon, he will die.'

She listened to the screech of a motorbike accelerating at speed and worked quickly to stem the blood as best she could, but her heart was banging against her ribs. She had exaggerated her concern for this man as a ploy to get Hugo back, but now the man *was* losing consciousness. She held his face in her hands. 'Stay with me,' she ordered. 'Stay with me!'

His eyes flickered and he turned dull blue eyes on her.

'It's all right,' she added. 'I've got you. I've called for the doctor.'

With one hand she stroked his hair from his forehead, with the other she pressed a cloth hard on his stomach to keep the blood loss at bay. She supposed she shouldn't care about the life of a German, especially not a Nazi, but in this moment, she was just a nurse caring for a patient. Besides, if any of them died or had been killed in the attack, it would be calamitous for the locals. The reprisals were swift and brutal. Field Marshal Wilhelm Keitel, chief of the Wehrmacht High Command, had given the order in 1941 that, for every single assassination of a German soldier, fifty to a hundred communists would be executed. There had been a huge outcry when it became apparent many of the executed men had not even been communists. Nobody Hélène knew agreed that even a terrible thing like an assassination should result in the deaths of so many. And nobody knew if the Vichy government's hands had been tied, or if the administration had been actively involved in the drastic repression. The order had been retracted to something less contentious but still distressing. In future only ten would be executed.

Whilst praying her request would be granted and that Hugo would arrive quickly, Hélène continued to comfort the German captain, who was floating in and out of consciousness. She did everything she could think of to keep him awake: smelling salts under his nose, tapping on the cheeks and constantly whispering that he would be fine. The little cottage hospital echoed with the moans and groans of the other men, although she felt sure most of their injuries were not life-threatening. She breathed a sigh of relief and leapt up when Hugo walked in, but faltered when she saw how dishevelled he looked. His face dirty, his hair uncombed, and purple shadows under his eyes. She could not suppress how upset she felt seeing him looking so spent, but the muscles round his eyes contracted as if to warn her not to speak.

'Looks worse than it is. I'm tired is all.'

Hélène didn't believe him, but decided this was not the time to pursue the subject.

Hugo came straight across to the injured captain. 'This is the man who needs my help?'

For the next hour Hugo worked on the man, stemming the blood loss, cleaning the wound, and stitching him up. He administered morphine and decided it would be preferable to keep him in their little hospital rather than sending him along bumpy roads to Sarlat. When Hélène argued that surely the larger hospital would be better, Hugo raised his hand to stop her speaking.

'It's still touch and go whether the man will survive,' he said in a low voice.

Hélène offered to keep an eye on the captain while

Hugo treated the other patients. They had to accept there would be German reprisals, but they'd be far less brutal if the man lived, so it was vital they take care of him. The work of the Maquis was always a double-edged sword – it was frightening when their actions were so close to home.

In a lull, she tried to question Hugo again, but the doctor just shook his head, with a wretched look on his face and his grey eyes sorrowful. With a pang, she reached out a hand to comfort him. He squeezed it and they gazed at each other. She was at a loss to know how to support him and then, at the end of the day still uncertain if the captain would survive, Hugo tried to send her home. When she demurred, he insisted.

'But Hugo,' she argued, looking at his bloodshot eyes. 'You need to sleep.'

'Marie and I will manage. Now go.'

'I want to stay.'

There was a long uncomfortable silence while she vacillated, still wanting to stay, and somehow knowing there was more to this than he was saying. Then he spoke again, this time in the most sombre voice she had ever heard him use. 'Hélène. If I don't save the captain, they will execute Marie. I need to be alone to do this.'

Hélène gasped. 'Surely . . . isn't it all the more reason for me to stay?'

'No. As I said.'

Although she would willingly have stayed in Hugo's place, she was exhausted and when he practically pushed her out of the door she gave in and went home, with an ache in her chest and misery in her heart.

CHAPTER 17

Half an hour later, Hélène climbed up into the attic and then she sat cross-legged on the floor with Jack. With tears in her eyes, she told him about the situation at the clinic – about what would happen if Hugo failed to save the captain's life.

'We need to do something to take your mind off things,' he said.

'I don't know what. I can only think of Hugo and Marie. I feel sick at the thought of what might happen.' Her jaw tightened and she screwed her hands into fists. 'Why do Élise and Victor never think of the consequences?'

She could feel his concentration as he looked at her. Again, she felt something flow between them. Compassion? Empathy? The unspoken words skimming just beneath the surface but not breaking through. He was not glancing away, not avoiding anything, and under his scrutiny she felt her defences weaken.

'It's war, Hélène,' he finally said and moved his oil lamp so he had room to shift his position.

'It's not just that I'm sick with worry for my sister, it's how the reprisals affect everyone else too.'

Because the light from the lamp had now thrown his face into darkness, she couldn't work out what else he was thinking, and it made her feel self-conscious. All she could see was the glitter of his eyes and she couldn't tell how much he could see of her. She moved the lamp onto a box. 'There. That's better.'

'So, what can I do to help?' he asked.

'I don't know. I want to keep my spirits up, but sometimes . . .' She shook her head.

'I know.'

'The threat goes on and on. I long for normal life, and for all the people I love to be safe, so much it hurts. Physically, I mean. Here.' She pressed a palm into her chest and took a breath, letting it out in a long sigh. 'And yes, I do feel low.'

'With something like this hanging over the doctor and his wife, it's hardly surprising,' he said. 'They're your friends.'

She bit her lip to hold back the tears. She didn't want to weep in front of him. 'I owe Hugo everything,' she said, her voice catching in her throat. 'Marie too.'

'Even without this, when we don't know what the next day is going to bring, it's easy to feel powerless.'

'But you don't feel like that.'

He snorted. 'Oh, I do, of course I do, and I have to fight it.'

'How?'

He narrowed his eyes, seeming to think for a minute, then his expression lightened. 'Do you have a pack of cards?'

'Of course. I'll get them.'

By the time Hélène had found the pack and then climbed back up to the attic Jack had laid out some cards of his own. 'This one is called 12 O'Clock High,' he said. 'A card game based on air combat. You just have to attack your opponent's aircraft.'

Hélène tried her best, but was not a natural card player and, despite his repeated instructions, she kept getting things wrong.

'I'll give it another go,' she said, but they ended up attempting to stifle their laughter at her incompetence. His face was entrancing when he smiled and, as animation transformed his features, his eyes shone. She felt a fleeting moment of happiness and reminded herself how, even in the worst of times, you could stumble upon a moment of peace.

'Glad you're not the one flying our planes,' he said.

'I'm more of a jigsaw girl,' she replied.

'Ah,' he said with a smile. 'Like my mother.'

She raised her brows. 'I'm like your mother?'

'Maybe. You look after everybody. My old Ma always did too.'

'Did?' She paused, unsure whether to ask or not.

He shook his head.

'Sorry.'

'One of those things. Although, of course, I remember her.'

'And you remember she looked after you.'

'Yes.'

'Thank you for distracting me,' she said, suddenly feeling guilty for having had those few minutes of respite.

He took her hand and when he kissed it, his moustache tickled. 'Any time.'

'You never told me what you were doing in France the last time you were here.'

'It was at the end of last year and early this year. Bloody cold it was too. As you know, the French rail system had become the focus of Allied bomber forces. It was called the "Transportation Plan" and the focus was to destroy railway centres to delay, impede, and prevent the movement of German troops through France. That's it.'

'We heard about it on Radio Londres.'

'What you might not know is the raids were resisted by the bombing chiefs, Harris at Bomber Command and Spaatz for the American air forces. Churchill baulked too, mainly because of French civilian casualties. However, they were all overruled by Eisenhower and President Roosevelt.'

'And now?'

'I'm here to train, as I said before, but also to liaise with the Resistance.' He paused. 'I can't say where, what or when, of course. But I guess people know what the Resistance is doing, and the Germans aren't stupid. Just knowing me puts you at risk of torture.'

'Maybe. But I don't want to think about it.'

'No.'

'So, you believe it won't be long before the Allies land?'

'Nope. But I also think the heaviest bombing is still to come.'

'It's hard to comprehend that one day this will all be over.' She sighed and shifted her position. 'Sorry, I'm getting cramp. I need to make a move. I'll go down and see if Florence has rustled up something to eat.'

'She's quite a girl, isn't she?'

Hélène smiled warmly. 'She's amazing. I don't know how we'd have survived without her.'

He tilted his head, giving her an amused look. 'Something tells me you would have found a way.'

'Maybe, but we'd all be terribly thin. I'm a dreadful cook at the best of times, whereas Florence is a culinary genius, even when she only has turnip and Jerusalem artichoke as ingredients.' She patted her stomach. 'We're all a lot gassier than we were.'

'Thanks for the warning,' he said with a laugh.

Down in the kitchen she found Florence muttering to herself. 'What's up?' Hélène asked.

'Nothing. I just wish I had some *Roquefort* or *Fourme d'Ambert*. They make all the difference to this dish.'

'You mean we're not having turnip stew?'

'Broccoli and potato soup actually.' She picked up the pepper grinder, gave it a few twists over the soup pan and then took it off the heat.

'No sign of Élise yet?' Hélène asked, trying to keep her voice calm.

Florence shook her head and they gazed at each other for a moment.

'Do you want to take some soup up to Jack?' Hélène said, changing the subject.

'Can I? I'd love to. He's great, isn't he? So handsome.'

'Is he? I hadn't noticed.'

Florence chuckled. 'Of course, you've noticed. We've all noticed. Even Élise, and she usually only has eyes for Victor. Victor's a bit too intense for me, but Jack, well he has a twinkle in his eye, doesn't he? I like that.'

Hélène was a little surprised and frowned. 'What happened to the young guy you were seeing?'

Florence looked ill at ease for a moment, then she seemed to pull herself together.

'Oh. You must mean Enzo. I wasn't seeing him. He can't fight because of the polio and I felt sorry for him. We just went for a couple of walks together, but now he won't leave me alone. You've probably seen him hanging round our gate.'

'Is he bothering you? I can have a word.'

'I can handle him. He'll take the hint sooner or later.'

'He was the tall one with the curly brown hair wasn't he, not the other one?'

'Yeah. Curly hair. Good-looking, but not bright. Anyway, I'd better get on.' She ladled some of the soup into a bowl with a handle on either side. 'Hope I can carry it up like this. Help yourself, will you?'

'Remind him not to move around. The attic floorboards creak.'

Hélène sat at the table, her mind curling round images she'd rather not see and desperately trying not to succumb to the dread in her heart. 'Hugo and Marie will be fine,' she whispered to herself over and over. 'They will be fine.' And Élise? She felt a burst of heat in her eyes, so closed them and rubbed her lids. Élise would be fine too. She had to be.

Then she thought about what Florence had said. It hadn't struck her before, but had her little sister taken a shine to Jack too? She still thought of Florence as a child, but of course she wasn't. She was a beautiful woman now, after all.

CHAPTER 18

Florence

Florence felt so guilty about putting her sisters at risk by insisting they hide Tomas, that it kept her awake at night. She was still feeling nervous as she wandered, disconsolate and lonely. When she was young, she'd often been left out of her sisters' games, so turned to her imagination to provide the companionship she longed for. Her magical inner world had been a comfort and a joy, but now reality was kicking in. How could she maintain a belief in the goodness of the world with everything that was happening around them? Injured soldiers, explosions at night, Élise becoming more active in the Resistance and still not back. She didn't know what to think any more.

But there was good and bad in everyone, wasn't there? The Nazis had been the cause of so much destruction and everyone else had been terrified into submission, but surely not everyone agreed with them? She turned off onto the track and walked beside the meadow where chalky milkwort grew along the verges, then threaded her way through the long grass to the picnic area. The woods were especially quiet today, with just the sound of her own footsteps and the leaves fluttering in the breeze. Ever since they'd come to live here, she'd loved the dappled heart of the woodland, especially in summer when it delivered a deliciously cool respite from the heat. But even in winter, when the ground was crisp and crunchy underfoot, it had been the one place to restore her. She felt she could hear the spirits of the trees and listened for them now. Nothing came. She tried again and when nothing came again, she felt sad. So much had gone. But then a single cuckoo called. She gazed around as more murmurings of the wood switched on as if in response, the branches creaking and whistling, the grasses rustling and the woodpeckers and thrushes flitting from branch to branch. When she glanced up at the patches of clear blue sky, she felt the sunshine on her face. She began singing to herself, avoiding treading on the wildflowers dotting the ground, especially the rosy-purple lady orchids, found only in the depths of the woods. Her mind and body relaxed a little and a small bubble of happiness bloomed inside her. She spun on the spot, stretching her arms out high and wide, twirling round and round until she was so dizzy it was impossible to stand up straight. And then she saw the young man watching her from between two trees.

'Anton! I wasn't expecting to see you again.'

'Florence.' He stepped forward and reached out a hand to steady her. 'I'm just out walking.'

She wondered how much he knew about what they were going through and felt the chill of fear. Surely he couldn't know anything about Tomas or Jack?

But he was looking away, seeming to be dealing with his own complicated emotions. He swallowed visibly then turned back to gaze at her. 'I know these are difficult times.'

She snorted. 'Difficult? You can say that again.'

He ran a hand through his short blonde hair and looked utterly mortified. 'I am so sorry. It was clumsy of me. I suppose what I meant was . . . now that we've bumped into each other, well, I was wondering if you might like to accompany me to the river.'

'You mean, be friends, despite the war?'

After a moment or two of gazing at his candid blue eyes as he nodded, and recognising his humble sincerity, she agreed.

He looked so openly pleased that his unworldly response warmed her heart. 'I can't tell you how happy that makes me. Thank you.' He held up a bag. 'I have beer and baguette.'

'Cheese?'

'Indeed.'

'Ah, you already know me so well.' She paused. 'Anton?'

'Florence.'

'How old are you? First you seemed older than me. Now not so much.'

'I am twenty.'

She smiled at him. 'So, I am two years older than you.'

'Does it matter?'

'Of course, not. We are friends, aren't we?'

He seemed delighted, his cheeks reddening a little.

Then he looked terribly serious. 'I wish to apologise.'

'You already have.'

'No. I wish to . . .' He struggled to find the words and stared at the ground before looking up and gazing straight into her eyes. 'I wish to apologise for what my countrymen have done, are doing, to your country.'

She bit her lip. 'Oh, Anton.'

'I didn't choose to come here. Because I have the command of French and English as well as my native German, they recognised I'd be useful as a translator. I am not a coward. I hope you appreciate that, but I could not have borne arms for the Reich.'

'I understand.'

There was a short silence.

'You live with your sisters?' he said.

'How do you know?'

'You told me, although you didn't say how many sisters. I imagine an entire coven of sisters, all blonde like you.'

For a moment she hesitated. Should she tell him? 'Just two sisters,' she said at last. 'Élise and Hélène. But I'm the only blonde one. Hélène is a nurse and Élise has a café. We're all very different. They call me their "little witch".'

'And are you?'

She raised her brows. 'A little witch?'

His eyes sparkled.

'Maybe I am.'

'Well, as it happens, I've always had a soft spot for witches.'

She laughed and he laughed with her and, in that moment, maybe *just* for that moment, she felt free of anxiety, the companionship between them warming her. These moments when people rose above the horror of war, when you could feel the common humanity uniting them . . . well, they restored her faith. She must never forget love was stronger than fear, stronger than hate and stronger than division.

'I'm so pleased we met like this,' she said and held out her hand to him.

'Shall we head on down to the river, then? It may not even be possible to privately hire a gabarre, if you'd like to do that. But we can ask discreetly and maybe hire one for Monday.'

'What about your job?'

He smiled. 'I can always take a day off.'

Although Florence had never been on one, she knew the gabarres were flat-bottomed wooden boats previously used for transporting goods along the rivers of the Périgord, until they were overtaken by the development of the railway and the automobile. But occasionally wine from the vineyards which ran along the Dordogne river was still transported in the old-fashioned way.

'I'd love it,' she said. 'But I don't know if we're allowed. Before the war we had a canoe. My sister Élise and I used to paddle. It was amazing, although rather scary, but you could see all the chateaux from a new perspective.'

'Let's find out,' he said and smiled at her.

CHAPTER 19

Élise

Victor needed his motorbike to move quickly between the Maquis camps and safe houses dotted around the Dordogne. A Motobécane M2, with a pillion for a passenger; he was justifiably proud of it. If stopped, he would say he worked in his father's garage in Sainte-Cécile and was out delivering spare parts. He always kept a few bits and pieces in his battered leather saddlebag just in case. But the bastide of Domme, protected by cliffs on the north side and encircled by ramparts on the other three sides, was tricky to get in and out of without being seen. It was early on Sunday morning and still not quite light, but even then not easy. Élise and Victor crept through streets lined with elegant houses towards the large square of *La Place de la Halle.*

'Quiet,' he whispered a moment before they reached the square. 'Germans.'

Élise could feel her heart pounding and held her breath as, with their backs against the wall, they waited for the soldiers to pass. When they had gone, she let out her breath slowly.

They then had to avoid a few more Germans soldiers in what seemed to be an all-night café. They slipped past and then turned off to pick up Victor's motorcycle, which had been repaired, repainted and given a false number plate after it had been involved in a collision with a German supply truck nearby.

After what had happened to Tomas in La Roque-Gageac, they had stayed at the safe house for two nights, partly to lie low and partly to help print leaflets. Élise now had a bundle of them tucked into her satchel, ready to take to the café later; then they would be distributed anywhere German soldiers might see them. The Maquis' aim to dishearten German soldiers so they would believe Germany was on the verge of losing the war, meant these leaflets played a crucial role.

Élise knew Hélène would be terribly worried about the delay, but she and Victor were finally making their way back home. They'd ridden the motorbike most of the way, but now Victor was wheeling it along a track as they reached the woods a few kilometres from Sainte-Cécile. Élise pulled him to a standstill. 'Look at the sky,' she said.

The sunrise was spectacular, pink, red and violet. Even when their country was sinking under foreign occupation, the world remained beautiful. He wrapped an arm round her shoulders as they took in the fresh new day, both feeling relieved they'd managed to complete the mission without being caught.

'Apart from Tomas, it went well,' he said and kissed her on the cheek. 'Thank you.'

'What's next?'

'There are two refugees we need to get out via the Pyrenees.'

'Well I don't know about you, but before I do anything else, I need to sleep.'

He yawned. 'What about if I come to your place? Just this once.'

'If we can slip in without Florence seeing, I don't see why not. Hélène will be leaving for work soon, so we will have to wait until then.'

'Is she up to all this, your sister? Will she cope? I've never felt too sure about her.'

Élise knew his dedication to the cause sometimes meant he found it difficult to tolerate people who were less fervent. So as soon as they sat down on a fallen tree trunk to rest, she leant against him and thought about how to respond.

'Hélène isn't one of nature's resisters,' she eventually said. 'But she'll cope, and she'd never breathe a word. She's sensible, you know, level-headed.'

He laughed as he ruffled her hair. 'Not like you, then.'

'She's like a mother hen to Florence and me. For a long time, she didn't want me to do anything and I had to keep quiet about everything. Now she's a bit more involved, whether she likes it or not.'

'She did well by agreeing to Jack staying.'

'She likes him.'

He looked up through the trees and exhaled slowly.

'Penny for them?' she said.

'Ah, nothing.'

'Go on.'

'Well . . . Florence.'

'What do you mean?'

'How would she stand up to—'

Élise butted in. 'Interrogation?'

He gazed at her.

She drew in her breath before speaking. 'Florence has an abundance of love. She would feed the Nazis to death.'

He laughed. 'Or maybe poison them with one of her herbs.'

'Maybe. But, you know, I can't help thinking how wonderful it will be when all this is over. When we can live a normal life again, have children, be happy.'

'The liberation won't be long now. The Germans are on the back foot. Once the Allied invasion happens, things will be different.'

'Hope you're right.'

'I'm always right.'

She laughed. 'Go on telling yourself that, Victor.'

'You'd miss me if I were gone,' he said and dug her in the ribs.

'I'd be inconsolable,' she said more seriously.

He took her face in his hands and kissed her gently on the mouth. She felt the love she was certain he had intended, but there was something else behind the tenderness of his kiss and she couldn't work out exactly what.

When his eyes grew suddenly grave, she tilted her head to the side. 'What?' she asked.

'You know I am already on the path to death,' he said, holding her gaze.

She pulled away and stood up abruptly. 'Why say that?'

He shrugged. 'The odds. Not exactly on my side.'

'Well I wish you wouldn't say such things,' she said and turned her back to hide the tears prickling her lids.

'I'm not invincible, Élise.'

There was a long silence. The unspeakable sadness of what he was saying, and maybe the truth of it, was something she could not process. Did not even want to process. And yet didn't she owe it to him? She paused in her thoughts. And, knowing there could be no resolution between his words and her feelings, she took a breath then turned back to him, and aiming for a more light-hearted tone, she reached out a hand. 'Come on, you fool, with your crazy ideas. I want to sleep, but I want your body even more. If I can stay awake, that is.'

He laughed as he rose to his feet. 'I think I know how to encourage a woman to stay awake.'

'Had lots of practice then?'

He raised his brows but didn't reply and then they carried on walking.

They had made love several times, but it had been out in the open or in a barn, never in a bed and, as it had always been cold, it had always been hurried. This would be their first time somewhere warm and comfortable and it felt momentous. Élise had not intended to fall in love with Victor or anyone else either, but it had happened when she least expected it. Victor had turned up in her life and the attraction had been instantaneous. She knew it. He knew it. And although they tried to resist it at first, they'd soon given up, tearing the clothes off each other in the back of his father's blue van when Victor had offered her a lift home. Who had made the first move neither could truly remember, so it had been sealed in her memory as a simultaneous explosion of passion.

Now she held his hand as they moved off. They were just nearing the village when they heard dogs barking and muffled laughter ahead.

'Sorry, angel. Might be the Boche,' he said. 'We need to split up. You go home, I'll turn back and hide out. Give me the satchel.'

'No. I need to take the pamphlets to the café. And they don't sound as if they're coming from the direction of my house. I can easily skirt around.'

'If you're sure.'

Élise hugged him then gathered up her courage and headed towards the village. Bloody Germans! No matter where you went, there *they* were, spoiling everything. She walked on as soundlessly as possible, still calculating how best to avoid them. She considered trying to conceal herself in the undergrowth, but it was sparse this near to the village and if they found her hiding, they'd only become more suspicious. Better to go on. She continued to tread carefully, but then a startled bird took flight right in front of her, flapping its wings and making a racket. Another followed, then another. Blast it, she muttered looking round for an escape. But it was too late. The soldiers were now heading towards the noise, their boots growing louder on the ground, and she knew she might have to steel herself.

They hadn't seen her yet so, step by step, she picked her way, avoiding anything that might alert them. She considered dumping the satchel but then, through a gap in the trees, she spotted them poking rifles into the bushes. If she dumped the satchel and they found her close by, they'd put two and two together. Who or what were they looking for? She was so nearly home, but it was too late to turn back and go the other way. She hesitated, smelling the smoke rising from the village houses at the same time as she saw there were only two men. Then one of them, an older sour-faced man with dreadful skin, spotted her. 'What you are doing?' he called out in halting French.

She stepped forward. 'Walking. I needed the fresh air. And I'm trying to find my dog.'

He held out his rifle to halt her progress. 'Ach so! On your own?'

She told him she was, keeping her answer brief and her eyes lowered to give an impression of meekness, even though she seethed from the familiar mixture of indignation and corrosive anxiety. How dare these foreigners treat people like this? She should be allowed to walk freely in her own country, at whatever time she wanted, without having to answer to them.

'You live in the village?' the other man asked. He had been smoking and now he ground the butt under his heel and coughed.

Her lips felt a bit dry, her mouth too. 'Nearby,' she said.

'Know anything about the attack on the bridge?'

'What attack?'

'The one when our captain was killed.'

'No. Why would I?'

He ignored her question. 'What you got in your satchel? Papers?'

'No, they're here.' As she dug in her jacket pocket, her heart began racing from an unnatural feeling of bravado. Any minute now they would open her bag and find the leaflets. What had she been thinking? She should have given them to Victor.

'Schnell! Schnell!'

She took a breath. Despite her fear, she knew her papers were fine, and she refused to fumble. These men with their daunting uniforms and visible weapons focused the mind. They want to frighten you, she told herself. Don't let them. Even though they provoked the same feeling of threat she'd experienced when the BNA thug had put a knife to her throat, she forced herself to stand firm. She extracted the papers and, emboldened, raised her eyes, and then handed them over with a confident smile on her face.

The man scrutinised them, then stared at her. 'You,' he said. 'You are Baudin?'

She choked back her fear, wondering what was coming next. Had something gone wrong at home?

But the man merely said, 'Your sister is nurse?'

'Yes.'

He seemed to consider and then he smiled. '*Gut. Sehr gut.*' And then he moved aside so she could pass. 'Your sister is a good nurse, fixed up my colleagues.'

Élise smiled to herself as soon as the men were out of

sight. Good old Hélène, you got me out of that one. But now don't look back, she commanded herself, though she still couldn't help casting a swift look over her shoulder before spitting on the ground and racing home.

As she arrived at their gate, panting and sweating, she saw a thin young man loitering in the lane nearby. She narrowed her eyes and recognised Enzo. The polio he'd suffered as a child had left him with a limp, but now, when he was able, he worked as a labourer on a local farm.

'What do you want?' she asked.

He shrugged and kicked at the leaves on the ground.

Élise opened the gate and began to walk up their path.

'I came for Florence,' the boy called out and when Élise glanced back, she noticed his friend, the boy with the thick spectacles, leaning against the trunk of an oak tree.

'I'll get her,' Élise said. 'Wait there.'

She carried on inside and a few moments later Florence came out and headed over to the boys. Élise watched and listened from the doorway. She had never liked Enzo, who was too shifty by half, and couldn't understand why Florence had befriended him.

'Enzo,' her sister was saying with a troubled look on her face. 'I thought I'd explained.'

'You said you'd see.'

'No. I think you must have misunderstood me. I said we'd see, and maybe we could be friends. Don't you remember? I'm sorry, but I'm not your girlfriend. I never have been. It was all in your head.'

He glowered at her. 'All in my head?' You think I'm stupid.'

'Of course, I don't.'

The bespectacled boy over by the tree began to guffaw and Enzo turned scarlet. 'Well, we'll see all right. Bitch!' He swaggered off, kicking the tree as he went and cursing obscenities as his friend continued to laugh.

When Florence turned back, Élise saw her eyes had filled with tears. 'Come on,' she said and took her arm. 'Boys are such a pain in the arse.'

Florence gulped back her tears. 'I only spoke to him before because I felt sorry for him. I didn't lead him on.'

'It's a pity his friend had to see. His pride is hurt, that's all. Now, I need to get this mud off my boots.'

'Back door for you then. But where on earth have you been all this time?'

CHAPTER 20

Hélène

Hélène had stayed up until two in the morning, talking to Jack and drinking Florence's home-made wine. She had expected to sleep late but had not, and now she felt as if she were in a kind of stupor. After slipping into a pair of grey trousers and a favourite lemon-coloured silk blouse, she came downstairs where she stood gazing out of the sitting room window, her eyes on the clouds and the distant trees, while wondering what to do next.

'Ah, there you are,' she heard Élise say.

Hélène swivelled round, almost dizzy with relief. At long last her sister was back. 'Oh, my goodness, you look the worse for wear. I've been so worried. Come here.'

'You don't look so great yourself,' Élise said as she crossed the room.

The sisters embraced.

Hélène held her at arm's length and studied her face. 'You don't know how happy I am to see you, but what happened? You've been gone so long.'

'We had to wait. I heard a German captain died in the bridge attack.'

'No. He's still hanging on . . . Or he was. What have you heard?'

'A couple of soldiers stopped me on my way back from the safe house. They said a captain had died.'

Hélène felt a burst of a panic, her heart speeding up. 'Oh my God, I hope they've got it wrong. He was still alive yesterday. Perhaps I should go. Should I go? I'll get my hat.' She moved towards the door, but Élise held her back.

'Hélène. It's Sunday. You need your rest. Hugo would have let you know, or Marie would come.'

Hélène bit her lip to stop it quivering. 'The dreadful thing is . . .

'What?'

'I can hardly bear to say it out loud, but they threatened to execute Marie if Hugo didn't save the captain. I just can't, well, you know . . . I can hardly breathe when I think of it.'

'Putains!' Élise exclaimed. 'The bastards.'

Hélène forced herself to take a long breath then exhaled slowly. 'But no news means good news, right?'

'Right, although maybe we should be thinking of getting Marie out of the village?'

'She won't go. She'd never leave Hugo.'

'The thing is . . .' Élise pinched the bridge of her nose,

which Hélène knew was a sign of reluctance in her sister. 'Tomas is dead.'

'Oh, Lord. What happened?'

Hélène held her breath while Élise explained. 'We saw it, or at least we heard it. The shots I mean. Victor is almost certain he's dead. We asked around in the morning and a couple of the village women saw him carted off looking lifeless.'

Hélène stood completely still, thinking of Tomas; so young, so scared. 'Poor boy,' she said quietly. Although she couldn't help thinking about the kind of future he would have had. Never able to go home, always on the run. 'Though he wouldn't have had much of a life,' she added.

'Not to mention how dangerous it might have been for us had he lived.'

The moments passed as Hélène allowed that to sink in. She had always known concealing Tomas in their attic had been a risk, but at this close brush with discovery she felt another flutter of panic. What had she been thinking, allowing Florence to persuade her otherwise?

'Are we safe?' she asked.

Élise insisted they were, but Hélène wondered, without seeing the boy's dead body, how could she know for sure? Even if Victor had been adamant the boy was dead, had Élise simply chosen to believe him?

Her sister looked keen to change the subject and added, 'Now listen, Victor wants Jack here a little longer. Can you cope with that? He'll be gone within a few days.'

'Yes. I can take his stitches out in a couple of days and then he'll be free to leave.'

'Good. You know he already goes out at night? But he's incredibly careful not be seen and I think we're far enough away from the village not to arouse suspicion.'

Hélène felt such a mix of emotions she hardly knew how to reply. She knew it would be much safer when Jack was gone, but she liked knowing he was there. 'He was here last night. I was . . . talking to him until late.'

Élise smiled knowingly. 'Talking?

'Yes.'

'If you say so. Anyway, Bill, the other SOE has still not been found but Victor is working on it.'

'Fine,' Hélène said. She looked pensively out into the garden, her mind churning.

'Why are you staring out of the window?' Élise asked.

'Just wondering why Florence keeps going out.'

Later that morning Hélène went through to the hall to see if she'd left her book on the table in there, but stunned by what she saw, she stood still. Élise appeared to be floating down the stairs in the red dress. Even though the skirt was still ripped, she looked every inch the lady and so like their mother it took a moment for Hélène to make sense of it. Hélène had seen the dress before, she was certain of it, and it had been worn by their mother. But a mother exposing a side to her character none of them had ever seen.

'What?' Élise said. 'I thought I'd try it on. But you look as if you've seen a ghost.'

'I think I have . . .'

'Really?'

'Now I remember. I saw Maman wearing it. She was

in the hall, just as you are right now, and she was drunk. Very, very drunk, and . . . weeping.'

'Where were you?'

'That's the funny thing. I think I was in the attic.'

'Oh crikey. I wonder why. You hated the attic.'

'Yes.' Hélène frowned. 'And I don't know how I could have seen her from up there.'

As the sun streamed in through the hall window and the dress shimmered even more brightly, Hélène decided to ask Violette to stitch it back together. She clearly had uncomfortable memories attached to it, but once mended maybe it could be a symbol of hope for them all. The captain would live, Hugo and Marie would be all right, and one day their lives would be patched up too. They would dance again and sing again; they would eat wonderful meals and they would be free. Hélène wasn't ready to proclaim that everything was going to be fine as yet, but as Élise spun on the spot, the skirt whirled out, sliced and ruined, but it still looked as if her sister was glowing on the inside. And in her beautiful smile Hélène saw not only her incredible spirit shining, but also that her sister was in love.

CHAPTER 21

Florence had missed lunch, and nobody knew where she'd gone. The day had not turned out as sunny as Hélène had hoped and the light early-morning clouds had grown heavier during the afternoon. By the time she spotted Florence arriving home in the late afternoon, it was raining. Hélène closed her eyes and took a deep breath.

'You were a long time,' she said, putting down her book and moving away from the window as her sister came in. 'You missed lunch.'

Florence flung herself down on the sofa. 'Did I?'

'Get up, you're wet, you'll soak the sofa.'

Florence puffed out her cheeks but didn't move.

'Look, I'm worried enough about Hugo,' Hélène said, and when her voice shook, she steadied herself. 'I don't want to have to worry about you as well. Where were you?'

'Out.'

Hélène shot her a quizzical look. 'I figured. I looked for you at the bottom of the garden, but you weren't there.'

'I went for a walk.'

'On your own?'

'Yes.' Florence sighed dramatically and began to plump up a cushion. 'Honestly, these are so lumpy.'

'Darling, I'm not sure it's safe at the moment to wander off on your own.'

'I like walking. It helps me clear my mind. Do you understand that?'

Hélène nodded. 'Yes. Of course I do . . . Did you need to clear your mind about anything in particular?'

With a hazy look in her eyes, Florence ignored the question. 'Best of all I like going barefoot in the woods.'

'What about ants?'

'With shoes on you can't feel the earth beneath your feet.'

'True.'

Florence stood up, dumped the cushion and gave it one last thump. 'You do realise I'm twenty-two, not twelve?'

Hélène raised her arms above her head, stretched, placed them on the top of her head for a moment and then sat down. 'Sorry. I do know – but it's hard.' All the reasons why she should try to keep a firm hold on Florence rushed into her mind. She was young. She was innocent, like one of the delicate fawns you saw in the woods. Surer-footed than a wobbly newborn, but not quite as robust as a yearling. She didn't see the world for what it was. 'I just want to keep you safe,' she added.

'Wrap me in cotton wool, you mean.' Florence came back to sit beside Hélène on the old sofa. 'You know I'd forgotten how badly this sofa needs recovering.'

'Restuffing too.'

Florence's eyes lit up. 'I know. Shall we do it together?'

'I was planning on reading.'

'You can read any time. Come on, let's do it. It will take your mind off things.'

Hélène groaned. 'You mean now? I'm tired.'

Florence rose to her feet and held out a hand. 'No time like the present, that's what you always say.'

Hélène heaved herself up reluctantly and saw Florence was gazing at her with a determined expression in her eyes.

'What?'

'Listen, Hélène, I don't want you sticking to me like my shadow.'

'All right, I'll try not to. Old habits die hard.'

'Especially with you.'

'What do you mean?'

Florence narrowed her eyes as she bent to examine the sofa. 'I think we need to get the cover off first and then we can work out how much it really needs restoring.'

'Florence?'

Her sister straightened up. 'Well you like to keep to your routine, don't you? Whereas I like to discover new things . . . Now where did I leave my scissors?'

'And have you?'

'What?'

'Discovered new things.'

Florence bit back a smile.

'There is something you're not telling me, isn't there?'

Florence started pulling at the covers, ignoring her. 'Look. There are holes everywhere.'

'You would tell me?'

'Of course. Now, I just need to get my scissors,' she said, and rushed from the room.

Hélène felt uneasy. She had danced attention on the needs and wants of her sisters for so long, thinking of them before herself, always hanging on to the reins holding them together. She pictured a circus ring, herself as ringmaster, top hat and tails, her sisters as prancing horses. Uncontrollable. And even though she'd like to let go a little, she realised she didn't know how. She had been the rallying point of the family for too long. And now there was this new resolve in Florence to withhold a part of herself, to keep it private, a part that was nothing to do with the family. A part that clearly signalled, 'back off'.

Hélène knew how to handle her patients, how to put them at ease, how to comfort them and how to encourage them to be brave. But, increasingly, she did not know how to handle her sisters as adults.

She shook her head as Florence entered the room brandishing her scissors and a knife.

'I found them . . .' Florence said and paused. 'Hélène, what's wrong? You look so sad.'

'Do I?'

'What's the matter?'

'I'm worried about Hugo and Marie.' She took a breath and pulled herself together.

'If anything really bad had happened, we'd know by now.'

Hélène sighed. 'Come on, this sofa. You do know how to do this?'

Florence's eyes sparkled. 'No, but it will be fun working it out.'

The pair of them cut the exterior fabric away and the inner fabric too, then they rolled the sofa on its side so they could remove the flaccid cambric from the base. Once the sofa was the right way up again, Florence examined the cushiony layer of sagging stuffing.

She bent her head and sniffed. 'Yuk! It stinks. This will have to go too.'

Hélène shook her head. 'I think we may have bitten off more than we can chew.'

'Wait,' Florence said. I can feel something down there. She dug her hand in deeper, then bought out a sealed envelope and waved it in the air. 'Ooh. Wonder what this is.'

'Probably a bill,' she replied without much interest.

Florence ripped it open and pulled out a single sheet of yellowing paper. She glanced at it and then looked up at Hélène, her face alive with curiosity. 'This, my dear sister, is a love letter.'

Hélène frowned. 'From whom?'

'I'll read it out loud. See if we can work it out.'

'All right,' she said, and Florence began to read.

My darling

This has been the longest wait of my life. I had hoped you'd reply to my last letter but can only think something must have happened to prevent you. Has our secret been discovered? Is that it? I cannot live another day without knowing you are safe. Call me and, if you can't, please write.

Your beloved. Always.

'Well,' Hélène said with brows raised. 'How intriguing.'

Hands on hips, Florence eyes widened. 'Isn't it romantic?'

'Romantic? I suppose. Sounds like an illicit affair to me.'

'Who could the "beloved" be?'

'Not Father.'

Florence smiled and Hélène understood why. Their father had many wonderful qualities, but romanticism was not one.

'But it could be a letter to Maman. Maybe when she was young?'

'Or her sister.'

'The one who ran away. Maybe she ran away because of this?'

Hélène turned back to the sofa. 'Well whoever wrote it, we still need to sort out this mess.'

'Would Violette have something to fix it?'

'Good idea!'

'Hélène,' Florence said after a pause. 'Do you really like Violette?'

'Of course. Why not?'

Florence shrugged. 'I don't know.'

Hélène laughed. 'Just because you didn't like the pattern she gave you to make a dress.'

'It was a silly childish dress.'

'If you say so. And now, Florence, I'm going to leave you to get on with the sofa.'

'Noooo!'

At that moment there was a knock at the back door and Hélène went through to the kitchen to open it. 'I was just thinking about you,' she said when she saw Violette standing there smiling.

'Oh, Hélène. I have news.'

'Come in.'

'No, no. I can't stop. I've left my boy napping. Marie begged me to come.'

'So?' Hélène said, hardly daring to ask.

Violette smiled. 'It's good news. Really good news. The captain has pulled through. He's out of danger.'

Hélène had not realised she'd been holding her breath until she exhaled loudly. 'Oh, thank God!' And trembling with relief she leant against the door frame for support.

Violette reached out to hold her, and the women hugged.

CHAPTER 22

Hélène lay awake in bed that night for hours. Her relief was so overwhelming she could have danced for joy. If anything had happened to Marie, Hugo would have been lost. Hélène would have taken it upon herself to care for him, do everything, organise the funeral in his place, if the Nazis had allowed her. But sometimes the bodies were simply carted away, and they never knew where to. Rumours abounded of mass graves, or of piles of bodies being burnt, and corpses being left out in the open for wild animals.

All this thinking of death brought back the days after her father had been taken so suddenly by a coronary. He had died at fifty-eight, the day before her twenty-first birthday. On the day of the funeral, when they entered the church and saw the pews so full of people, her mother had hissed in her ear, 'The spectacle of sudden death. How they love it.'

Hélène sighed at the memory of her mother's heartlessness and was instantly back there with the awful smell of lilies so redolent of grief. They had smelt pungent, sickly, sitting atop the coffin. Oriental lilies, known for their strong perfume, with large creamy white blooms and a pinker edge around the petals. It was raining. Of course, it was raining. How could the sun have shone? Her father had not been religious, and her mother was a lapsed Catholic, but the funeral was to be a traditional one. All for show. The expensive silk-lined coffin – Claudette had been proud of that – was carried from the hearse by six unknown men, all wearing top hat and tails. Hélène had known the coffin was the most expensive kind, not because her mother had shared the choice of it with her, but because she'd seen it marked up in the catalogue. The congregation was silent as the men bore the coffin in on their shoulders, with the family following behind. As she slowly placed one foot in front of the other, Hélène glanced from side to side, surprised by the strangers in the church all craning their necks for a better view. Her mother twisted round and narrowed her eyes at Hélène. A clear reprimand. And then Claudette carried on walking, dry-eyed, dressed head-to-toe in black and looking pale, glancing neither to the left nor to the right. Hélène followed with her sisters as they slowly edged towards the front pew.

The priest looked like a movie star. Glamorous, with smouldering Clark Gable eyes. Hélène stared open-mouthed and her mother prodded her in the ribs. What a waste for such a man to be a priest, Hélène thought irreverently and glanced at Élise, who widened her eyes in agreement. Then they sat up straight and tried to listen.

Hélène didn't hear a word; instead she gazed at the coffin, trying to imagine what her father looked like inside it. Was he pale and waxy, or had they painted him to be pink, unlike himself? Either way she would never set eyes on him again. As that truth sank in, she couldn't help crying. She felt as if a part of her was in there with him. But seeing her mother glare at her, Hélène, ashamed of her tears, surreptitiously wiped them away.

Then, without warning or any prior agreement, Élise got up and strode to the front of the church. Facing the pews, she took out a piece of paper from her pocket and began to read in a beautiful clear voice:

'Do not stand at my grave and weep,
I am not there, I do not sleep.
I am in a thousand winds that blow,
I am the softly falling snow.
I am the gentle showers of rain . . .'

Hélène didn't hear the rest of the poem. She was thinking about her father and worrying about what their mother would do to Élise as punishment. Judging by Claudette's face, she was incandescent with rage. Then Hélène tuned in again and heard Élise read the very last line:

'Do not stand at my grave and cry.
I am not there; I did not die.'

Élise did not return to their pew. She marched straight out of the church and Hélène felt proud of her.

When it was all over and the mourners were leaving, Hélène thought she could smell cucumbers. How odd. Incense yes, but cucumbers? Could it be a perfume? Surely no one would have brought their shopping in with them? It was a fresh, unlikely smell to find in a church on a soggy wet day.

Hélène's palms were clammy as she accepted people's condolences at the door of the church, and her mother's smile remained fixed as she held out a black-gloved hand. Whenever Hélène looked as if she were about to cry, Claudette pinched her skin or grabbed her by the elbow and pulled her away from anyone within sight or earshot.

At the graveside, as the coffin was lowered into the hole, the sky cleared and birds began singing. It surprised Hélène, the proof that life could go on without her father. When it was over, Florence elected to go in the car with Claudette, but Hélène and Élise walked home through the churchyard, reading out loud some of the words on the older headstones. As they walked, Hélène's limbs felt heavy, weighed down by sorrow. Élise didn't cry or speak, but she took Hélène's hand and squeezed it.

All that day Hélène had wanted something more from her mother, some acknowledgement of who her father had been, what he had meant to them all, and how much he would be missed, but there had been nothing. All she'd had to comfort her was her sister squeezing her hand in solidarity.

During the wake there was one moment when

Claudette's careful control began to slip. Hélène caught the look on her mother's face before she quickly turned away, but it had been down to gin not grief, Hélène thought, and it was anger not love that she had seen in her eyes.

Hélène had returned alone to the grave the next day and seen it piled high with flowers, most with little cards attached, all of them with beautiful words written from the heart. It had moved her to see how well-loved her father had been and she had sat on the grass and wept freely until her eyes were stinging and swollen.

Sometimes, even now – all these years later – the memory made her feel desperately sad. She never stopped wishing he was alive. There was a fancy headstone in England bearing his name and, much as she might want to, she would not be able to visit it until the war was over.

CHAPTER 23

Florence

On Monday, Florence was already waiting when Anton turned up laden with a heavy canvas bag. It hadn't been a lie when she'd told Hélène she'd been out for a walk the day before, she really had wanted time to think. Today she had chosen to wear a floral silk dress in lilac, that she'd altered from one of the dresses her mother had left behind. Claudette had discarded all her glorious French clothes from her younger years and, while they fitted Élise perfectly, *she* rarely wore a dress. So Florence had nipped in the waist of this one, cut off the slightly puffed sleeves at the elbow, kept the pleating at the shoulders, taken the seams in a little so the skirt skimmed her body, and altered the hemline to fall a little below her knee. She was delighted with the result but, until now, had no reason to wear it.

'You look nice,' he said.

She gave a little curtsy, happy to see him, and spun on the spot so the skirt swished and swirled around her.

'What's in there?' she asked, indicating the bag.

'Treats!'

She whistled. 'I can't wait.'

'We can swim if you like,' he said, 'but I've actually managed to arrange a river trip.'

'Really?'

'Indeed. I have my motorbike to take us to Limeuil. Does that suit you?'

'Of course.'

'It's a lovely day for it and I'm told the most beautiful stretch is between Souillac and Lalinde where the cliffs force the river to make horseshoe loops.'

'I know Limeuil. It's where the Vézère river joins the Dordogne.'

She climbed up behind him onto the bike and clung on as he made his way up the hill. She was not going to live her life in fear. And this outing, this adventure, this breaking free, felt a little like a rebellion – not just against Hélène, who wanted to keep her safe at home, but against the war itself. She would not be intimidated by it. And Anton had been sent to show her the way; she saw it in his eyes.

She'd always looked for signs to show her the way. Little things she liked to interpret as omens. A feather here. A flower there. And she was superstitious too, especially fond of the one when two people pulled the dry and brittle chicken wishbone apart and the winner could make a wish. She liked making wishes, hugging them to herself, and knowing they were secret. And she loved throwing spilt salt over her left shoulder and would sometimes spill some just so she could, although spilling salt was said to bring bad luck. People believed the devil sat on your left shoulder, but God perched on your right, so if you threw salt over your left shoulder it would blind the devil and reverse the bad luck. That was her favourite, although she also never walked under a ladder, and saluted Mr Magpie daily. She fervently agreed that to give someone a knife would be tremendously bad luck for your friendship, unless you offered the knife with a coin attached to it. The friend had to give you the coin straight back in payment for the knife, thereby saving your friendship. So far, she had not tried it out.

'It's about thirty kilometres,' she heard Anton shouting over the engine noise. 'Are you all right?'

'I'm happy,' she shouted back. And she was. She really was.

Once they reached their destination, Anton parked the bike and untied his bag from where he'd attached it at the back.

Florence gazed around her at the enormous trees, at a vineyard circling a chateau, and at the view of the undulating green meadows and beyond them the amazing confluence of the two rivers. They began to meander down from the top of the hill, passing stone houses and timber-framed cottages built into the hillside. Then they passed through the gateway of the *Maison du Porche,* which separated the upper town from the lower.

'On our way back up Rue du Port, we'll pass the convent and then, if we go under the gateway into Grande Rue and bear left, we'll reach the Porte du Recluzou which leads out of town.'

'Are we going to walk out of town?'

'No. I just want to show you something amusing. If we go uphill from there and bear left to the church, we'll find the *Maison de tolérance.*' With a twinkle in his eye, he told her about the lovely old house with a wooden terrace, where certain types of local girls used to entertain lonely boatmen.

'You've been reading up,' she said and laughed.

'Actually, I already came here to investigate. I have to find some way to impress you.'

She didn't tell him how much she already was impressed.

As he led her down a set of stone steps to the spot where a small craft was bobbing on the water, she smiled at the sight of swans gliding and ducks dipping about on the river.

'Not a gabarre then,' she said as he got into the boat and then held out a hand to help her climb in.

'The man in charge of the boat is retired,' Anton said, when she was seated. 'But for a few francs he agreed to this. It's only a short trip, but long enough to spot castles on high rocky cliffs and the fortified towns around them.'

'My favourite villages are Beynac-et-Cazenac, la Roque-Gageac, and, of course, Domme,' she said, picturing the fortified honey-stone *bastide* or fortified hilltop town, with its old stone walls built so high.

'Yes, they are breathtakingly beautiful,' he agreed as they began to move off.

'There are ghosts here, you know,' she said.

'You believe in ghosts?'

'Maybe. I know the past is still here, still with us. You can almost smell it. Don't you think there are moments when that happens? When the history of a place seems to sit right alongside us.'

He looked misty-eyed, as if she were touching on something that was important to him too.

'You feel as if you could reach out and touch it,' she added. 'And there they'd be, the English and the French still battling it out.'

He laughed. 'I so know what you mean, and one day this war will be part of the past too. I wonder if people will even remember.'

'Yes, I think of that too. And when you look at the hazy river early in the morning, it feels so ancient with its little islands and high banks. And then the sun, when it comes, and the river turns silver. Nothing changes that.'

They remained in silence for the remainder of the trip, enjoying the languid twists of the river and the spectacular surrounding scenery and, perhaps most of all, the sunlight breaking through the clouds and speckling the free-flowing water. He reached out a hand to her as they glided past plum and walnut orchards and tumbling walls festooned with ivy and cascading wisteria. Florence held on to his hand as she gazed up at the ancient chateaux and honey-hued villages and listened to the birds singing along with the gentle thrum of the motor, and she felt at peace. If only for this moment.

When she arrived back after her river trip, she spotted Enzo watching as Anton parked a little way from the house. Why was Enzo hanging around again? Deliberately, she pushed the annoying lad from her mind, despite a twitch of unease. In the house she was surprised to find her hairdresser friend, Lucille, sitting in the garden, her face streaked with dried tears and Élise attempting, rather half-heartedly, to comfort her. Élise had little time for the shallow tears of girls, and who could blame her? But Lucille was a good soul and Florence, always more generous than her sister in judging another's pain, felt instantly sympathetic.

'She isn't quite making sense,' Élise said. 'But I think she's fallen out with her mother.'

Lucille rose to her feet and ran to hug Florence. 'Oh, I'm so glad you're back. Where have you been?'

'Just out,' Florence said, avoiding the curious look on Élise's face. Had she heard Anton's motorbike leaving right before Florence appeared?

It's true,' Lucille continued. 'I have. Oh Florence, it was awful. I called her terrible names and she said I was an ungrateful brat and she never wanted to see me again.'

'It will blow over. She'll come round.'

'That's just it,' she said, gulping back what looked like a second round of tears. 'I . . . d . . . don't want her to come round. She's hateful and wicked and I never want to see her again.'

'You feel bad now, but she's your mother and I'm sure she needs you.'

'I'm staying with my aunt Lili, but it's my job. I love my job. What am I going to do?' And now her narrow shoulders began heaving and she started crying again in earnest.

Florence wrapped an arm around her friend and exchanged looks with Élise who, backing off, held up her hands as if to say 'over to you'.

'Come on, let's get you inside. You can wash your face and then I'll walk you back to your aunt's house. There will be a way through this, I promise.'

Lucille went along with that, and while she was in the laundry room splashing her face Florence thought back over her day. She and Anton had talked about maybe meeting another time at a disused sixteenth-century mill on the edge of the Vézère river. Hidden in a valley between meadows, tall bushes of hydrangea and oak trees, he said it was the perfect place to get away from the war. She was still surprised she had accepted Anton's friendship so readily, after all she couldn't forget he was German, and she understood the danger. But he was such a sweet, kind person, one of those special people who had the ability to make everything feel better. Although she could hardly admit it to herself, the risk was also a little thrilling.

Lucille joined Florence in the kitchen.

'You look better already,' Florence said.

'I feel it. Thank you.'

'I've had an idea.'

'What?'

Florence smiled. 'Well, if your aunt Lili will let you stay on, why not start a new business of your own?'

Lucille frowned. 'I'm not with you.'

'You could be a sort of roving hairdresser. Offer haircuts, or whatever people need, in their own homes. With fewer buses running, it gets harder and harder to get around these days, but you could easily travel by bicycle.'

Lucille's eyes lit up. 'You think I could do it?'

'You'd need some equipment. But it would be lovely. We could see each other whenever we liked.'

'I have some savings. But where would I get the stuff from?'

'Bergerac, or Sarlat maybe? Or perhaps Lili might persuade your mother to set you up. That would be best.'

Lucille hugged her. 'You, Florence Baudin, are a genius.'

Florence glanced at the door to the hall. 'Shall we go to the woods before you go back?'

They went out and chatting continuously, walked to the picnic area in the woods where they sat on the bench.

'So,' Lucille said. 'What have you been up to lately?'

'I've made a new friend,' Florence said, unable to keep it to herself.

Lucille's eyes widened. 'Someone new around here. Who? What's she called?'

'It's a boy. He's called Anton and we get on brilliantly.'

'Where did you meet him?'

Florence laughed. 'At the bottom of the garden.'

Florence went on to describe Anton and told Lucille about their meetings and how she'd been on the river with him. 'He's such good fun,' she added.

'How nice. Where does he come from?'

'Nowhere near here.'

'Oh,' she said with a curious look.

Florence ignored it. 'It's great to be able to get out for a bit without Hélène breathing down my neck. He has a motorbike.'

'Lucky you. Wish I had a boyfriend with a motor.'

'Oh no, he's not my boyfriend. We just get on like a house on fire and I feel as if I've known him for ages.'

'A friend then.'

'Yes.'

'So, is he from Sarlat?'

Florence shook her head. 'Not exactly.'

'You're being cagey.'

Florence looked at the ants running in trails along the ground. 'Well if I tell you, you have to promise never to breathe a word.'

CHAPTER 24

Hélène

On Tuesday evening, after an unexpectedly damp day, the clouds had at last cleared. Just after Hélène had taken Jack's stitches out – he had gazed into her eyes and called her a nightingale – and while it was still light, she was on her way to Violette's house for supper. But as she was about to cross the road, she saw from her vantage point the faded blue front door open and an SS officer come out. He turned to look back inside and speak to someone. Then, after the door had closed, he took several strides in Hélène's direction. She scanned the street and glanced up at the armies of swifts skimming the rooftops and screaming as they swooped and dived in pursuit of insects. On seeing this timeless sight, no one would guess everything was not exactly as it should be; it seemed like just another evening in a sleepy French village. Except for the

SS officer. She twisted her head to look the other way so as not to catch his eye and as she heard him walk away, she frowned in uncertainty. Was her friend all right?

She clasped her bag tightly against her chest. She had planned to ask Violette to mend the red silk dress and had brought it with her in the hope that, if it were made whole again, she'd be able to peel back the layers of her life. Her memory, or this particular memory, was capricious and she didn't know how to grab hold of it. But every time she thought of the dress, an image of the attic also slid into her mind. As a child the attic had been a shadowy place full of scratching and scampering and she had always avoided it, so why was it so strongly associated with the dress?

Violette answered her knock quickly and ushered her into her sewing room.

'I hope you don't mind sitting in here. I need to finish this hat by tomorrow.'

Hélène considered the pink and purple helmet-shaped hat, made from wool felt with a delicate netted veil.

'Who is it for?'

'Nobody special.'

Hélène studied her friend. There was a slight pause as she decided whether to pursue the topic. In the end she decided she would. 'Come on, Violette,' she said. 'Surely you can tell *me*.'

Violette glanced up at her and sighed. 'If you must know, it is for a German officer.'

Hélène looked at her askance, taking in the felt flowers Violette was sewing onto the hat. 'He wears hats like that?'

Violette raised her brows 'Of course not. Hideous, isn't it?'

They both laughed.

'It's for his wife. Once he discovered I'd worked in couture in Paris, he hot-footed it here.'

Hélène frowned as Violette bent her head and carried on sewing. 'But I thought we had both agreed not to do anything for them.'

Violette looked up again and narrowed her eyes. 'You nursed the injured Germans.'

'With good reason. I wanted to see Hugo released.'

'Look, I know you disapprove, but I have my reasons too.'

'Reasons?

'Dresses are not selling so well these days. I have Jean-Louis to think of.'

'His medications?'

'Yes, and the specialist I take him to.'

'You still go to Paris?'

'No. A man in Sarlat, now.'

Hélène remembered when Violette had first arrived two years before. It had not been an easy fit between an old-fashioned French village and this chic Parisian woman with her high heels, elegant dresses and fur coats. Why she had come here in the middle of the war she'd never said. They all had secrets, it was only natural, but Violette never mentioned her past. But because she was a brilliant seamstress and designer – adept at cutting up a pair of old curtains and turning them into the prettiest of outfits, or reviving an old dress so it looked like new – she had eventually been embraced by the village. Violette always looked beautiful, and was smartly dressed, *soignée*, and charming to everyone. Hélène had sometimes thought her a little vain, but maybe only because she herself could never aspire to such sophistication. In fact she had already developed frown marks between her eyebrows, whereas Violette's face was entirely smooth.

Hélène frowned now. 'I saw an SS officer leaving. Is everything all right, or . . . is he your hat man?'

Violette nodded. 'Hat man.'

Deciding to drop the subject for now, Hélène picked up her bag and took out the red dress. She held it up so Violette could see the ripped skirt.

'Oh, my goodness, what happened?'

Hélène shrugged. 'We found it like this. Could you mend it?'

Violette reached out and examined it closely. 'I can't make it look the way it was before, but I can stitch it together with inserts of new fabric.'

'The same colour?'

'No. Not exactly. If we were in Paris, yes, but here my stocks are low. I only have a length of burgundy silk. But it could work.'

Hélène felt doubtful.

Violette patted her hand. 'Don't worry. I can make it beautiful again.'

'I'll pay you.'

'Not at all. We're friends, are we not? Whose dress is it?'

Hélène scratched the back of her neck. 'I think it was my mother's.'

Violette was looking at it admiringly. 'It has a Parisian label. Look.' She held it out for Hélène to see.

'You must miss Paris,' Hélène said, seeing the wistful expression on her friend's face.

Violette didn't meet her eyes.

'Are you lonely here, Violette? I mean, do you feel lonely.'

'Oh, it's not so bad. There are worse things, and I have my darling boy.'

'You have me too. You know that.'

'I know.' Violette smiled at her. 'Thank you.'

Hélène thought about it as she gazed at Violette's perfectly symmetrical face, carefully shaped brows, high cheekbones, and swan-like neck. Hélène had her sisters and her work with Hugo but, apart from her son, Violette's life was so solitary. She appreciated she should have asked her friend why she'd left Paris, but so many people had left the capital, maybe she hadn't felt safe. Hélène glanced around at the little sewing room, taking in the artfully arranged coloured threads, the piles of folded fabrics, the braids and the three half-finished hats. She wondered who they were for, but decided not to ask. Violette had to make a living somehow and who was Hélène to judge her for it?

Violette put the strange hat aside. 'Let's go through. I have a rabbit stew bubbling away.'

'Oh, I almost forgot.' She picked up her bag. 'Florence made these biscuits for Jean-Louis.'

'How kind.' She reached out to take them.

Hélène gazed at her for a moment then just came out with it. 'Why did you choose to leave Paris, Violette?'

'Choose?' She laughed bitterly. 'I had no choice,' and then, right on cue, her little boy woke with a cry. Violette sighed. 'Ah sorry, I'll have to go up. He's been waking a lot lately. It's the coughing. Go through to the kitchen.'

Hélène did as Violette had said and wandered into the tiny room. She looked around her friend's kitchen. The shutters were closed, and the back door locked. A tiny two-person table was pushed up against one wall, already laid for a meal, and a glass with just the dregs of red wine in it had been left on the draining board. She gave the stew a stir and sat at the table to wait.

It didn't seem at all like the kind of place her friend would have been accustomed to in Paris. Violette had arrived in Sainte-Cécile in 1942, but the mass exodus from Paris had been in the summer of 1940, when millions had streamed along the roads while German planes strafed them mercilessly. Violette must have carried on sewing and embroidering in the atelier of the couture house she worked for until she came here.

When Violette came back down, Hélène remembered she hadn't asked about the sofa. 'We are trying to re-upholster and restuff a sofa. Florence and me. It's not going well.'

'You need help?' her friend asked.

'Well, if you wouldn't you mind?'

'Of course not. I'll come tomorrow. I'll have to bring Jean-Louis, but I can let you have everything you'll need and give you instructions on how to stuff it. And I can easily run up some new covers if you have the fabric.'

'I think we've got enough of the blue-and-white stripe

we used for the curtains. We bought far too much when we first moved in.'

Hélène gazed at Violette. 'I was wondering about your life in Paris. Did you ever meet Elsa Schiaparelli?'

Violette looked astonished. 'Good heavens, no. She would have been way above a humble seamstress like me.'

'I love the pictures of her designs in the magazines.'

'The thing about her clothes is they let women move freely. They don't constrict you.'

'But they're beautiful too, aren't they, especially the shocking pink dresses and the tailored suits which have no business being so pretty?'

Violette laughed. 'I didn't think you were so interested in fashion.'

'I'm not. I just like her. The practicality *and* the glamour.' She grinned. 'Possibly the only personality trait I've inherited from my mother.'

Hélène had read about how the Italian designer fled France early on and that the Nazis had intended to shift the entire couture world to Berlin, but it had proved unfeasible. She knew many of the fashion houses had remained open in Paris including Pierre Balmain, Christian Dior, Lanvin and Nina Ricci, so maybe Violette had continued working for one of those.

Hélène decided to bite the bullet. 'Who did you work for in Paris, if you don't mind me asking, that is?'

'Oh, only a small designer. You wouldn't have heard of him.'

As they drank their wine, they gossiped about the villagers, especially their only confirmed bachelor,

Maurice, the handsome blacksmith, who was about forty and still lived with his parents.

'Do you think he'll ever marry?' Violette asked.

'Why? Are you interested?'

Violette laughed. 'No!'

Then they talked about crazy Madame Deschamps who went out in her slippers and hair curlers, poor soul, leaving her daughter Amelie to run around looking for her. They talked about tall, thin Pascal the clerk, who they at first had suspected of spying, but whom they now trusted. And they talked about how hard it must be for Suzanne and Henri to be living with the Nazis.

'Do you feel nostalgic about the past?' Hélène asked her.

Violette shook her head. 'Not really, though I was happy in Paris, at least to begin with.'

Just before they began to eat their dessert, Violette gave her a quizzical look. 'I was wondering if Florence has a boyfriend yet.'

'Florence?'

'I was thinking earlier. Surely it's time for her to have a beau.'

CHAPTER 25

Florence

Florence didn't mind that the day had brought rain. It was good for the garden and now the sky had brightened, even if only for a little while before it grew dark. She was alone in the kitchen and Élise was just outside the back door preparing to move the goats back into their shed when there was a knock at the front.

'Are you all right to answer?' Élise asked Florence, popping her head round the door. 'I've got my hands full of goats.'

Florence smiled at that image.

The sisters had hoped that because Hélène had helped treat the injured German soldiers, and the captain too, they might now be left in peace, rather than be subject to yet another identity check.

'Yes,' she said. 'Of course. But don't put the goats in

their shed, take them back to the woods, just in case soldiers have come to demand food. Go.' Her first thought was always for the goats and their precious source of milk.

Élise slipped away.

When Florence opened the front door, she swallowed her breath. It wasn't soldiers but two hard-faced BNA thugs, one dark-skinned and tall, one older, white and shaped like a bull.

They were both armed and the older one pushed her into the kitchen.

'You stand here,' he ordered.

'Where is your dog?' the taller one asked, glancing round while his companion pointed his rifle at her.

Florence felt flustered. 'Dog?'

'We heard your sister was out looking for him the other day.'

Florence ran through the options quickly. 'Ah, right. I'm afraid I don't know. I haven't seen him.'

'And your sisters?

'Still at work.'

He gave her time to elaborate, but heart thumping, she remained silent and resolved not to give any indication Élise was outside. She thought about shouting for Jack to come down, but if she did, Élise might hear and the men would find their goats.

He walked around the room poking at things with his rifle. 'Nice place you've got.'

'We like it.'

'I'm sure you do.'

She hardly dared ask why they were there, but knew she had to.

'Ah now . . . depends,' he replied.

'On what?'

Well, well, well, let's see,' he said with a sneer and eyes glittering with hostility. In a flash she saw how much he was enjoying this casual bullying. 'All alone?'

With an expression of what she hoped was defiance rather than capitulation, she nodded.

After looking suspiciously at Florence's herbs, the bull-like man knocked them from the ceiling with his rifle then trampled them beneath his boots. When he found her store cupboard, his eyes lit up, but instead of stealing her carefully nurtured and preserved supplies, he cruelly hurled them one by one onto the flagstone floor, smashing the glass jars. Florence flinched as the scents of rosemary, dried tomatoes, asparagus, artichokes, olive oil and lemon rose in the air, and the mess slowly congealed on the ground. She had lovingly planted, taken care of, and cooked the contents of every single jar; her way of helping her sisters survive. He glanced at her stricken face and laughed; his enjoyment of her pain even worse than the ruin of her prized supplies. Distraught, she ran across to try to save some of them, but the glass had spread everywhere and as she tried to pick some of it out, she cut herself. When she sat back on her heels, she lifted her palms and saw the blood. He snorted and she felt a flash of anger at his intention to reduce her to nothing.

'Why would you do such a thing?' she demanded.

He smiled and strode over. 'Been keeping it all from us, eh?' He grabbed her by the elbow and pulled her up.

She forced herself to think, her gaze sliding across to the back door.

'Oh no you don't,' he said, and then he traced a finger down her cheek and neck. Feeling a wave of disgust, she recoiled from his touch, her chest heaving.

'You don't like?' he said, eyebrows raised in mock surprise.

She tried to control her breathing, but her breath was coming too fast and her heart was hammering against her ribs. Then the real panic rose. Her chest constricted, her muscles tightened even more, and she felt as if she might never be able to breathe again.

'Maybe you will like this better?' This time her pulled her head back by the hair and licked her neck.

She gasped and then, repulsed, she cringed, turning her head to the side, and shying away. As the other man came closer, she struggled to keep a hold on herself.

'Now you see what we do with little girls who hide food from us.'

'Please,' she implored, trying to look at one then the other in the frantic hope of discovering a trace of compassion. What went through the minds of these men? Had they no sisters, mothers, wives? Her own mind was spinning out of control, darting desperately from one alternative to another as she fought to find a way out. This. That. No. Not that. Maybe? Maybe what? And then a blank. Stripped of any dignity, she saw it was hopeless.

'Please,' she said again

'Shut the fuck up,' the tall man said.

As the older man chucked her under the chin, he ripped open the front of her blouse and fondled her breasts. The revulsion and bile rose up. She fought the impulse to vomit, her breathing completely erratic now as if she were fighting for oxygen.

'Well now, aren't you the pretty one? How old are you?'

'Twenty-two,' she managed to stutter.

'But you look younger.' He inclined his head at his friend. 'Fresh meat, I'd say.'

The tall man guffawed.

'How about it, eh?' He took off his jacket and cap, began to undo his belt and then, seeing the terror in Florence's eyes, her tormentor laughed and lifted her skirt. She tried to push him off, holding on to the hope he was just enjoying frightening her, but the other man held down her arms. She knew then and fought against it, even as the bullish, muscular man put a hand under her skirt and pulled down her knickers. Then he dragged her into the middle of the room. 'Bend over the table.'

In this incomprehensible, terrifying moment, ice ran through her entire body and she froze.

With his back to the door he hit her across the cheek and then forced her over the table, twisting her head to one side, squashing her cheek against the wood and pushing her arms flat out above her head. She heard him undoing his clothing and making sure he was able. There was a moment of sheer terror when he used his fingers and then he slammed himself upon her. She felt the terrible weight of him, smelt the stale tobacco and sour wine on his breath. The walls pressed in on her. As he treated her as something less than human, her mind and body began to split. Her thoughts collided and began to still. She felt the pain, but at the same time did not feel it. She was in the woods by the river, feeling the summer sun on her skin, and running through the fields in autumn. She was somewhere else. She had to be somewhere else. She did not scream but went completely silent as he heaved and grunted. After a few moments, at the back of her mind, as if in a far-distant place, she heard the other man approaching the table. 'Me now, I think,' he said and laughed. 'Then we search the house to see what we can find.'

CHAPTER 26

Élise

Slowly, Élise edged open the door to the kitchen. The men heard nothing, their backs to her, one of them speaking. She raised her pistol, hesitated for just a moment, then squeezed. A shot rang out and then, immediately after, a second one. Both men fell to the floor as Élise roared in. 'Fucking bastards! Fucking, fucking, bastards,' she bellowed, still holding the gun. She wanted to scream, hurt them some more, but as they writhed on the floor, she simply put another bullet into one neck and then the other, dispatching them both.

She took a breath and ran to Florence.

'Darling,' she whispered. 'Let me help you.'

Florence didn't respond.

Élise stroked her hair. 'Come on, let me get you away

from here,' she said, her voice almost breaking with the pain of it.

Florence remained exactly where she was, catatonic, soundless, barely breathing, her skirt bunched up around her hips. Élise heard Jack running down from the attic and saw his face drain of colour as he entered the kitchen. 'I heard the shots.' He let out an enraged howl when he saw what had happened. 'Oh God, I should have come down earlier.'

They stared at each other in horror for a moment, then Jack turned away while Élise pulled at Florence's skirt, covered her breasts with a tea towel and picked up her underwear. Then he went to Florence and spoke softly.

'Will you let me help you?' he asked.

She made a slight movement which he took as agreement, and was able to gently ease her away from the table. As blood dripped from her hands, she saw it and began to shake, then her legs gave way.

'Water,' he said to Élise, whose eyes were stinging with rage. 'Bandages too, and a blanket to wrap her in. And something sweet. She's in shock. I'll carry her.'

'Men who use their dicks as weapons should get a taste of their own medicine,' snarled Élise through gritted teeth.

As Jack carried Florence through to the sitting room, Élise fetched what he'd asked for and then followed them in. He had lain her sister on their smaller sofa, the more comfortable one still in bits, so Élise covered her with the blanket and perched on the edge gently bandaging her hand. Florence's hand was limp, as if the life had gone out of her.

Jack motioned Élise to come over to him. She got up, still quaking from a mix of fury and sorrow and a depth of loathing she had never in her life felt before. He pulled her aside, just out of Florence's earshot.

'We need to decide what to do,' he said. 'And quickly.'

'I know. I have to fetch Hélène, but I can't leave Florence.'

He shook his head. 'You know I can't go.'

'Yes. I know.'

'And we need help. Those bodies need moving and fast. Can you get Victor?'

'I'll have to find him first, won't I, before I can go for Hélène I mean?'

'I think so.'

'You'll stay with Florence. Look after her?'

'Of course.'

'I hate leaving her,' she said, her voice breaking.

He reached out and held her shoulder. 'I know. But we need Victor.'

Élise wanted to cry. To scream. To shout out her revulsion and her rage. This should not have happened to Florence. Her hands clenched and unclenched repeatedly as adrenaline coursed through her. 'I'll kill them, she muttered. 'I'll kill them.'

'Élise, you already did.'

Once in the kitchen again she stared aghast at the blood and the lifeless bodies of the men, and the implications of what she had done hit home.

She went out to find Victor. He and Jack would have to remove the bodies in Victor's father's blue van and then dump them far away. God knows what the reprisals would be. But if they could make it look as if the men had been killed nowhere near Sainte-Cécile that would help. And if they could prevent them from being found at all, so much the better. Then she remembered their truck. 'Oh shit,' she said, then ran back inside the house, picked up the clean jacket of one of the men, and then the cap, before tucking her hair inside. She found the keys in the jacket pocket, picked up their rifles, ran out to the truck, got in and drove off. At least it was getting dark.

CHAPTER 27

Hélène

Hélène arrived back just before curfew. She pushed open the front door to find Jack pacing back and forth in the hall, his face grim, his jaw pulsing and the skin around his green eyes taut with worry, or something much worse. Despair maybe? Or anger? Whatever it was, she took a quick breath and, feeling alarmed, allowed him to take her by the arm and move her further away from the sitting room door.

He put a finger to his lips and spoke in a rapid low voice. 'I heard the gate. Thank Christ it's you.'

'What's going on?'

'You need to stay strong, Hélène, now more than ever.' And as quickly as he was able, he explained what had happened to Florence.

Hélène felt as if she'd been punched, her stomach

muscles clenching and her mind beginning to shut down. She blinked rapidly to stop the tears already burning her eyes.

'Why didn't you come downstairs sooner?' She pounded her fists on his chest as if to beat the pain away. 'You should have come down.'

'I know. I'm so sorry, but I didn't hear the men come in.'

Despite her efforts not to cry, her hand flew to cover her mouth as she felt her face crumpling. No! Not this. Not to Florence. She wanted to stay calm, yet no matter how hard she struggled, she couldn't prevent silent tears from spilling down her cheeks.

Jack wiped her tears away and then held her tightly for a moment. 'I'm sorry,' he said again. 'So sorry.'

'But why didn't you hear anything?' she whispered as he let her go.

'I must have been asleep. I came the moment I heard the shots. I knew Élise was here as well as Florence. I didn't know Élise had gone outside.'

Hélène shook her head.

'Do you have any sedatives?' he asked. 'Florence isn't speaking, and more than anything she needs to sleep.'

Hélène tried to swallow the lump that had appeared from nowhere and wouldn't leave her throat. 'I'll get something,' she managed to say. 'Where is she?'

'On the sofa in the sitting room. But look, Victor is outside waiting for me. I couldn't leave her on her own.'

'I saw the blue van. Why is *he* here?'

Jack gave her a pained look. 'I'm afraid Élise shot both the men dead. BNA men.'

Hélène gasped as she drew in her breath. '*Nom de Dieu!*'

'You'll need to clean up the bloody mess in the kitchen and the trail where we had to drag the bodies out through the back of the house. And burn anything with blood on it.'

She put a palm to her forehead and felt herself sway. This simply could not be happening. As her teeth began to chatter, he held her firmly by the shoulders and looked into her eyes. 'I need you to do this. Can you do this, Hélène?'

She took a breath. He had remained calm and collected and she knew she must do the same. 'Why didn't Élise come and fetch me? Where is she?'

'She went to find Victor and then to get rid of the BNA truck.'

Once he had gone, Hélène checked on Florence who was lying curled up into herself, her eyes closed and her breathing shallow. Hélène touched her forehead, but the girl didn't respond, almost as if her brain and body had withdrawn at the unspeakable brutality she had suffered. It grieved Hélène beyond words to know her sister would never be able to see the world in the same open-hearted way again.

In the kitchen she stared in horror at the blood and mess on the floor, table and wall, and had to choke back the rising feelings of nausea. Then she filled a bucket, got out the mop and poured in the bleach, ready to begin the laborious process of mopping, rinsing, slopping out the red water, refilling, again and again and again. As she worked, she was plagued by a stream of images, imagining how terrified Florence must have been. How alone. Until, trembling from the grief inside her, Hélène's tears fell onto the flagstone floor where they mingled with the discoloured water. But then came the rage. The more anguished she became, the more vigorously she mopped, as if she might somehow release the fury with each stroke. She straightened up, took a long slow breath, and listened. The house was deeply silent, but it was not a good silence; it was a silence that caused so much noise in her head she didn't know what to do. For how long would the repercussions from this violation and killing hang over them? And, as well as the silence, there was a new darkness in the house. Darkness. A place where you could hide. A place where evil could hide too. Even before this, their lives had been turned upside down, but now appalling things were crawling beneath the floorboards, seeping out of the walls, and echoing in the kitchen. From now on she would sleep with a knife beneath her pillow.

From time to time she checked on Florence and after she had wiped all the surfaces with Lysol and the cleaning was finished, she sat beside her sister and rubbed her icy feet. The only sound was the ticking of the clock, marking the passage of seconds, minutes, and hours. Hélène's tears came and dried up, came again and dried again. But there was a new and foreign feeling of numbness in her chest, almost an ache but not quite an ache. A constriction perhaps. She didn't know how to feel, how to process what had happened to Florence and what Élise had been forced to do. It shook her. Every few minutes she slipped into a brief mental and emotional respite, when her mind wandered into the past or invented images of the future, but it shocked her anew every time she came reeling back to the present. She felt something shifting inside her and knew nothing could ever be the same again. She could never look at her sisters in the same way knowing what they had both experienced, and that she had not been there.

CHAPTER 28

Early the next morning, while Hélène boiled pans of water, Élise filled the tin bath in the laundry with cold. Then, as Hélène added the boiling water, Élise led Florence through from the sitting room wrapped in a warm blanket.

'Can you manage to get in, sweetheart?' Hélène asked. 'We've added some of your rose water and here's the last of the lavender soap you made.'

Élise took the blanket and Hélène forced herself not to show any emotion at the sight of blood and bruising on Florence's thighs. Her sister's vulnerability, so apparent now in her downcast eyes and trembling legs, broke Hélène's heart. She was so slight, so young, so innocent; no one who saw her could blame Élise for shooting the men.

After Florence had gripped the edges of the bath and lowered herself in, she bent forward, and Hélène held up her hair. Élise gently washed her back and arms with soothing repetitive movements as if she were a young child in need of tender care. Then Élise handed Florence the soap to wash between her legs. As she did what she had to, her sisters looked away, both biting back tears. Hélène glanced at Élise who, with sorrow in her eyes, was also chewing at her trembling lip. Hélène shook her head, just the slightest shake, but Élise gulped and then silently agreed. Florence had not cried in front of them and so neither could, nor should, they.

Élise sang an old lullaby as Florence sloshed the water between her legs and then, when she stopped, the room went silent. To Hélène it felt momentous. They would always remember this. The three of them together in circumstances they could barely countenance, and all they could hear was the sound of a bird singing in the chestnut tree and the two goats bleating at the side of the house. Hélène took a long slow breath. Nature would heal their sister. She hoped for it and she prayed Florence would instinctively know it too. Eventually. But before then, what?

When Florence was ready, she bent her head back and Élise washed her hair, rinsing it with fresh water from the kitchen and then they both helped her out and wrapped her in towels.

While Élise stayed with Florence, Hélène went through the whole house sweeping up every broken thing and neatly folding clothing, towels, blankets and bed linen, then lifting it all back into cupboards, drawers and store-rooms where it belonged. Hélène liked order. It made her feel safe and in control, even at a time when they were neither safe nor in control. When the world you relied on became unreliable, you did what you had to do. And this was her way of maintaining internal sanity. So, as she tried to restore whatever vestiges of normal life she could, she didn't hurry. When she was done, she went out to feed the chickens and goats and then joined her sisters.

'I'm going to bed,' Florence said in a small voice and they both jumped to assist her.

'No,' she said, rising to her feet and batting them away. 'I will go unaided. If you help me now, I may never be strong enough to help myself again.'

They watched her leave, listening to her slow footsteps as she climbed the stairs and then the squeak of her bedroom door opening and closing.

When they were sure she was safely in her own room, Élise collapsed against Hélène and then sobbed in her sister's arms, her body shuddering and shaking as if she might never stop.

CHAPTER 29

The next few days passed in a blur. Hélène had sent a message to the surgery saying she was unwell the day after the rape, but had to go back after that, partly so as not to arouse suspicion, partly because she needed to do something useful. The reliance and desire for routine was enshrined within her; a strategy for living she'd learned from her father, but she missed Jack's presence in the house and had waited, hoping he'd return. He hadn't.

Élise had abandoned the BNA truck but didn't know where Jack and Victor had dumped the bodies, and she was currently staying at home with Florence, her café closed. They were all traumatised. Neither sister knew how to help Florence, other than by holding her when the day might come when she finally broke her silence and released some of the pain. Hélène worried incessantly. What if the killing of the two men was traced back to them? And worse, she feared if Florence were to be interrogated, she would break down.

Neither Hélène nor Élise knew why the BNA had come to the house to search. The Germans had let Hugo go, they did not know about Jack, and the deserter boy was gone. Unless, of course, he was not dead. Tomas lurked at the edges of Hélène's consciousness, thin, pale and terrified, more wraithlike than before. The boorish, bullying BNA were a law unto themselves, so the search could have been completely random. But maybe she was wrong. Could someone have been eavesdropping, maybe have overheard them talking? She'd heard a few of the village houses had also been searched before theirs, so maybe it had been indiscriminate after all. How dreadful it was to be forced to live with this never-ending pervasive fear, she thought, as she washed her hands.

Hugo's call stopped her fretting and she went back through to the surgery.

'Many patients waiting?' she asked.

Hugo shook his head.

So far, she hadn't questioned him much about his brief incarceration at the castle, but now she asked if he'd seen Henri while he'd been there.

'No. They blindfolded me except for when I was in the cell. Or dungeon. It seems so medieval to say that, doesn't it?'

'Did you hear any non-German voices?'

'I think I did, briefly. Why?'

'Just curious. Maybe it was Suzanne or Henri. Did the Germans say why they'd arrested you?'

He rubbed his chin then shook his head. 'I think someone had told them I had the machine and they suspected me of printing all the pamphlets for the Maquis. That's all they spoke about.'

'But you hadn't printed them?'

He gave her a sheepish smile. 'Not since they got hold of their own mimeograph machine.'

'So you had printed pamphlets in the past?'

'Of course.'

'And now they're watching you, what are we going to do about helping injured Maquis?'

He scratched his head. 'Tricky.'

'I could help.'

'Maybe, but it isn't safe for them to come here, nor to your house since you were searched. How are your sisters, by the way? I notice Élise hasn't been opening her café.'

Hélène took a breath and calculated what to say. Florence had begged them not to tell anyone what had happened to her. The humiliation would be too awful, she said, and she couldn't bear to be the subject of gossip.

'Like me, Élise has been a bit off colour too, nothing serious. She'll open the café again soon.' She paused and took control of the conversation. 'So, injured Maquis? What do we do?'

'There's a doctor in Sarlat we can rely on.'

'It's a bit of a way to go if they're hurt.'

He shrugged, but not uncaringly, and she knew he was right. There was no alternative.

* * *

When she arrived home in the evening, Hélène was surprised to find Florence at the stove, wearing her apron and stirring a pot of something. The shock of the violation and the killing of the two men continued to ricochet through the three of them, but each was finding their own way and it looked like this was how Florence was going to do it.

Hélène decided not to make a big thing of her sister being back in the kitchen and simply said, in a matter-of-fact tone, 'Something smells good.'

'Onions and garlic,' Florence said.

'What are you cooking?'

'I dug up some of my finger carrots and I've added them to the winter spinach and what's left of the turnips. It should be tasty. I chopped in the tiniest bit of dried ham I'd stored in the outside larder.'

'All right,' Hélène said, drawing out the vowel as she felt her way into the conversation, trying to work out not only the right words but also the right tone of voice. 'And how are you feeling?'

'Angry.' Florence turned to face her, and Hélène could see the rage in her sister's usually gentle eyes.

'Oh Florence.'

'And, as I said before, I don't want anyone to know. Ever. Do you understand?' she added, her voice chilly.

'Of course.'

'And I won't speak of it ever again, not to you, not to anyone.'

Hélène was aware of treading a fine line between her sister's hurt and her bravado. 'But darling, are you sure you're up to cooking? If you're in pain, one of us could do it.'

With her hands on her hips, Florence took on a combative stance. 'I'm fine, Hélène, and what the hell else am I supposed to do? You and Élise can't cook to save your lives. I'd rather not starve on top of . . .'

Hélène watched as her sister swallowed in the effort to control her emotions.

'On top of everything,' she finished flatly, picking up the pan.

'At least let me help you then.'

'No, Hélène,' she snapped and slammed down the pan. 'I'm not an invalid. When I think about it, which I don't want to do any more, I feel so enraged I hardly know how to cope with it. I don't think I'll ever feel clean again. But I am not going to let those vile animals ruin the rest of my life.'

'Well good, it really is good, but don't bottle it up, will you?'

'I am not a child. I know you think I am, but I'm not. And, as soon as the summer vegetables are up, I'm going to make preserves again. That's *all* I'm going to bottle up.'

'I'm glad to hear it.'

'I shall dry more herbs too. Growing things and cooking them makes me happy. I've already planted lots of seedlings: aubergine, tomatoes, lettuce and so on.'

'Wonderful.'

'And in case you are worrying about it, I am not pregnant.'

Hélène pressed a palm to her lips to hold back a gasp of relief.

Florence gave her a stern unfathomable look. 'But listen to me, Hélène. You can't make everything all right, all the time. So, don't try. Just stop, will you?'

Hélène, feeling a little redundant, watched as Florence turned back to the stove. But how brave her little sister was being. She had been so frightened for her, but this new spirited anger was driving her right now and it was a step forward. Had Florence sunk straight into a decline, the feelings of dejection and powerlessness might have overwhelmed her, and Hélène would have been far more frightened for her. What might follow once the anger faded was impossible to tell at this stage, although Hélène guessed the terrible acknowledgement of hurt would have to come. Possibly a feeling of helplessness too, but for now her sister was right; gardening and cooking would see her through.

All the same, Hélène climbed the stairs up to her own bedroom and there, sitting on the bed, she allowed her own feelings of disbelief to surface and she silently wept. She wasn't even sure what she was weeping about. For Florence, of course, but also for *all* their lives. For the normality they had lost the day the Nazis arrived in France. For the changes over which they had no power. For all those poor souls who had been torn from their lives and herded off in trains and sent to God only knew where. For the lovely little things of life. For peace. For hope. For goodness.

When she was done crying, she wiped her eyes. They were all changing, not just Florence. Hélène herself had become more involved since Tomas arrived and now she wanted to fight back. Do whatever she could to help get rid of the Nazis. She'd been so concerned about looking after the other two, she hadn't been able to see how strong they both had become. Élise with her letter box took terrible risks every day of her life and now here was Florence being incredibly brave.

She decided to climb up to the attic in the vague hope of seeing Jack, but when she got there, she saw his rucksack had gone. He'd left with Victor to move the bodies that terrible day and she hadn't seen him since. Not knowing if he had gone for good, she felt a pang of loss. Would she ever see him again? She closed her eyes and summoned his uneven smile and his eyes so full of warmth. As everything about him came back to her, she felt tears burning her eyes again but pulled herself together and went back down to the kitchen. Giving in to tears again would do nothing to help.

'Do you know anything about Jack?' she asked Florence.

'Yes, I forgot to say. He turned up with Claude to pick up his rucksack. He said Bill had been found and he'd received new orders.'

'Do you know what they were?'

Florence shook her head. 'No, he just said it was all systems go, something like that.'

Hélène watched as Florence rubbed her jaw and then lifted her face, the expression in her eyes unfathomable. 'He was kind to me, after . . . you know. Jack, I mean. You'll see him again, Hélène. I'm sure of it. We all will.'

'Well, I hope so. But . . . darling, are you . . .' she said, and shot Florence a look of concern. 'Are you in pain at all, now? Physically, I mean.'

'A little.'

'Can I help?'

Florence's response was emphatic. 'No. I don't need your help. I don't need anybody's help.'

Élise came into the kitchen.

'I didn't know you had a gun,' Florence said, turning to her.

'Neither did I,' Hélène added.

Then Florence let out a weary snort. 'I'm so bloody glad you shot the bastards though.'

'I think we can agree on that,' Élise said with a wobbly grin.

'Listen. You've both been brilliant, but I want you to understand, I don't need babysitting.'

Hélène stared at the floor. Of course, Élise had had to shoot to protect Florence from the second man, but this wasn't going to go away, and she couldn't shake the feeling that something awful was still going to happen.

When she looked up, it was to see Florence searching her eyes as if trying to find an answer there. 'We don't have dreams of the future any more, do we? We don't have dreams. We used to talk all the time about the things we were going to do.'

'Darling, we will again,' Hélène said, holding back her misgivings. 'When all this is over, I promise you we will have dreams again, better ones than before.'

But Florence just shook her head and turning her back on them, ran up the stairs.

CHAPTER 30

Élise

Almost two weeks later, Élise was crossing her fingers as Hélène tried to persuade Florence it would do her good to get out of the house. Florence was still not speaking about what had happened, but it was the Saturday market day in Sarlat and Hélène had been allowed to borrow the doctor's creaking eighteen-year-old Citroën 5CV car. Hugo was not a stupid man and had clearly seen Hélène had been withdrawn and unhappy. Élise guessed the offer of the car had been his way to try to support her. He didn't know it was Florence who most needed his help.

Too nervous to leave the house, Florence resisted at first, but eventually, tempted by the possibility of buying plants and meeting up with her hairdresser friend Lucille, she reluctantly agreed. Lucille was going to be there to persuade her mother to help her set up a roving business in the village on her own.

An hour after they left, Élise was pacing the kitchen while waiting for Victor, although she didn't know exactly when he'd turn up. Earlier she had cycled to the garage and left a message, but he didn't yet know they would have the house to themselves so might not come immediately. Thrilled by her plan and the thought of being with him, she felt restless. They hadn't seen each other since that awful night and now she couldn't wait. *He will stay for the day. He will*, she repeated. Ever since she was small, Élise had clung to the belief she could make something happen by putting enough effort and imagination into it. So, she did that now, imagining him next to her as they lay on her bed together, the heat of him beneath her hands and the joy of feeling his skin against hers. In her bed! How wonderful would that be?

She opened the back door and glanced around as clouds covered the sun. Was it her imagination? Or were they being spied on? Was it worse now, or was she more suspicious than before? As she felt the soft breeze on her skin and the clouds moved away, she took in the glorious blue sky, and spotted a black kite cruising the thermals. She listened to the starlings and finches singing in the pear tree and heard the hum of buzzing insects. It felt like summer, peaceful and bright, yet things were still playing on her mind. Hard-edged things. But what was actually eating away at her? It felt like guilt. Surely it couldn't be guilt over the killing? Even though she had never killed before, she'd had to do it. And what she'd done she could not undo, nor would she want to.

But all the same, she had expected to feel *something* more after the shooting; an intense thrill fizzing in her blood maybe, or a burst of energy making her feel more alive, but instead she'd felt empty and deflated.

Most troubling, of course, was the sight of what had happened to Florence *and* what had been about to happen again had she not intervened. Victor had given her the gun a few weeks before, but she hadn't told her sisters since she knew what Hélène would say. When she pictured her sisters in Sarlat, she hoped Florence was enjoying her day – she deserved that at least – and although withdrawn, her little sister had proven more resilient than they dared expect.

A knock at the door interrupted her thoughts. She ran to open it and when she saw Victor, she pulled him into the kitchen and into her arms.

'Well,' he said. 'What have I done to deserve this?'

She raised one brow, bouncing on her toes as she drew back. 'My sisters are out. For the day!'

In those few seconds before he properly touched her, every nerve in her body tingled with anticipation. He ran his fingers through her hair and pulled her head back, then gazed into her eyes as he manoeuvred her against the back door. 'I'll just lock this,' he said, reaching behind her. Then he buried his face in her hair.

'You smell,' he said.

'Smell?'

He frowned, pretending to think. 'Is it oranges? Roses

perhaps? Maybe lavender . . . Noooo, none of those, it's a rather stronger, not exactly pleasant tar-like scent.'

She laughed. 'Carbolic soap.'

'You know what, I don't care what you smell like, but I thought your sister made the gorgeous stuff.'

'She does, but we're almost out.'

He traced her collarbones with the tips of his fingers. 'So where do you want me?

'I think you know,' and she turned and began to race upstairs. He thundered up behind her and, with his hands around her middle, pushed her to her knees before they reached the top.

'Let me go, you heathen,' she yelled.

With his full weight on her, he laughed. 'Why? Don't you want me?'

'On the staircase? No, I bloody don't.'

She laughed as he let her go and she led him into her bedroom where she had already closed the curtains and lit a couple of candles.

'Ah,' he said.' You were planning on romantic.'

She pulled off his jacket. 'You know I was, so stop teasing and let's get to it. And by the way, you smell too.'

'Of?'

She thought about it. There was the tang of sweat, tobacco and something else. 'I know. You smell of liquorice.'

He put his hands on her shoulders and kissed her tenderly. The feel of his mouth on hers was sweet and produced a tingling feeling all over her body and he *tasted* of liquorice too. Liquorice and salt.

'You, Élise Baudin, are the most impossible woman

I've ever known,' he said when he stopped kissing her. 'You are also the most beautiful and the bravest, and I love you.'

She blinked up at him and lifted her hands to cradle her face, then standing on the tips of her toes, she stretched up to kiss him on his forehead. He loved her. He'd never said anything like that before. But could they even speak of love?

'You do?' she said, increasingly dizzy, as her insides seemed to liquefy.

He steadied her and smiled. 'So now?' He raised his brows and leant forward to kiss her. Then he picked her up and carried her to the bed where he lay her down before coming down beside her and resting his weight on one elbow so he could gaze at her. She thought of the BNA and the Gestapo and how their dominance and hatred of women and their lack of empathy was a vile expression of their warped masculinity, even to the extent of relishing violence. Victor was not like them at all.

'So, stop thinking,' he said.

'How do you know I am?'

'Because you are *not* paying attention and I am now going to punish you by peeling off all your clothes, item by item.'

She smiled up at him. 'Yes please.'

Once they were both undressed, she took his free hand and placed it between her legs. As he began to move his fingers she gasped and felt the heat rising. The reality was rarely as good as the imagination led you to believe, but with Victor it was better. After a few moments of this she couldn't wait and pulled him down on top of her. She lifted her head for a moment then, raising her knees and opening her legs more widely, she reached out behind her head and, clutching the pillow with her fists, she pushed her hips up against him. The sex was fast and visceral, all the fear and anger of their war-torn lives releasing as their furious bodies drove each other on. To feel him inside her, here in her bedroom, felt like a miracle and now her breath was coming too fast and her knees were shaking and she wanted this moment to go on for ever and she wanted it to end before she lost every connection with reality. The bed was creaking, the room was expanding, and then came the moment of unbearable intensity when something switched, and she couldn't hold on to the mounting sensations any longer. Three beats and then the release swept through her, hot and cold, the waves of energy pulsing through her entire body.

It was over and they had both been too wired to take things slowly.

Without speaking she wrapped herself in a robe and went downstairs to find a bottle of Florence's home-made wine. When she arrived in the bedroom holding it aloft, he was standing naked with his back to her, his hands clasped behind his head, as he looked out through a gap in the curtain. His back was smooth and muscular, his thighs sturdy and she longed to touch every part of his beautiful body. He looked unimaginably graceful. Just the sinewy lines of him, the smooth flowing lines of him, and the firm power of his body was enough to make her want him again.

'What do you see?' she asked.

He turned. 'I see you.'

His chest was smooth, the dark hair on his head kept short and he had stubble on his chin. His eyes were deep, darker than ever, softer too as he gazed at her. She saw the love in them, the spirit, the warmth, and she was shaken to see the vulnerability too.

'Take off your robe,' he said.

She let it slip to the floor and shook back her hair feeling his eyes on every part of her. She gazed back at him. Now, as they stood there naked, they were cocooned in their own private world and she knew they were truly seeing each other. More than that they were seeing *into* each other in a way they never had before, seeing not only who they were, but seeing who they had been and even who they might become. She felt tears filling her eyes.

'We'll remember this moment,' he said. 'Whatever might come next.'

'We will.' And she put down the bottle and went to him, laying her head against his shoulder. All her thoughts had stopped and there was only this now, this sense of connection, this love. He stroked her hair, speaking soothingly and then drew her face to his. 'No matter what, we will always have this,' he said.

And they walked over to the bed where she pushed him down onto the mattress. He sank back into the pillows laughing and they made wonderful leisurely love for the rest of the day.

CHAPTER 31

Hélène

Before the war, Hélène had adored exploring the Périgord. She loved taking her time as she climbed the jagged hills, meandered through deep dark forests, or crept along the chalky clifftops where the sheer drops, lined with shrubs and clinging moss, took her breath away. She loved the dozens of enchanting villages and peaceful hamlets scattered among the hills, and the fields of sunflowers in summer. Even during the war, she had sometimes been able to use the doctor's car, taking the back roads to visit patients in sleepy parishes of just a few stone houses gathered around a tiny church. But today she had not only borrowed the car, but had been given some precious rationed petrol too, and was taking Florence to the market at Sarlat.

The market these days wasn't a patch on the atmospheric

pre-war ones the sisters used to love, when every market day had felt like a festival, but as they slowly walked arm in arm, Hélène could feel Florence trembling.

'Do you remember,' she said, hoping to calm her, 'coming here on a spring morning back before the war and buying *chocolatines* to eat on the hoof?'

Florence didn't speak.

Hélène gazed at beautifully ornate stonework of the fifteenth and sixteenth-century mansions lining the street. The lovely mix of medieval and Renaissance buildings never failed to raise her spirits, but it would take something more to lift Florence out of her present state. It seemed to Hélène that today the anxiety had inhabited her sister so deeply, she could barely put one foot in front of the other.

But as she watched Florence glance up at the lauze roofs of the buildings, at their honey-coloured limestone facades and faded blue-grey shutters, her sister spoke. 'It's still lovely, isn't it?' she said, and Hélène felt so moved at the sound of her sister's voice, her own throat dried up. She squeezed Florence's hand then turned away to hide her damp eyes and looked at the cobbled streets and old-fashioned shopfronts, no longer buzzing with the sound of chatter as they once would have been.

She couldn't help thinking of happier times. She pictured the huge varieties of fish they used to see lying on beds of ice, the cheeses, hard and soft – *Bleu de Causses* or *Cabécou du Périgord* – the freshly cut flowers, the jars of foie gras, the brightly coloured apples, and the sweetest of strawberries. The chickens too, and quails roasting on spits and, in the winter, the intoxicating scent of truffles or 'black gold' as they were often called. This had been a land of plenty, where women carried straw panniers full of produce and men sat outside the cafés putting the world to rights while wearing berets, smoking Gauloises and drinking Bergerac wine.

'You're safe, you know,' Hélène said. 'I'm here and nothing bad will happen to us.'

Florence gazed at her feet for a moment, then looked around. 'Are you sure?'

'Yes, I am . . . Do you remember the delicious *pommes de terre Sarladaises*?' Hélène asked.

Florence was still glancing about. 'We used to have them for lunch in the hotel,' she said in a small voice.

Hélène felt pleased that Florence was at least engaging. And she could taste those potatoes, sliced into coins, sautéed in duck fat until luscious and crispy, mixed with garlic and wild mushrooms or even truffles in the winter and sprinkled with chopped parsley. 'Yes, we did,' she said. 'Oh, and the gorgeous pastries in the market. Remember those?'

'*Gâteau-mousse au chocolat et aux noisettes* – that was my favourite.'

'You and your chocolate hazelnut mousse cake. You ate so much you made yourself sick.'

Florence blinked rapidly. 'Did I?'

Hélène raised her brows and attempted to smother her laughter at the sight of her sister's disbelieving face.

They had arrived in time to catch the early-morning sunshine on the glistening yellow sandstone buildings as they walked the part of the Rue de la République which ran through the old town. They bypassed the maze of narrow streets on either side and turned into the Rue de la Boétie, then arrived at the Cathédrale Saint-Sacerdos where the sun shining on the stained glass windows made the world feel like a better place.

Florence found a stall selling seedlings and, although still clinging to Hélène, she bought some new herbs to add to her collection. The cathedral to the south-east of Sarlat, alongside the Place de Peyrou, led north-east via the Rue de la Liberté to the larger Place de la Liberté. The girls walked through to the second square and then into the wonderful winding street of the Rue des Consuls, where they stopped at their favourite small café. They seated themselves inside, ordered a tisane each and then waited patiently while the owner, an elderly lady with grey-speckled hair and raisin-like black eyes prepared their drinks.

'Are you glad you came?' Hélène asked tentatively.

Yes,' Florence said. 'I know I needed to get out. But it's hard, you know. I keep feeling I have to look over my shoulder.'

Hélène reached over and squeezed her sister's hand.

As soon as they'd finished, Madame cleared the cups away and they felt obliged to make room for other customers.

Then they were back on the Rue de la République where Florence's friend, Lucille, would be at her mother's hair-dressing salon.

Florence shuddered as they walked swiftly past the

Hotel de la Madeleine, an imposing four-storey building where German officers were billeted. From its shuttered windows on the first and second floors, red, black and white Nazi banners fluttered in the breeze, each displaying a huge swastika. The hotel, situated at the entrance of the medieval city, could not be avoided as, just a few doors away, was Sandrine's salon.

Lucille's mother, Sandrine, was universally acknowledged to be a staunch Vichy supporter. Lucille and Florence had been friends for years and rarely talked politics. Mainly they did what girls generally do. Lucille was, however, a lot more hard-headed than Florence. She wanted more than anything to be rich and so escape the clutches of her demanding mother. Hélène didn't know how Florence's experience at the hands of the BNA might affect her relationship with the other girl. She doubted Florence would breathe a word of it, at least not in the salon, and from the moment they arrived, she could see Florence bravely sporting a cheerful face.

Lucille offered to trim Florence's hair while she was there, so Hélène sat in the waiting area flicking through an old magazine and listening to Sandrine openly savaging the Maquis as she set a client's hair.

'They do us all a disservice,' she was saying. 'They disrespect Pétain and the whole of the Vichy administration. If it were up to me, I'd slam them up against a wall and shoot the lot of them.'

The other woman murmured a response and Hélène wondered how long Lucille could possibly remain impervious; so far, she had not been infected by her mother's vitriol. There were constant rumours about Sandrine, who was always showing off her new stockings, fancy lipsticks and expensive perfume. Some town gossips claimed she was having an affair with one of the Germans billeted at the hotel. Maybe even two. Hélène wanted to get out of there before she might say something she'd regret and anyway, the chemical smell of perming lotion was giving her a headache.

She gestured to Florence that she wanted to go outside. Florence signalled it was fine and then Hélène left, breathing in a lungful of fresh air with relief.

On their way home, although still subdued, Florence seemed a touch brighter. 'Thank you. I enjoyed it.'

'Now Jack has gone, Lucille can always come and stay the night, just as she used to. As long as we warn Élise in advance.'

'I'll ask. She's staying with her aunt Lili who lives in the village and even if Sandrine won't let her stay with me, Lili would.'

'Why wouldn't she let her stay with you?'

Florence looked embarrassed. 'She heard Hugo had been arrested.'

'Ah, so, as I work with Hugo, I am no longer safe to be around her daughter.'

'Stupid, isn't she? There's no one safer than you. By the way, Lucille stole a teeny piece of dry-cured duck breast one of the German soldiers had presented to Sandrine, and she gave it to me.'

'You'll make something delicious with that.'

'Maybe.'

Hélène put an arm around her sister and the car swerved.

'Careful, you nearly drove us into a ditch.' And Florence sounded a little more like her old self.

CHAPTER 32

Hélène had still not replied to her mother's letter. It wasn't that she didn't want to exactly, but it was so hard deciding what to write when so much could not be said. Even though the letter was destined for England, via Geneva, strict censorship controls meant there was still a chance it would be opened long before it had a chance to get there. But on this lovely Sunday morning, she sat in the kitchen chewing the end of her pen with a tisane at her side.

Dear Maman, she wrote as the sunlight spilled across the table and she watched a fly buzzing around a smear of strawberry jam that hadn't been wiped away. She dipped her finger into it and rubbed. She and Élise were doing their best to keep the meals going and the kitchen clean, but they had neither Florence's flair nor her diligence when it came to domestic duties. Florence did still cook, but sometimes they found her just sitting in the garden, gazing at nothing with a bowl of half-peeled potatoes on her lap. Hélène took a breath and let it out in a puff. Thinking about Florence was still painful. She carried on with the letter.

> *I was pleased to receive your letter and to read all your news. You'll be glad to hear we are all well despite the occupation. Élise is still running the café and I'm still working for Hugo. Florence . . .*

She listened to the sound of church bells. What on earth could she say about Florence? It seemed wrong to say nothing at all, but what had happened was far too private and distressing to bluntly write about it in a letter. *Oh, and by the way, Maman, your youngest daughter was recently raped*. Just seeing it in black and white would be beyond appalling. Nor could it be couched in euphemisms. Not only would the knowledge upset Claudette terribly, especially when she could not come to France to comfort her daughter, but Hélène also loathed the thought of *anyone* reading about it. And more, importantly, Florence would too.

Hélène had no idea how long it would take her sister to properly recover or even if she would 'properly' recover. It didn't seem possible she could find her way back to her once-innocent self. And, if she was honest, her sister was paler than ever, practically devoid of colour. Even after their visit to Sarlat, it seemed as if she was still withdrawing from life. Always fair, her skin had become virtually transparent and tinged with the blue of her veins which were almost visible. Hélène would feel more confident if Florence could express her feelings but, for now, she was far from able to do so.

In the end Hélène simply wrote that Florence was busy in the garden as usual and they had plenty of vegetables. When something that you could not mention dominated your mind, it seemed to trap everything else you might have been able to say, so that nothing came out at all. But it would have to do. She didn't even dare mention the goats which should have been handed over to the Nazis ages ago. Perhaps a few more bland words about the weather or the village and that would have to suffice. She made sure there was nothing her mother could read between the lines and signed her name.

Once finished, she went through to her desk in the sitting room, slipped the letter into an airmail envelope, and found a stamp in the top drawer. Before she left the room, she glanced out of the window to see what the weather was up to. Excellent, she thought. Wall-to-wall sunshine.

'Do you fancy coming into the village with me?' she asked as Élise walked in. She wafted the letter about in the air. 'I need to post this.'

'Sure. I'll ask Florence, shall I?'

'Yes. Better had. Do you think she'll want to?'

Florence, not relishing being alone, didn't take much persuading and so the three set out together. It was a lovely day, the sky bright blue, everything shining, and it seemed so peaceful Hélène found it hard to credit they were at war. When they passed the warren of houses and gardens and reached the centre of the village, Hélène felt

Florence's hand tighten around her own and she glanced at her sister's face.

'You all right?'

'Yes.'

'At least you've got a little colour in your cheeks now.'

The square was not busy, but there were a few people out and about in their Sunday best. Most said hello and shared a few words as they always had done. A few children clustered around the fountain egging each other on to race in and out of the water which, miraculously, was flowing again after months of absence, but the large families who used to gather for a leisurely lunch in the restaurant rarely came nowadays. The restaurant was open, but many of the officers billeted at Suzanne's chateau used it and that put people off, even though the food was good. The fellowship when everyone gathered around shared tables at harvest time might still happen, though with a distinct lack of men. And, unfortunately, with so little flour available, there was not even the chance of a delicious buttery croissant from the village boulangerie.

The sisters stopped to talk to Maurice Fabron, the blacksmith, a man who usually kept himself to himself. They talked about how living in rural France had once been so idyllic, but now was different.

'And yet, on a day like this, you can still feel a little of the old atmosphere, don't you think?' said Élise, glancing around.

'Maybe,' Maurice said. 'But the old days weren't all perfect, you know. Doesn't seem to matter how secure I make their enclosure; the foxes still get in and kill the chickens. Just as they always did.'

'And remember when bees invaded my bedroom?' Hélène added, thinking of the time before the war when they'd needed Maurice's help getting rid of them, and the pandemonium when Élise was badly stung and had to be rushed to see Hugo.

He laughed. 'Right old caper that was.'

After a few more words they said their goodbyes and sauntered on through the streets, past clusters of smaller creamy-coloured stone houses where they met up with Arlo, a man with piercing black eyes. Tall and a touch too thin, he more than made up for it in heart.

'Out for a stroll, ladies?' he asked with a broad smile on his tanned face.

'We are,' Hélène said. 'What about you?'

'My dog has done a runner,' he said, with a look of resignation. 'Can't find the bugger anywhere.'

'We'll keep an eye out for him and bring him home if we see him.'

Arlo was from Alsace, but had to flee his home and come to the Périgord Noir when the Germans invaded. Florence had helped feed him so, in return, he'd been kind to the sisters, mending their ancient wheelbarrow and handcart until they finally gave up the ghost. He'd even fixed Hélène's bicycle after she had fallen off and twisted the wheels. Many of the men who'd arrived with him from Alsace stayed for a year but then were sent back to their ruined village. Arlo had remained and married Justine, a tiny bright-eyed and rosy-cheeked local girl who worked as a cleaner for Doctor Hugo and the priest.

'Be seeing you then,' Arlo said, 'enjoy your day.'

And they walked on towards the fields and the woods.

'I would love the markets to go back to the way they were,' Florence said, 'I miss the colour and smells.'

Hélène and Élise glanced at each other.

'There's no need to look at each other,' she added. 'I haven't lost my voice.'

Hélène thought how right Florence was about the markets. But at least there was still the honey stall now and then. So many kinds of honey. Lavender, eucalyptus, thyme. And flowers too, scenting the air with rose, magnolia and iris. But she missed the combination of colour you got from freshly baked loaves, home-made lemonade, newly harvested bright green peas, juicy yellow melons, duck eggs in baskets, Périgord walnuts, confit de canard, truffles and the most flamboyant of strawberries.

She missed the sounds too. The general hum and buzz of conversation, the shouts of children, followed by the shrill admonishing voices of their parents. The bustle of feet on the cobbles, and the laughter of friends greeting each other. The sounds of waiters as they wrote down orders and clattered about clearing the plates from pavement tables outside the restaurant. She sighed. It was lucky they still had the birds. So many thrushes and blue tits still singing in the trees, and the tinkling sound of goldfinches calling as they flew overhead.

They reached the meadow close to their home where a slight breeze was blowing the grass about. 'Shall we sit here for a bit?' Élise asked.

'We haven't got a blanket to sit on,' Hélène said.

'It doesn't matter.'

'Ants?'

But Florence was already lying down on the grass with her hands clasped behind her head and staring at the sky. 'I'm going to make biscuits when we get home,' she said quietly, but with a hint of steel in her voice.

Hélène joined her and lay down, looking up into the infinity of a deep blue sky dotted with just one or two fluffy white clouds moving slowly.

Élise was the last to stretch out. 'It is revitalising, isn't it,' she said, 'to get out and simply laze the day away. Makes things feel more normal.'

Florence twisted her head to the side to look at her and let her arms fall beside her body. 'Will it be normal again?'

And Hélène knew she was really asking if *she* would ever feel normal again.

Élise sighed and reached for Florence's hand. 'It will.'

Hélène felt the sun on her cheeks and closed her eyes. It was good lying on the ground and feeling the earth beneath her. Calming somehow, connecting her to the timelessness of life, rooting her in what could not be destroyed. The breeze had dropped now, the only movement coming from buzzing insects and soon she grew drowsy and felt herself drifting off.

It didn't last, because a few minutes later Élise sat up abruptly. 'Ouch,' she said scratching the back of her thigh. 'Damn it. You were right.'

'Ants?' Hélène said, and then they all rose to their feet. 'I've got something at home that will soothe it.'

They walked on to connect with the track leading to their house, but as they neared home, Hélène slowed a little, hoping to preserve the moment, and not wanting the day to be over.

'What is it?' Élise asked.

Hélène glanced up at the only fluffy white cloud left in the sky. 'Just remembering what a peaceful world feels like.'

'Wonderful, isn't it?'

'Gives me hope.'

After they entered through the front door, Florence headed straight for the kitchen and Élise went into the sitting room. Hélène fetched the cream for Élise's ant bites but when she took it into the room, she found her sister staring out of the window.

'It's been a good day, hasn't it?' Élise said.

Hélène agreed. It had and the sun had shone throughout.

Later they got together to help Florence concoct a meal of pasta flavoured with a drizzle of what remained of their walnut oil, plus some well-sautéed garlic. Then they made a salad of shredded cabbage and tiny slivers of Lucille's smoked duck. Florence tossed in the walnuts and dressed it with olive oil. They all ate their fill and Hélène understood how the act of preparing food together had not only reinforced their unity as sisters, but had also breathed new life into Florence. Aware of how swiftly these precious times could be torn away, Hélène treasured them. Things would surely get better now.

'To us,' she said and held up her glass of wine.

* * *

In the night, when Hélène woke to the sound of screaming, she knew it was Florence. She grabbed her robe, lit an oil lamp and, carrying it, ran to Florence's room, where she found her crouching in the corner, on her hands and knees, eyes wild with terror, her skin slippery with sweat. Hélène put the lamp down then bent to reach out her arms. But Florence did not move, did not even seem to see it was Hélène who had come to help.

When Florence began to cry, Hélène knelt on the floor beside her, stroking her hair to try to soothe her. Gradually, after a few more minutes, Florence's eyes began to lose the wild look and she was able to focus on Hélène, although her breath was still too shallow.

'I—'

'Shhh. You don't need to speak. It was only a nightmare.'

'The men. So real and it got worse and worse. I was so scared.' She pressed a palm over heart. 'Feel,' she said, her voice shaking.

Hélène did as she was asked and could feel her sister's pounding heart. She helped her up and sat her on the bed, but now Florence began rocking back and forth. Rocking and rocking.

'I felt . . . I felt I was going to . . . to actually die from the pain in my heart,' she whispered, her sentence fragmenting. 'I couldn't . . . wake up. I was screaming. Did you hear me? I was screaming.'

'I heard you, darling, I'm here.'

Florence screwed up her eyes as if to shut out the memory and Hélène began stroking her back with slow soothing movements, just as you might calm a frightened animal.

'Dearest, I know it feels real, but it isn't. They aren't coming back. And we'll find a way to ensure you're not alone here. Maybe one of Victor's men might help, at least until you feel comfortable again.'

'I don't want anyone I don't know.'

'Perhaps Enzo?'

Florence looked horrified. 'God no. He isn't my friend. Didn't I tell you?'

'Oh gosh, yes. Sorry, I'd forgotten. Well not Enzo then. Maybe we can contact Claude. He may know if Jack is still around. You'd be all right with Jack?'

Florence seemed to like the idea, but added, 'I won't be able to go back to sleep now.'

'Come in with me.'

While Florence had remained numb and withdrawn, she had barred the door to all her feelings. Today she had allowed some happiness to return, but in doing so had also opened the door to some of her darker emotions. And yet, Hélène thought, despite the nightmare, it was a hopeful sign. No one could deaden their feelings forever and still live a full and happy life.

CHAPTER 33

Élise

Élise was alone in the kitchen the next morning, when she was startled by a light tap at the back door. She opened it and found a freckled village lad, blue-eyed and skinny with a large nose, and wearing boots that were far too big for him. He shifted his weight from one foot to the other while glancing about curiously.

'I have a message,' he whispered, with a suppressed smile playing around his mouth, clearly thrilled to be engaged in clandestine business. Élise guessed he would have no idea what it was about.

'Oh?'

'From Victor. He wants you to meet him at the café.'

'Right now?'

The boy's eyes were wide and round. 'Urgent, Victor said.'

Élise thanked him and, as he left, he saluted.

She smiled, amused by the gesture, then prepared to leave. She went outside, uncertain whether to speak to Hélène before she left or not. The weather had changed and after their lovely Sunday sunshine, the sky was now grey and the day felt sombre. It was blowy too, so she went back in to fetch a jacket and then hesitated in the doorway to the hall. She could hear the floorboards creaking as Hélène moved about upstairs as she got ready for work, but decided against telling her. Back outside again she was surprised to see Florence digging near the bottom of the garden as early as this. 'Just going out for a bit,' she called out but didn't linger, which felt mean, after having overheard her sister's night terrors.

'Hey, wait,' Florence called back, but Élise didn't respond. She could not risk delay, even for Florence, so carrying a basket over her arm, she left her sister behind. Hopefully, she wouldn't be gone for long and Hélène would still be at home for another half hour, so Florence need only be alone briefly. She felt guilty though, for the plan had been Hélène would go to work today but she, Élise, would stay. She told herself it couldn't be helped, that Florence would be fine and might not even notice.

She walked briskly through the village, greeting the blacksmith with a wave, and then came across Angela cleaning the windows of her sweetshop, even though she had no sugar to make sweets and could not open up. The woman always wanted to talk, but with a smile Élise walked swiftly past. She passed Doctor Hugo's house and the town hall and then reached her café. The shutters were closed, and no light could be seen from within. The café looked deserted.

But inside she found Victor and another man, a maquisard Élise knew by sight but not by name. They had fallen silent when she walked straight in, and as she did, she also spotted Violette standing in the gloom at the back with Suzanne, the sinewy blonde chatelaine, who lived with her husband Henri at the castle. No one was seated and Élise could feel a tense atmosphere.

'What's going on?' she asked Victor. 'Why are Violette and Suzanne here?'

There was a momentary silence, then Suzanne glanced at Victor who seemed to give her the go-ahead.

'I have news from the castle,' she said, her voice grim.

'I see,' Élise said, wondering what was so important it needed them all to meet so early.

'Yesterday the Nazis captured three maquisards. They were ambushing a German supply truck and one of the Germans was killed during the gunfire.'

Élise grimaced. Oh God. Capture was always a risk for the Maquis, which was why they worked in small groups, with as little information as possible. She put the basket down. 'That's awful.'

Suzanne shook her head. 'It is, but that's not all.'

'So?'

'Soon after, during the search of the area, they came across two bodies. Two well-hidden and partially eaten BNA men's bodies. They were still in BNA uniform.'

Élise tried to disguise the waves of shock threatening to ruin her self-control. Only Victor and Jack knew where the two BNA thugs she had shot had been dumped, but she had to assume these were the same two men. She glanced at Victor who gave her a barely perceptible nod.

'The Germans have accused the three people they captured of that crime too and they will all stand trial for triple murder,' Suzanne added.

Élise felt sick. Innocent people were now accused of what she had done. This was beyond dreadful.

'So, you see we need to help the men escape,' Victor said, and Élise knew he understood how she was feeling and, therefore, how desperately she would want to be involved.

'Two men and one woman, actually,' Suzanne said. 'She is one of the local leaders in Domme and has information that could put several others in the gravest danger. The SS are waiting for the Gestapo to interrogate the prisoners, but as far as I can work out, they won't arrive until tomorrow.'

Suzanne had spoken calmly, but Élise knew she must be desperately worried. They all knew the brutal results of being handed to the Gestapo.

'So, you're saying we only have today?'

'Tonight, that's the plan. There's just one guard outside both cells. They aren't expecting anyone to find their way in there because the grounds of the castle and chateau are regularly patrolled. Victor and I will meet at the bottom of a shaft they haven't yet discovered, that leads to a tunnel. It's an ancient shaft, not the more recent one excavated during the Great War. I think you know it, Élise.'

Élise frowned. 'Remind me.'

'One of my dogs found it on the day you and I were out for a walk together before the war.'

'Ah yes.'

'You go up through the woods directly behind the castle, and near the top there's a crumbling wall, partly covered with creepers. You have to climb over it and on the other side there's heavy circular iron lid, again partially covered with creepers. That's the entrance. Do you remember?'

Élise did remember. 'Yes,' she said.

'Victor needs you to show him the back route to the shaft. I know you don't normally go out on operations but there's no one else.'

Violette sighed. 'Apart from me. Sorry, Élise. I do know of it too, and Suzanne asked if I would do it, but I can't leave my son.'

Élise exhaled slowly. So that's why Violette was there. 'It's fine. I'll show Victor the way.'

'Meanwhile,' Suzanne continued, 'I will be distracting the guard and as soon as Victor arrives, he will knock him out. Once the guard is out cold—'

'Or dead,' Élise interjected.

'Yes. We'll unlock the men and then try to get up to the chapel without being seen. That's the riskiest part.'

'So, you only have to show me the way and then leave,' Victor said.

'From the chapel it's easy,' Suzanne continued. 'We'll take the concealed limestone staircase. It extends underground and into a hidden room in the cellar of the main chateau.'

'Isn't it where the ghost hangs out?' Élise asked, thinking

of the story of Isabel, the unfaithful wife who was imprisoned by her husband in the castle until she died of a broken heart.

Suzanne smiled grimly. 'No, she's in one of the towers. The men will wait in the hidden room. The Gestapo will arrive to find the prisoners are missing and I will be safely back in the chateau. There will be a search, of course.'

'A hue and cry, more like,' Élise said. 'This is a big operation.'

'Yes. One of the most difficult rescue attempts we've made so far. But they won't find anyone. When it is eventually safe to leave, they'll crawl out through a drain which opens out much lower down the hill.'

'How do you conceal a staircase in a chapel?' Violette asked. 'Isn't it rather obvious?'

Suzanne frowned 'Well it—'

She was interrupted by a knock and everyone except for Élise began to disperse, heading for the back door. Before Victor left, he tenderly caressed Élise's cheek, and smiled for her alone. Élise pressed her palm to her cheek as if to preserve his touch, just as Hélène walked in from the front of the café and began busily unwrapping a loaf of bread.

'Hope you don't mind. I used my key. Florence asked me to give you the bread.'

'Thanks, but I'm not opening.'

'Then why are you here?'

'I can't say.'

'Oh, Élise. You're worrying me.'

'Well stop it. I'm heading back home now.'

As Élise walked home, she thought about the danger of being caught. She would have to say something to Hélène to explain her absence that night, but resolved to keep it vague. Tonight would be so much riskier than the night they had tried to take Tomas to the safe house and was a far cry from running the letter box. But she truly longed to become more actively involved. And, as she'd been the one who had killed the two BNA men, it was only right she play a part in helping the ones who now stood accused. She knew a few of the maquisards now, and Victor not only trusted her but was actively training her to take part in operations when the Allies landed. Besides, although the night's work was bound to be difficult and dangerous, she would be with Victor. And that was what mattered. Together, she was sure they would make it through.

CHAPTER 34

Florence

Florence had been digging for over an hour and a half by the time she heard Élise coming home. She straightened up and, wiping the sweat from her brow, she glanced down at herself. She'd forgotten she was still wearing her nightdress, and it was now stained with earth and patches of sweat. After her nightmare she had slept again but had woken early and, not wanting to disturb Hélène, had crept out of the room, slipped downstairs and left the house by the back door. She still loved the early morning in the garden when the birdsong was just beginning, and the air smelt so clean and fresh, but even though she was exhausted emotionally she hadn't been able to sit and enjoy it.

And digging was a good way to make things go away, at least for a while. While working, she didn't hold her breath, her thoughts didn't race, she didn't get bursts of heat, nor did she feel dizzy and nauseous. So, she carried on pressing the spade into the ground with renewed force.

But when she straightened up a little later, the thoughts came tearing back, and she felt the worst thing of all. Shame. Self-disgust. Even though it didn't make sense, she felt she must somehow be to blame. She knew if she told Hélène about this, her sister would try to persuade her differently, but Florence had to work this out for herself. Up until now she hadn't wanted to talk about the rape at all; if she didn't talk about it, then it hadn't happened. But she knew she would never recover if she went on avoiding the truth. She had to unravel everything that was tangled up inside her. Rationally, she knew she'd done nothing to bring on the rape, knew the fault absolutely lay at the hands of those men, and it was wrong to blame the innocent victim . . . Victim. What a terrible word that was. She hated it.

She watched Élise walk into the house wrapped up in her own thoughts and wondered what had drawn her out earlier. She wished she were more like her sister. Braver. Bolder. More determined to fight. And yet, when she'd woken this morning, it *had* been with a new resolution. She'd known she was going to find a way not to become a victim and, if that meant she had to toughen up, then she would. If she was going to live any kind of life, she needed to regain a sense of control. Not easy at any time, and harder still at a time of war. But, if she were ever to feel good about herself again and not some small, dirty, ruined thing, she had to do it.

She sighed deeply, put away her spade, and after washing the dirt from her hands, she slipped up to her room.

Still in her nightdress, she reached under the pillow and pulled out her little notebook and began to write down how she felt, chewing the end of her pencil when it became too painful. She wrote about her anger and her shame. She wrote about needing to become resilient and gave a bitter little laugh to herself. No longer so innocent, nor so trusting, she had already changed. And now she didn't even know if she could trust herself. So she wrote about that too, and about her fears for the future. She wrote about her determination to recover and the things she still loved: her garden, nature, her sisters. And then, finally, when she could no longer put it off, and with tears pouring down her cheeks, she wrote about what those men had done to her.

CHAPTER 35

Élise

It was going to be a long day for Élise, waiting for the night. She turned the plan over in her mind again and again, visualising the route she'd need to take to the concealed shaft and praying they would succeed. No matter how many times she glanced at her wristwatch or looked out of the window, time seemed to be standing still. She felt a mix of trepidation, expectation and anxiety, but forced herself to lie on her bed and close her eyes. The suspense made it hard to relax. While acutely aware of the usual sounds of the house, creaking shutters, groaning pipes, shuffling in the attic, she also picked up something different. Not outside, but also coming from within. And then she realised it was Florence sobbing. She waited, unwilling to intrude on her sister's private grief, but when the crying didn't stop, Élise went to her. She tapped on Florence's bedroom door then pushed it open and tiptoed in. Her sister was sitting cross-legged on the floor and scribbling in a notebook while tears slid down her cheeks and dripped on to her hands. Élise sat down beside her and murmured sympathetically when Florence leant against her. But she wished Hélène were there to help.

'I can try and see if Hélène could come home,' she said.

Between her sobs, Florence managed to say no, so Élise remained sitting silently with her until her sister's tears dried up.

'Is there anything I can do?' she asked when it was over.

Florence sniffed. 'I could do with a clean hankie. But I'm all right. Honestly I am.'

Élise brought her a clean handkerchief and, as Florence was busy writing again and only reached for it without a word, she decided to leave her to it. In any case, besides helping her sister cope with her understandable distress, Élise had to prepare herself mentally and physically for the night ahead. She wondered how the others were spending the day, felt sure Suzanne would be checking everything was in place and ready for them. Gradually the hours passed. Élise and Florence shared a simple lunch, just some bread and tomatoes, neither of them saying much, and eventually Élise did manage to snatch a drifting half-hour's sleep. The afternoon slid into evening and when Hélène came home, Élise took her by the arm and drew her aside.

'Look, I need to put you in the picture. I can't say much, but I will be out tonight.'

Hélène responded to her gravitas by not interrupting.

'It could be dangerous, but I really do have to go.'

Hélène placed a hand on her shoulder and gazed into her eyes. 'I'm not going to try to stop you.'

Élise hugged her in gratitude. The last thing she needed was an argument with her sister on such an important night for them all.

Now, while Élise was waiting in the woods for Victor, she glanced up into the velvet inky blackness of the sky and the millions of stars punctuating its depths. She listened to the sounds of night – an owl hooting, creatures snuffling in the undergrowth, a few night birds moving in the branches – and confessed to herself how bone-tired she felt already. Nervously pacing back and forth in the small clearing, her brain and body needing rest and her soul needing calm, she knew she could not give in. Victor was late and she was worried.

She heard Suzanne's whistle, the agreed signal that it was time to find the shaft, and then heard light footsteps softly crunching the leaves and twigs on the ground as someone approached. She stepped back into the gloom and waited, praying it was Victor.

And then, a moment or two later, he was there.

'Thank God,' she whispered as she hurried over.

He kissed her lightly on the cheek.

'Follow me,' she said. 'We need to get further up the hill.'

'The shaft isn't so close to the castle, is it?'

'Yes, it is,' she said. 'The one Suzanne meant.'

'You're sure?'

'Of course. Come on.'

As Élise led him through the woods, she felt her heart thumping and her spirits lifting. The blood was surging through her veins and she felt excited. It was incredibly thrilling to be out in the dark, making her way along the overgrown track through the woods with Victor, listening out for footsteps that weren't theirs. There was something magical and otherworldly about it too. But my God, she thought, doing something this dangerous certainly made you feel alive. When they reached a crumbling wall, only partly hidden by undergrowth, she pulled the creepers away and climbed over it.

'It's there, I think,' she said.

On the other side they found a heavy circular iron lid, well-disguised, and not previously visible. Nobody would have guessed it was there if they hadn't known where to look. Together they raised the lid.

'I'll go down,' Victor said. 'You close the lid after me.'

'I'm coming too.'

'No, Élise. That's not the plan.'

'I'll just make sure you're okay and then I'll come back up and close it when I'm out.'

He caressed the soft skin of her hands and then slid himself into the darkness.

'Can you find the footholds in the wall?'

She waited; her fists clenched, and nerves so taut she felt they might snap. Her armpits grew cold with sweat as the seconds ticked by. What was delaying Victor? Why hadn't he answered her? Everything in the woods around her was rustling and yet she waited suspended in time. And then, alerted to a new sound in the woods behind her, a feeling of dread lifted the hairs on the back of her neck. She held her breath, glancing back, then moments later breathed a little more freely. Just a fox.

'Ah,' she eventually heard him say. 'There's actually a ladder.'

'Suzanne didn't tell us about that. I'm coming down. Can you use your torch?'

'Not yet.'

'But it's dark and leads to a tunnel, so surely nobody will see the light?'

'I'll wait until I get to the bottom,' he whispered.

'Okay.'

They carried on cautiously for several minutes. She held her nose from time to time against the musty dank smell of the shaft. Things have died down here, she thought.

'Almost there,' he said. 'You go back up now.'

She saw the light from his torch as he switched it on and then heard German voices shouting. 'Halt! Halt!'

'Get back up!' he ordered in a thin tight voice. '*Now.*'

She froze for a second, her heart beating in her throat. Then, knowing she had no choice, she climbed the ladder in a frantic rush, blood crashing in her ears and her breath feverishly fast. As she scrambled out at the top, her ankle buckled. She tried to put her weight on it, almost shrieking out loud in pain. And now she could not walk, only limp.

She thought of Victor as bulletproof; his bravery endless, his strength immense, but in the end, he was only human like the rest of them. At the trees, she paused for second, staring back at the shaft and wanting desperately to see him emerge unscathed. Come on, Victor, she mentally implored, come on.

And then she heard a shot ring out in the darkness. Her heart lurched. No. *No.*

CHAPTER 36

Hélène

That night, after checking Florence was sleeping soundly, Hélène could not rest. Feeling as if the walls were closing in on her, she got out of bed soundlessly, avoiding the creakiest of her room's uneven floorboards. She made her way to the kitchen where she stoked the boiler, put some grain coffee on to brew, opened the back door and went outside. It was still dark, but the kind of darkness that persists for only minutes before the sunrise. She waited, listening to the nocturnal world and watching the mist fade and the sun begin to rise, something she had done so many times before. She wiped the morning dew from the old cast iron bench under the chestnut tree and sat down, hoping to keep an eye open for Élise. But it was chilly this early, so she nipped back inside to find a woollen wrap and to bring out her coffee.

By the time she was outside again, the sun had risen, the sky a glorious pink and gold, and the mist melting into gossamer strips that now lay in swathes across the valley. How could it be that this eternally beautiful landscape looked even softer and more magical than ever? 'Nobody can take it away from us,' she whispered, 'nobody'. She sat nursing her coffee and staring at the emerging view. She heard a cockerel crow and, as the sky turned palest blue, she felt a sense of belonging, relieved, even with everything going on, she could still feel so rooted. But if belonging came from being yourself, and Hélène felt sure it did, how was it possible, when none of them were being themselves anymore? Weren't they all playing versions of themselves, adopting the armour of bravado and courage even when fear gnawed at them? And belonging wasn't simply about where you felt you belonged; it was also about what belonged to you, and there was the problem. They were fighting to repossess their country from the invaders, the occupiers, the people who had stolen what did *not* belong to them. Men who had taken cherished belongings, beaten and killed entire families, trampled over dreams, destroyed aspirations, and left broken lives in their wake. The villagers were getting through this by the skin of their teeth and, she feared, even when it was over, the legacy of war would not simply fade away.

But then she thought about love and the way it made her feel.

She loved Florence and Élise, although they drove her insane at times, but the ties of blood between them were powerful and she would defend her sisters until her dying breath. An unbreakable thread wound from her heart to theirs, binding the three of them together. Forever. If it hadn't been for the war, at least one of them might have been married by now, become a mother perhaps. Maybe all of them might have. She tried to imagine how it would be but kept seeing Jack's smiling face before her. It was more than a faint hunger driving her, it was a longing deep inside. She loved Jack; she was sure of it.

While she did her best to cheer up her sisters when they needed it, she knew her persistent good humour masked some rather more difficult emotions. The helplessness, the rage, the feeling of inadequacy, and the loneliness. She felt them all, even when dwelling in the heart of a family she loved.

And now, once again, she was worrying. This time about Élise, who surely should have been back by now? She rose to her feet and walked over to the gate, lifted the latch, and began to move on down the track. She could see a figure heading towards her, but too far distant for her to see who.

She thought about drawing back but didn't and continued to watch. Whoever it was, they were making slow progress. She waited a little longer, eventually turning back to go inside, but then heard her name being called. Hélène narrowed her eyes, trying to see more clearly as she peered down the track. Could it be Élise? And now she hurried towards the figure. Goodness, it *was* Élise, and Hélène saw she was hobbling and wincing with each painful step. She ran to help her sister.

'What happened?'

'They've got Victor,' Élise said. And then she fell into Hélène's arms.

Somehow Hélène managed to support Élise into the house and then half carried, half dragged her through to the sitting room, where she eased her into a chair.

'I'm going to check your ankle first,' she said, kneeling on the floor.

Élise bent down to rub her leg. 'I can't put any weight on it. It's taken me ages to get here. I heard the Germans in the woods, and their dogs. I was so scared.'

Hélène removed Élise's boot and then manipulated her foot. 'It's not broken,' she said after a few moments, and glanced up at her sister's pinched face.

'You're sure?' Élise asked, her voice shaking.

'Yes, you'd have been screaming when I did that. Now I'm going to get you something sweet to drink and then I'm going to bandage your ankle. You've twisted it.'

'Okay.'

'And you're sure they have got Victor?'

Élise looked haunted. 'I followed Suzanne's instructions perfectly. I just don't get how they knew. I'm sure I sent Victor down the right shaft. But what if I didn't?' And then she bent forward and buried her face in her hands.

CHAPTER 37

After leaving Élise finally sleeping, Hélène cycled into work early, hoping to hear news of what else had happened during the night. First, she called on Violette, who answered the door still wearing her dressing gown and her hair in curlers.

'Come through to the kitchen. I have some real coffee on the go.'

'Where on earth did you get it?'

'Just some I had saved. I didn't sleep much last night, so really need something to wake me up.'

'Me neither. Do you know exactly what they were doing, because I don't?'

Violette explained what the plan had been.

'Oh my God. So that's what Élise meant about the shaft. She says the Germans have got Victor.'

Violette gasped. 'Is he dead?'

'I don't know. Élise is in a terrible state.'

'Do you think Suzanne is all right?'

'I hope so. We'll find out soon enough, I suppose.'

'Will they hold a trial?'

Hélène shrugged helplessly. 'It won't make any difference if they do. The trials are a joke. I've heard of plenty where the whole thing was a complete sham. They're just a cover-up and they simply execute whoever they want, whenever they want.'

Violette looked ashen. 'Let me know if you hear anything.'

'You too.'

Hélène kissed her friend on both cheeks and wheeled her bike on to the surgery. The door was unlocked, but the place felt deserted, so after taking off her coat, she walked through into the small attached cottage hospital and found the captain sitting up in bed.

'I am aware you may have saved my life,' he said. 'Thank you.'

He spoke relatively good French.

'I think it was Doctor Marchand's doing,' she said. 'He was under a great deal of pressure to keep you alive.'

He gave her an embarrassed smile. 'I heard. Anyway, I am most thankful for your prompt action.'

'Will Hugo have to go back to the castle?'

'No. I think I can ensure he will remain here. Although I can't promise he won't be closely watched. We are all a little sick of this war, no?'

She inclined her head in agreement.

'May I speak frankly?' he asked.

'Of course.'

'I miss my children,' he said, then he added, 'my life too.'

'We didn't ask to be occupied,' she retorted. 'Don't you think we all miss our lives?'

'I'm sure you do. I'm sorry. You have been most kind.'

'It's my job. I'll get you some breakfast.'

He reached out a hand to her and she took it cautiously.

'I'll do what I can for you. My name is Captain Hans Meyer.'

'Hélène Baudin,' she said, and then let go of his hand.

Without knocking, an SS officer walked in, clipped his heels together and nodded at the captain. 'We have a few questions for Nurse Baudin.'

Hélène blinked rapidly and stepped away from the bed. 'Of course. How may I help?'

'A young German man by the name of Tomas Schmidt. Know him?'

She frowned, digging her thumbnail into the pad of her left hand behind her back, aware that Meyer could see what she was doing from his bed. 'No. Why would I?'

'He was a deserter who was caught by a night patrol. He mentioned Sainte-Cécile.'

'Oh?'

'You don't know him?'

She shook her head.

'We think he might have been assisted by someone in this village. Concealed by them.'

'Why would anyone here want to conceal a German deserter? Nobody would do anything so crazy. We'd be more likely to give them up.'

He raised his brows. 'I see.'

'Anything else?'

'No. We are questioning the whole village. We have already spoken to the doctor and his wife. There may be nothing to it. This Tomas Schmidt was rambling.'

'Could he have just found somewhere to hide here.'

'Anything is possible.'

He walked away but then turned back. 'Do you have a barn?'

'A garden shed. Is he dead now, the deserter?'

'That, madam, is none of your business.'

After he'd gone, Hélène had to fight to control herself. Now, on top of Victor having been caught, and possibly shot, there was this. What if Tomas was still alive and he led them straight to her home? She turned away from the captain and busied herself with rolling a gauze dressing strip to hide her trembling fingers. Images of Tomas haunted her. Tomas alive. Tomas dead. Tomas turning up at their home. Tomas laughing at her. Tomas in his coffin. And, worst of all, Tomas sitting up in his coffin and pointing at her. As her mind whirled, she clapped her hands over her ears to try to stop the stream of images.

'Miss?'

She became aware that Captain Meyer was speaking to her.

'Don't worry,' she heard him say. 'They're only trying to put the wind up you all. Nobody cares a fig about a deserter, I'm afraid to say. In all probability they shot him.'

An hour later their local policeman, Leo, turned up at the surgery asking for Hélène. Already overwrought and holding her breath in anticipation of what he was about to say, she led him through to a private room at the back where it was safer to talk.

'There is to be a trial in two days' time,' he said.

Hélène gasped. 'Forty-eight hours. No more?'

'At nine in the morning. The three who were already imprisoned at the chateau, plus Victor.'

'Oh God!' She felt physically sick.

He didn't speak.

'So Victor is alive. Do you know if he's injured?'

'As far as I can gather, no.'

She pressed her lips together and, thinking of Élise, her heart faltered. 'But he will have been interrogated?'

'Most certainly. But he knows to resist telling them anything for forty-eight hours, no matter what they do. He's tough.'

Hélène covered her mouth with her hand to hold back the groan. She longed to release all the fear building inside her – to scream, shout, beat her fists against the wall – but knew she could not.

'It'll be all right,' Leo said and touched her on the shoulder. 'Élise wasn't at her café, so I've alerted Violette and she's passing messages on to everyone to disperse.'

'The safe houses?'

'Yes. The whole group will break up for a while.'

'And Victor?'

'I'm afraid it's too late for him.'

'But how did they capture him? Did they know about the plan? Did somebody betray us?'

Leo shook his head and shrugged.

Hélène thought about Élise and her fear that she might have sent Victor down the wrong shaft. If it were true her poor, poor sister would be plagued with guilt for the rest of her life.

CHAPTER 38

She came home from the surgery at the end of the afternoon, but unable to relax, wandered from room to room, the trial plaguing her mind. She wanted to talk to Élise about it but couldn't find her.

Cleaning seemed like a funny way to find yourself when you felt most lost, but it usually worked for Hélène and she hoped it would keep the horrible sick feeling at bay. There was something calming about methodically cleaning the house. The rubbing, the rhythmic swishing of the broom, the vigorous polishing. You didn't have to think, all you had to do was focus. She began in the sitting room, the room where the girls let down their hair, had a drink, read a book, or just sifted through their day. Hélène had a routine. She surveyed the scene: cushions thrown haphazardly and then abandoned on the floor, books lying open and unread on the recently refurbished sofa – in the end Violette had finished it for them – curtains needing straightening, an overflowing wastepaper basket, and cups and glasses lying empty.

First, she gathered up everything not in its rightful place. She collected the cushions, energetically plumped them, and then settled them neatly in a row on the sofa. She stood back to admire. Perfect. Then she removed the used glasses and cups and took them through to the kitchen where she washed them up. Back in the sitting room, she slotted the books into the bookcase, ensuring they were in alphabetical order for, if not, how could you quickly find what you wanted? And after that she dusted every surface, every lamp, every ornament, and every painting with meticulous care. Even a fine layer of dust was unacceptable. She took special care of her mother's porcelain figurines and Florence's favourite, a cast iron outdoor ornament. Her sister had fallen in love with its weathered green patina and had spirited it away from their Richmond garden, insisting it should be kept indoors. Since then it had gravitated from Florence's room to the kitchen and finally to the sitting room, where it sat on the sideboard. Claudette would not have approved. But to Florence, this whimsical statuette of a resting fairy with outstretched leg, a small dove on her foot and delicate features on the wings and face, was charming.

Sometimes, transported into a kind of meditative state by the cleaning, lost in *not* thinking, Hélène forgot what she had already done and what she had not. Had she already finished the floor? Surely not. To Hélène cleaning was like painting. You stopped thinking. That was the thing. While cleaning or painting, she felt as if she were in a trance. For her mother, Claudette, the same could be said for writing. Hélène recalled coming across her mother when she'd been sitting at her desk supposedly writing, but in fact had just been staring out of the window, pen abandoned, as if in a trance too. She hadn't even noticed when Hélène asked what they would be having for tea. From then on, she had imagined her mother writing down secrets in her diary and had longed to find out what they were.

Years later, when they packed up the Richmond house, her mother had piled up all the junk in sacks outside. Hélène had been curious and when it was dark, she had nipped outside to see what she could find. To her amazement, one of her mother's diaries poked out from beneath a cardboard box. Hélène had carefully extracted it and hurried up to her bedroom, intending to share it with Élise, but as she read, she felt like a thief stealing her mother's heart. Because the thoughts and feelings, the *secrets*, were unrecognisable as Claudette's, because everything in the diary was about lost love, lost passion, and the death of spirit and desire. No names were ever mentioned.

Hélène came back to the present and the cleaning and the thought of the trial. She closed her eyes and forced herself to breathe deeply.

At least the room felt fresher.

She took another deep breath and dragged the rugs out to the garden to give them a good beating. Back inside, she swept the floor and when the pan was full, she emptied it and brought the mop and bucket through from the kitchen. Her favourite part came after washing the floor. Florence had concocted the citrus-scented polish out of beeswax and olive oil, to use on furniture and floors. Hélène, on her hands and knees, rubbed it in then polished and polished until her arm ached, and the floor shone. The intoxicating scent of oranges and lemons wafted through the air and she breathed deeply, filling her lungs. Home to Hélène meant a safe place where familiar sights and smells mingled together, a cosy, comforting place, an inviting place where they all could freely express themselves. And the beautiful, random colours of the room were a testimony to their *mainly* harmonious life together, a place of hope and love, but now also a place of vulnerability.

She went to check on Florence, who had been asleep all afternoon.

Florence was now sitting up in bed, rubbing her eyes. 'Gosh. I've been asleep for hours.'

'I'm surprised you managed to with all the noise I've been making.'

'Doing what?'

'Cleaning. Do you know where Élise is?'

'She went to the woods with Claude.'

'With her ankle so bad?'

'He was talking about the trial.'

'Ah.'

'Oh, Hélène, it's so awful. Élise looks completely broken.'

'I know.'

'Shall we make supper together? Give me a few minutes and I'll be down.'

Hélène went down to the kitchen to tidy up a little. She had dreamed of a different life, travelling all over the world. Of seeing India, Italy, America, New Zealand and Greece. Especially Greece. One of those startling white villages you saw in magazines, shining so brightly against a cobalt blue sky. She had dreamed of being an artist too, with exhibitions in London and New York. And she had dreamed of freedom.

As she tidied away the dried crockery, she let her mind wander, sifting through the early years when Florence had been fifteen and Élise just seventeen. Little more than children; it had felt like playing house, especially after Claudette had gone home to England. But it was here, where these old stone walls had slowly wrapped around her and kept her sisters safe, that she'd turned from an imaginative girl into a responsible woman. And now she felt rooted in this life, even though those roots were constantly being threatened – and never more so than now.

CHAPTER 39

The next morning the sun shone brightly, but with the trial now only twenty-four hours away, a heavy black cloud hung over the village. Hugo, seeing Hélène staring into space and barely hearing a word that was said to her, took her to one side.

'Look,' he said patiently, as he handed over a package. 'Get a breath of fresh air and deliver that to Clément's wife, Gabrielle.' He picked up another package. 'And take this one to Madame Deschamps and her daughter Amelie. Don't get them muddled up.'

She smiled, grateful for a reprieve.

While she was out, she bumped into black-eyed Arlo, who gazed at her sadly and asked how she and her sisters were coping.

'We're all worried about the trial,' she said, trying not to betray quite how terrible she felt.

Neither needed to say they knew what the likely outcome would be.

'I know Victor well,' he said. 'Along with you and your sisters, he was good to me when I first arrived. My wife and I are devastated.'

'How did you know Victor was among the arrested?'

'The Nazis posted a list at the town hall.'

'So everyone knows?'

'Pretty much.'

Hugo kept her duties light and let her go early.

She arrived home at four and saw Élise hobbling towards the woods again. She called out, but her sister either didn't hear or didn't want company. Florence was already in the kitchen, chopping carrots, onions and potatoes, so Hélène changed and, at about five, headed towards the woods to sit with Élise. She saw her at their old picnic table, gazing at the ground, but when she drew close Élise just waved her away. Victor was due to be tried in only sixteen hours' time and goodness knows what torment Élise was going through.

Hélène didn't know what to do. She wanted to comfort her sister but felt torn. If Élise wanted to be alone, there was not much point her hovering about. And with all the anxiety over Victor and the trial, she needed a good long walk to tire herself out.

She turned away and set off grimly, not noticing where she was going and was surprised when she eventually looked at her watch and found it was already six and a thick mist was drifting into the valley. From the higher ground she glanced up to see the curve of black kites gliding and soaring on thermals as they searched for food. As she neared another stretch of woodland, she spotted a dark figure slipping from tree to tree and she froze, uncertain whether to go back or to carry on. She didn't know if the man had seen her, but he was heading towards the denser woodland. Maybe if she just stood still until he had passed. But then she saw him veer to the left and take a few steps in her direction. She stepped back, ready to run, but as he came very slightly into the light, she gasped.

'Jack! You gave me the fright of my life.'

He put a finger to his lips. 'Shhhh.'

'I thought it was you,' he said, when she walked over.

She felt the flush rising and her heart speeding up, but managed to prevent her tone from sounding too eager. 'I wasn't sure I'd ever see you again.'

'Proverbial bad penny, that's me.'

She pointed in the direction of the *manoir*. 'Are you staying through there?'

'For my sins. Safest place for now. I'm with Bill.'

'Ah, so glad you found him. Right. Good. Well . . .'

'Weather not looking too good,' he said. He gazed across at the approaching mist and then up at the darkening sky and held out his hand, palm uppermost. 'Heavy rain on the way, I'd say. Why not take shelter in my place? Sit the rain out.'

The scent of grass and earth was growing stronger in the drizzle. Shouldn't she be getting home before the storm broke? Although Élise wasn't talking now, she might need support later.

He examined her face with narrowed eyes. 'You look terrible.'

She heaved a sigh.

'The trial tomorrow morning?'

'Yes.'

'I'm so sorry,' he said.

She couldn't speak.

He came closer and wrapped an arm around her shoulders. 'Come on, old girl, you look as if you need a stiff drink.'

She smiled, unable to stop herself. She *was* worried sick about the trial, but now, right in this moment, she was ashamed to admit she ached for the release of spending some time with Jack.

'I'd like that.'

When they arrived at the tumbledown manoir, Hélène could see it wasn't as bad as she'd expected. Yes, the exterior was totally obscured by creeping ivy and parts of the roof had clearly fallen in, but once he'd lifted the foliage aside and ushered her through a small gap in the wall, it was as if they'd entered a sanctuary. She found herself in an outside courtyard, in the centre of which was an old-fashioned well. The stone walls of the yard were festooned with hanging sprays of gorgeous, light purple wisteria on one side and budding pink clematis on the other. In this partly sunny and partly shady location, the plants had done well.

'It works,' he said, 'the well. In fact it's the total extent of our water supply. Come on inside.'

With a hand firmly on the small of her back, he took

her through a hallway and into what remained of a kitchen. The ancient stove seemed to give out some heat and as the rain began to fall, she walked towards it.

'Are you cooking on this?' She felt stupid for falling back on pleasantries when she really wanted to say how much she had missed him.

'You mean aren't we worried the smoke will give the game away?'

'I suppose.'

'Well, we only light it at night, if at all, and we're mainly surviving on food the Maquis bring us.'

She gazed up at the high ceiling and then looked around her. 'Is there somewhere to sit?'

'Let me show you. We have to make it a bit tricky for Jerry to find us.'

They left the kitchen and passed into what must have been a larder, with a heavily studded wooden door at one end. From beneath a small stone slab he withdrew a key, 'Here we go,' he said.

The opened door led to a narrow, twisting stone staircase. He locked the door and indicated she should go up ahead of him.

'Servant staircase, I suppose,' she said. 'We have one too.'

'There are only the two floors, but it's built in a U-shape, so it's quite easy to cover up where we are. We need to go through to the other side now.'

They went through several high-ceilinged rooms, the beams looking as if they'd been taken directly from a tree without much alteration. Faded cream shutters, closed or hanging half open where they needed repair, let in dull slivers of light that striped the floor.

'We go up to one of the attics from here,' he said.

'Isn't it more difficult to get away quickly?'

'No, it joins the other attics and ours has an external staircase into a high walled garden. I should say, what was once a garden, completely unkempt now, and the staircase has missing treads, so you must take care in the dark, but we've forged a path through the undergrowth. It's impossible to see the staircase unless you know it's there.'

When they finally reached the attic via a dicey wooden ladder, she saw a small window on one side of the sloping roof.

'I didn't expect a dormer window.'

'It overlooks the walled garden. You can't see it from the nearest road, or from anywhere really.'

'Right.'

'Take a pew,' he said.

There were two mattresses in the room, with a pile of blankets and several cushions. She also spotted a bucket. 'All mod cons,' she said with a smile.

He bowed. 'You're welcome.'

She headed to one of the mattresses and sat crossed-legged.

'I have cognac. Will it do?'

'Sure.'

He went to a small wooden box and took out a bottle and two chipped china cups. ''Fraid it's not Waterford Crystal.'

He filled a cup and handed it to her, then he sat about a foot away on the same mattress.

'I'm so scared,' she said. 'It's almost certain Victor will be executed.'

He sucked in his breath.

'I'm worried for Élise. She acts tough, but she loves Victor and it will just . . . just . . .' She paused, unable to say the words.

'Yes,' he said. 'I know. It will devastate her.'

Hélène felt her face crumple as she tried to stop the tears.

'She feels guilty, I think, although none of it was her fault. I don't know what to do.'

'Hélène, there isn't anything you can do.'

'But Jack, I feel so helpless.'

He listened carefully without interrupting. It reminded her of her father when he would usher her into his study and ask her to tell him everything about her day. Her little concerns must have sounded incredibly pedestrian to him, but he'd always listened and made her feel she was the most important person in the world. And it reminded her of Julien too. He had listened, or at least he had tried to, and she had loved him for it.

Jack reached out a hand to Hélène and she took it. Then he passed her a handkerchief. 'It's clean,' he said.

'Thank you.' She wiped her eyes and pulled herself together. 'I wanted to ask if you might be able to come back to us. Florence insists she's fine, but I'm not keen on leaving her alone. The trouble is Tomas, the German deserter we concealed, may not be dead.'

'Blimey! Not good news.'

'No, especially if they can force him to reveal who was responsible for hiding him. It's all getting too much for me. I feel as if I'm going round and round and the net is closing in tighter and tighter every day. They all expect me to know what to do, but I just want to run away.'

'I know. I feel like that sometimes.'

'Really?'

He dipped his head then glanced up. 'Listen. About Tomas. You don't know anything for sure. He may be dead and if he isn't, he may not remember. I recall you said he was in quite a state.'

'Practically delirious.'

'And Victor blindfolded him on the way out, didn't he?'

'Yes.'

'You'll have to stick it out, I'm afraid. I wish I could help, but we're in the middle of an operation. Just make sure the attic looks as if it has been untouched for years. And all of you deny it.'

'He may not be able to find our house again, but he may be able to recognise our faces.'

'Then claim you probably saw him in the village. Say he must have seen you there.'

There was a rumble and then a crackle of thunder. She shivered and automatically shifted closer to him. Jack wrapped an arm around her shoulders as the rain began to batter the roof, sounding as if a million bullets were hitting the tiles. The room had darkened too and, this close to the eaves, the deluge felt primal. Zeus, the ruler of the heavens – God of rain, thunder and lightning – was angry. Jack said something but Hélène couldn't hear above the din. A bolt of white light illuminated the attic and she jolted in surprise. In those few seconds, she saw Jack's eyes glittering as he gazed at her. The thunderclaps came only a few seconds after, followed by a howling wind as the rain worsened.

Hélène closed her eyes. She wasn't scared of storms exactly, although her sisters always claimed she was. Florence even liked running outside during a storm, but Hélène *was* afraid of being hit by lightning. As a child she'd read an article about a man who had been struck by lightning and had been left with tree patterns on his back and chest.

The torrent of rain and the screaming wind went on and on. It felt like an elemental struggle between land and air and beyond the blackness, Hélène felt even the stars would be weeping. She heard a tree crash to the ground, but with Jack by her side, she found herself lulled into a kind of cocoon. She snuggled up, feeling the heat of his body warming her. Normal life had vanished, and it was now just the two of them. She felt safe. In fact, she liked so much about how they were together that, in a way, she wished the storm might never end. She didn't want to have to face the outside world again. Didn't want to feel the burden of responsibility resting on her shoulders. Didn't want to be the one who knew what to do. But most of all, she couldn't bear to think of the inevitability of what would be coming tomorrow morning.

As the storm gradually calmed, Jack gently edged her down onto the mattress where he kissed her. It was a long, slow kiss and as her stomach tightened, she closed her eyes, surrendering to the moment. His lips tasted salty and somehow peppery too and she felt his moustache tickling her. But then she felt him pull away.

'What?' she said, confused and scrabbling to make sense of it.

'I'm sorry, I shouldn't have done that. I like you Hélène, very much. You're a fine woman, but we can't.'

Her heart lurched. 'Why not?'

'Because I may not even be here tomorrow, and it wouldn't be fair.'

Her throat constricted and she chewed the inside of her cheek, willing herself to be mature about this, although she felt ghastly inside. She didn't want to be a 'fine' woman, she wanted him to tell her she was beautiful, declare he was besotted by her, and that he longed to be with her.

'Where do you come from, Jack?' she asked eventually. It was the only way she could guide them on to safer ground, where she could hide the shame she felt at the nasty tight knot of disappointment inside her.

He smiled. 'Devonshire born and bred. My father has a townhouse in Totnes, where I grew up, but my favourite place is my grandmother's home in East Devon.'

'Tell me about it.'

In a quiet voice he spoke. 'It's a thatched cottage surrounded by meadow grass and wildflowers and it looks as if it somehow grew out of the field. A fairy-tale place.'

'Florence would love that.'

'Oak woods flank the hill at the back and one side of

the house, and a brook borders the front. There's not even a tarmac road. Actually, she's left the place to me.

'She died?'

'Yes.'

He'd spoken so wistfully about his grandmother and the cottage, and she fully understood the desire for connection with a special place.

'Would it be all right if you just held me?' she asked in as even a tone of voice as she could manage.

'Of course.' And he gathered her up into his arms and held her there. It was something, but not nearly enough to assuage the darkness growing inside her as the hour of the trial grew ever closer.

CHAPTER 40

It was a little after ten at night when the rain lessened, and Jack walked through the woods with Hélène. At the beginning of their track he gave her quick a peck on the cheek.

'I'll have to leave you here.'

She watched as he walked away.

He clearly meant what he'd said in the attic of the manoir, so she might as well give up all hope of anything more intimate happening between them. It felt like an end, even though there had never really been a beginning. Was it all right to mourn something when it only *might* have been?

'She's been like this for hours,' Florence said with a look of frustration as Hélène walked into the kitchen. 'I can't get her to eat.'

Hélène could see Élise was drunk, swaying and singing at the top of her voice. She walked across and attempted to take the bottle, but Élise resisted furiously.

'Get her some water, could you, Florence?' Hélène said.

As Florence filled a glass and then placed it on the table, Élise swept it aside, spilling water all over the table.

Hélène tried again. 'Darling, if you carry on like this think of the state you'll be in tomorrow.'

Élise glared at her. 'Of course I'll be in a state. I'm already in a state.'

'But you'll have one hell of a hangover as well.'

While Florence wiped up the water, Élise muttered something nobody could hear.

'Could you try to eat something?' Hélène asked.

'Oh for fuck's sake, Hélène, would you listen to yourself? You're not my mother. If you'd ever been in love and had someone love you back, you'd understand how I feel, but no, strait-laced Hélène would never stoop so low as to have sex before marriage.'

Hélène swallowed hard. She must try not to take this personally. Her sister was hurting and didn't know what she was saying. They were all under terrible pressure, fearing the worst.

'Even Julien, that man you saw for a while. You went around with such a silly smile on your face, when all the time—'

'Élise,' Florence interjected. 'Don't . . .'

But Élise didn't listen. 'You thought he liked you, didn't you, but why would he like plain old Hélène, when he could have elegant, chic Violette?'

Hélène felt confused. 'I don't know what you mean.'

'I saw him kissing Violette.'

Dumbfounded, Hélène stared at her sister. 'I don't believe you.'

'Look we're all overwrought. I'm sure Élise is exaggerating,' Florence said.

But Hélène had seen her sister's face when Élise had mentioned Violette.

She stared at Florence. 'It's true? You knew?'

Florence bit her lip. 'I never liked Violette anyway.'

'You both knew, and you didn't think to tell me?' She gazed from one to the other. Florence looked crestfallen and Élise just stared at the floor.

Then Florence glanced up with tears in her eyes. 'I'm so sorry.'

Hélène fought to control herself. 'So you let me make a fool of myself. And laughed behind my back, no doubt.'

'We didn't want to hurt you,' Florence said, shaking her head.

'And you think hearing this now doesn't hurt me? I loved Julien; do you realise that? And you let me make an idiot of myself. Well, thanks a lot.'

Élise and Florence looked at each other with uncertainty.

'I'm so sorry,' Florence said again, looking aghast.

'Do you think all I wanted was to be a nurse and constantly bear the responsibility for you two?' Hélène said, ignoring her sister, her voice rising dangerously and her cheeks growing hot. 'Do you think I never wanted my own life? I put everything aside for you.'

'Hélène,' Élise said, raising her head.

But in the full flow of anger Hélène couldn't stop. 'Oh

sorry, don't you mean "plain old Hélène"? You little bitch! It's all about you, Élise, isn't it? But I had my dreams. I wanted to paint. I loved art. It was the one thing that made me feel truly alive – apart from Julien.'

'But you could have . . .' Florence began

'No, I couldn't. If it wasn't the surgery, it was you two. I never had the space or the time. You have no idea. Neither of you. You just went about your lives.'

'We're sorry,' Florence said. 'Really.'

And now Hélène truly lost her temper. 'Too little, too bloody late. All either of you ever think about is yourselves.' And then she left the room, slamming the door behind her and running up the stairs.

Once in her bedroom, she stamped about, muttering angrily. She felt terribly betrayed by her sisters. By Julien. By Violette. How could Élise and Florence not have told her? How could Violette have done that? She'd known about Julien. She'd known that she, Hélène, was in love with him. What kind of friend did a thing like that? What kind of sister kept quiet?

She thumped her fists into her pillow and then held it to her face, allowing the tears to flow.

And when she finally stopped crying, she dried her eyes and felt even more terrible. Not just because of what Élise had said, but because she was a person who did not lose her temper. A row was the last thing any of them needed and Élise needed her support right now. Of course, it had been triggered by what she'd felt was Jack's rejection and her own overstretched nerves. She'd tried to suppress her distress, but it had all come pouring out in the worst possible way. She paced her room with no idea how to fix things. The only thing that mattered was their little family and she hated falling out with her sisters.

What a horrible, selfish person she was to be unable to control herself when Florence had suffered so terribly, and on the eve of Victor's trial. The worst night of their lives. She gulped back tears at the thought of an execution, of Victor losing his life in that way. While they all prayed there would be a reprieve, she knew in her heart it was unlikely. No wonder Élise was beside herself.

And Élise had been right. She should have known Julien didn't really want her. He had been the most handsome man she'd ever seen, strong with glowing brown eyes, dark hair and such a winning smile. And she had been charmed by him. Well, it was water under the bridge. What mattered now was to find a way to help Élise get through the next day.

Most of the night Hélène listened to Élise pacing her room. She wanted to knock on her door, find some way to comfort her. Sometimes her sister's fierce energy scared her, but that wasn't what was stopping her. This was Élise at her most vulnerable, more wounded than defiant, and Hélène felt she needed to be alone.

She slept little but when she awoke, she gasped for breath and felt as if she were choking. She clasped a hand over her throat and tried to force herself to breathe. There was no air in the room, and she began to panic. But eventually the tight band around her chest released, and at last she sucked in a breath.

At six in the morning, with only three hours to go, she

went through and found her sister staring out of the open window.

'Élise,' she said softly.

Her sister turned a tear-stained face towards her and then she ran and threw her arms around Hélène. 'I'm so, so sorry,' she whispered over and over. 'I didn't mean what I said.'

'I'm sorry too, darling. I feel awful losing my temper at such a terrible time. It was unforgivable.'

Élise pulled away and wiped her eyes with her sleeves, then shook her head. 'No. We're all on edge. I'm nearly out of my mind, but none of us wanted this day to come.'

Hélène gulped back her emotions. 'Shall we forget about last night and somehow get through the day?'

Her sister's face was so white and pinched that Hélène felt the sting of tears.

Élise gazed at her, pursed her lips, put her hands on her hips and then spoke in a different voice. *'Don't cry, darling. It'll spoil your face.'*

'You sound just like her,' Hélène said, and they both smiled because *don't cry, darling. It'll spoil your face*, was what Claudette had always said when any of them became tearful.

'What are you smiling about?' Florence asked as she entered the room.

'We're not really smiling,' Élise replied. 'It was only a memory.'

Florence frowned.

'Listen,' Hélène said and pointed at the window. 'Is it a nightingale?'

They all listened to the trills, whistles, and gurgling sounds.

'It *is* a nightingale,' Florence said. 'That's a good sign.'

She crossed the floor, holding out her arms to them both. And the three clung to each other in an embrace.

When they finally pulled apart, Florence looked at them in turn. 'Do either of you want any breakfast?'

'I'd be sick if I tried to eat,' said Élise, while Hélène shook her head.

'Coffee then?'

Élise closed her eyes. 'I feel so dizzy.'

Hélène helped her to the bed. 'Lie down for a little while and then I'll help you get dressed.'

'How am I going to get through this?' Élise asked, eyes still closed. 'I feel so sick and I just can't take in what's happened. Was it my fault?'

'Élise, it wasn't. I told you I spoke to Suzanne. You went to the correct shaft. Someone betrayed us. The Germans knew. It's as simple as that, I'm afraid.'

'Who though?'

Hélène shook her head.

With an hour to go they were all finally outside, dressed in a mix of grey and black clothing cobbled together from their own wardrobes and their mother's old clothes. Marie had offered to bring the car as it would be impossible for Élise to walk all the way with her ankle still so painful. The wind had got up a little and Hélène watched the trees, their leaves fluttering. She thought of the times gone by, their arrival in France, and their hopes for their futures. None of them could ever have foreseen something like this.

There was a long silence as they waited. Any words would have been redundant. There was a sudden strong gust and Hélène heard a window banging in the house.

'Oh, sorry, it's mine,' Florence said. 'With the wind blowing like this I'd better nip back in and close it.'

Hélène felt every fibre of her being commanding her to run away, but she remained rooted to the spot, her eyes fixed on the door, waiting for Florence to come back out.

When the bright little car pulled up, it looked out of place given the dark gloomy clothes they were wearing and the reason they were wearing them.

Hélène took a breath and exhaled slowly. 'We'd better do this then.'

Marie got out and opened the front passenger door for Élise.

Élise took a step back and shook her head. 'Sorry. I can't. I just can't.'

Hélène wrapped an arm around her shoulders. 'Darling, you don't have to, you really don't, but we will be with you all the way. And I think you might regret it if you don't.'

Élise stared at the ground and all they could hear was the sound of the birds singing and the wind whistling through the trees.

CHAPTER 41

When they were eventually standing in the town square, nerves stretched taut, Hélène heard a window slam shut behind her and, as she twisted round to look, she saw curtains twitching at several others. The small crowd faced the front of the town hall, which was now festooned with three banners with Nazi swastikas, rather than the usual one. Despite the wind, it was a beautiful day, the kind that only happens after a storm. But there was an eerie silence; not even the birds were singing, not a single dog was barking, and no cockerels were crowing. Heads bent; people did not catch each other's eyes.

The minutes ticked by slowly.

Hélène stood beside Élise with an arm around her waist, and with Florence on the other side. They all wore dark hats, and Élise had insisted on wearing a bright red scarf inside her thin cotton jacket. An inner talisman to give her strength, even if only she and her sisters knew it was there.

Eventually, a German soldier opened the main door of the town hall. Hélène's heart banged against her ribs and she heard Élise gasp and then felt her grip hold of her hand. The crowd slowly climbed the steps in single file under the scrutiny of a row of four German officers standing outside. Hélène listened to shuffling feet, people murmuring, complaining about the wind as they held on to their hats to stop them flying off, and then, once inside, she heard coughing and chairs shifting as they took their seats. She felt sick herself, so couldn't imagine what Élise was feeling.

The room was painted white, and four SS men in uniform sat at a long highly polished mahogany table. She heard a door at the side of the room open and turned to see a guard standing there. The sun streamed in and the murmuring in the room died away. Élise had not made a move to look and was staring at the SS men. They all waited while another guard entered the room and went to speak to the men sitting at the table. They heard hushed voices and then an exclamation. The waiting went on for ages. Élise was still staring at the seated SS men and Hélène prayed her sister would not do anything impulsive. For now, at least, her face remained impassive. Élise could not and must not reveal even the slightest hint that she was, or had been, involved in any of this. Nor that she had a connection with any of the prisoners. Her sister was not stupid, and she knew the cost of giving the Nazis even the slightest reason to suspect her, but could Hélène trust her not to show anything on her face? Maybe they should not have come. Élise hadn't wanted to and perhaps they should have listened to her.

At last, the three men and one woman were brought in with their hands tied behind their backs. They looked terrible. Hélène heard sharp intakes of breath at the sight of the prisoners' bruised faces, swollen eyes, and blackened hands beaten almost to a pulp. It was as if the entire group of onlookers had taken the same horrified breath. She squeezed Élise's hand tighter than ever.

The crimes were read out. Then the Nazis who had arrested the three who had been part of the ambush – and responsible for the murder of a German soldier and the murder of two members of the BNA – testified against them.

Hélène knew it had really been Élise who had shot the two BNA men, but she also knew that even without that they would still be executed for killing a German soldier. The testimony was in German, so nobody knew what was being said, although they could guess.

Then it was Victor's turn and a couple of local shop-keepers who had known him all his life spoke up for his good character. Nobody was called to speak for the other three. It was the most perfunctory of trials and Hélène was shocked to realise it was finishing so quickly. To be alive at a time like this was to be terribly vulnerable, as today was making abundantly clear. Hélène gazed at the prisoners, wishing she could find some way to send them strength. Faced with the threat of imminent death, the youngest of the men began to cry, but they all looked defenceless standing there knowing what was coming. Knowing everything was lost. Everything they'd ever known and everyone they had ever loved.

The four SS men sitting at the table exchanged a few words among themselves and then eyed the assembled courtroom. The most senior among them rose to his feet and, with the stoniest of faces, began to speak in French. Ice ran through Hélène's veins as he read each prisoner's name, one by one, followed by the sentence of death by firing squad.

'As a warning to you all,' he continued, eyeing each one of them. 'The execution will be carried out in the square with immediate effect.'

There was total stunned silence. Everyone had expected the killing would be carried out away from the public gaze in the yard behind the town hall, as others had been.

'Court dismissed,' he proclaimed, and he and the other three turned on their heels and swiftly left by a door behind the desk.

At first Hélène was unable to move, but people began pushing past so she, Élise and Florence were forced to rise and file out. The first thing they saw was that while they had been inside, four poles had been erected in the ground. The sisters staggered along behind the others, but Hélène led them to wait at the edge of the square just behind the rest of the crowd. Most people were staring at the cobbles and weeping silently.

When the men, including Victor, and the one woman were marched out at gunpoint with hands tied behind their back, Hélène felt Élise shudder. Her own heart was thumping so hard she felt at any minute she might pass out, but forced herself to remain strong for her sister.

The condemned maquisards, their heads uncovered, stared into the crowd where some had now raised their heads to look. She saw Victor fix his one good eye on Élise and smile. Who could fail to grant leniency at such a heartbreaking sight? But the Nazis had no mercy. Nothing was going to stop this. She noticed Enzo and his useless crony smirking and longed to slap their stupid faces. She saw Suzanne and then, for a moment, her heart faltered when she thought she'd spotted Jack too. When she looked again, he was gone. She tightened her arm around Élise, who was now holding Victor's gaze, mirroring his unflinching stoicism. Her sister would be broken by this, but Hélène understood that Élise wanted Victor to know that she would endure whatever came next and would carry on resisting with every fibre of her being. Élise didn't know the meaning of giving up.

There was nowhere to hide from what was coming. Victor had made his choice, one he was about to pay for with his life. Experience had taught Hélène it was better to step back in the face of danger but, after this, there could be no stepping back. Everything had changed. And now they must all fight back in any way they could. The Nazis, instead of frightening the people with this terrible thing, were only going to make the Resistance and all who supported them even more determined.

She felt a sickening jolt of fear as the prisoners were lined up, each one tied loosely to a pole. It was as if the world had stopped spinning as they waited.

And then, on a command, the firing squad took aim. What came next went on forever, even though it could only have been seconds. One by one, as the shots rang out, three of the prisoners went limp, their bodies sagging as they slid down the poles, their heads drooping. Lifeless. Stunned by it, Hélène watched their lives end. Overwhelmed by the horror of what was happening, her mind was unable to process it and she retched at the stink of blood and death. It was cruel. Worse than cruel. One minute they were breathing human beings, hearts beating, alive, and then they were not. They had families, people who loved them. She heard sobbing behind her.

There was only Victor left. Was there any chance he would be spared? she couldn't help thinking, desperately. After all, he had not killed anyone.

The firing squad took aim again. There would be no last-minute reprieve. It was Victor's turn.

Élise made a low inhuman groaning sound, like nothing Hélène had ever heard. But just before he fell, Victor sang loud and clear, the first line of '*Le Chant Des Partisans*', widely recognised as the unofficial anthem of the Resistance. He died still singing it as the shots rang out across the square. The crowd joined in, humming it under their breath until the firing squad were ordered to turn and point their rifles at them. Then, silenced by the threat, the people slowly backed away and orders were barked out in bad French that they should all immediately disperse.

In the space of a heartbeat, Élise's life had changed. Rigid with shock, and with a painful ankle, she was unable to properly put one foot in front of another and leant against Hélène, who, with Florence's help, managed to drag her away from the sight of her dead lover. Horrified by what she'd seen, Florence's eyes were wide with disbelief.

Marie helped Élise into the waiting car.

None of them were able to speak.

CHAPTER 42

Victor was dead and nothing could ever be the same again. During the following days, the sisters lived in a kind of vacuum. Life had to be lived, but none of them knew how to do it. Hélène glanced at Élise, who was sitting in the kitchen staring out of the window. Her sister looked terrible, her cheeks sunken, her eyes haunted.

Hélène opened her mouth to speak but closed it again. She wanted to say Victor's spirit would watch over Élise and that he would always live in her heart, but it was too soon. It was too raw, too visceral for words of comfort, no matter how well-meant or heartfelt. They would just sound crass, like empty platitudes. The loss had to be felt as deeply as the love had been. They came together; love and the possibility of loss. It was a part of life, even without a war.

'Is there anything I can get you?' she asked instead.

Élise shook her head.

Hélène didn't know how she would face death herself; none of them knew. The execution had snatched Victor far too young, but he had stood proud and tall right to the bitter end. That kind of death could not distinguish between young and old and Victor's father had even offered to go in his son's place, but the Germans had laughed in his face.

Hélène made a mint tea and placed the cup in front of her sister. Then she patted her on the shoulder and went outside.

She had taken time off work again but, increasingly, with empty days on her hands, she found herself thinking about grief. Élise's grief above all others. But Hélène also thought about the grief they all felt. And it made her remember her father's early death. Absorbed in her own feeling of rage, had she even considered her mother's grief? Claudette had neither cried nor displayed any outward expressions of sorrow. The girls witnessed no wringing of hands, no quivering lips, and no trembling chin. Her sleep did not appear affected nor her drinking habits. *'Just one small sherry before supper, darling, and one glass of wine with the meal.'* That had always been her mantra and it didn't change. She had not been afflicted with a loss of appetite, her make-up had remained flawless, her hair tidily chignoned, and her clothing immaculate. She wore high heels, as always, and a pencil skirt, neat blouse, plus earrings and a brooch. She had become so quintessentially English that Hélène felt Claudette was the one with an English mother and not their father.

She had warned them all, in a crisp unequivocal tone,

that outward displays of emotion would not be tolerated, neither at home nor, even more crucially, at the funeral. Hélène had suppressed her heartbreak. She, above all of them, had adored their father; hardly surprising, so alike in looks and in temperament they'd been. Even when she was tiny, she'd loved nothing more than to curl up in his study pretending to be old enough to read while he worked.

Now Hélène wondered if Claudette's mask had been just that – a mask to conceal whatever she might really be feeling. It had been so hard to live up to her mother's expectations and she had tried, she really had tried. And now Élise needed a mother and Hélène didn't feel up to the job.

When Hélène went back inside, she found Élise had isolated herself in her locked room. Florence tried to tempt her with her favourite meals, leaving a tray outside her door, but the food remained untouched, to be collected later congealed and cold.

When Élise did rouse herself from her torpor, it was to wander the house like a wraith, usually in the night when her sisters were in bed. Hélène would hear her footsteps and decide that Élise had to be left to work this out in her own way. She thought about Victor who, from the start, had been such a zealot. It was hardly surprising Elsie had been drawn to such a passionate man, but now . . . what now? When the trauma subsided, what would Élise be left with?

Florence still hadn't talked about her own experience, but on the face of it, seemed to be coping. Yet Hélène felt that although the external bruises had faded, the internal ones still needed more time to heal. By comparison, her own disappointment over Jack was nothing. She resolved to buck up and go back to work, where Doctor Hugo must no longer be left to deal with everything alone.

But first she told Florence of her fear that Tomas might not be dead. She explained that Élise was right and he had indeed been shot, but nobody would confirm if he had been killed outright or not, and then she told her what Jack had said to say and do if there were any consequences. Florence agreed to make the attic look as if it hadn't been touched for years.

When Hélène went back to work on Monday, she discovered much of the village had come down with something a bit like influenza. It was unlikely, given the season, but she was dispatched to treat people in their homes and report back on anyone who might genuinely need the doctor's help. In parlour after parlour she listened to stories of dismay and sadness. Even those who had not previously supported the Resistance now told her they'd changed their minds.

'We can't take this sitting down,' Madame Deschamps' daughter vehemently proclaimed when Hélène went to see her mother at the hotel. Madame Deschamps herself was hysterical and had to be pacified with coffee and a slice of lemon cake.

In his own home, Clément stood to attention and offered to join the Resistance. 'I know I'm old,' he said, 'but I can still hold a gun. Look.' And from his jacket pocket he pulled out an ancient weapon he must have kept since the Great War. Hélène watched his hand shaking as he held it and had to smother a smile.

'So very kind,' she said soothingly. 'But I think it's best if you put it away, Clément, before you do someone an injury.'

The old boy looked at her askance but then settled back in his chair with the gun back in his pocket.

'It isn't loaded,' he added.

Seeing the young people killed in front of their eyes had shaken the village. Angela, the sweetshop owner, had known Victor since he was a baby and had been comforting his father who had not been able to witness the killing and had stayed at home crying.

'Now the poor man has a broken heart,' she said.

Hélène had always thought Victor's father a hard-hearted, petty-minded man, always wanting to shift his mistakes onto others, but she felt sorry for him now. People wanted to help and asked what they could do. Much of the time Hélène was at a loss for words. After all, most of them were old and the best thing they could do was to keep themselves safe. Their village had become a frightening place where people hid and rarely spoke, a place where they waited for something to change. And now it had. Some of the older men still stressed caution, but the women had become more militant.

A middle-aged woman called Inès patted Hélène's hand as they sat in her tiny salon. 'Listen, my dear. I want to give you this.'

She held out her hand and gave Hélène a key.

'What's this for?'

The woman took a long breath before speaking again. 'My son's little house is tucked away in the woods outside the village. I thought the Resistance might be able to use it as a place of safety.'

'That's so kind. Are you sure?'

'My boy is dead, and his wife and child have gone back to her parents' place in Toulouse, so it's empty.'

Hélène took the key and, holding back tears, she wrote down the details.

As she left the house she thought of Jack. Maybe that little house could be where SOE might hold their meetings with the Resistance. There had been no further arrests, which made it seem likely none of the executed had given away too much to their Gestapo interrogators. It was generally acknowledged that under extreme torture everyone would eventually give the Nazis what they wanted. The SS appeared to enjoy the torture – nails ripped out, electrodes attached to sensitive parts of the body, whipping, water torture, prisoners being made to carry their full body weight, hanging from hooks by their arms pulled back into an unnatural position, and so much more. The Gestapo knew that their victims, faced with such indescribable agony, would always talk in the end. This was why no one was party to vital information beyond the concerns of their immediate group.

That evening Hélène followed Élise into the kitchen, longing to ask her how she was feeling, but not wanting to have her head bitten off.

'Do you want to eat something?' Hélène asked instead, worried by how drawn her sister was looking.

'No. I feel a bit sick.'

'I'll make you a ginger tisane. It does help.'

Hélène busied herself brewing ersatz coffee and boiling water for the tisane, but after a few minutes she turned to face Élise and saw her standing with a look of inexpressible sorrow in her eyes.

'I don't understand how the sun can still come up,' she said, her voice scratchy and unnatural, as if it hurt to speak.

The constriction in Hélène's throat prevented her from replying.

'I don't know what to do with myself. I don't know how to feel. How am I supposed to feel, Hélène? Tell me.'

She swallowed. 'Oh darling, I'm so sorry.'

Élise shook her head. 'I've never known anything hurt like this before. I can't eat. I can't sleep. Sometimes I feel I can't breathe. I don't even want to breathe. There's a pain here.' She punched herself in the chest. 'Right here. And it doesn't go away.'

Hélène came across to her sister and held out her arms. Élise allowed herself to be held. Then she pulled away. 'I can't even cry,' she said. 'And yet my heart is breaking.'

'There's nothing I can say. I wish there were.'

'No.'

Hélène gazed at her sister, who was lost in the hinterland between a world in which Victor lived and breathed, and one in which he did not. 'It's trite, I know, but try to take one day at a time.'

'Not sure I can manage a whole day.'

'Maybe one hour at a time then.' She paused. 'Look, I'm going to the woods. Would you like to come? We can walk very slowly.'

Élise shook her head. 'No. I'll stay home, maybe sit in the garden for a bit. I'm going to open the café tomorrow, even if I have to hobble there.'

'Florence said you were. Are you ready?'

'I don't feel I'll ever be ready, but I'm going to do it anyway. I need to find my way back from this.'

Hélène understood.

'I can't stop loving him,' Élise added. 'He's here, you see. In my heart. I want to plead with him not to be gone. I want to get down on my knees and tell him I love him. I didn't. I didn't tell him. I held back and now I never can. I never, ever, can Hélène.'

'Victor knew you loved him.'

'Oh God, I think I'm going to be sick,' Élise muttered and rushed outside.

CHAPTER 43

During her afternoon break some days later, Hélène called on Violette. She hadn't seen her since before the execution and there was something on her mind.

'Oh, I am pleased to see you,' Violette said. 'I've got something for you. I know nothing can really make things better, but I'm hoping it will cheer you up a little bit, at least. Just wait in my sewing room, would you?'

Hélène did as she was asked and sitting in the window, heard Violette's footsteps as she first went up, and then down the stairs, and then came back holding the red dress up for her to see.

'Oh!' Hélène gasped, jumping up from her chair, astonished by the transformation.

'I hung it in my wardrobe so it wouldn't get creased lying around in here.'

'It's so beautiful. I can't believe what you've done. Can I take it with me today?'

Violette smiled and held it out for her. 'Of course. I'm glad you like it.'

Mesmerised by the shifting colours of the silk, Hélène fingered the fabric, smoothing it beneath her fingertips. 'It might lift Élise's spirits to see it. Although I'm not sure if anything can right now.'

'She must be devastated by Victor's death.'

'Yes,' she said. 'It's very raw. Not just his death but the manner of it. But she's a survivor and she'll find ways to cope. It won't crush her, not in the end, but she's facing demons, I think.'

'How do you mean?'

'I'm not sure. It's just a feeling.'

'A thing like . . . well . . . shocking for everyone, but think of watching the one you love, above all others, being put to death . . .' She blinked rapidly, paused, and looked away.

There was a brief silence.

'Violette,' Hélène tentatively began. 'How did your husband die? He wasn't shot too, was he?'

She searched Violette's face but her friend looked uncomfortable, twisting her mouth and not meeting Hélène's eye.

'Violette, I'm sorry.'

'Pierre didn't die, Hélène.'

'Oh, I always thought . . .'

Violette shook her head then looked at Hélène directly. 'I'd rather not talk about it.'

'I'm so sorry. Forgive me. I shouldn't have asked.'

'It's okay. But let's change the subject.'

Hélène cast around for something to say. This dress. It had meant something; maybe it still did. She imagined her mother whirling on a moonlit night, the skirt rippling like the waves of the sea, flowing, rising, falling. She saw the blue of the ocean and the white crests of the waves slowly turning red.

Distracted, she blinked rapidly and felt a little breathless. She folded the dress over the back of a chair and steadied herself. There was something she still needed to say.

'Are you all right?' Violette asked.

Both she and Violette began to speak at the same time.

'You first,' Violette said with a laugh.

Hélène drew back her shoulders. She would just have to come out with it. 'This may not be the right moment, but I wanted to ask how well you knew Julien.'

'Julien?'

'Yes. Julien from Domme? You knew I was in love with him, didn't you?'

There was only the slightest hesitation then Violette smiled. 'I must admit, I'd forgotten.'

'I told you about him though?'

Violette looked a little uncomfortable. 'Yes.'

'We sat in your garden.'

'Yes.'

'So . . . did you know him well?'

Violette gazed at her feet and then looked up. 'I'd been seeing him on and off for a few weeks before you told me how much you liked him. I put a stop to it then, you know, ended things.'

'You should have told me.'

Violette shrugged. 'I'm sorry. Really. I didn't want to hurt you or set hares running. I knew he was a bit of a ladies' man and thought it would just blow over with you.'

There was a prolonged silence. Hélène didn't know what to think, but felt a bit let down. She wished Violette had told her from the start.

'Can we put it behind us, Hélène?' Violette said. 'Please? I'm so sorry.'

Hélène absentmindedly examined the lines on her palm as she was thinking. Violette was her friend. Who else would she enjoy a good gossip with, if not her? But not to say a word? It wasn't what you'd expect from someone who was supposed to care about you and who you cared about too.

'What were you going to say?' she eventually asked.

Violette shrugged. 'I've forgotten.'

Hélène decided to let it go, after all Violette was here and Julien was long gone. There was no point clinging on to resentment. 'Thank you so much for fixing the dress.'

'It was nothing.'

Hélène kissed her on the cheek and then Violette showed her out.

Back in the surgery, Captain Meyer came in to have his stitches removed and to bestow gifts of wine and chocolate in appreciation for his treatment.

'There's no need,' she said, but his warm smile and gratitude gave her pause for thought. Perhaps they shouldn't hate all the Germans; they had to focus the hatred on the Nazis.

'If there's anything I can do in return, please ask,' he said.

'Do you mean it?'

And she went about her work wondering if there was a way he could, in fact, help. Impossible, she thought. His hands were tied, but he then surprised her by leaving a contact phone number on his way out.

'What happened to the deserter they were talking about?' she asked.

He frowned as if not grasping what she was saying.

'Don't you remember? I was questioned about him when you were here.'

'Ah, yes. I believe he is still alive.'

She felt a prickle of fear as Tomas appeared before her, clear as day, his face white and pinched, his eyes icy. He lifted a hand and pointed his index finger. She had to blink the image away.

That evening Hélène and Florence were sitting on a flat rock by the river with their bare feet dangling above the sparkling water. Florence had painted her toenails pink, saying it made her feel better. Here at this point in the river, although the water was flowing quite rapidly, it was safe, and Hélène found she was longing for a swim, wanting more than anything to be in that water and in control of her body, if nothing else. Feeling the timeless peace of the river valley, Hélène could tell how desperately she really needed to relax.

'Are you hot?' she asked.

'Oh yes, and I want to swim,' Florence said, echoing Hélène's own thoughts. 'Will it be warm enough?'

'It won't be as warm as July or August.'

'No. But it might be warm enough.'

They continued to stare at the river that rose in the Massif Central and ended at the Gironde estuary near Bordeaux but crossed much of the south-west on its way. At almost five hundred kilometres, it had been an important part of daily life in the Dordogne, having once been the only means of transport. The people still loved it. There were sturgeon, salmon, and families of otters, and Hélène wished she had not only brought her swimming costume but also her fishing rod or, at the very least, something to drink.

Florence rose to her feet and began to cast off her clothes. 'I can't stand it. I'm going in,' she said excitedly. 'Coming?'

Hélène shook her head.

Florence shrugged. 'Suit yourself.'

Hélène watched as her sister clambered down to the water's edge and slipped in. 'Mon Dieu,' she yelped. 'It's freezing.'

Hélène laughed. The sun felt warm on her skin and she lifted her face to feel it even more. Such a simple thing but how good. After that she watched as Florence floundered at first, gradually became accustomed to the temperature, and then began to swim with a strong confident crawl, lying flat on the water with her face half submerged and gasping for air as she took alternate overarm strokes. She swam fluidly, stroke after perfect stroke. Hélène rose to her feet just as Florence called to her to come in too.

'It's wonderful,' she shouted. 'Come on, Hélène. Don't be a spoilsport.'

Hélène hesitated but then undid her buttons and ripped off her skirt and blouse. She gazed at the water for a moment longer and then rashly removed her underwear too. In for a penny . . .

'Wow,' Florence shouted, 'You're really going for it, Hélène.'

She stumbled as she picked her way to the water's edge and when she slid in over the stones that skittered about beneath her, she gasped. It really was cold. She splashed about to warm up a little then began to swim across to Florence, who was laughing and spluttering as she trod water.

'Race you to the bend,' Hélène said. 'By the abandoned houses.'

Florence grinned. 'You're on.'

And they swam, glancing occasionally at each other, pushing on as fast as they could, the river water whooshing and swooshing around them, spray flying outwards as they cut through it, kicking their legs and feet. Hélène felt she could swim forever and, if she did, everything would be all right; she could forget everything that had happened, stop worrying about the future, and exist only in the present. Florence got there first, whooping and waving at the same time.

'I won! I won!' she exclaimed delightedly.

She swam to the edge and hauled herself out to dry in

what remained of the sun. Dripping, she shook herself like a dog, and the droplets fanned out and fell to the ground like rain. Hélène followed her as the remaining windowpanes of the old red-roofed houses turned to an eye-watering gold. She glanced at the overgrown apple, pear and fig trees growing in the gardens, their leaves also shimmering in the low sunlight. Still beautiful, she thought, while her heart pumped furiously, and she panted for breath. Everything else went quiet. The light changed a little, softened and shifted until there was only pink, and a timeless, ancient world seemed to break through to the present and, for a brief moment, she saw the world as Florence did. Magical. Extraordinary. Limitless. Oh, Florence, she thought. I have misjudged you.

'My goodness I needed that,' Florence said. 'Doesn't it feel marvellous? And look how lovely the river is, the way the trees are dancing in the water. Just like an underwater world. And the dragonflies. See?'

And Hélène did see, and she blinked because what else could she do, unless she wanted Florence to see her tears. And she did not. She picked up a smooth stone and rubbed the dirt away. Still wet from her fingers and her dripping hair, it revealed a mix of purple, yellow and green, like the woods on the other side of the river.

Then she nodded, her breathing calm now. 'I'm not as fit as you,' she said.

Florence smiled. 'It's all the gardening I do.'

Hélène stretched her arms out wide and, feeling free, didn't mind her nakedness at all. 'Oh, I wish I could stay here forever.'

'Me too. Let's do it again soon and try to bring Élise. I know it won't make anything right, but it would do her good. There's something about swimming in the river.'

'Yes.'

'But now we'd better get back before the sun goes down completely,' Florence added. 'Walk or swim?'

Hélène laughed as the sky turned red and orange, feeling better than she had in ages. 'You are in your sopping wet underwear and I'm stark naked, so I rather think we'd better swim and pick up our clothes from where we left them.'

CHAPTER 44

That night Hélène slept soundly. And when morning came, she was glad and rose early. Feeling revitalised, she made herself a simple breakfast, got dressed and went to work, intending to make an early start to compensate for some of the time she'd lost. She had started to tidy the dispensary in a desultory way – it was too early for patients – when Marie came in, already dressed in a pink flowery frock and smiling broadly.

'Good morning,' she said. 'How about a coffee in the garden?'

Marie was one of the few people who thought ersatz coffee tasted good and Hélène was about to decline, but as she and Marie hadn't had a good chat for a while, she agreed.

'Go on through. I'll bring it out.'

Hélène went into the hall and then slipped out through the tall glass doors at the back that opened outwards into the walled rose garden. She made herself comfortable on one of four little cast iron chairs beside a matching table, painted pale green. It was warm and wonderfully peaceful sitting in the sunshine and listening to the buzz of insects, with the delicate scent of roses drifting in the air. Two large blue butterflies hovered over some early hollyhocks flowering against the wall. Her mother was a keen gardener too and had grown hollyhocks and foxgloves because, she said, they'd attract hummingbirds. For years Hélène and Élise had kept a lookout for those elusive birds, fighting to gain their mother's approval by being first to sight one. They never did.

A few minutes later, Marie came out again with a silver tray and set it on the table. The table wobbled. 'Oh dear, I'll get something to stop that.'

She marched indoors, coming out again with a cork mat which she slipped beneath the offending table leg. 'There we are. I baked some oat biscuits. A bit dry and crumbly, but not too bad.'

She passed Hélène her coffee in a little white cup and offered her the plate of biscuits.

Hélène shook her head. 'I've only just had breakfast.' Then she sipped her drink, trying not to screw up her face. 'I don't know how you can like this stuff,' she said.

Marie laughed. 'I suspect it's an acquired taste.'

Hélène put her unfinished coffee on the table.

'So, tell me how you all are,' Marie said. 'Is Élise beginning to come to terms with what happened?'

'It's still sinking in. She will come through and is opening the café, but it's as if she's sleepwalking at the moment.'

'Terrible for her.'

But Hélène was thinking not only of Élise, but Florence too. She hadn't told anyone about what had happened to her sister at the hands of those men. She still wanted to talk to Marie about it and opened her mouth, but then closed it again. She could not betray her sister.

'Do you hear from Claudette?' Marie asked.

'Not much. The post, you know . . .' Of course, Hélène knew it wasn't the only reason, but didn't want to elaborate.

'Quite.'

'Did you see much of her when she was younger?'

'Not when she was a child, but when I married Hugo and moved here, we'd say hello when she was here during the summer. Mainly she kept herself to herself and had her hands full with you girls.'

'Did she seem happy?'

'Happy?' Marie pulled an uncertain face. 'Maybe. It was hard to tell with Claudette. I think she probably was, in her own way. She never said much. I had the feeling that something was going on.'

'Really?'

'I wasn't sure what. She used to take you children to the river, I remember that.'

'Hmm. Talking about the river, I—'

She was about to tell Marie about her glorious swim with Florence the evening before but was interrupted by the sound of raised voices in the hall. She exchanged a look with Marie, who just raised her eyebrows and twisted round to look.

'Is it a patient?' Hélène asked.

Marie pushed her chair aside and rose to her feet, but before she could go to see who was there, Hugo entered the garden flanked by two heavily built Nazi officers.

'You are Marie Marchand?' one of them asked and pointed at Marie.

Hélène noticed her friend had gone pale and was gripping the back of her chair, her knuckles white.

'Yes. I am Marie Marchand.'

The officer reached inside his jacket pocket and with a look of contempt, he pulled out a sheet of paper. 'You are to report to Gestapo headquarters in Périgueux. You have one week to provide us with a certificate of Aryan descent.'

'But that's ridiculous,' Hélène protested, determined not to be intimidated as she stood up and glared at the man. 'Marie isn't Jewish.'

But Marie held up a hand to silence her.

'The doctor's wife fully understands.'

'But it isn't true,' Hélène objected.

The office stood stiffly, shoulders back, posture perfect, manicured fingernails. A preening sort of a fellow, Hélène thought as the anger coiled inside her.

He flashed her a disingenuous smile, flicked his fingers at her as if she were no more than dust, and then spoke. 'And *you* are?'

'Doctor Hugo's nurse,' she said, still defiant, drawing herself up tall.

When he next spoke, his words were delivered coldly, detached. 'While investigating the doctor before, during, and after his brief incarceration with us, we came across something unexpected about his wife. Therefore, we are here.'

The other man gave Marie a sharp look. 'If you cannot come up with the requisite paperwork in time, you will be sent to a labour camp.'

He inclined his head and the other man gave her a half smile. 'One week, madame.'

'I'll show you out,' Hugo said, a nerve in his jaw pulsing.

He raised a hand in dismissal. 'No need, we will find our own way,' he replied, and the two men swiftly left.

Marie sank into her chair. 'It was just a matter of time,' she said, sounding defeated. Then she dropped her head and buried her face in her hands.

Hélène glanced at Hugo, who was standing behind his wife's chair, his hands grasping her shoulders. He was blinking rapidly, and his face had clouded.

'It's true?' Hélène asked, and her voice caught. She couldn't believe she was even asking this.

Hugo wouldn't look at her and closed his eyes.

There was a short, terrible silence as fear ripped through Hélène. She ran through the options in her head. There had to be something they could do. There had to be a solution.

'Élise knows the forger,' she said eventually. 'Maybe we can get Marie a fake document?'

Now Hugo opened his eyes and shook his head. 'It would take too long. You need birth certificates going right back to her grandparents on both sides. Her grandfather, on her mother's side, was a Jew. Marie has Jewish blood. That's all they need.'

'I don't understand why you didn't you organise a fake one before, when there was time.'

'We hoped it would never come to this and we didn't want a single soul to know, not even a forger, because who could you trust with it? It would have made her too vulnerable.'

Hélène could hardly breathe with the shock of it, but her mind was still whirring. 'In that case,' she said, 'we'll have to find a way to get her out of here.'

Marie shook her head. 'I can't leave Hugo.'

'You'll be sent to labour camp if you stay.' She headed for the door. 'I'm going to speak to Élise. It may take a little while, but we'll find a way.'

Hugo gazed at her with damp eyes. 'Take whatever time you need.'

But when Hélène went to the café, she found the door locked, so instead she tore home at breakneck speed, heart pounding, head bowed and ignoring anyone who attempted to waylay her.

Back at home she told Florence what had happened and how desperately worried she was for Marie.

'Élise has just gone to tie up the goats somewhere in the woods,' Florence said. 'I'll try to find her. Don't worry, Hélène, I'm sure we'll think of something.'

So Hélène sat at the sunlit kitchen table to wait for Élise and considered the situation. If the terrible rumours about the labour camps were true, it was unthinkable that Marie could be sent to one of those godforsaken places.

How were she and Hugo ever to survive this? Stalwarts of the village, they had helped everyone one way or another for years and it simply wasn't fair.

As the familiar comfort of the kitchen wrapped itself around her, she remembered how she used to sit with her father in their Richmond kitchen, she drawing comfort from his reassuring smile and he seeming to enjoy their companionship. How she wished he were here now. She fiddled with her watch, checking it every few minutes. Surely Élise wouldn't be much longer.

She rose to her feet and prowled around the kitchen, her mind in turmoil, then opened the back door to glance outside. Nothing. Just the wind blowing the trees about. She sat down again and forced herself to stay calm.

Their Richmond kitchen came back to her again. It had been in the basement, overlooking a small terrace at the back where they used to eat in the warmer weather. In the summer the terrace was a riot of colour with jasmine and climbing roses, pots of pelargoniums, and hanging baskets filled with impatiens and petunias, much like the garden Florence had made for them here. She pressed her lips together to stop herself crying and, as she did, she found some strength. No matter what it took, and she still didn't know how, she was going to find a way to help Marie.

At last she heard the back door swing open and Élise came in. 'Florence told me,' she said as she unlaced her boots before kicking them off.

'Is there anyone who can help us, Élise?'

'You mean to get her away?'

'Yes.'

'The local maquisards have scattered since . . .' She visibly held back the flood of grief that lay just beneath the surface and then continued. 'Since Victor. They've disbanded temporarily. Nobody knows what information the Nazis got out of the ones they murdered, so nobody feels safe enough to stay.'

'Do you know where Claude and Jack are?'

'I'm sure I can find out. I'll put my boots back on and go now.'

'How's your ankle?'

'It's fine.'

The rest of the day passed slowly as Hélène tried to work out the options and waited for Élise to come back with news. They needed someone who knew the ropes well enough to get Marie across the Pyrenees into Spain and then to England. Though what would happen from there she had no idea.

The hanging around was awful and yet by evening Élise had still not returned. Trying to kill time and overcome her growing feeling of panic, Hélène made herself a chamomile tisane and went outside to breathe the flowery scents of the garden and the green earthy smells of the forest beyond. She felt a sudden burst of optimism when she spotted Jack approaching in the shadows beside one of the sheds at the side of the house. She beckoned him forward and he came towards her and although her heart was racing, she faced him calmly.

'Quickly. Let's go inside before anyone sees you. We need your help.'

He glanced around. 'There's nobody here. I don't think the birds or rabbits will tell. What's this about?'

She resolutely led him by the elbow to the back door. 'I am so glad you're here.'

'Angel of mercy, you know me.'

She took him through to the sitting room where they perched on the window seat.

'Right. So, tell me what this is about. I had a message from Élise, via Claude, telling me to come here as quickly as I could.'

'It's not good news. The bottom line is we have to help Marie get out of France.'

'Because?'

'The Germans know about Marie's Jewish ancestry.'

'Christ!'

'She only has a week to come up with a certificate of Aryan descent.' She gazed at Jack then bent over, hiding her face in her hands. 'Oh this is hell. I just can't bear it.'

'And I suppose there isn't time to raise a false document?' he said.

She felt sick but took a long slow breath before looking up and speaking. 'I've thought and thought, but no.'

'Tell me what I can do?'

'We need to get her out of France quickly, but there are no maquisards around to help.'

'Well the local Maquis wouldn't necessarily know how. It's complex navigating this kind of escape. But I have done it before.'

'Are you saying you might be able to take her?'

'If there's no one else to do it she'll be sent to a labour camp, won't she?'

'So you will?'

'I'll need Élise's help.'

Hélène drew in her breath and felt as if the shadows of the house were spinning around her. 'No,' she said. 'Élise can't go. She's too fragile. This soon after Victor's death she would not be—'

'Level-headed enough?' he interjected.

'She needs time to recover before she takes on anything like this. If it needs two of us, then I'll come.'

'Are you sure? It's a big ask, Hélène.'

'I know.'

Slowly he stood her up and then very deliberately placed his hands on her shoulders. 'You'll be away for a while.'

'How long?' She stared into his eyes and held her breath.

'Hard to say.'

She let out her breath slowly. 'Would your father be able to help her once she reaches England?'

He dropped his hands. 'I'll make sure of it. If you accompany us as far as the Pyrenees, I can organise the local network to see her across the mountains and then to the ferry. But unless something goes wrong, I won't be crossing the mountains with her. There's too much on here.'

She covered her mouth with her hand, not wanting him to see the emotion she was feeling, a combination of relief that Marie had a chance to get away but also anguish at the thought of leaving her sisters.

'It will be a dangerous journey,' he said. 'You're sure?'

'I'm sure.'

'Good. I think it's best if we go as man and wife, with Marie as your mother. If you travel in uniform it will focus the attention on you, not Marie or me.'

'And the false papers?

'I'll arrange those. I know people weren't certain at first, but Pascal Giraud, the clerk, will provide travel permits. We can trust him.'

Hélène retreated inside herself as she thought about it. There was no question of not going, but her hands were clammy and she could feel the trepidation already mounting. Élise and Florence were both so vulnerable right now, but however reluctant she might be to leave them, she had to do this.

'We'll need a vehicle,' he said. 'You can drive, can't you?'

'Of course. I'll ask if Victor's father might lend us his blue van.'

'Great. We'll take it in turns to drive and Marie can rest in the back. We only need tell them she's your mother if they make us all get out. We'll say we are returning west having just visited relatives and we're bringing back a motorbike.'

Hélène couldn't help feeling torn. With the war raging, nobody enjoyed straying far from home, and this was something so much more than a daytrip to Sarlat.

'I know you can do it,' Jack said, clearly aware of her state of mind.

She stared at her hands, twisting them over and over. 'You really think so?'

'Of course.'

'My sisters?'

'They'll be fine. They're both adults and stronger than you think. Have faith, Hélène.'

She bit back her fear. This was not what she wanted but she ordered herself to buck up and get on with it.

'Okay?' he asked.

'Okay.'

'Don't pack much. A change of clothes will suffice. If we have to abandon the van, we'll need to travel light.'

'Why would we have to abandon it?'

'Any number of things, but mainly lack of petrol. Now there's one other thing . . .' He paused and took a breath. 'I want you to know nothing is guaranteed. We may fail.'

Her chest tightened and she felt as if she couldn't get enough air.

'Hélène, you *can* do this,' he said and took hold of both her hands.

She stood there for what felt like ages, not thinking, just breathing and feeling him holding her hands in his.

'Yes,' she finally said in a more resolute tone. 'Of course I can. And I will.'

'You'll need to lie low for at least three days before we go and not be seen in the village or at work. Do you visit sick patients occasionally?'

'I travel to nurse patients who can't be moved, sometimes for several days at a time, so it is feasible.'

'We have to make it clear that you left the village several days before Marie, so they don't associate you with her disappearance.'

CHAPTER 45

Early the next morning, Hélène went to speak to Leo at the police station to ask if she could make a phone call. Then she went straight to Hugo to tell him of the plan, requesting enough time off work to carry it out. He took her hands in his and squeezed them. 'Anything that will help Marie.'

Once that was done, she and Florence set off to find the isolated house Inès had spoken of. The woman had said that it was hidden in woods outside the village, but they walked for nearly an hour and kept losing their way. Hélène's limbs felt heavy as she walked, and so were her spirits, but she had to do this today. If the girls needed to hide while she was away, this would be the best place. It proved tricky to find but she felt relieved when they eventually stumbled across the tall bushes and trees concealing the house.

'A Little Red Riding Hood house,' Florence said as they pushed through and caught their first glimpse of it.

'Or maybe not,' Hélène replied with a laugh.

'Let's see if there's a granny inside.'

Hélène unlocked the door and when she opened it the dust awoke, lifting in the breeze and spinning in the shaft of sunlight. The place was small but comfortable, a little musty through lack of use, but there was a kitchen and a small sitting room. They braved the creaky stairs and found two bedrooms. Back outside again, they discovered a lavatory and a barn.

'The whole place feels as if it's stuck in the past,' Hélène said.

'But you can almost sense the people are still here.'

'Yes, you can,' said Hélène taking hold of Florence's hand. 'Please show this house to Élise when she's feeling stronger.'

Florence chuckled. 'If I can ever find my way again. I thought we were going to be lost forever and sleep in the woods for a hundred years.'

'You can see it would make an excellent rendezvous for the Maquis, can't you, or for you two? And not a wolf in sight.'

Florence explored the small overgrown garden while Hélène locked up and then they left to begin the walk home.

Haunted by the feeling in the house – that sensation of lives left hanging – Hélène was turning her own history over in her mind as they walked, and Florence grew quiet.

Before Florence was born their parents had laughed a lot, taken walks in the park with Hélène and Élise, pushing them on the swings as they shrieked 'higher, higher'.

They'd gone to the seaside in summer, usually Devon – Hope Cove or Lannacombe Bay. Sometimes they made it to the Roseland Peninsula in Cornwall. And there had been the odd weekend in Brighton too. Their mother smiled and sang and ran along the sand with them. A precious and magical time, so when her father withdrew from the family, it had left Hélène confused, angry, and wondering what she'd done wrong.

Once they reached the age of eleven, she and Élise had been enrolled at a minor independent school near their home in Richmond. Hélène remembered it as a lonely time, with their mother focusing her attention on Florence and their father being increasingly absent from home. For Hélène and Élise, the good times were over.

Their mother had lost a vital spark and no longer forgave her older children their failings. And as their house became a shadowy place, Hélène had quickly learnt bricks and mortar did not make a home. She closed her eyes to try to recapture their happier past, but like the hummingbirds, it was elusive.

She wondered what her father would say if he could see her now. He had taught her that learning from her mistakes was the best way to get on in life. That nothing was impossible if you believed in yourself. And if you fell, you picked yourself up. Would he be proud, praising her fortitude and courage, pleased with how she had held the family together and what she was about to do to help Marie?

As for her childhood relationship with Florence, she had relished making her little sister cry, pinching her skin, pulling her hair. Once or twice she had prayed Florence would just disappear or die. And all Florence ever did was look up to her big sister with so much light and admiration in her eyes it made Hélène hate herself. Then one day, Florence had got in the way of a cyclist in the street and Hélène had rushed for help, her heart pounding in fear that her little sister really would die. It hadn't been serious, but it taken the accident for Hélène to work out the envy she felt was not Florence's fault and from that day on she had sworn to love her.

And now here they were about to be parted and she loved her so much it hurt.

'Penny for them,' Florence was saying. 'You seemed very absorbed.'

'Sorry. I was thinking about Marie. And about the old days. Funny how the past won't lie down and die.'

Three days later, Hélène kissed her sisters farewell. Florence flung her arms around her and would not let go, while Élise patted Hélène on the back. When Florence did eventually release her, Hélène saw her youngest sister was silently weeping.

'Darling, you'll be fine without me,' she said, her voice cracking, but with an effort she pulled herself together and continued. 'Honestly, you will.'

Florence sniffed and wiped her face with her sleeve. 'It's not that.'

'What then?'

'I'm scared for you.'

'Oh sweetheart, we've been through that. I'll be with

Jack and back in no time. Jack knows what he's doing. Now,' she narrowed her eyes, 'promise me you'll look after each other.'

They both nodded.

'Good luck,' Élise whispered. 'Stay strong. You can do this and come back safely. We need you.'

Hélène's heart fluttered and she smiled. 'I never thought I'd hear you say that.'

Élise wobbled her head with 'a wonders will never cease' look.

Hélène picked up her bag and, turning on her heels, left the house before they could see how terrified she truly felt.

She walked quickly through the village glancing left and right. It was not yet light so nobody was about, but you couldn't be too careful. She spotted the bulk of the blue van already waiting at the back entrance to the surgery. Oh God, she thought, it's actually happening. She opened the back door and went through the surgery to the house.

Inside the hall Marie was sobbing into Hugo's chest, but turned as Hélène entered the room.

'I can't leave him,' she said. 'Tell him. We've been together for thirty-five years. I won't leave him.'

Hugo stroked her hair. 'I'll be perfectly fine,' he said.

Marie didn't look as if she believed him.

'You have to go, Marie,' Hélène said. 'You either choose to go now, or you let them take you. It's as simple as that. This way you will have a fighting chance.'

'But I don't want to have a chance without Hugo, and what will they do to him once they find I'm gone?'

'If Hugo came with you, I think the Germans would smell a rat and be after you so fast you wouldn't even be able to draw breath. As it is, he will say he had no idea what you were planning, and I'm sure Captain Meyer will speak up for him. I think he will confirm Hugo had no prior knowledge.'

It had been a risk asking for Meyer's help, but she had phoned him the morning after Jack's visit. She hadn't told the captain of the plan, only that in the days to come Hugo might need his support because, unfortunately, she herself would be away nursing a sick relative on the coast.

By lying low, she'd made it seem as if she had left three days before Marie, a fact that was reinforced by Hugo explaining the reason for her absence to his patients and everyone else too. Meanwhile Marie had made her presence very much felt by helping Hugo in the surgery. As soon as Marie's disappearance got out, Hélène hoped it would become quickly apparent to the captain that he must claim to believe what Hugo was saying.

And now it was the fourth day, and they were ready to go. The day after next, the Nazis would be back to check if Marie had a certificate proving her ancestry was, in fact, Aryan – but they would be long gone.

Hélène watched Marie, the woman who had been a mother to them all, clinging to her husband. How could such evil exist in the world for this to happen to such good people? How was it possible Hitler could have manipulated an entire nation into thinking this was right? It was unbelievable and yet it was happening.

Hugo was clearly agitated and frightened, although he was trying to conceal his emotions for Marie's sake.

Marie turned to Hélène, took a breath, and picked up her pitifully small canvas bag. 'We are meeting Jack at the van. He has the keys.'

Hélène watched the unspoken love and anguish passing between Hugo and his wife, then Marie flashed him a confident smile and left the house.

Hélène ventured a final look at Hugo whose face had now crumpled, all bravado gone.

'Don't worry,' she said and went to kiss him on the cheeks. 'We'll look after her. I promise.'

Outside she saw Jack helping Marie into the back of the van. Hélène glanced inside it and saw it was packed with garage equipment, tools; spare wheels and so on, plus the motorbike, behind which he had fashioned a resting place for Marie. Dry-eyed, Marie climbed in.

'Sorry it smells of engine oil,' Jack said. 'Tap on the partition if you need anything.' And then he closed the back of the van and went to sit in the driver's seat with Hélène by his side. He touched her hand. 'Ready?'

'Ready,' she said, comforted by his attention to detail and his charm, and smiling despite her fears.

He started up the van and they left the village. It was still dark, and they should make good headway if they took minor roads and stayed away from known Nazi-occupied towns. They would head in the direction of Bergerac, avoiding the German garrison, and then travel due west on the back roads. They had originally planned to go further south and then west, but now they were travelling towards Bordeaux instead. It was more dangerous but should take less time. There was a *Propagandastaffel* – a propaganda squadron – in the town of Bordeaux, in charge, obviously, of the propaganda but also controlling the French press. And there were submarine bunkers and the Mérignac-Beaudésert internment camp nearby. They would need to avoid the Gurs internment camp too, not far from Pau, used mainly for Jews, as well as people considered dangerous by the government.

For safety's sake they would turn off before reaching Bordeaux and then head south towards the Pyrenees. Marie was not young, and she had been warned the trek across the mountains to Spain would be arduous. But hundreds of Frenchmen, British and American airmen, and fleeing Jews had escaped along the same route and succeeded, every one of them assisted by a string of local men and women who had fed and hidden them while running the risk of capture themselves. Hélène tried not to think how Marie would cope, especially when Jack told her that nowadays there was a greater risk of ambush than previously and a number did not make it.

For the first part of the journey they passed little traffic and managed to talk. Hélène could tell Jack understood how frightened she was, and he'd been keeping up a steady stream of conversation for her sake.

'What did you do before the war?' she asked him during a lull.

He blew out his cheeks. 'I was a restoration architect, believe it or not, working mainly in London, but also in Bath, Cheltenham and so on.'

'Will you go back to it?'

'I don't know. I always wanted to farm. Sheep, dairy, I don't know. Maybe fruit.'

'So why didn't you?'

'The lure of something more, I suppose.'

'So, after all this?'

'I may go back to Devon and stay put. What about you?'

'Well, this is our home.'

'And when one of you, or indeed all of you, marry?'

She scratched the back of her neck. 'I can't think about it. I like to imagine the three of us together forever, but I know things will change. I guess we'll see when the time comes.'

'Would you ever go back to live in England?'

She shrugged. 'Who knows?' she said and then gazed out of the window so he couldn't see her burning cheeks because, of course, she had imagined herself living in England with him.

They reached their first stopping point in the late afternoon. Jean-Michel Poitiers, a village priest, was providing food and a bed for the night, Marie in the house and Jack and Hélène in a barn. They had maintained the pretence of being a married couple, so he was billeting them together. The house was two-storey, with such a steep red roof Hélène thought it must have a usable attic. She took to the priest instantly, a tall thin man with a hooked nose, a shock of curly white hair and extraordinary smiling blue eyes.

During a meal of mainly potatoes, he told them he had

been helping refugees for the last two years, had been arrested once but then let go. After eating, he gave Jack a bottle of wine and some blankets to take to the barn, and Hélène an oil lamp. They followed him out of the house and across the yard to a hay barn hidden behind a row of poplars.

'Nobody comes here,' the priest said. 'You'll be safe. But if you hear a prolonged whistle that'll be me. You can get out through there.'

He indicated a small door at the back and then, after he'd left them alone, they found an old mattress in one corner with an upturned crate beside it, with two mugs and a corkscrew.

'Wine, madam?' Jack asked, brandishing the bottle.

They drank the wine quickly, and in fact Hélène could have done with more. Much more.

'Time to sleep, I think,' he said, and lay back on the mattress, pulling one of the blankets over him.

She followed, and although her breath quickened at their proximity, Jack began snoring gently within seconds. She lay awake, as her need for him heightened unbearably. With her mind in turmoil, she forced her body not to touch his, while at the same time longing to do so. In the end she gave up and nestled close, comforted by his warmth, and breathing in the male smell of him. Sweat, wine, tobacco. He turned over, and in his sleep he wrapped an arm around her.

She woke in the night, tears spilling down her face but with no idea why. A savage pain had gripped her. She couldn't breathe properly and felt as if a well of accumulated emotion was pouring from her. Grief, fear, anger, despair. Feelings she had tried to keep under control, now out of control and jeering at her. *Ha, ha, ha. Thought you could hide from us? Well take that!*

In her distress she whimpered.

'Shhh,' Jack said, stroking her hair. 'Everything will be all right.'

She tried to reply, but her throat ached.

'Never give up, my girl,' he said, and she turned to look at his face just visible in the moonlight coming in through one small skylight.

'My father used to say that,' she said, finally able to speak. 'Exactly that.'

'Wise man, your dad.'

'I sometimes feel as if I'm never going to be who I was meant to be, nor have any chance of knowing who I could be.'

'Because of the war?'

'Yes. And then I feel guilty and petty because what right have I to be sad?'

'I don't think you realise how brave you are.'

'By coming with you and Marie?'

'Well yes. But also because of what you do, day in and day out. The care you take of other people.'

'It's my job.'

'No, it's the bravery of ordinary people that touches me. In the face of everything that's wrong, remaining human. That's what really matters. None of us know what we are going to be faced with and yet we carry on.'

She sighed. 'I think of the stories I've heard. People

have actually seen children herded like animals into cattle wagons. Innocent children. It makes me weep.'

'What are *you* most frightened of, Hélène? For yourself I mean.'

They were startled by the sound of an owl's screech and there was a pause as she thought.

'I'm frightened of being taken in the night and never seeing my sisters again.'

'You have to actively fight the fear. We all do. Fear is good only so long as it galvanises us into action, not if it paralyses us.'

She considered what he'd said, and feeling encouraged by his quiet compassion, she asked, 'What do you fear, Jack?'

'I fear the Nazis are even more evil than we realise. It will all come out eventually . . . but now do you think you could try to sleep?'

'I'm not sure I can.'

'When I can't sleep, I recite poems I learnt at school until I doze off.'

She laughed. 'I sing to myself.'

'Maybe we could sing something together, quietly of course.'

Hélène, like her father, had a fine singing voice, although she had never shown it off or sung in front of people she didn't know well. But she took a breath and began to sing. After all, she was beginning to feel she did know Jack well.

CHAPTER 46

The next morning, Hélène eased herself off the mattress, desperate to go to the lavatory but equally desperate not to disturb Jack. She glanced at his face bathed in sunshine streaming down from the skylight, then she spied a metal bucket but felt too embarrassed to use it. She investigated the main barn doors but, of course, they were locked from the outside. Feeling trapped, she scratched her head, thinking it might have to be the bucket after all, but then she remembered the little door at the back. She hurried across to it, slid the bolt and went out into a small clearing surrounded by trees. She slipped into the shade of the trees and squatted down, sighing in relief at being able to empty her bladder.

When she had finished, she rose to her feet, stretched her arms above her head and took a leisurely breath of cool morning air. She glanced about, surveying the peaceful scene. In the distance she heard the noise of a village waking, dogs barking, children calling out, a motorbike revving. It felt comforting to hear signs of normal life and she allowed herself to relish it for a moment or two. But then what? Wake Jack, or find her way to the house and, hopefully, breakfast? She decided on the latter. The intimacy of the night spent so close to Jack made her feel warm inside, but she wasn't sure how to respond to him when he woke. The words she might say circled in her mind. Maybe she should say how grateful she was or perhaps just ask if he'd slept well? Or should she try and look indifferent?

On her way around the barn she met Marie, who smiled and wished her good morning, then added, 'I was on my way to unlock you.'

'I came out the back way. Jack's still asleep.'

'Go on into the house and I'll rouse Jack.'

Hélène walked through a yard where a dozen scraggy hens scratched at the dry ground and a solitary goat was tied to a post near a patch of yellowing grass. She turned the handle of the door Marie had pointed out and found herself in a large farmhouse kitchen with a typical red-tiled floor, where the priest's bustling housekeeper was brewing coffee and pulling a tray of baking from the oven. The room smelt of cooking, smoke, tobacco and wine.

'Smells delicious,' Hélène said.

Kitchen implements and copper pans hung from low black ceiling beams and on the other side from the oven a rough stone fireplace lay empty. The woman inclined her head but did not speak. She placed a cup of coffee in front of Hélène and a couple of the buns she'd made.

'Thank you,' Hélène said. 'Is it just me for breakfast?'

'You, your husband and your friend.'

And as she was speaking, Marie returned with Jack in tow, rubbing the sleep from his eyes, his hair tousled, and a broad grin on his face.

'Morning,' Jack said, and patted her on the shoulder as he passed.

She glanced sideways at him, acutely aware the eyes of Marie and the housekeeper were upon her.

The talk at breakfast was low-key and when Marie said she'd like to take a walk to stretch her legs, Hélène jumped up to join her.

Outside, they made their way to the woodland clearing behind the barn and then into the trees where the dappled light was dancing patterns on the ground. They didn't speak at first, their boots crunching on springy ground, fallen twigs and dead bracken. The woods smelt earthy and rich with new growth, the oak trees a beautiful bright green and the sky beyond a seamless blue. As they made their way deeper into the woods, they heard the gurgle of running water from a stream and the long grass rustling in the breeze. They stood for a while simply enjoying the day and trying not to think about what lay ahead, until Marie said, 'Better turn back.'

'I wish I could stay here.'

Marie patted her hand. 'Come on.'

The breeze came in gusts now and the birds began shifting in the branches overhead. Giant ferns and small white flowers growing in clusters nearby marked their way back.

'You never told anyone?' Hélène asked as they moved off.

'Well Hugo, of course. He wanted us to flee to England or America right from the start. It was I who insisted we sit it out.'

'What happened to the rest of your family?'

'As you know, I don't come from the Périgord. Like your friend Violette, I was born in Paris but moved here when Hugo and I married all those years ago.'

'And your family remained in Paris?'

'Yes, my parents and my younger brother, Jacques. Like me, my mother has never been a practising Jew. My father is Catholic and a dentist.'

'And where are they now?'

Marie shook her head grimly. 'They were deported early on.'

'I'm so sorry.'

'I only found out because an old school friend of mine wrote to tell me. It was risky because if the letter had been intercepted, the Boche would know about me too.'

'How *did* they find out about you?'

Marie shook her head. 'I don't know. The thing is, my parents are elderly and my mother already frail. She has respiratory problems and I feel sure the journey in one of those awful cattle trucks will have finished her off.'

'And your father and brother?'

'Both strong. My brother never married so didn't have a family to worry about. He looked after my parents. Should have been me.'

Hélène reached across and took her hand.

'But we listen to the news from England, illicitly of course. I cannot make sense of it.'

'So you think—'

'Yes. I'm afraid they may be dead. It breaks my heart to know people I love have been treated as if they were nothing. They call the Jews vermin, you know?'

Hélène shook her head. 'We have to believe in a better future when this is over.'

Marie heaved a sigh. 'I didn't want to leave Hugo and I feel terribly lonely without him.'

'We just have to get you to safety and I'm sure Hugo will be waiting for you when it's all over.'

Hélène had been looking at the ground and thinking about Hugo as they walked back to the clearing and hadn't noticed Jack approaching.

'We need to get going,' he called out to them and she looked up. He flashed her a smile as they stood facing each other. It felt like a light turning on in her heart. 'There's a washroom with a lavatory two doors down from the kitchen if you need it, but be quick. The priest has given me the location of our next safe house.'

He was businesslike, focused on the task now, and both Marie and Hélène headed for the washroom.

A little later and they were on their way again and for much of the day neither Jack nor Hélène spoke, the hours bleeding into each other. Lulled by the rhythmic bumping of the van as they travelled along winding back roads through the countryside, Hélène thought about what Marie had said about her parents. And it put her in mind of her own mother.

One day when Hélène had been about eleven, Claudette had been arranging some flowers she'd picked from the Richmond garden. Hélène asked if she could have one, a pink rose, to put in her hair and her mother had turned and given her a strange smile. 'What would be the point? Your hair is too thin. The flower would just fall out.'

'I could pin it,' she'd replied.

Claudette had laughed. 'No point trying to make a silk purse out of a sow's ear. Now run along dear, and stop bothering me.'

An hour later, Florence ran into the garden to join Hélène at the swing, a beautiful pink rose pinned in her hair. In a rage, Hélène had swung as high as she could and then jumped off. The swing carried on its momentum and hit little Florence on the head. Shocked by what she had done, Hélène froze.

Florence screamed and Claudette came running, instantly taking in what had happened and turning on Hélène.

'You vicious little bitch,' she hissed. 'Go to your room and stay there. Your father will hear of this.'

Hélène had stumbled off weeping. She hadn't intended to hurt her sister, had she? It had been an instinctive response to her mother's little cruelty. When her father came to see her, she blurted out the whole story. He'd stroked her hair and told her she must not mind her mother, but it wasn't fair to take it out on Florence.

'What are you thinking?' Jack said, breaking into her memories. You seem distracted.'

'I was reminiscing.'

'Anything in particular?'

'My childhood. I had a tricky time of it with my mother.'

He laughed. 'Didn't we all?'

'Why is that though?'

He shrugged. 'Search me. My mother was loving but a little too protective.'

'I don't think I'd mind.'

'You would if you'd known my old mum.'

She laughed and turned to look at him, but his face had grown grim. 'Look ahead,' he said. 'I don't think I can turn off in time.'

Hélène looked and felt a band tighten around her head.

CHAPTER 47

Aware her heart was speeding up, Hélène inhaled sharply. The German roadblock was maybe two hundred metres ahead, but before that she could see a tractor and then another two vehicles a little way in front of their own blue van. She glanced about, desperate to spy out a side road. Other than his jaw stiffening, nothing in Jack's face revealed any fear as he gently applied the brakes, his eyes focusing steadily on the road ahead. The tractor near the front was moving slowly, which could work to their advantage, as the Germans at the control point were intent on yelling at it to move along. In front of the tractor, Hélène saw a hay wagon and an automobile, possibly German, had now pulled up, but the guards were dragging people from the car, so maybe not German after all.

'Let's pray they don't stop us,' Jack said.

Hélène's heart was hammering now as she swivelled

left and then right growing more and more determined to find a way out as they gradually edged forward. Then she saw it. 'There. Look! Quickly. A farm track to your right. It was hidden by the trees.'

'Right,' he said and immediately swerved into it. 'It's a narrow one. Better pray it's not a dead end.'

'Must go to a farm. Did they see us?'

They heard a vehicle, and she felt her entire body tense, her nerves completely frazzled now. Was it following them down the track? She listened carefully and so did Jack.

'Might be okay,' she said, feeling a burst of elation as it seemed to go past.

'And we're not so far from Bordeaux, but we won't be able to get to the safe house now.'

He drove on, the track growing narrower and narrower. She began to breathe more easily when it became clear the vehicle had not followed them, but it had been a close shave, and sooner or later, they really would have to survive a checkpoint. Eventually they arrived at a crossing of sorts and after a slight hesitation he shrugged and took the turning to the left. It was growing darker now and he didn't dare use the headlights.

'You need to pull up,' she said. 'We can check out the map tomorrow, but these tiny tracks are not marked. It's impossible to know where we're heading in the dark.'

He pulled a face but did come to a stop.

'We'll have to sleep in the van.'

'You can bunk in with Marie in the back, if you like, and I'll get some kip here.'

'Can we just find a place to park the van less conspicuously first? I'll get out and have a look.'

She jumped down and went off to see. After several minutes she returned, told him what she'd found and then he drove on and stopped beside a gateway into a field. She opened the gate, and then he drove the car into the field, parking it behind a line of tall trees.

'This will have to do,' she said.

'Can you let Marie out? Call of nature. See you in a mo.'

When Hélène opened up the back, she saw Marie was looking pale. She reached out a hand to help her climb out of the van.

'Are you all right?'

'I'm stiff and sore and I spilt my water when Jack swerved. I didn't know what was happened. Are they after us?'

'No. We avoided a roadblock by coming this way.'

'Do we know where we are?'

Hélène shook her head. 'We'll try to work out the route in the morning. I'll get you some more water but we're going to have to sleep in the van.'

'I'm starving. Is there any food left?'

'Afraid not.'

Jack came striding up. 'Sorry about the picturesque detour. Have you got space to stretch out in the back, Marie?'

'Yes. First I need the lavatory.'

He waved at the bushes. 'Be my guest.'

While Marie was gone, Hélène told Jack she'd rather

try to get some sleep in the front of the van. 'I'd feel claustrophobic in the back. At least there are windows at the front.'

'You won't see anything. It'll be pitch black soon.'

'I'll know they're there.'

He scratched the back of his head. 'Fine by me. Do you want to grab a couple of blankets from the back?'

Hélène found the spare blankets a moment before Marie returned. 'Will you be all right? You're very pale.'

'I'll be fine. See you in the morning. But can you leave the back of the van unlocked, please. Just in case.'

'Sure. Will do. Goodnight,' and she kissed Marie on both cheeks.

But it wasn't possible to find a comfortable way to sleep sitting in the front of the van and Hélène, never a good sleeper at the best of times, fidgeted and shifted around so much that in the end Jack said, 'Look, I can sleep anywhere. Upright even, so why not try to lie with your head in my lap, if there's room? Come on.'

He pulled his blanket up to his chin and she managed to lie in a tricky sideways position but at least her neck muscles had a chance of loosening up as she lay against him. She'd had a headache since she first spotted the German checkpoint and the relief at being able to lie down was immense, even if various parts of the van were sticking into her. Once again, she felt comforted by his proximity and the warmth of his body and from where she lay, she could see stars peppering the night sky. She began to properly relax, her heart now beating out a steady rhythm. And gradually she felt less afraid.

Everything would be all right. With her head in his lap, she was not in a position to have a cosy chat and Jack obviously just wanted to sleep, so she remained silent and eventually drifted off too.

A tapping sound woke her. It took her a moment to realise where she was but when she did, she struggled upright and saw Jack was already awake and staring out of his side window where a dark-haired child was gazing in.

Jack wound down the window to say hello. The child smiled and opened the van door. Hélène thought he looked about seven and wanted to ask his name, but the dog who'd been by his side now began to bark hysterically. Jack and Hélène climbed down from the van and opened the back door wide to find Marie was not there.

'Oh,' Hélène said. 'Where is she?'

'Well, I hope not far.'

Hélène glanced around. It was a ravishing day; sunny, bright and fresh, the field where they'd parked a riot of wildflowers with a few desultory goats now investigating the van. Jack was patting the dog who had quietened down and then they heard a woman calling. 'Paul. Paul. *Petit déjeuner.*'

'Your maman?' Hélène asked as the woman came running.

'Oui,' the boy said.

The woman, whose frizzy yellow hair was flying out around her, stopped a couple of metres away. 'What's all this?' she said with narrowed eyes. 'You don't have permission to park in our field.'

Hélène stepped up. She couldn't tell if the woman was hostile or if she was merely wary. 'My apologies, madame. We lost our way. I am travelling to take care of a sick relative in Bordeaux. This is my husband.'

The woman looked pointedly at Marie, who had just walked out of the bushes.

'My mother,' Hélène said.

'It takes all three of you?'

'Come,' Jack said, and showed her the motorbike in the back of the van.

'My husband is delivering it to a customer in Bordeaux,' Hélène said, knowing she hadn't kept to their original story.

The woman appeared to melt a little. 'Well I am Francoise. I expect you must be hungry, so come along now. I'll see what I can rustle up.'

While they were eating the eggs and bread the woman had shoved in front of them, she left the room, taking Paul with her. Jack withdrew the map from his pocket and tried to work out which track they had taken. He shook his head. 'It's not marked. I'll ask Francoise when she comes back.'

But after a few more minutes it was not Francoise who came back but a man wearing a cloth cap, farmer's overalls, an angry face and pointing a rifle at them.

Jack stood up quickly and raised his hands. 'Whoa,' he said. 'Put down the rifle and we'll be on our way.'

The man's answer was to fire a shot at the wall.

'You will be on your way, all right, with the Milice, who I will be sending my son to alert in a few moments.'

Hélène rose to her feet now. 'Good morning, I am—'

'I don't give a monkey's who or what you are.'

Francoise entered the room also holding a gun, a pistol this time, although she kept glancing at it as if there was something wrong, or she didn't quite trust it, or didn't know how to use it, which for a farmer's wife would have been strange.

'You are escaped prisoners on the loose,' she said, her voice shaking. 'We heard about it on the radio. The militia and the Germans are looking everywhere for you. Do not think you fooled me. He . . .' and she pointed at Jack, 'is not French.'

'Please let us go,' Hélène pleaded. 'Surely you can see my mother is not well. We really are not escaped prisoners.'

The man took over. 'Put your van keys on the table.'

Jack did as he was asked.

'And your motorbike keys.'

Jack hesitated and the room went so quiet Hélène could feel the tension in the air, but when the man gestured with his gun, Jack dug in his pocket.

Hélène knew Jack was armed, but there were two of these people and only one of him. She had no way of knowing if he might be about to use the gun, or how it would turn out if he did. She longed to whisper to him, but all she could do was trust him. The moment stretched on for ages, but then he took out another key.

'Right,' the man said. 'On the table. Now you can go on your way.'

'Our bags?' Hélène said.

'At the side of the road.'

Jack and Hélène exchanged glances, but it was clear there would be no compromise here. It was either walk away with nothing or be arrested.

'So how do we get to Bordeaux?' Hélène asked.

'You walk. Follow the track for a few miles and then you will meet up with the road into town. You can get a train from there.'

'Look,' Jack said. 'Keep the van, but let us have the motorbike. My mother-in-law cannot walk so far.'

The farmer's wife scratched her head as if considering this, but the man just glared at Jack.

Right then the little boy ran into the room and flung his arms around his father's knees.

'I told you to wait in the hall until I called you,' he growled and bent down to pull him away.

With split-second timing, Jack withdrew his gun and shot the farmer in the foot. In return the man, cursing, raised his rifle, but keeled over before he could use it. His wife ran to him and Jack grabbed the van and motorbike keys and told Hélène and Marie to run and get into the van. The woman held up her gun, but Jack had already worked out it was a bluff. He reached out and knocked it from her hand and then grabbed the man's rifle and followed Hélène and Jack.

They leapt into the van and Jack drove like a maniac until they reached the road.

'They will alert the militia,' Hélène said. 'So we'll have to abandon the van.'

'You're right. The motorbike, I hope I can get away

with. But we'll need to split up. Thank goodness you didn't tell him you were a nurse.'

'I was about to.'

'I know.'

She thought quickly. 'I'll put my uniform on now, and you can drop us somewhere near the station. Marie can wear her other hat and her coat.'

'I've got a pair of tortoiseshell glasses she can use too.' He pulled them from his pocket. 'She's got her knitting with her, hasn't she?'

'What about you?' she asked.

'I shall ride hell for leather for Bordeaux. If you're stopped, make sure you have your ID, train tickets and ration cards at the ready.'

'Will do.'

'I'll meet you at this address.' He scribbled on a piece of paper. 'Memorise it and then destroy it. We were not planning to go there this time, so they will be suspicious, but I know them, or I used to last year. Tell them Jack sent you and say, "The Germans look like they are winning the war." They should reply, "Well you are an optimistic one."'

'And if they don't say that?'

'Make a dash for it.'

CHAPTER 48

Hélène squeezed the skin between her brows as she watched Jack ride off. She absolutely would not cry, but would he reach Bordeaux safely? Would they? Even at midday, the streets of the small town they'd arrived at stood half-empty, with only a few women selling vegetables from their baskets, and even the children looking tired and dispirited. Hélène had memorised the address in Bordeaux and now she and Marie, moving purposefully, went to purchase their tickets from the unsmiling railway clerk at the counter. He looked them up and down, suspicion narrowing his eyes, and feeling sure everyone could see through their subterfuge, Hélène's throat ached with tension. But, eventually, he handed them two tickets and told them which platform to take.

They had a twenty-minute wait, during which Marie wore the tortoiseshell glasses and focused on her knitting, while Hélène kept her eyes peeled for anyone who looked

German. The platform was busier than she'd expected. Women carrying baskets of produce stood talking, among them here and there a widow dressed in black, as well as three small children playing tag and a dozen old men. A harried young woman appeared, glancing left and right as if she were looking for someone, or maybe she had just missed her train. Hélène wondered where they were all going, after all they couldn't all be running away, or pretending to be something they weren't. As the whistle blew, she stood up, smoothing down her creased nurse's uniform, and Marie put her knitting away.

Once on the train they found an empty carriage and made themselves comfortable. Hélène felt dog-tired and was sure Marie must be too. She closed her eyes until she heard the whistle again and felt the carriage judder and the shriek of metal on metal as it began to move. Her hair had loosened from its tight bun so she pinned it back as best she could and wiped the beads of sweat from her forehead, then feeling thirsty, she gazed out of the carriage window. Why hadn't she thought to buy something to drink?

But soon she gave in to the rhythmic rocking and rumbling of the train and allowed her thoughts to drift. First to her sisters, still worrying that by coming she had left them in the lurch, but then she glanced at Marie's furrowed brow and it strengthened her determination to succeed. She had to do this. Previously, she had been merely stoic in response to the German occupation, but now it was very different.

Her jaw clenched when German soldiers mounted the

train at the first stop, but she was determined not to show her fear. She worried the pulsing in her neck might be visible, but the two soldiers checked their papers and barely gave them a second glance. So, their first checkpoint had passed without incident and Hélène felt almost triumphant.

They were not checked again until they reached their destination and, even then, nobody questioned why they were there. It looked as if a middle-aged woman accompanying a nurse did not give rise to suspicion.

The trouble began when they finally reached the address Jack had given her. She and Marie stared at the bombed-out building in horror. The houses either side were riddled with bullet holes and had no glass left in their windows, but Hélène saw people still looking out from them. The house she had come to find was in a far worse state. The roof and most of the beams had caved in and were balanced at odd angles close to the ground. Heaps of bricks, sections of plaster and lumps of concrete had exploded all over the place, even onto the pavement where people simply walked around them. Bordeaux had been bombed by Germany at the start of the war and later by the Allies, their aim being to destroy the submarine base. Hélène knew it had been the target of heavy British and American raids, especially early in 1943, but to her eyes this looked more recent. And anyway, Jack had been in France earlier this year and the house must have been standing then. Almost bent double, she picked her way across the rubble, squeezed under what remained of the roof, crossing her fingers the building had settled, and nothing would suddenly give way and fall on her head. When she reached the other side, she came across what must have been a garden. A door lying on the ground suddenly shifted and a dusty young woman with dark brown hair appeared as if rising from out of the ground.

'Oh,' she said, looking guarded and narrowing her eyes at the sight of Hélène.

Under the woman's scrutiny, Hélène shrank back, then she tried the password, but the woman continued to stare.

'I was supposed to come here,' Hélène said.

'They've all gone. You know, the ones who were here. They were taken. There's only me and my boy.'

'My mother and I need somewhere to stay.'

The woman narrowed her eyes again. 'You are a nurse?'

'I am.' 'You help my boy and I'll show you where you can sleep.'

Hélène agreed and made her way back to let Marie know she should come through too.

When the woman lifted the door Hélène saw beneath it a narrow stone staircase that was still more or less intact. She and Marie followed the woman who held a torch in front of her. At the bottom they dipped their heads and picked their way through a warren of small cellar rooms with low ceilings. In some the beams had caved in but others were intact and eventually they arrived at a room with blackened walls and a small glassless window just beneath a broken beam. When Hélène stood on the tips of her toes, she could see a strip of sky, so at least the room had a source of air. And yet, despite that, it smelt of mould, damp and decay and, whatever the floor had once been, it was now covered in earth.

'You can have this,' the woman said. 'I'm Mathilde, by the way. But now I take you to my boy.'

Hélène glanced at Marie and at the one musty mattress in the corner, gritty with grime. 'Can you bear it here?'

'We can take it in turns to look out for Jack. If we go somewhere else, I don't think I'll ever get to the mountains.'

A single bare bulb dangled from the yellowing ceiling, but when Hélène tried the switch nothing happened. How could it when the house above had been blown to bits?

She glanced around. 'Do you think it's safe though?'

Marie's chin trembled but her voice was firm. 'I think everything that could fall has already done so.'

'I hope you're right. There's still a ton of bricks and debris above us. But look, I have enough to pay for a small pension for a couple of nights.'

'No. Let's just try to stick it out here until Jack turns up.'

CHAPTER 49

For two days, Hélène and Marie waited in Bordeaux for Jack, growing more and more uncertain about what to do if he didn't turn up. As well as worrying about what that would mean for Marie, Hélène was also feeling terrified for Jack himself. Was he safe? Had the Nazis caught him, interrogated him? Had they hurt him? Although he didn't seem to feel quite the same way about her as she did about him, a strong connection *had* developed between them. She twisted her hair at the back, then let it fall loose.

If Jack didn't turn up soon, she'd have to contact whoever the people were who could accompany Marie to the mountains herself, although she had no idea how to find them. When she did, they would then be able to pass Marie to the network of local guides and helpers who'd help her cross into Spain and onward to England. Hélène knew the main escape routes had been used extensively to get Allied airmen out of the country, especially soon after the fall of France to the Germans. Now, with more secure internment camps and Spanish guides who demanded higher prices, it was harder and people were being forced to take increasingly unknown routes higher up in the mountains. As far as Hélène knew, Marie would have to reach Pau by train, but after . . . she wasn't sure. Maybe she could walk to Oloron-Sainte-Marie? But when she had risked sharing her concerns with Mathilde, the woman whose boy had been sick, she was told they'd come the wrong way.

'You should have made for Perpignan from Toulouse,' the woman muttered.

'We thought of it but there are too many German troops based near Toulouse,' Hélène replied.

The woman shrugged.

On the third day of waiting, Hélène had been out to get hold of some food using her ration card but, on her way back – just before she turned the corner into the street – she was shaken by the sound of an explosion. She ran around the corner towards the house and found Mathilde and her little boy standing on the other side of the street in the swirling dust, staring at the debris. Three German soldiers were laughing as they turned their backs on the devastation and climbed into a truck.

'What happened?' Hélène asked.

Mathilde pulled a face as the truck moved off. 'Bastards threw a hand grenade into the cellar.'

Hélène looked around in a panic. 'Marie. Where's Marie? Was she with you?'

Then she heard footsteps coming up behind her.

'I'm here,' Marie called out. 'Right behind you, and look . . . I've found Jack.'

Hélène stared at him, relief flooding her body.

He smiled back at her. 'Sorry I took so long.'

'What kept you?' she asked, aiming for a light tone of voice, not wanting to betray how frightened she had been.

'Had to take a circuitous route. Nazi patrols and checkpoints where I least expected them.'

'Well . . . thank goodness you made it. I was getting worried.'

He laughed. 'You? Surely not!'

And she couldn't help smiling.

Jack took them to a safe house, and that night Marie went to bed early while he and Hélène stayed up talking by the light of a single candle. She gazed at him in relief, inexpressibly glad he'd escaped capture. In the flickering light, his green eyes darkened and she imagined she could see right into his soul.

'Are you all right?' she asked.

'I'm not sure. I keep thinking.' He heaved a sigh and paused for a moment before carrying on. 'Love is what makes us who we are, don't you think?'

'I've never heard you talk about love.'

'Your love for your sisters, for Marie, for Hugo. That makes you who you are.'

'I suppose.' She cleared her throat before asking. 'So, what makes *you* who you are?'

'Love of my country,' he said, but then frowned, giving

her the impression he was not certain. 'It's my duty to defend my homeland, but in the end, it's love you see, not duty.'

'And not hate?'

'Well, hate can motivate. But indifference is the most destructive, I think. It lets us off the hook. I've always tried to be the best version of myself I can be. When I was bullied as a child, after my mother died, my grandmother taught me to face my fears and my tormentors.'

'And you did.'

'I never looked back.'

She reached for his hand. 'Jack, don't you long to have a family of your own one day?'

'I . . . well.' He stroked her hand and gazed at the table, not looking at her. She held her breath, feeling certain he was about to say more.

'What?'

'There are things . . .' His shoulders hunched, and he shook his head as if changing his mind. 'I can't think of anything while we are at war.'

'And yet people still fall in love, marry, have children. Even during the war, they do.'

'I can't,' he said, and now he looked up and gazed at her, his eyes softening. 'Until, well . . . there's so much you don't know. I'm just not ready. Can you understand?'

'Of course.' But she didn't know if he meant he might one day be ready for *her*, or ready in a more general way. She didn't want to humiliate herself by asking such a direct question, especially if the answer was unlikely to be what she hoped for. But she loved how he'd spoken slowly, as if reaching for the truth, not wanting to get it wrong or be misunderstood. There was a prolonged silence during which Hélène listened to the sounds of the clock ticking the night away. Morning would soon come and then he'd be gone. She berated herself for her lack of courage.

'So how long until you get back to us?' she eventually asked.

'It depends.'

Her heart skipped a beat. 'You might not come back?'

The tiny muscles around his eyes flickered. 'I'll receive new orders. But I *will* need to come back here, to Bordeaux at least, to pick up the motorbike, if I can.'

'I could wait for you, and we could ride back together.'

He shook his head. 'Too risky.'

'But it's risky for you.'

'It's my job. What I'm here to do. And you're needed back home. Hugo will be longing for news of Marie and your sisters will want to know you're safe. They'd never forgive me if I endangered you any further.'

Yes, she thought. He was probably right. 'Well. Let us know if you do come back.'

He grasped her hand. 'You have been an absolute brick through all of this. I can't tell you how much I admire you.'

Hélène was pleased but also a little disappointed. It wasn't his admiration she wanted.

He rose to his feet and picked up the candlestick. 'Time for bed, I think. We're all in one room together. Will that do?'

They went up to a room in the attic where Marie was already fast asleep on a single mattress in the corner. The wind rattled the window frame and a draught whistled around the room; the candle flickered casting shadows across the walls and ceiling.

Jack glanced around. 'Looks like you and I are bunking up together again.'

Hélène lay down first and then Jack settled himself beside her. He didn't extinguish the candle straight away and for a few moments they faced each other. Then he cradled her face in his hands and she tasted the salt and the wine as he kissed her on the lips.

'You, Hélène Baudin, are not only beautiful, but you're one hell of a woman too.'

CHAPTER 50

Hélène caught the milk train from Bordeaux to Sarlat, stopping at every single station. Not all of the tracks were still good, so the train was forced to stop for hasty repairs and took longer than usual. She felt pleased with herself, proud she'd found the courage to help Marie get to safety, and now that Jack was taking her to the people who would help her cross the mountains, Hélène felt some relief. Despite the creeping fear she had felt, she'd done her best for her friend. Part of the journey ran close to the Dordogne river so it was picturesque and she enjoyed gazing out while losing herself in Jack's words and reliving the thrill of his kiss. Thus, the journey passed quickly enough. There was a moment of anxiety when the French police boarded the train, but when they saw her nurse's uniform, they accepted her reason for travel and left her alone.

Once she arrived at the station, she then had a thirty-minute walk into the centre of Sarlat, from where she caught the only bus home. She sat on the rattling vehicle with a conflicting mixture of emotions: glad to be coming home, sad Jack wasn't with her, and praying Marie would cope with the mountain crossing. At least it wasn't winter.

She arrived home to find Florence sitting at the table in the kitchen, knitting.

'You're back!' Florence shrieked, throwing down her knitting and bouncing on her toes. 'I'm so happy you're home.'

Hélène dropped her bag and held out her arms. 'Come here.'

Florence flew into her embrace and then, obviously having heard the noise, Élise came into the room. 'Well done,' she said, grinning from ear to ear. 'I knew you'd make it. I'll put some coffee on.'

'Actually, I could do with a real drink.'

Élise laughed, her eyes shining. 'That's my girl. Do we have anything left, Florence?'

Florence disentangled herself and went out to her stores while Hélène and Élise hugged.

'You look fantastic,' Élise said. 'Wilder. Danger clearly suits you.'

'Not sure I'd go quite that far.'

A few moments later, Florence brought back an unopened bottle of cognac.

Hélène raised her eyebrows. 'Where on earth did you get it?'

'I've been saving it.'

'Well, I'm overjoyed to come home to such a welcome.

How've you both been and what on earth are you knitting, Florence? It looks tiny.'

Hélène felt confused when she saw Florence glance questioningly at Élise and then Élise giving her a slight nod in reply.

Florence drew a long breath as if to speak then shook her head. 'No, you tell her, Élise. It's your news.'

There was a pause and a blanket of silence fell before Élise eventually spoke.

'Well,' she said, glancing down and looking unusually shy. Then more boldly, more herself, she raised her head and held Hélène's gaze. 'The thing is . . . I'm expecting a baby.'

'And I'm going to be an auntie,' Florence added. 'You too.'

Hélène, who had been standing at the table, pulled out a chair and immediately dropped onto it, unsure how to respond. She felt odd, a little dislocated, possibly a little envious too. Was this good news? She wasn't certain. Moments passed as she gazed at Élise. 'I'm not sure what to say.'

Florence held up her knitting. 'Bootees, you see. I've only got blue wool, so it has to be a boy.'

Élise had turned her back at Hélène's response and was now staring out of the window into the darkness.

'Is the baby Victor's?' Hélène asked cautiously.

Élise spun round, eyes blazing. 'How could you think it isn't? Of course it's his.'

'Sorry I—'

'Can't you just be pleased for me?'

'Oh, darling, I am pleased for you, but—'

'But what?' Élise interrupted. 'There isn't a *but*.'

'Well, I suppose I'm a little bit worried. A baby without a father isn't an easy choice. Look at Violette.'

'She seems to cope alright. Anyway, I don't know why you're calling it a choice. It's hardly a choice.'

'Sorry I—'

Élise interrupted again. 'I didn't plan this, and I certainly didn't want Victor to die, but now it's happened there's no going back. I'm happy about it, Hélène. Don't you see? I'll always have a part of Victor with me.'

'I do see that. Really, I do. I didn't mean to sound unkind. It was just a bit of a shock, okay?'

'Okay.'

'So, are you still running the letter box?'

Élise gave her an elated smile. 'I'm doing a little more now.'

Hélène frowned. 'What about the baby?'

Élise gave her a look and spread her hands in exasperation. 'The baby won't be here for months, Hélène. I'm not a bloody invalid.'

'Of course.' Hélène realised she was getting this all wrong. She smiled and altered her tone to sound more supportive. 'So how long have you known?'

'I suspected before Victor was killed but Hugo confirmed it this week.'

'Well, I'm glad. Really I am. It's wonderful news.'

Élise nodded.

'How is Hugo?'

'Like a lost soul without Marie. Anyway, even more importantly, how did you get on? Is Marie all right?'

'And Jack?' Florence added.

Hélène told them the whole story to gasps of astonishment from Florence and hand-clapping approval from Élise.

'So, what about here? What else has been happening while I've been away?' she asked.

'Nothing much,' Florence said. 'Madame Deschamps has been wandering again.'

'More than usual?'

'I found her halfway down our lane.'

'Poor old soul. Anything else?'

Florence shook her head. 'I don't think so.'

'That's not true,' Élise said, turning to her younger sister with a smile. 'Florence has a new friend, haven't you? That note pushed through the door yesterday *was* from him, wasn't it?'

CHAPTER 51

With a cushion tucked under her arm, Hélène, wrapped in a blanket and bearing her latest novel, crept down to the sitting room. Unable to sleep after the news of Élise's pregnancy, she lay on a rug with Florence's cast iron fairy beside her, but instead of reading, she stroked its surface. She'd always tried to be practical, not wanting to indulge in what she considered to be useless nostalgia, but she was thinking about the past again. It kept intruding even when she didn't want it to. With an unfocused gaze, she sifted back through the years, seeing them all at various times in their Richmond home until the images clicked into place on one specific day. The day their mother vanished and the girls had come home from school to an empty house. Looking back, Hélène could see their characters already well-defined. She put Florence's fairy down and closed her eyes, extracting the memory from where it had lodged for so long. The day sprung into bright, vivid life.

Élise had gone in first by the back door, followed by Florence and finally Hélène. Claudette didn't work and was always at home when they came back from school, but when Florence called for her, the house remained strangely silent. Claudette wasn't there and neither was their father. More importantly, their mother's daily, Mrs Frobisher, had already gone home so they really would have to fend for themselves. Florence turned the radio on and danced around the kitchen, delighted at the unexpected freedom, while Élise banged about savagely, and Hélène looked in the pantry to see if she could work out what there might be for tea.

'We can have cake,' Florence said enthusiastically. 'There's no one to stop us. Maman made a ginger cake yesterday.'

Élise turned on her. 'Have you already had some?'

Florence bit her lip. 'She said not to say.'

Élise threw down her satchel. 'Honestly, she lets you get away with murder. It isn't fair.'

'You could try to be nicer to her.'

'Nicer? I am nice.'

'Élise, you are not. You are mean to her and you are mean to me too.'

Hands on hips, Élise frowned. 'When am I mean to you?'

Florence pulled an astonished face. 'Er . . . only *all* the time. Hélène's mean too.'

Hélène closed the pantry door with a bang. 'There's nothing to eat.'

'I told you, there's cake,' Florence said, now beginning to look tearful.

'Where?'

'In the cake tin, stupid!'

'Well that's hardly *nice*,' Élise said.

'What?'

'Calling Hélène stupid. I thought you were the *nice* one.'

'Oh, shut up, Élise. You know, I really hate you sometimes.' And with that parting shot she fled the room and stomped up the stairs.

Now, with slow languid movements, Hélène got up from the floor, caught unawares by this unexpected snippet from the past. All of them had felt at sea, their mother's brief disappearance even worse than her acid tongue, but when had that sharpness started? Those barbs. The sideways digs. Whenever it was, and whatever her mother's dreams had once been, Hélène knew they'd never been fulfilled.

She was losing track of time, and while in some ways she longed to revisit the past for a little longer, it felt like an indulgence. How strange the three of them should still be living together. In some ways not much had changed; in other ways the changes were huge. There was the war and there was this now as well; a baby and her own unresolved love for Jack. Feeling her joints aching, she went over to the window to pull open the curtain. Still dark. She longed for the first signs of dawn because sometimes she couldn't bear the long darkness of night. And she longed for Jack too. From outside she heard the hoot of an owl. What was going to become of them? Where would they be in a year's time? Two? More? The war continued unrelentingly and tonight she'd had enough of feeling their lives were slipping through their fingers. Despite her deep-seated exhaustion, she began to rub away the ache in her leaden limbs.

CHAPTER 52

Florence

When she'd received the note from Anton apologising for not having been in touch but suggesting a meeting now, Florence had felt ambivalent about seeing him again. Yet, nevertheless, she felt she needed to. It would be the first time since her ordeal at the hand of those dreadful BNA men, but she reminded herself that Anton wasn't like them. Not like them at all. She owed it to him to see him one last time. So she stood at the beginning of their track as he had suggested in his note and waited apprehensively. When he arrived, dressed in cream trousers and a blue short-sleeved shirt, with his face shining, she smiled hoping she'd made the right decision.

'Would you like to come to a Red Riding Hood house I know?' she asked, ignoring a sudden sinking feeling.

He raised his brows. 'Red Riding Hood?'

'A little empty house, that's all.'

She had told Élise about it and shown her the way to find it and she knew it wasn't being used as a safe house yet, although it might be at some point in the future. She hesitated, nervous now and perhaps a little scared. What if it wasn't such a good idea?

'I would love to,' he said. 'Sounds intriguing.'

It will be all right, she told herself. It will be all right.

Now Anton wheeled his motorcycle along a track that bordered an unkempt field, while Florence picked her way over the stones. She felt tongue-tied and wasn't sure what to say.

'Is something wrong?' he asked. 'Is it because I took so long to contact you again? I had to work in Bordeaux for a while.'

She shook her head. 'No, not at all.'

This wasn't the moment to explain. Maybe there never would be a moment. In a way she was pleased to see him, but she felt ill at ease being alone with a man. Even a man like Anton.

'It's just . . . well, you're very quiet.'

'Sorry,' she said.

It was a beautiful day, warm and sunny, the meadows bursting with wild daffodils and small yellow tulips. A few fluffy white clouds floated in the otherwise seamless blue sky and white butterflies drifted over the long grasses, while a gentle breeze carried hints of wild herbs. In the near distance you could see the elegant towers of a chateau, and the woods lining the estate were alive with pheasants. It should have been a perfect day, Florence thought, as she batted away the teeming flying insects and then tripped over a small boulder.

'Oops,' he said and stretched out a hand to steady her.

'Thanks,' she said. 'I'm fine. I think it might be best if you leave the motorbike here, behind these trees.'

Anton did so and they carried on without it. Eventually they pushed through the tall bushes and trees concealing the little house, and he asked why she'd wanted to come here particularly.

She thought about it and then said, 'I wanted to be somewhere quiet. I've been here before and it's so out of the way.' The truth was she'd thought the little house was a good idea because nobody would see them together.

'Oh?'

'Let's go inside and have a look.'

Florence knew where Hélène had hidden the key so fished it out from beneath a terracotta tub, now full of weeds, but which must have once featured a fine display of summer flowers. She turned the key in the lock and pushed open the door.

'Come on,' she said, as she went across to open the window and the outside shutters, trying to keep her tone light and breezy. 'We can play at keeping house.'

He laughed as he followed her inside the kitchen. 'Is that what you did as a child?'

'Playing house? No, not really.'

'What *did* you do?'

She puffed out her cheeks exaggeratedly. 'I mainly remember following my sisters around in the hope they one day might actually *like* me.'

He looked surprised. 'Your sisters do not like you?'

'They do now. But I was the youngest and . . . well, my mother paid *me* far more attention than them. I didn't have a clue then, of course. I just thought there was something wrong with me.'

'They were jealous?'

'Resentful, I think.'

'Ah, childhood. It can be a tricky time. My father wanted me to become an engineer like him, but I had no aptitude for it. Languages have always been my love, although my father also speaks English and French, like me.'

'You're much cleverer than I am,' Florence said. Although to her he was not only clever, but cultured too. And yet, even though a man who enjoyed romantic castles and gardening could not be bad, she still felt wary. He was German after all, and she had shown him the way to what might become a safe house. Oh God! What had she done? Had she been a reckless fool to have even come with him on her own?

'You are clever in your own way,' he said.

'What?'

He laughed. 'You were miles away. I said you're clever too, just in a different way. It's what my father could never comprehend.'

'That we are all clever in our own way?'

'Exactly.'

'Hélène is clever. She plays the piano and paints, or she used to, as well as being a nurse. And Élise likes history. Puts me to shame, I'm afraid.'

'I don't think that can be true.'

She sighed, but with the ease between them gone, didn't know how to reply. She felt her chest tighten a bit but eventually managed to say, 'I did make this dress myself.'

'There you are then. You sew, you garden and what else?'

'Well I like reading, and I do all the cooking, pickling, jam making and baking.'

'The perfect wife,' he said.

'I know. Sickening isn't it, but it's what the government expect. When I first arrived here, I was only fifteen and I had to go to obligatory classes in housekeeping. It was hilarious. We didn't have to do anything like that in England. And the boys here, when they're twenty, must go to forest work camps to be indoctrinated. They called it *Chantiers de la Jeunesse*.'

'You lived in England?' he said and she quickly realised her mistake.

She spotted he had ignored her comment about indoctrination, because everyone knew about the Hitler Youth movement. Maybe he was ashamed of that.

They had been sitting on a bench in the window, where the sun was now streaming in. He turned towards her as if to speak. For a moment she felt fine but then suddenly, overcome by an urge to run, she jolted, angling her body away from him. Hair hanging in a curling curtain, she shielded her face.

'Won't you tell me what the matter is?' He reached out a hand.

Tremors coursed through her and she shuddered. 'I can't explain.'

'What is it, Florence? What's troubling you? I know there's something.'

She turned her head to look at him and tears filled her eyes. 'I just felt a bit . . .'

'What?'

She bowed head. 'Please don't make me say.'

'I don't want to make you say anything, but can I help?'

She glanced at him. He had clasped his hands together and was looking concerned and confused, but all she could do was shake her head again. 'No.'

'Florence?'

She held up her hand, palm facing towards him in a kind of final rebuttal. 'I can't talk about it . . . I don't think I'll ever be able to.'

He gazed at her helplessly, but she stood abruptly and went to the open door. 'Do you mind if we drop it?'

He rose to his feet too. 'Of course.'

Outside it was warmer than before so they headed for the shadier woodland before picking up the bike, then walked in silence for a few minutes with her, keeping a few steps ahead.

Feeling calmer now, she turned back to smile at him.

'I saw my father this weekend,' he said, after a while.

'He's in France?'

'For a bit. Between autumn 1941 and summer 1943 he was seconded to the German military to oversee the construction of the Bordeaux submarine bunkers originally established by the Italians.'

'And now?'

'Now, because of Allied bombing, a second roof must be fitted over the submarine base. He's here for that. I told him I'd made friends with a French girl.'

'Oh?'

'He was curious and said how much he had enjoyed France when he was here many years ago. I'm seeing him for dinner tonight.'

'So, how have you been able to find the time to come and see me today?'

'Well my work as a translator and French teacher at the German garrison at Bergerac and in Bordeaux is done. They wanted to send me to Paris, but I begged for a fortnight's leave during which time I'm hoping to figure out a better plan. The town hall at Sarlat may need a translator.'

'I love Sarlat. Or . . . I used to before the war.'

He almost winced. 'I'm sorry.'

They headed back, skirting the village and making for the track leading to her home. About halfway there, Florence spotted Lucille coming the other way.

'Lucille,' Florence called and waved at her friend. 'Hello.'

'I just called at your house,' Lucille said, keeping her distance.

'Well now you're here, come and meet Anton.'

Lucille glanced to one side and then the other, looking nervous.

Florence laughed. 'He won't bite, you know.'

Lucille gave them both a brief nod and backed away.

'Another time. I've got to go. Sorry.' And then she scuttled off up the track towards the village.

'What's got into her?' Florence said, feeling troubled.

Anton left her at the gate, and she stood for a minute watching him retreat. She felt stupid and childish and she'd behaved out of all proportion, hadn't she? Or was it normal for someone like her? She stiffened but couldn't pretend she felt fine. So, *was* it normal to feel sick at the thought of being touched by any man? Even as a friend. Would such a feeling ever go away? She felt cold and sad, wanting to go back and do it differently but, of course, she could not.

Florence gazed at their front door and, at that instant, Hélène opened it and she and Élise came down the path, both looking curious.

CHAPTER 53

Hélène

'Was that your friend?' Hélène asked, keeping her voice nonchalant. She waited, rubbing the tight muscles of her neck and eyeing her sister, but Florence glanced away.

Hélène frowned. 'Florence?'

In the moments during which Florence didn't reply, her hands curled almost into fists and then uncurled repeatedly as if she were trying to suppress her response. Something was definitely going on, Hélène thought. 'Well?' she said, feeling hot and impatient in the increasingly humid air.

When Florence eventually spoke, it was with a steely look in her eyes. 'Were you watching me from the window?' she said. 'Spying on me?

'He looked nice,' Hélène continued, not wanting to admit she had been watching. 'Who is he?'

'It's none of your business. He's just a friend, nothing

more. He's called Anton and . . .' She sighed deeply and pressed her lips together.

'And?' Hélène prompted.

Florence almost winced. 'Well I suppose there is something I maybe ought to tell you.'

Hélène felt a stab of concern. 'He's not married?'

Florence shook her head.

'That's a relief. So, tell us. It can't be that bad.' She paused and then gasped. 'My God, you're not pregnant, are you?'

Florence widened her eyes in horror.

'Sorry. I wasn't thinking.'

Florence ran her hands through her hair and didn't meet Hélène's eyes.

'Look, you don't have to tell us anything if you don't want to. I'm going inside. It's too hot out here and I've got things to get on with.' She began to move away.

'No,' Florence said, reaching out but not actually touching Hélène. 'Wait.'

Hélène wanted a good look at her sister. Was she going to lie? The lies that worried her the most were the ones that appeared to be so close to the truth they seemed believable. She heard a dog barking and a horse snorting in a nearby field and wondered again if her sister was going to tell her the truth.

Meanwhile Florence was twisting her heel into a clump of dry grass. 'If you really must know . . . the thing is . . .'

There was a short silence.

'Yes?'

'Well . . . Anton is actually . . . well, he's German.'

Élise whistled. 'You're kidding!'

The air seemed to thin and for a moment Hélène felt as if she were suffocating. At a loss for words, she bowed her head while she considered what to say, then she looked up and saw her sister's face, a picture of misery.

'Florence,' she began gently. 'You know it's not safe to have a German friend. If people find out you've been cavorting with the enemy—'

'He's not the enemy,' Florence broke in defensively. 'He's kind, and I'm not *cavorting*. And anyway, like I said, he's just a friend. He enjoys nature, like me.'

'How long have you known him?'

'A while.'

'Why didn't you say anything before?'

Florence lifted her chin in defiance. 'Because I knew what you'd say. I knew it would confirm all your prejudices.'

'Good grief!' Élise said. 'That's a bit brutal.'

Hélène ran her fingers through her hair in frustration, not wanting to have to deal with this. It would be too easy to be unkind and then the damage would be done. She had to find a way to convince Florence without them falling out.

'Listen to me,' she said as gently as she could. 'There will be retribution when the liberation comes. You must know there will.'

Florence gave her a look, her eyes sad. 'I suppose.'

'Darling, there's no suppose about it. Come on Florence. They'll hurt you! Shave your head. Humiliate you.' Hélène could feel a vein pulsing in her temple.

'They need never know.'

'There's already talk of vengeance. You know that, don't you?'

'We'll keep it quiet.'

Hélène raised her voice. 'No! The Resistance will punish any woman who has been seen socialising with a Nazi.'

Florence's bottom lip began to wobble. 'Don't shout at me. Anton isn't a Nazi.'

'It won't matter. He's German. That will be enough.'

Feeling terribly bleak inside, Hélène looked across at Élise who shrugged and raised her hands helplessly. Hélène glanced at Florence, who at twenty-two was behaving like a belligerent fifteen-year-old. Any minute now she'd be rolling her eyes. But she had to get through to her.

'Florence,' she said more calmly.

'What?'

'Please don't let us argue.'

'For once in your life, Hélène, can you please quit with the sanctimonious attitude. You are not my mother. Don't pretend you are.'

'That's not fair,' Hélène said feeling hurt. 'I'm not—'

'You are, you do,' Florence burst in. 'Anyway, chances are I won't see him again.'

'For God's sake, you expect me to believe that? I'm only trying to watch out for you. Élise, say something please.'

Élise just shrugged again. 'I don't know what to say.'

'Well I give up. I don't know what else I can do,' Hélène threw her hands up in the air, turned her back, and walked away feeling a need for solitude.

She heard Élise talking, the gentle rise and fall of her

sister's words and Florence's irritable responses fading in the background as she went back to the house and then into the kitchen. After all the drama of getting to Bordeaux and everything that had happened there, she'd had enough. More than enough and she felt properly riled. How could Florence be so stupid? And how could so much have happened in such a short space of time? It was insane. Élise pregnant, the baby's father dead, Florence friendly with the enemy. What else? She shook her head in exasperation. How could she ever go away and leave them again? What might happen next? It was intolerable. She imagined further disasters, as more and more babies arrived, screaming in cribs littering the house, and long-limbed, blonde German men began to leap from broom cupboards and wardrobes, so many that for a moment she had to stifle a smile. Other absurdities flitted through her mind. Florence marrying a goose-stepping Nazi and going to live in Germany and giving birth to the perfect Aryan baby, complete with swastika emblazoned on its forehead. Herself growing white-haired, alone, and quite possibly mad. She gulped at the air to regain control and felt as if she was going to cry. But no. Her stomach muscles were heaving. Oh crikey, she was going to laugh. She covered her mouth. No way was it appropriate and she bit her lip trying to stop it, but a wave of laughter was forcing its way up from her belly. When Florence and Élise entered the kitchen it erupted as a guffaw. She attempted to speak, explain herself, apologise, say that she knew there was not a funny side to this, but she couldn't get the words out.

'It's not funny, Hélène,' Florence said, echoing Hélène's

own thoughts and looking so indignant it only made everything worse.

Now in the grip of unstoppable laughter, Hélène clutched the back of a chair and bent double. Élise began to chuckle too. Hélène almost managed to quit, but when Élise caught her eye, the laughter erupted again. Irresistible, wild laughter. And yet Florence was right; it wasn't funny. None of it was. But now with a stitch in her side, Hélène could do nothing but clasp her sides and swallow air. After a moment she stretched out her arms as if she were reaching for something so important her life depended on it, but then she let them fall.

'I . . . I . . .'

Florence was staring at her in disbelief. 'What's the matter with you?' she demanded and then she marched over and slapped Hélène's face. 'You're hysterical. Stop it.'

Rendered speechless, Hélène just shook her head and wiped her stinging eyes, her laughter only subsiding now because of her need to finally draw breath. And when she *had* finally sobered, the really funny thing, the really extraordinary thing, was that it seemed as if a burden had suddenly been lifted from her and she felt she could do anything. Anything she wanted.

CHAPTER 54

That evening the sisters avoided the subject of Florence's German friend and the house felt cold and unnaturally quiet. The next day, soon after an equally silent breakfast, Hélène spotted a silver-haired man in civilian dress standing at the gate and glancing at the house, as if unsure about something. His suit was elegant, double-breasted, the colour a muted navy. He sported a cream lightweight fedora and carried a brown leather briefcase. She continued to watch as he placed a hand on the gate but then immediately withdrew it. He took a few steps away, removed his metal-framed spectacles, wiped them with a handkerchief and then, with a frown, looked as if he was evaluating something further down the track.

They had to be on their guard, Hélène thought to herself, keep an eye out for watchers – either the professional observer type or simply the collaborators. Both a source of constant danger. Easier were the ones you could identify, the ones who stared overtly, usually older men, their eyes following you down the street while you felt the heat on your back. Harder were the inconspicuous watchers, the passive collaborators made up of those who kept their heads down and closed their eyes to what was happening *and* those who acted as if nothing *was* happening. Hélène suspected that, after the liberation, these same people would be the first to claim active involvement with the Maquis, and she already despised them for it. There were collaborators who felt they had no choice if they were to survive but, more and more, Hélène felt that was no excuse. On the journey to Bordeaux she had learned you had to stand up and be counted, no matter what.

'I've never seen him before,' Élise said, coming up behind her. 'Have you?'

Hélène focused on her sister. 'No . . . Gestapo do you think? They sometimes wear civilian clothing.'

'Too hesitant to be Gestapo.'

'I think he was probably lost. Look, he's going now.'

Florence was still uncommunicative, despite Hélène's attempts to engage with her. And however much she searched her mind for something positive to say, her sister's answers were curt. Most of the time Florence remained in the garden, bending over as she planted seedlings or reaching up to prune the top of the shrubs. Now she was banging about in the kitchen and when Hélène asked if she'd like to go for a walk, Florence refused to look up.

'Leave me alone, can't you?' she snapped.

So Hélène backed out.

'He's there again,' Élise said a little later on. 'That man we saw. Just standing facing away from our gate.'

'What do you think he wants?'

'No idea . . . Should we ask Florence if she has seen him before?'

'Best not. She's very prickly.'

But Élise called for Florence anyway.

'What?' came the irritable reply.

'Can you come here?'

'I'm busy. I'm baking.'

'Please.'

Hélène felt wary as her sister came through from the kitchen wiping her floury hands on her extra-large bib apron. Parisian blue with crossover straps at the back and so soft and so comfortable she wore it from morning to night.

She pushed the blonde curls from her disgruntled face. 'So?'

Élise pointed at the window. 'You seen that man before?'

Florence joined the other two and glanced out guardedly. 'Don't think so, but I can only see his back. Are we safe?'

'I'm sure he won't do anything. But we don't often get strangers coming this far down our track.'

Florence squinted at the man. 'Oh, no he's turning around.' She took a step back into the room.

The man had indeed turned around and, as he approached the gate, he stretched out a hand to lift the latch.

'So? *Have* you seen him before?' Élise whispered.

'No. And he can't hear us so there's no need to whisper.'

'I'll go out,' Hélène said.

Élise shook her head. 'No, we'll all go. That is if you want to, Florence? Do you think he looks German?'

Hélène allowed Élise to lead the way outside. Florence had hesitated but only for a moment, and in the end, she did follow them and stood a little behind Hélène.

When the man saw the three of them together, he appeared surprised. 'Good afternoon. I beg your pardon for the intrusion,' he said, and gave them a little bow. His French was immaculate, with the merest hint of a German accent.

'You speak excellent French,' Hélène said, feeling instantly more suspicious.

He inclined his head in response. 'I learnt as a child.'

'How can we help?' Élise asked in an equally polite tone of voice, though Hélène could tell Élise was still wondering if the man worked for the Nazis and had come to spy on them.

He glanced around him. 'I am not sure if I am in the correct place.'

'For what?'

He smiled at her. 'Well I am actually looking for Claudette Baudin.'

The girls exchanged surprised looks. 'Really? What do you want with her?' Hélène asked.

'Well nothing much, just to say hello. I was passing and remembered she lived hereabouts. I was last in the area many years ago, and on my little stroll I thought I recognised this house.'

'She lives in England,' Élise said.

'Ah, she must have sold the house. This was hers, yes?'

'Still is,' said Élise. 'But we live here. She's our mother.'

He gave her a long curious look and then blinked when he noticed Florence standing further back than the other two. 'Ah. So, you must be the youngest.'

'How did you know?'

He laughed. 'Nothing sinister. You just look like the youngest.'

Florence smiled and looked more relaxed. Perhaps the talk of their mother was cheering her up.

'So, you knew our mother quite well?' Hélène asked.

'Oh . . . well, not . . . As I said, I was just passing through the village and felt it was only polite to—'

'To?'

'Drop by. Nothing more.' He took off his hat, dipped his head, then put the hat back on. 'It has been a pleasure, but now I have business to attend to.'

He turned and swiftly walked away, leaving the girls mystified.

'We should have asked his name,' Élise said.

Hélène shrugged. 'It hardly matters. He won't be back.'

'How do you think he knew Maman?'

CHAPTER 55

It had rained a little, leaving the air feeling fresher, and from where she sat on the window seat Hélène could see water dripping from the lacy hydrangea petals. But inside the house the atmosphere was still strained. Hélène settled down to read while Élise let out her grey cotton trousers to fit her better and began mending a man's brown jacket to wear with them.

'Are your clothes already getting tight?' Hélène asked, putting down her book and not minding. She couldn't concentrate on it anyway.

'Across the bust and tummy. Yes, a little bit. But this jacket is perfect.'

Hélène laughed. 'Except for the holes.'

'Make do and mend! Isn't it what they say in jolly old England?'

'Yes. Wish I was there now, don't you?'

'Truthfully? No.' Élise paused. 'Have you managed to talk to Florence?'

Hélène took a sharp breath in. 'I've tried but she isn't really speaking to me.'

'Nor me actually. But she'll come round.'

'I've never seen her like this before. So . . . so . . .'

'Aloof?'

'Yes. It worries me.'

Hélène felt that Florence's state of mind was being affected not only by their argument but also by what had happened to her at the hands of the BNA. Something so harrowing could hardly just fade away.

'I'm going to nip into the village to pick up some biscuits I forgot to bring home. Coming?' Élise asked.

'I was going to do the laundry.'

'Can't it wait?'

'I suppose.'

In the village Élise slipped into her café and Hélène sat on a bench in the square to wait. Arlo came by, towering over his tiny wife Justine, and both of them wished Hélène a good day. They talked for a few moments then dear old Madame Deschamps wandered over, interrupting them by asking if Hélène had any lemon cake.

'Cake, madame? Sorry, I don't. Would you like to sit with me instead?'

The old lady shook her head. 'No. I don't want to sit. It's cake I want. Have you got it?'

'Perhaps your daughter has baked a cake? Have you looked in your kitchen?'

'What a good idea,' she said.

'Come on. I'll walk you back over.'

As Arlo and Justine took their leave, Hélène linked arms with the old lady and walked her across to the hotel where she pushed open the door. Sure enough, the buttery aroma of baking greeted them as Amelie hurried through from the kitchen, wiping her hands on her apron and sighing with a mixture of relief and exasperation.

'I don't know, I turn my back for five minutes and she's off. She gets these ideas in her head, you see.'

'I am here, you know,' Madame Deschamps said.

'Thank you for bringing her back. Just wait a minute and I'll cut you some cake to take home.'

'There's no need,' Hélène said, holding up a hand. 'I was only waiting for Élise.'

'All the same.' Amelie turned and was a back a few minutes later carrying a beautiful golden cake on a patterned plate. She set it on the hall table to show it to Hélène. Despite the shortages, you could smell almonds, honey, vanilla, and lemon zest.

'It's an absolute triumph,' Hélène said with a smile.

'I do my best,' Amelie said, looking pleased, then she wrapped a large slice in a tea towel and handed it to Hélène. 'Last week I made a spiced cinnamon and apple cake, with ground walnuts. We have to experiment with the lack of flour.'

'Yes, my sister does that too. I'm no cook myself.'

Amelie patted her hand. 'But you, my dear, are a nurse. That is more than enough.'

'There you see,' the old lady said interrupting her. 'I told you there was cake.'

Hélène and Amelie exchanged smiles.

On her way back across the square Hélène spotted a stranger on the opposite side, near the town hall. She was still smiling about what had happened and sniffing the cake too, so it took a moment for her to see it was the same man they'd met outside their house earlier. Noticing her, he tilted his head and walked across, extending his hand, and smiling.

'Friedrich Becker. Hello. I met you and your sisters outside your house.'

'Yes,' she said, noticing he wasn't wearing the cream fedora now and she could see his silver hair properly. 'Hélène Baudin,' she eventually said, remembering her manners.

'Claudette's eldest?'

'Yes.

'Delighted.'

There was a momentary silence as she tried to think of what to say.

'Will you be in Sainte-Cécile for long?' she asked finally.

He shrugged. 'Oh, no. I just have a little business. But I was hoping I might bump into one of you. How are you?'

'I'm fine, thank you.'

'And your sisters?'

'Very well, considering everything.' God, she sounded stiff, more like a matron than a young woman.

'I remember the youngest one. What was her name again?'

She raised her brows. 'You mean Florence. I don't believe we exchanged names.'

He smiled. 'I must have imagined it. Florence is a lovely name. Would you have time for a coffee, Hélène? I would love to talk more about your mother. And I do have some things I'd like to discuss with you.'

'You do?' Hélène said, feeling a little perplexed.

'I see there is a café just over there.'

'My sister's café, actually. It isn't open today but look, here she is now.'

Élise marched up to them swinging her bag of biscuits and looked puzzled when Becker stood up to greet her.

'This is Friedrich Becker, Élise. You know, the old friend of Maman's we met outside our house.'

Her sister's mouth twisted into a wary knot.

There was a moment of unease.

Élise did not hold out her hand but eventually replied politely enough. 'Nice to meet you again.'

'Herr Becker has some things he wants to talk about.'

Élise gave Hélène a sceptical look. 'Really? With us?'

'Yes.'

'Well we can hardly talk here in the square for all the world to see.'

Hélène knew she actually meant they couldn't be seen in the heart of the village apparently socialising with a German.

'Is it important?' Élise asked.

Becker gave her a small cautious smile. 'I rather think it is.'

'Then, you'd better come to our house,' she added rather ungraciously.

'That would be ideal.'

'Tomorrow evening?'

'Thank you.' He paused. 'It was lovely seeing you both. Do have a good day.'

'Well,' Hélène said, once he was out of earshot. 'That was strange.'

'Indeed. What the hell does he want?'

CHAPTER 56

The next evening the sky was clear, which augured well for an excellent drying day to follow. In anticipation of that, Hélène was pinning out the washing in the back garden when she heard the front gate squeak as it swung open.

'I'll go,' Élise called out from where she'd been sitting on the bench outside the kitchen.

Hélène heard her striding around to the front and then a snatch of conversation. After a moment Élise came back. 'It's him,' she hissed, her manner churlish. 'Becker,' she continued. 'Waiting by the front door.'

Hélène walked around to the front and saw him standing stiffly. 'Well,' she said and held out her hand, then realising it was still damp from the laundry, withdrew it and wiped it on her skirt.

'Herr Becker. Shall we go in?' Élise suggested.

Just then Hélène spotted Florence slip round from the back garden too. She called to her, but her sister didn't reply and carried on down the track towards the spot where a blonde young man was standing motionless, staring at the ground.

'Anton,' they heard Florence say. 'What are you doing here?'

Hélène, Élise, and Friedrich Becker all turned in unison. Élise and Hélène exchanging perplexed looks.

They watched as Florence reached the young man and held out her hand to him, but instead of taking it he put up his own hands in a gesture of resistance and stepped back.

'What is it?' Florence said, looking bewildered.

Then Friedrich Becker spoke. 'Anton, I asked you to wait in the car, but now you're here, you'd better come inside.' He glanced at Hélène. 'If that is acceptable, Miss Baudin?'

So this was the famous Anton. He didn't look a bit pleased to see Florence; in fact he looked at a complete loss.

'Everyone should come inside,' Hélène said. 'Élise will put the kettle on.'

Becker gave a slight bow. 'You have English tea?'

Hélène shook her head. 'I'm afraid not, just tisanes or ersatz coffee.'

He turned to the young man. 'Come, Anton.'

Anton obeyed immediately, skirting around Florence. She looked even more bewildered than before and then trailed behind as they all went inside.

Hélène led everyone through to the kitchen where Élise busied herself filling the kettle and then putting it on the hob where she remained with her back to it.

Hélène indicated their guests should sit. Anton did so, but Friedrich Becker chose to remain standing. She inclined her head. 'As you prefer, Herr Becker.'

'Please call me Friedrich.'

But Florence was staring at him wide-eyed. 'Becker? Are you Anton's father?'

'Indeed. He is my only son.'

Anton, meanwhile, was staring at his hands, twisting and turning them round and round. Hélène felt a twinge of fear; after all, the Germans were still their enemy, no matter how convivial. What the hell was going on? Maybe they were here to tell them the friendship between Anton and Florence could not continue. Did Friedrich Becker disapprove? If so, that might be the best outcome. At least *she* would no longer be the villain of the piece. She glanced at Florence, who was hanging back and leaning against the back door.

'You have a lovely home, Miss Baudin,' Friedrich said, glancing at Hélène.

'Thank you. We like it.'

'But I have been here before.'

'We saw you at the gate,' Élise said.

He shook his head. 'I meant long before. I spent a couple of weeks here one summer.'

'In the village?'

'In this house, in fact.'

Élise pursed her lips. 'How come?'

He took off his spectacles and wiped them. 'It is a long story. I think I will take a seat now, if I may?' He glanced at Hélène, who nodded.

While he settled at the table, Élise prepared the peppermint tisane and brought Claudette's Moroccan glasses over to the table. There was an atmosphere of expectation in the room and Hélène knew both of her sisters were as much in the dark as she was.

'I shall start at the beginning,' Friedrich said as he ran his thumb around the rim of his glass.

And he went on to explain how he had got to know their mother at the Conference of Genoa during the April and May of 1922.

'It was the first conference Germany was permitted to take part in after the First World War. Claudette was there accompanying your father. As a civil servant in the Foreign Office he was part of the British delegation. We spent quite a bit of time together, your mother and I.'

'You and she?' Hélène said, jumping to conclusions. 'You were—'

'You're not trying to tell us you had an affair with our mother?' Élise burst in, her jaw jutting angrily.

'I'm not making excuses, but she was left alone for hours in what she described as an already cooling marriage.'

Hélène braced herself but didn't speak.

'So how did you come to be here?' Élise asked.

His eyebrows knitted together either in concentration or embarrassment. Hélène wasn't sure which.

Then he carried on speaking. 'It is not easy to talk about this, but we fell in love, your mother and I . . .'

'But she was married.'

He blinked rapidly. 'Yes, she was.'

Hélène frowned. He seemed nervous, as if he were

gathering his courage. He glanced out of the window, blinked again, then turned back to them. He still didn't speak, and she felt unease growing inside her.

'Yes,' he finally said. 'She was married, and because of Anton's friendship with Florence here, I have to tell you the truth.'

'Truth?' Hélène said. 'What truth? And what's it got to do with Anton?'

'This,' he said and swallowed visibly. 'Some months after our brief relationship your mother gave birth to our baby girl.'

Baby girl. What baby girl? Hélène's heart was pounding. What was he talking about? She felt light-headed and tried to steady herself, but the room seemed to be suddenly dipping and moving. She drew in a long breath and then slowly letting it out, she tipped her head to one side to study his face for tell-tale signs of falsehood. He had hesitated, but perhaps it was normal given the situation and his hand gestures were not flustered. But still she felt suspicious and unnerved.

'When was that?' she asked, stiffly.

'The child was born at the end of 1922.'

The sisters all went still as that sank in. Hélène felt as if the house itself had frozen and that she had frozen with it. It sat there, the question. None of them able – or willing – to take the initiative and demand to hear the awful inevitable truth.

The silence went on, but in the end it was Florence who spoke, her voice tremulous. 'On what day?'

'December the thirtieth.'

Florence flushed and slid to the floor, where she sat with her knees drawn up to her chest, shoulders hunched around her and her head bowed. Élise stared in astonishment, a hand covering her mouth and her eyes wide.

Hélène's eyes began to sting. 'So . . .' she said.

He cleared his throat nervously. 'Yes. Florence is my daughter. Anton is her half-brother.'

The shock didn't immediately affect Hélène. For a few moments she felt dislocated from the room, from her sisters, from herself. Then, as the truth slammed into her, she felt a burst of anger. Her ragged breath hurting her, she weighed up what he'd said, then she glanced at Florence. How was she going to protect her from this? She shot furious glances at Friedrich. It couldn't be true. How dare he come here and upend their lives like this? And now Florence was staring at him, the skin pinched around eyes filling with tears. Hélène opened her mouth searching for something to say to help her sister but struggled to find the words.

'Darling . . .' she started to say, but Florence held up a palm and shook her head, a look of anguish on her face.

Hélène's breath quickened and her mouth twisted. She pointed at Becker. 'You need to go. I don't believe a word of this. Go. Now!'

CHAPTER 57

Élise

Immediately after Hélène had asked Becker to leave, Florence went to bed. At the front door, he had pleaded with Hélène, adamant that he needed to return the next day to finish his story. Unable to deny him at least that, Hélène had eventually relented. The landscape of their childhood had changed dramatically when Florence was born and now, if all this was true, they knew why. Élise was relieved to have some time to think before he returned. It was a lot to take in. Florence, meanwhile, had closed her bedroom door and would answer neither to Hélène nor Élise's entreaties to eat or drink.

In the morning, the atmosphere was gloomy as they gathered in the kitchen.

'It can't be true,' Hélène repeated more than once.

'How could he come here with this outrageous story and upset Florence like this?'

'You sound like you're trying to convince yourself,' Élise said, shaking her head. 'But you know the date does add up.'

Hélène turned to the sink and faced the window and Élise could hear her sloshing the water noisily around the cutlery and banging clean crockery down on the draining board. Taking it out on breakfast things from a meal left untouched.

Élise stifled her annoyance at the racket and went over to touch Hélène on the shoulder, but her sister shrugged her off.

Florence, who was sitting at the kitchen table tracing the grain of the wood with her thumbnail, stifled a whimper. Élise drew up a chair and tried to hold her, but Florence flinched and leant away. Élise glanced across at Hélène but she remained as she was, even her back looking prickly.

'Florence, it will be all right,' Élise said in a placating voice and glanced again at Hélène who now did at least turn towards them. And thank God she'd stopped with the annoying clattering.

Florence's shoulders began to shake and then she gulped back a tear. 'I hate him. Why did he have to come? He can't be my father. Can he, Élise?'

'I don't know.'

Then Florence started to sob.

Élise shrank from the pain she heard in those tears. A kind of primal, visceral despair. Too awful for words, it was as if Florence was grieving for a part of herself she could never recover, a part of herself that had vanished overnight. Her sobs came in waves, erupting again and again, engulfing her and separating her from her sisters as she sat hunched up and alone. A chasm had opened and Élise had no idea how to bridge it.

She waited, staring at the floor, then out of the window. She heard their goats bleating and from further away, a cockerel crowing. Sunlight crept into every corner of the kitchen and she longed to be outside striding across the grass, along the track, and into the woods – anywhere but here and this awful torrent of emotion she could find no way to halt.

But after a while, Florence gulped again and her tears subsided. 'How could Maman do that?' she said, her mouth twisting in anger. 'How could she?'

Élise shook her head. 'I don't know. But listen, we still don't actually know if he's telling the truth.'

She tried again to offer comfort, yet still Florence would not allow it and pushed her away.

'What am I going to do?' Florence whimpered, her shoulders drooping. 'What?'

She began sobbing again. Helpless in the face of Florence's pain, Élise's own eyes began to smart. She didn't want to be swallowed up by this distress, but how could she just get up and leave?

'Darling, you don't have to see him again,' she said. 'It doesn't have to change anything.'

Florence glared at her, the anger returning. 'How can you even say that? It changes absolutely everything.'

Élise felt so out of her depth she glanced at Hélène again, but her sister was still leaning against the sink, watching white-faced, her arms hanging loosely at her sides, and she showed no sign of intending to move. Élise frowned at her.

'Can't you say something?' she said, but Hélène just screwed up her face as if to stop tears.

Élise didn't understand. She'd never seen her older sister like this before; Hélène was the compassionate one, the caring one, the one to step in and take command of any crisis. Why was she holding back? Had this shocked her so much she simply couldn't speak?

'I never want to see him again,' Florence said as her sobs receded once more.

'You don't have to if you don't want to,' Hélène finally said, at last coming back to life and intervening. 'None of us have to.'

Florence's body went limp, as if all the tension were draining from her. And now she allowed Élise to wrap an arm around her and pull her close. Élise glanced across at Hélène who gave her a sad, broken kind of smile and it seemed to her that Hélène was conceding defeat, and perhaps letting go a little.

'Oh God. I wish he had never come here,' Florence said, then wiped her eyes with her fingers. 'I'd better splash my face.'

As she got up and went to the laundry room, Élise began to breathe more easily. Maybe the worst was over.

'Well done,' Hélène said.

Élise smiled and inclined her head. 'Perhaps I'll train as a nurse too.'

'I wouldn't go that far,' Hélène said and sighed. 'I never expected anything like this. Did you?'

'No. I wish I hadn't invited him in. How do you feel?'

'Shocked. Angry. Frightened for Florence. I mean how will this change things? And worst of all, if it is true . . . her father is a German.'

In the afternoon, they heard a knock at the door. Hélène caught Élise's eye then looked away before smoothing down her blouse. Her sister retied the band holding her hair in a ponytail at the nape of her neck. 'Well then,' she said.

'We don't have to let him in,' Hélène said.

Élise felt her throat tighten. 'I think we do.'

Hélène looked at her. 'Why don't you go?'

And once again Élise felt Hélène letting go of control. They had taken her so much for granted and she felt a shiver of shame that she hadn't appreciated how much.

She went to the door and showed Friedrich in. 'No Anton?' she asked.

'Not this time. I think he might like to talk to Florence later, if she is willing.'

Élise dipped her head and this time invited him into the sitting room. Good-looking for an older man, he was dressed now in a pale summer suit that emphasised the blue of his eyes and the silver in his hair. Their father had never been so dashing or as sophisticated as this, and Élise could see how her mother might have been tempted. Friedrich seated himself on the larger of the two sofas and looked around eagerly. For Florence, Élise thought.

There was a long silence.

Élise was about to speak but then Florence came in, dragging her feet and barely even glancing at Becker, her eyes still red from crying and her skin blotchy. She took the furthest chair, kept her head bowed, and picked at her nails. Élise remained standing and Hélène perched on the window seat.

In the end Élise broke the silence. 'You still haven't explained how you came to be here for part of a summer.'

'You're right.'

'So?'

'Your father had intercepted a letter from me to your mother in the spring of 1924. He found out Florence was not his child.'

Élise's eyes stung at the thought of this. It was hard to imagine her father opening her mother's post, although for that matter, it was hard to stomach the thought of her mother having an affair.

'He gave Claudette an ultimatum; to choose to either stay or leave without any of her daughters.'

Hélène was leaning forward shaking her head and Élise could see how much this was hurting her.

'As I'm sure you recall, your mother often came on holiday here with you girls while your father worked on in London,' Friedrich continued. 'I arrived in Sainte-Cécile in the summer of 1924, and Claudette and I spent a couple of weeks together. I wanted to see Florence and I tried to persuade Claudette to leave with me.'

'She didn't though,' Élise said.

'No. You should know I was happy in my marriage to Anton's mother, and I am proud of my son, but Claudette was the love of my life, my soulmate.'

'Without Hélène and me?' Élise asked pointedly. 'You wanted her to go with you and just take Florence?'

'Yes, I'm ashamed to say . . . However, she would not.' Becker looked at Élise and then Hélène. 'I'm so sorry.'

Élise gazed at him, unable to speak.

Hélène excused herself and left the room. While she was gone nobody spoke. It was late afternoon now and the sun's shadows had lengthened. As Élise stared out of the window, she felt the events of the past shifting and colliding as they slotted into a completely new pattern. Her mother had changed, and this man was the reason why. She had stayed with their father for the sake of Hélène and herself, but had never been happy again. And for the first time, Élise felt an aching pity for her mother. No wonder she had resented them.

When Hélène returned, she asked Élise to come with her. In the hall Élise spotted the red silk dress hanging over the banister rail.

'What?' she said.

'Put it on,' Hélène whispered. 'Quickly.'

'Why?'

'Just do it. I need to see.'

'See what?'

Hélène sighed. 'Please, Élise. And hurry up.'

Élise went into the kitchen to change and when they both walked back into the drawing room, Friedrich stared, open-mouthed.

'Did you ever see our mother wearing this?' Hélène asked.

He stared, seeming unable to tear his eyes from Élise. 'Yes. I saw it the last time I was with Claudette. We'd had dinner together here in the house.'

'Why?' Florence demanded. 'Why did you have to see her again?'

He looked at her, as if searching her face for something. 'It was to talk.'

Apart from shaking her head, Florence did not respond and stared down at her empty hands.

'So, what happened?' Élise asked.

He glanced around the room, his eyes resting on Florence again. 'I always wanted to know you,' he said. 'But your mother . . .'

'Are you saying she wouldn't let you?' Florence said, her voice tearful.

'She had her reasons.'

There was a prolonged silence.

'So?' Élise eventually said, acutely aware they were all waiting. 'My mother was wearing the dress?'

'Yes. She looked so beautiful and I can see that you, Élise, are the image of her. But Florence, like Anton, takes after me. For a while, Claudette did send me photographs of a blonde, curly-haired little girl. It broke my heart, but she forbade me to see you . . . or . . .' He hesitated. 'Maybe it was your father?'

'My father was a good man,' Hélène broke in. 'How dare you infer he was not.'

'Of course.' Friedrich held up his hands as if in defence.

'I didn't mean . . . Anyway, she was wearing that dress that night and we drank two bottles of red wine between us, so I guess you could say we were both quite drunk. I repeated my request for her to leave your father, but she continued to refuse.'

'Surely it was the right thing to do?' Hélène said.

'Maybe, but tell me, was your mother happy?'

Hélène shook her head. 'When we were little, yes, but not after Florence was born.'

'So it's my fault?' Florence said, looking angry and hurt.

Hélène's face crumpled. 'Of course not. None of it was your fault. If our mother chose to be unfaithful to our father, then it was her fault.'

'But people don't choose who they fall in love with,' Florence said.

'Life is all about hard choices. We can't all follow our instincts or desires just because we feel like it. You'll learn that one day.'

Florence looked taken aback at Hélène's sudden sharp tone of voice and her chin began to tremble.

'It is not helpful to apportion blame,' Friedrich remarked.

Hélène bristled and glared at him. '*You* do not get a say.'

He sighed. 'I'm sorry.'

'Go on with the story,' said Élise.

'She refused to come with me. She said she couldn't leave her eldest two girls. I suggested she come with all three of you, but she said it would break her husband's heart.'

Élise glanced across at Hélène, who was opening and closing her mouth, tears glistening in her eyes.

'Instead, she proposed we carry on our affair in secret. I told her I could not. I explained I had met Liv, a woman in Germany of whom I had become fond. I certainly couldn't countenance deceiving Liv as well as your father. But neither could I commit to Liv while there was a chance Claudette might relent. This was to be my last-ditch attempt.'

'So how did the dress get ruined?'

'Claudette began shouting, screaming, ripping the dress in front of my eyes. "Go to your Liv then," she kept yelling. "Go to her."'

Élise took a long slow breath. This was awful.

'And then one of the children who had been asleep upstairs began to shriek.'

Élise glanced across at Hélène who was looking ashen.

'Hélène?' she said.

Now Hélène was screwing up her eyes. 'I think I must have been on the landing.'

'You were crying?'

'I remember shouting at her, begging her, "*Mummy, stop, please Mummy, stop.*" I was frightened.'

'Do you remember anything else?'

Hélène looked uncertain.

Élise knew what it was like to retrieve a memory she didn't want to find. It usually happened in the no man's land between sleep and wakefulness, when repressed images would arise unbidden from somewhere deep inside. She certainly didn't want to push Hélène into remembering something so painful. 'It's all right,' she said. 'You don't have to.'

But Hélène held up a hand to stop her. 'She marched up the stairs, like a mad woman. I remember saying, *"No, Mummy."* But she yanked hold of me, pulling my arm so hard my shoulder hurt, even though I was pleading with her.'

Hélène gazed into the distance as if seeing the scene unfold somewhere out there. Élise came across to her, but Hélène didn't seem to notice.

'I was clutching her skirt, trying to stop her, but she pulled down the attic ladder and shoved me up the rungs and into the attic. I was begging her not to, imploring her not to close the hatch. But she closed it anyway. She knew I was terrified of the attic, the dark, the creatures.'

Friedrich hung his head for a moment. 'I didn't know.'

'Didn't you?'

Friedrich looked appalled. 'I'd have prevented it. I thought she'd put you back in your bedroom. She came back down weeping, sobbing, doubled over. Hysterical. She had a bottle in her hand. I don't know where she got it from. She threw it at the wall and told me to get out.'

'And you left her in that state?'

'I refused to go at first, but she just got worse. I knew while I remained, she would not calm down.'

Hélène was still pale, but she nodded. 'She did calm down eventually, or at least I heard the yelling stop but . . .'

'What?' Élise asked.

'She left me up there all night. I was so terrified I wet myself and she never said sorry. That's what I remember most, the sting and smell of urine and wanting her to say sorry so much.'

Élise could see her sister's eyes had a flat, narrowed look in them, as if she were holding herself in, and she felt a burst of anger on her sister's behalf. But dear God, it was hard to square the composed, controlled woman her mother had become with the wild drunken woman Friedrich had described.

Friedrich buried his head in his hands for a moment, then looked up again sadly as he turned to Hélène. 'I'm so sorry for what happened to you. I called the next day, but she wouldn't open the door. I called every day for the rest of the week, but she wouldn't even speak to me. I blamed myself for telling her about Liv, but I wanted her to realise we could not go on as we were.'

'So, between Florence being born and all that happening you had carried on seeing each other?' Élise asked, knowing she sounded angry and judgemental.

'No. Only those two weeks, that summer.'

'What happened with Liv?' Florence asked, lifting her head now.

'I married her. She is Anton's mother. I had told her about Claudette and she said she would wait. She was a good woman.'

'Was?'

'She died last year.' He gazed at his hands and Élise, thinking of Victor, felt desperately sad.

'I only came back now to see if Claudette and I could come to some agreement about Florence. I longed to know my daughter.'

Florence rose to her feet and left the room, slamming the door behind her. Élise could see Hélène watching, blinking rapidly; she felt tears burning her eyes too, but she swiped them away with her knuckles.

'And Anton did not come with me today because I've already told him everything.'

'How does he feel about this?' Élise asked.

'It's complicated. He was drawn to Florence, felt a connection, but he will understand. He is supportive, my son. I think he sympathises.'

Hélène glanced at her watch, as if wanting to bring all this to an end and looking to Élise, as if she'd had enough. 'Gosh, it's six o'clock, already,' her sister said.

'I am overstaying my welcome,' Friedrich said and rose to his feet. 'Thank you, but if Florence is willing, perhaps we might see her tomorrow after lunch? Anton and I will wait at the gate at two. We shall be leaving for Germany soon after.'

CHAPTER 58

Hélène

It had been traumatic to hear the events of the past laid bare, and despite feeling some sympathy for her mother, Hélène felt enraged on her father's behalf. Her mother's love, passion – whatever it had been – the awful consequences had lasted a lifetime. And if the villagers had known what had happened, her mother's behaviour must have seemed scandalous. She felt scandalised herself and wished they could turn the clock back and never have spoken to Friedrich Becker in the first place.

Florence knocked then entered Hélène's room looking washed out. 'Hélène, can I talk to you?'

'Of course,' she said and patted a spot beside her on the bed.

'I've been thinking about it.'

'Me too.'

'Do you believe him?'

Hélène sighed. 'I don't want to believe him.'

'At first, I didn't want to either but now I do believe him. I can't think of him as my father though.'

'You don't have to see him again. He's going back to Germany anyway.'

There was a brief silence.

Florence sighed deeply. 'I feel sick whenever I think about it, but I do have to see him again. Him and Anton, before they go. I might never get another chance.'

Hélène knew she couldn't stop her, and probably shouldn't. Nobody could prevent whatever the impact of this was going to be.

'Friedrich Becker seems a decent man,' she said and held out her hand.

Florence squeezed her hand and then let it drop. 'Despite the affair?'

'It takes two, doesn't it? I just wish he wasn't German.'

'Do you blame Maman?'

Hélène considered it carefully, but her thoughts were all over the place and it was her father who appeared in her mind. Her sad, lonely father. How she longed to talk all this over with Marie, but of course she was gone.

'I think I need to get out for a bit,' Hélène said as she rose to her feet. 'Clear my head. Will you be all right?'

Florence nodded and kissed her on the cheek. 'Sorry, to have been so bad-tempered lately.'

Hélène patted her on the shoulder, then left the room.

In the absence of Marie to confide in, Hélène decided

to call on Violette, so she picked a few cornflowers from the garden and set off.

As she walked, she thought about Friedrich's revelations which had, at least, thrown some light on Claudette's later behaviour too: her distance, her slow withdrawal, her closed heart. Hélène faintly remembered her mother as a vibrant young woman – full of laughter and fun – but that mother was shadowy, tricky to grasp. Hélène could only catch hold of her mother's ghost and a yellow summer dress, drifting through a shifting past that never quite solidified.

She stood still on the track, screwing up her eyes trying to focus and then suddenly it was as if a light turned on, and a vein of memory opened up, all colour and brightness. And she was a child again on a dry sunny day when they were staying in the countryside, Claudette, Élise and herself. Hélène could not see her father there. Had they been on holiday without their father? She took a long deep breath and willed the memory to unfold. She could see herself running down a narrow lane with Élise, feeling free and breathing in the floral summery scents. They were going to pick lacy creamy elderflower sprays, 'Only those, mind,' her mother said and warned them not to touch any browning ones or the cow parsley, which looked similar. The good elderflowers were their treasure, Élise declared, as they carefully slipped the flowers into their canvas bags, each trying to be the one who picked the most. And, when they went home, they helped Claudette make elderflower champagne. A few days later they packed the bottles carefully and wedged them between cases in the boot of the car to take home to Richmond where they had to remain unopened for several weeks.

Hélène remembered checking every day to see if the cloudiness had cleared. And now she tasted something. Mint. The small sprigs of mint her mother had used to garnish the delicious sparkling drink. They had polished off the first bottle and eaten slices of Victoria sponge cake until they were satiated.

She would have loved to have remained in that golden memory but was brought back to the present by the sound of dogs barking in the village.

Violette answered the door straight away, looking a bit strained. 'Oh,' she said. 'You'd better come in.'

'Are you all right?' Hélène asked.

Violette had purple shadows beneath eyes and she looked worn out. Hélène felt she had called at the wrong time and almost decided to bow out and call back later, except something made her stay. Perhaps she thought Violette might need her or perhaps, more selfishly, she couldn't let go of the urge to talk herself.

'Is Jean-Louis well?'

'Not brilliant. He's complaining of pains in his chest again. Neither of us slept much.'

Hélène handed her the cornflowers. 'I'm sorry. I can come back another time.'

For a moment Hélène could have sworn Violette looked relieved but then she smiled. 'No, come through. I'll put these in water.'

She found a pretty white vase which showed off the brilliant blue of the cornflowers perfectly. With her special flair, Violette knew exactly what would go with what and even though she was clearly tired, she had on a smart two-piece suit with a skirt and fitted jacket that showed off her slim waist. In a lovely soft green, it was both practical and versatile, and she had knotted a spotted scarf at her neck.

When they were both sitting in the little kitchen, Hélène told her everything Friedrich had revealed.

'I feel as if my family has changed forever,' she concluded tearfully. 'It's so upsetting. And I don't know how it's going to affect Florence.'

Violette appeared to listen, nodding in the right places, exclaiming where she ought, yet Hélène didn't feel heard. This listening-but-not-listening was upsetting and unable to properly articulate her fears about Florence, she could barely hide her frustration.

Her friend glanced at her watch and stood suddenly. 'I need to put the oven on.'

'Am I keeping you from something?' Hélène asked a little curtly.

'No . . . no. It isn't that. I'm sorry. I just have a lot on my plate right now.'

Hélène glanced around. The kitchen was untidy. Most unlike Violette who, like Hélène herself, was obsessed with cleanliness.

'And I have a client arriving in a moment.'

'To collect a hat? Or to order a hat?'

'Of course,' Violette said, but her posture was defensive, and she didn't sound convincing. 'Look, we can talk about Florence any time you like, but I'm sure she'll be fine.'

With an awful sinking feeling in her stomach, Hélène felt as if she had been dismissed. She brought Jack's face to mind. At least he would listen; if only she knew where he was.

'It's just . . .' she said and paused for a second, but determined to get it out, continued. 'What I mean is, I wonder how much being half-German might affect her position here.'

'You mean afterwards?'

'Yes. During the liberation.'

'And you're sure there will be a liberation?'

'Yes.'

'Best if she keeps it to herself, don't you think?'

Hélène stood up as if by a tacit agreement between them. 'I'll go now. I don't want to hold you up any longer.'

Violette came to the door and the two of them hugged briefly and then Hélène walked away wondering what was up with Violette.

She passed the town hall and on the steps, saw a German SS officer talking to the clerk, Pascal. After a moment, the officer headed over in the direction of Violette's house. He stopped outside and then rapped on her door. Come to collect a hat, Hélène thought. How awful for Violette to have to deal with a man like that.

As she watched, her mind drifted back to Friedrich's revelation again. It was hard to comprehend her father issuing an ultimatum, although he must have done it to keep the family together. Had he been right to do so? Perhaps not. Staying had infected her mother with such acrimony it spilled into lifelong bitterness. And she and

Élise had harboured resentment at the favouritism, for Claudette had always loved Florence the most.

She watched as Violette opened the door and let the officer in, a fixed smile on her face. It made Hélène shudder.

CHAPTER 59

Florence

As they picked their way through the woods, Florence felt so light-headed it seemed as if a puff of wind might blow her away.

'Come on,' said Anton, gently beckoning her forward.

Under a brilliant azure sky, they jumped over tangled tree roots and avoided crushing the wildflowers underfoot, all the time their hands never touching. She usually loved all the different greens – the moss, the lichen, the grasses – but today she couldn't connect, and confusion festered just beneath the surface.

When they sat on the bench in the picnic area they looked at each other nervously, all ease between them gone. Like strangers, Florence thought.

'I . . .' she started to say, but then she chewed the inside of her lip, consumed by a feeling she couldn't properly name. Shame, fear, sadness. But more than that, she couldn't shake off a forlorn longing to properly belong. And instead she felt something had dislocated inside her and now she didn't belong anywhere.

'Well,' he said a moment later. 'This is rather strange, isn't it?'

She felt a throbbing pain at her temple. It was so much worse than strange. But if she spoke, she would cry, and she didn't want to cry again. She looked up into the canopy, where leaves flickered in the sunlight. Her throat hurt to swallow but she tried again.

'I . . .' but still her emotions overwhelmed her.

He remained silent.

'Who am I?' she eventually managed to say, curling her hands into fists. 'I feel like someone I don't even know!'

'You are the same person.'

'But I'm not. I'm half-German now.' But that wasn't all of it. 'I feel so jumbled. It hurts you know. It really hurts.'

He tried to take her hand, but she pulled away. There was so much she couldn't explain or even fathom. She wanted to be part English, part French. Not this. She wanted the father she'd always loved, not Friedrich Becker.

'You just need to get used to it,' he said.

'And what if I don't?'

He shrugged and looked so sad she felt selfish for not considering how this might be affecting him.

'What about you?' she said. How are you? After all you've only known the truth a day longer than me.'

A nerve pulsed in his temple and he took a sharp breath

before speaking. 'It's a lot to take in but it's easier for me. I have gained a sister. Do you see?'

She didn't speak.

'I have something for you,' he said, and reached in his pocket to pull out a silver locket and a chain. He clicked it open and handed it to her. 'My father wanted you to have it.'

She took the locket and looked at the photos inside it, glancing up at him in puzzlement.

'Don't you see?' he said. 'The baby on the right is you and the one on the left is me.'

She listened to a burst of birdsong and managed not to cry. 'I thought they were both pictures of you.'

He shook his head. 'We looked like twins. Did you ever wonder why you resembled neither your father nor your mother?'

'I knew Hélène looked like Papa and Élise like Maman. I just thought I must take after my English grandmother. She's dead, of course, but now . . . well, I didn't even have an English grandmother.'

He gazed at her and she saw such compassion and gentleness in his eyes. She had to hold on to the fact that Anton and Friedrich were good men. But still it felt awful to discover she was the child of the enemy.

'We do look alike even now, don't we?' Anton said.

'I suppose. Although I didn't see it before.' She paused and spotted a red squirrel darting up a nearby tree trunk. He followed her gaze.

'So much life in these woods,' he said.

'We desperately need more rain.'

She wanted to ask him questions, not slip into small talk, but she wavered. Did she really want to know about his life? Wouldn't knowing make it feel more real? She didn't want it to be real. She wanted to wake up and find it had all been a dream.

'I used to want to believe in forest fairies – I can't believe that now.'

'What changed?'

'Life, I suppose.'

This deep in the woods the air was still moist and she breathed in the fragrance of leaves and earth and watched the green ferns unfurling in the breeze. But she sighed at her own cowardice. Deciding she would kick herself afterwards if she didn't try, she asked him what his mother had been like.

'She was funny, kind, good-natured,' he said. 'Always smiling.'

'You must miss her.'

She saw him swallow the lump in his throat.

'I'm so sorry.'

They were still being cautious with each other. The goalposts had shifted and she sighed deeply.

'That sounded heartfelt.'

'I feel so uncomfortable.'

'With me?'

'With myself.'

He smiled. 'Me too. Kind of.'

'Your mother sounds lovely. She was not like my mother. My mother was kind to *me*, not so much Hélène and Élise.'

They sat together for a little longer and then he glanced at his wristwatch and said it was time to rejoin Friedrich.

'He seems . . . nice,' she said, then puffed out her cheeks at the lameness of the remark. 'What I mean is, I can't call him *Father*. It would feel . . . disloyal I think.'

'He won't mind. Really.'

She took a breath and then exhaled slowly, knowing she had to ask. 'So, when are you leaving for Germany?'

'Tomorrow.'

Oh, she thought. So soon, and with no idea of when they'd be back, if ever. Maybe it was a good thing. She wasn't sure.

'I have this for you too,' Anton said and handed her a small notebook. 'I wrote my favourite poems inside it and see, there's our address. I hope you will write. After the war.'

She felt terribly forlorn again. 'Will you be all right? I mean if Germany loses the war?'

'It looks increasingly likely.'

'So?'

He took hold of her hand and squeezed it gently. 'We'll be fine. But we need to leave while we still can. Promise you won't forget us?'

When they met up with Friedrich, he took hold of both her hands and gazed at her. 'Your hands are cold,' he said and let them go.

He was right. They were, but she stared at her feet and couldn't meet his eyes.

'I am so happy to know you,' he added.

Then she glanced up and saw he was smiling and that he had lovely eyes, just like Anton.

'And Florence, you are even more beautiful than I ever imagined.'

She felt the colour rising to her cheeks but managed to smile back.

'And from what Anton tells me you are extremely accomplished too.'

'I cook a bit,' she said, and he laughed.

'Modest too. If at any time you need anything, let me know. Or get in touch with Anton. I will not let you down.'

She wanted to say something, but her breath grew ragged and she was forced to gulp instead. He clasped both her hands inside his to warm them. 'Goodbye, sweet girl. Until we meet again,' he said, and then they were gone and she felt inconsolable, so much like crying she didn't know what to do.

In the end, feeling loath to face her sisters or spend the time alone, she called for Lucille.

Still teary, she told her friend everything. But as they walked further from the village, Lucille remained entirely silent and Florence, wanting her to respond, gripped hold of her arms.

'Why won't you say anything?'

Lucille looked at her in amazement. 'How can you even ask?'

Florence frowned, her heart constricting.

'You're German!' Lucille hissed.

Florence winced.

'Listen to me, Florence, you cannot tell anyone. Not a

single soul. People will be shocked; people will be angry. They won't believe you didn't know. Everyone hates the Germans, and some of them might want to hurt you.'

'I'm half-French too.'

'It won't matter. This is terrible. You have a German brother. A German father. If this gets out, it makes you the enemy.'

Florence swallowed her distress and tried to speak but she felt too sad and frightened to say a word. What was she going to do? What could she do? She didn't want to be the enemy. It was completely impossible.

'Look,' Lucille said. 'I have to go. Please don't tell anyone. Right?'

Florence nodded and her friend kissed her on both cheeks.

After Lucille had gone, Florence kicked her heels and walked home the long way round. She listened to the birds singing in the trees and waved away the hordes of buzzing flying insects, but nothing wholly reached her. She felt cut off and terribly alone. Just as she reached the lane to the village, a Nazi staff car, a black Citroën, passed her, heading in the direction of the chateau and castle. She was surprised to see two people she knew sitting in the back. What were *they* doing there?

CHAPTER 60

Élise

Élise was sitting on the bench, drowsy and very nearly asleep, listening to the wind growing more blustery and carrying the fragrance of wildflowers from the fields. She could hear the birds singing too, and something scratching in the bushes. But then, more importantly, she heard the gate as Florence arrived home.

'Hello,' she called out. 'I'm round here in the garden. How did it go?'

Florence came to sit on the bench with her. 'It was . . . I don't know. Uncomfortable, awkward. Sad.'

Élise gazed at Florence. She looked tired. There was something different about her eyes and to Élise it looked as if the light had dimmed a little and been replaced by something more wary. She seemed less ethereal and there was an edge to her. Élise felt wretched, as if things had shifted between *them* and might never be the same again.

Florence fingered the locket at her neck. 'Anton gave me this. They are both going back to Germany tomorrow.'

'How do you feel about that?'

Florence looked away. 'I don't know. One minute I'm glad they're going, the next I feel miserable. But I wouldn't be able to spend more time with them anyway, not now when there's so much hatred. Well, it's justifiable isn't it – hatred against the Germans.'

Élise bowed her head. 'Yes.'

'I'd be condemned if I met them again and people saw me with them. Hélène has already spelled out what would happen, especially if the liberation is truly coming.'

'It is,' Élise said. 'Really. It is.'

'And Anton and his father don't want to be here when the Allies come.'

They gazed at each other in this odd, strange moment.

'We are still sisters, right? I . . .' Florence said, attempting to sound confident, although her trembling voice gave her away.

Élise, now standing, pulled her sister up and wrapped an arm around her. 'Always sisters. Never doubt it.'

'And Hélène?'

'Of course. Her too.'

'I feel tired, but not tired in a good way. I mean I couldn't sleep even though I wish I could. I want to sleep for a hundred years in fact.' She shook her head. 'But I guess I'll have to dig instead or find something to cook.'

'Be my guest, little witch.'

Florence smiled and Élise felt hugely relieved to see it.

'Oh, I almost forgot, I saw Violette and her little boy in an SS staff car. It looked as if they were being taken to the chateau.'

The next day Élise wound her way silently down the track. For the first time since the trial she was due to meet with Claude and two of the maquisards, and anticipated working on a plan that might help Violette. She prayed the seamstress was safe, but despaired to think the Germans might be punishing people in advance of being forced to retreat. Still, she patted her belly and whispered urgently to the baby growing there. 'Everything is going to be fine. Just one last push to get the Nazis out. That's all.' Then she headed in the direction of the safe house and was surprised to pass Enzo who called out to her. 'How's your sister?'

She had never liked the shifty boy but paused. 'Which one?'

'Florence of course.'

'She is well, thank you.'

He narrowed his eyes and smirked. 'I saw her.'

'You did?'

'With a young man and a grey-haired man, older than her. Oh yes. Pally they were. Your father?'

'No. He is not my father. Now if you'll excuse me.' She walked briskly on ignoring his further questions.

But as she entered the safe house a little later, the first person she saw wasn't Claude, it was Jack.

'I wasn't expecting you,' she said in surprise.

He drew her aside so they could talk quietly without the others hearing. 'I got back last night.'

'And Marie?'

'Well on her way, I hope.'

'Good. Hélène will be relieved. Hugo too, of course.'

'She had the best guides, but I don't know how the mountain crossing went.'

Élise nodded.

'I hope she's all right, but the Germans are becoming more unpredictable now,' he added.

She glanced at the two maquisards over at the table. She already knew Mathius, who had been a friend of Victor's; a tall, skinny man with broken veins on his cheeks and a shock of black curly hair. He smiled at her and introduced the other. A young man, more of a boy really, blonde-haired and chunky, who eyed her curiously and said she was to call him Louis. They seemed to have silently accepted her presence at the meeting.

'I invited Élise to join us,' Claude said. 'She will be taking a more active role now.'

He pulled up a chair for her and she joined them at the table where they had been poring over a map. She decided to talk to Jack about Violette once the main business was completed.

'So, what's the plan?' Mathius asked. 'Is it really true there is an Allied landing happening? We've heard so many rumours before that haven't come to anything.'

'I can't tell you much, and I don't know any more than my orders have confirmed. Here in the Dordogne, our goal is to slow the march of the 2nd SS Panzer Division, known as the "Das Reich". A tough, hardened bunch if there ever was one.'

'Do we know when?' Élise asked, thrilled to be involved in the plans to at last turf the Nazis out of their country.

'Not yet,' Jack said. 'But we have radio connection with London and any of you can listen to Radio Londres if you have access to a set. The great thing is, because of the bombing in Germany, the morale of German troops is sinking. Works to our advantage.'

Claude nodded.

'And the Das Reich are based in Montauban now?' Mathius asked.

'Yes. About fifty-five kilometres north of Toulouse.'

'We've been busy here, following your plan,' Claude continued glancing across at Jack. 'Bumping up the campaign of sniping, sabotage, roadblocks. Plus there have been four times the number of parachute drops of arms.'

'Good,' Jack said.

Claude pulled a face. 'Trouble is, half the maquisards still don't know how to handle the weapons properly.'

'But everyone is raring to go?' Jack asked.

'Absolutely. There's a level of anticipation I've never felt before. Fever pitch I'd say.'

Jack raised his brows. 'Let's hope their passion will make up for their lack of skill.'

'The German reprisals have been terrible,' Mathius said. 'Not just shootings. They set fire to houses in Montpezat, burned farms, and the entire village of Terrou was razed to the ground.'

Jack puffed out his cheeks and let out his breath. 'It will

get worse. These men are dangerous at best; merciless when thwarted.'

There was a brief silence as they all took that in.

'Right.' He tapped at a point on the map. 'So the idea is to cut off the Germans in Bergerac, here.' And then he continued to discuss the rest of the plan answering specific questions from Claude, Élise and the two maquisards.

Before they left, Élise told Jack about Florence having seen Violette being taken to the chateau and asked if they might be able to at least, find out why.

'Unless Suzanne can throw some light on it, there's little hope of us doing anything at this stage,' he said. 'I'm really sorry, but it's much too risky, and now we have to prepare for the Das Reich we can't afford to lose any men on an operation that would most likely fail.'

She was worried for Violette but, of course, he was right, and if Suzanne knew anything at all she would let them know. So she just shook his hand and said goodbye to the others.

On her way home, she took a diversion through the village so that people would spot her collecting a few things from the café. She'd have to avoid leaving any hint that something suspicious was going on, so must look as if everything she did was business as usual. It was a bit cooler now, the breeze sharp, and she was turning over everything Jack had said, hoping that tomorrow they would put out the call for the volunteers from outlying farms and villages to pick up their weapons and come to the Maquis. These people, known as the SA or *Armée Secrète*, were men and women carrying on with their normal lives until the signal came to take up arms.

As she arrived at the streets on the edge of the village, something stopped her and she stood still for a moment, trying to work out what it was. She heard someone yelp in pain then laughter and jeering voices. She leant forward, concentrating. Where the noise was coming from? The voices grew more aggressive and when she heard a loud shriek her focus settled on a small nearby square. She marched on and rounded the corner. At first, she could only make out the backs of two men who were hurling insults and stones at someone hunched up and trying to hide behind a bench. Élise hated bullies and vowed to give them a taste of their own medicine. Coming closer she recognised Enzo and his friend and heard the words, *German bitch* and *Nazi whore* repeated like a chant.

She slipped around the edge of the square to see who they were mocking, and her worst fears were confirmed. Florence, wearing a white sundress, was cowering like a trapped animal, her arm covering her face and pleading with them to stop. Élise whipped out her gun and strode towards the boys.

'Get away from her now!' she shouted, pointing the gun at them.

They swaggered on the spot, squaring their shoulders, and sticking out their chests. 'Why don't you make us?' Enzo crowed. 'Bet it's not even loaded.'

She cocked the gun and pointed it at his heart. 'Believe me, I'm an excellent shot.'

He went a little pale. 'You wouldn't dare.'

'Want to bet on it?'

He opened his mouth, a bit more uncertain now.

'I'm not averse to a spot of killing, in fact I rather enjoy it, especially when my target is lowlife scum like you two.' And, in the split-second before she pulled the trigger, she pointed the gun at the sky.

'*Putain!*' one of the boys said, jumping out of his skin and backing away.

'Now listen good. If I hear of you going anywhere near my sister again, I will kill you. And *that* is a promise. Now fuck off, imbeciles.'

They both turned on their heels and ran, swearing as they went.

Florence levered herself up from where she had been crouching and came round to fall back onto the bench. She took an uneven breath and let it out slowly.

'Bastard little bullies!' Élise said. 'How long had that been going on?'

'Not long.'

'Are you hurt?'

'Just a little bit. One of their stones caught me on the leg before I hid behind the bench.' She showed Élise the place on her leg where a trickle of blood was now visible. 'But thank goodness you came when you did.'

'Can you stand?'

Florence said she could and Élise helped her up.

'Let's get you home then.'

Florence gazed at her. 'The thing is, how did they know?'

'Have you told anyone?'

'Only Lucille, and she wouldn't say a word.'

Élise didn't reply. She didn't have Florence's faith in Lucille.

They walked along the track to their house and found Hélène asleep in the drawing room.

'Don't wake her,' Florence said and began to turn away. 'I'll make some coffee.'

'I'm not asleep,' came a murmur from Hélène.

Élise folded her arms. 'In that case . . .'

'Honestly, Élise, it doesn't matter,' Florence said, pulling at her elbow.

Hélène sat up. 'What doesn't matter?'

Élise pulled up Florence's skirt to show the blood. 'That little arse Enzo and his friend were taunting her, throwing stones.

'Honestly, it was nothing,' Florence still insisted.

'Tell her what they were saying.'

Florence hung her head, but Élise carried on. 'The little foul-mouthed shits were calling her a German bitch.'

Élise gazed at Hélène and saw a range of emotions slide across her face: anger, fear, upset, guilt. She knew Hélène was trying to curb her instinct to fix everything for all of them, but she'd want to fix this and yet how could she?

Hélène rose to her feet and caught Élise's eye before turning to Florence. 'I'll just clean the cut for you. Let's go.'

'Do you think . . .' Élise said. 'I mean, would it be best if Florence didn't leave the house for a few days?'

'Let's talk about what to do after I've seen to her leg. Okay, Florence?'

CHAPTER 61

Hélène

Hugo had said they wouldn't make an early start so, still at home, Hélène flung the kitchen window wide open and then proceeded to gaze at her sister, who was busy wiping the table. 'Is there nothing we can do about Violette and her little boy?' she asked her.

Élise stopped wiping and glanced up then she shook her head. 'Not just now, I'm afraid.'

'Are you sure? Have you seen Suzanne?'

Élise shook her head. A gust of window blew the curtains about. 'For goodness sake, shut the window,' she said. 'It's getting windy again.'

'But it's stuffy inside,' Hélène replied, though she closed the window anyway. 'I'll open the back door instead.'

Élise shrugged and finished off what she was doing and then went to the sink to rinse out the cloth.

'I called at Violette's house but there was no reply,' Hélène said. 'They must still be held captive at the chateau.'

Élise folded the cloth over the sink to dry. 'Well, we can only pray they haven't come to any harm.'

'I wish there were something I could do. I hate not knowing.'

Élise swatted at a fly but missed it. 'Hélène, there isn't anything we can do. Wishing won't change it. I know it's awful, but the focus is on preparing for the next few days. I tried, but nobody is free to do anything else.'

Hélène nodded and couldn't help thinking about what had happened the last time they attempted a rescue.

'Have you heard anything from Jack?' she asked, glancing at Élise.

'Yes. He's back.'

Hélène's heart lifted. 'Really? You saw him?'

'Yesterday.'

'You didn't tell me.'

'It was a planning meeting. I'm not really allowed to say.'

'Well, did he say anything about Marie?'

'Only that it went well. She had good guides. The best.'

'Oh, thank God. I'm so glad.' And she thought how relieved Hugo would be. Marie's absence had been hard on the old doctor, even though he always put a brave face on it and continued to put everyone before himself.

'There's going to be a big push,' Élise said after a moment. 'As soon as we know where the Allies have landed. Jack's heavily involved.'

'Right. Did he send a message for me?'

'No but . . . look, Hélène, as I said, it was a planning meeting not a chat. He wouldn't have said anything personal; you know. He thinks the Das Reich, a huge SS division, will be moving through this area to try to fight the Allies.'

Hélène couldn't meet her eyes. It wasn't easy to talk about Jack. 'Fair enough,' she said. 'Look, I need to let Hugo know the news about Marie.'

'Sure. Give him my best.'

Hélène gathered her things and headed into the village. Hugo had been desperate for news of Marie and now she had something to relate, Hélène didn't want to delay a moment longer. Florence's friend Lucille was just crossing the square as Hélène arrived and she raised a hand to wave, but the girl swiftly turned on her heels and retraced her footsteps. Hélène sighed, wishing Florence hadn't mentioned anything to her about having a German father.

As she neared the surgery, she heard muted cheering. She pushed open the door and saw Hugo and Pascal, the clerk, grinning like Cheshire cats and Leo, the policeman throwing his hat up into the air. Arlo was there too, with an arm around his wife, Justine, and Madame Deschamps and her daughter Amelie were wide-eyed and glowing. She spotted that each one of them held a glass and saw three bottles of champagne on the side table. Hélène laughed at the cheerful sight.

'Oh my dear girl,' Hugo said, beaming as he filled a glass for her and came across with it. 'This day! This day! You haven't heard?'

'What?' she said, taking the proffered glass.

He put an arm around her shoulder. 'I can hardly speak for excitement. They've landed. The Allies have landed.'

She gasped in disbelief. 'Oh my goodness, really? But that's wonderful. Where?'

'Normandy. They've landed in Normandy. I just heard it on Radio Londres,' he added.

'Thank God for the BBC!' Hélène said. She knew they broadcast entirely in French to Nazi-occupied France. And that it was operated by the Free French who had escaped the occupation.

'Remember this day, Hélène, 6 June 1944. It's the beginning of the end for the damn Nazis. Time now for a toast.'

Everyone raised their glass as Hugo thought about what to say. 'To us,' he finally declared. 'To every last one of us who has lived through this hell and survived to tell the tale, and to all those who lost their lives.'

'To us,' they all repeated.

'To Allied success,' Hélène added. 'And Nazi defeat.'

Each one nodded and raised their glass to the Allies.

Hugo opened the second bottle with a flourish and the cork flew right across the room, narrowly missing Madame Deschamps' right earlobe. She looked surprised but not upset. They were all euphoric, smiling and laughing as he poured a little into their glasses.

'I have news too,' Hélène whispered after a few moments and pulled him away from the others to tell him the latest about Marie.

He looked visibly moved, his eyes full of longing. 'Has she reached England yet?'

'I doubt it, but she will soon. It's fortunate the Nazis gave up the search for her.'

As Hélène carried on talking with the doctor and his friends, the blacksmith came into the surgery and told them he'd heard rumours of wide-scale insurrection in the area around Bergerac. Bridges blown up, roads blocked, railway tracks wiped out, points and turntables destroyed. Hélène felt proud of Jack's role in it. She hoped it would be impossible for the Das Reich, the SS division Élise had told her about, to proceed with much speed. And that they would only be able to *crawl* north-west from Montauban.

As she headed home, her footsteps light and bouncy, Hélène could hardly believe the news. She realised she was crying, but these were happy tears. Wonderful tears. The Allies really had landed. At last it was happening, and she felt elated. Finally, perhaps, France could be free again. Genuine happiness had seemed lost back in the time when they had taken freedom for granted, but now it was within reaching distance again. The Nazis would be gone, not today, but one day soon. And the possibility of life in a free France seemed so much more than a distant dream.

CHAPTER 62

The next day Hélène had only just arrived at the surgery but was already working with Hugo on preparing medications to deliver to patients. Every surface was spotless and she worked with unhurried efficiency.

'There have been even more explosions around Bergerac,' Hugo said. 'Fires too.'

'Germans setting fire to things?' she asked.

'I don't know. Could be. Unless it's our guys. Could you reach up for that bottle of penicillin, please? It's our last one.

She opened the medicine cupboard and took out a large brown glass bottle.

'Best put a week's worth in each of the smaller bottles.'

'Can we get hold of more penicillin?'

'It's looking unlikely. Supplies are still not getting through.'

She nodded. 'Did you listen to Radio Londres last night? Is—'

'Absolutely. The Allied landing has held firm.'

She closed her eyes for a moment, and her shoulders relaxed as a feeling of relief flooded her body. 'Thank God. I can't imagine how awful it must be for the troops.'

'Pretty terrifying, I'd say. And they'll be soaking wet too. The newsreader said more than 150,000 American, British and Canadian forces landed on five beaches.'

'Five?'

'Yes. All of them along a fifty-mile stretch of Normandy coast. The rumour is the Germans were duped into thinking the landing would be elsewhere.'

'They said that on the radio?'

'Implied it.'

She felt speechless, almost dizzy, wishing so much she had a radio too. So she could hear it all unfolding day by day, although she had to admit the suspense might be awful.

'It's the beginning of the end, you mark my words.'

'Oh . . . with all my heart I do hope so.' She felt tears in her eyes and held still for a moment, anticipating an end that wasn't yet with them but might, just might, be soon, and then she drew in her breath and carried on. 'Are we short of anything else?'

'We have plenty of barbiturates. Pentobarbital and butabarbital. You'd have thought during a war we'd be using more rather than less, wouldn't you?'

'Quite.'

'We have enough sulphapyridine, I think. Could you check? We'll need it if we have to treat any casualties.'

'Did you hear something then?' Hélène asked, glancing up.

'You're just feeling a bit jumpy. It was only a car backfiring.'

But Hélène took a breath and chewed her lip. 'I hope whatever it is isn't anything to do with me.'

'Why would it be?'

Hélène gulped. 'The thing is, Hugo, I could do with your advice.'

He tilted his head to the side. 'Go on.'

'You see we recently learned Florence has a different father from Élise and me.'

Hugo's eyes widened. 'Goodness me. Do you want to talk about it?'

At a loss for words, Hélène flopped into a chair. 'I don't know. Yes. No.'

'Well,' he said. 'Finding out must have been a shock but—'

'I'm afraid there's more,' she interjected. 'Her father is German.'

'Ah. Well . . . let us consider for a minute.' He gazed at her and then at the floor before he spoke again. 'Firstly, it might not be as worrying as you may fear.'

'Oh, Hugo.'

'Keep her home for now. Then let's see.'

'I don't know how long it will be before the liberation and the recriminations that are bound to follow.'

'A while yet. The Allies still have a hell of a battle on their hands.'

'The thing is, Élise will be needed, and I'd rather not leave Florence at home alone at the moment.'

'Take all the time you need,' he said and patted her hand. 'Unless we have more casualties, I can easily manage.'

They both heard the screech of tyres as more vehicles arrived. They exchanged troubled looks as car doors slammed and then they heard the shouting begin.

'I'll just see what's going on,' Hélène said as she went to glance out of the window. At the sight of the village square filling with armoured vehicles – all bearing the Nazi insignia – her shoulders slumped. She stepped away from the window to look at Hugo and pressed a palm to her chest. 'The square is swarming with German soldiers.'

Hugo had turned pale. 'Das Reich?'

'No, it's too soon.' she said. 'This could be because of the derailments, the attacks.' They both knew it meant the Germans would be out for revenge.

'Where's your sister?'

'Élise?'

'Yes. Is she at the café?'

'Don't think so. She's been at meetings out of town.'

'Safer that way.' He paused. '. . . I never thanked you, Hélène.'

'For?'

'For accompanying my wife.'

'You did thank me, Hugo. Please don't worry, I'm sure Marie is in safe hands.'

Hélène knew she sounded more resolute than she felt but she didn't want to spread alarm.

'Hope you're right,' he said. 'Should we show our faces out there?'

She shook her head. 'They'll be pounding on the door soon enough.'

The derailment of a train on its way to pick up supplies from a huge German depot had been a success. Hélène had watched, heart in mouth, as her sister had sailed off in a truck with several maquisards the night before, their excitement and expectations high. This was exactly the sort of operation Jack had been here to organise, but she knew better than to hope to see him now, although if she was honest, that didn't stop her.

As she waited with Hugo, she gripped the side of the counter and thought about Jack. Since their last night together she'd felt there might still be a chance for them after all. Maybe only a small chance, but she had felt the warmth of his love. She was sure of it.

'Maybe they won't come in,' Hugo said.

Her hands felt clammy. 'I can't stand this waiting. Should we just get on with finishing the medications?'

She picked up one of the glass bottles again and began filling it. As she did, she thought about Élise's pregnancy and the danger of her involvement in Maquis activities. Yet when Hélène had challenged her, she'd simply scoffed.

'I have to honour Victor's memory,' she'd said, a glint of defiance in her eyes.

'Isn't carrying his child enough?'

Élise had stood, hands on hips, and stared at her pityingly.

But Hélène had begun to see all choices were not equal and if Élise was already cradling a child in her arms, she might well have been forced to make a different decision.

Was it possible to choose to do something that might endanger your own beloved children?

A scream coming from outside stopped her in her tracks. 'Oh Hugo,' she said. 'What's going on out there?'

He went across to the window to look out. 'Chaos. Is what.'

As Hélène wiped away the beads of sweat above her lips, Violette came into her mind. She must be so frightened at the chateau. Her friend had not wanted to make hats for German officers but had chosen to do so for the sake of her child. But if the Allies won, would she be safe?

And, as the Allies pushed forward, where did that leave Florence, with a German parent?

She heard the side door bang. Two men ran through the hall and came into the room. One, who she recognised as Enzo's older brother, a boy called Emile, was limping from what looked like a flesh wound in his calf. The other was older, painfully thin and haggard. Both were clearly on the run.

'Help us, we beg you,' Emile implored, fear in his eyes.

'Take them both through to the cottage hospital,' Hugo ordered her. 'Put them in bed.'

'With their clothes on?'

'There's no time to undress them or to bandage that man's wound. Pull the covers over them and come back here as quickly as you can.'

Hélène's heart was thumping as she did what he'd asked, then she unlocked the back door and left it open so it might seem as if the men had let themselves in that way and had hidden there without Hugo's knowledge.

Just as she came back through there was a thunderous rapping at the door. Hugo handed her a bottle of castor oil.

'Measure it out. Look busy, but calm.'

As she lifted the bottle, five soldiers carrying rifles burst in.

'Out,' their leader said. 'Everybody out.'

'There are sick people in our hospital,' Hugo said.

'How many? They must come out.'

'Let me—' Hugo tried to say.

But their bullish leader pushed him aside and marched through to the little ward where five men were now installed. The three who were genuinely ill and the two who were on the run. Hugo and Hélène followed, both fearful of what would happen next. Using their rifles, the soldiers tore the blankets from the first bed, hurling the bedding to the floor while the occupant, an old boy of eighty, shrank back in fear. They continued one bed after another until they reached the last but one, which was occupied by Emile, the injured man.

'Why is there blood on the floor?' the German demanded.

Emile instantly climbed out of bed and held his arms up in surrender. The older man slipped out of his bed and raced for the door. Before he reached it, a shot cracked the air, making everyone jump. He crumpled to the ground.

'This is a hospital,' Hugo said. 'You can't—'

The soldier turned on Hugo and pointed his rifle directly at him. 'Shut your mouth, grandpa. I can do whatever I like. You know the penalty for aiding a terrorist.'

Hélène stepped forward. 'Please, neither of us knew

those men were in here. Look, the back door is open. They must have stolen in while we were out at the front sorting out medications. Please, Doctor Hugo would never do anything wrong.'

The man gave her an unyielding look.

Another man entered who Hélène instantly recognised as Captain Hans Meyer. Hélène tried to read his expression and was relieved to see he appeared to have grasped the situation.

He gave a directive in German and the soldier pointing the rifle at Hugo lowered it. The soldiers were then commanded to arrest the injured maquisard and then remove the dead man from the clinic.

They all left except for Captain Meyer, who gazed first at Hélène and then at Hugo. 'You must be more careful whom you let in. Keep your doors locked. I won't be here much longer.'

Hélène tried to say they hadn't known about the men, but he shook his head. 'I wasn't born yesterday, isn't that what you say?'

Hélène avoided his eyes.

'Well, let us just chalk this one up to experience.'

'Thank you.'

He gave her a meaningful look. 'In case you hadn't heard . . . the young deserter, Tomas, I think his name was. He has pulled through and it is hoped today he will be able to identify those in the village who helped conceal him. His life may be spared if he can do it. But listen carefully, it is possible they may already have at least some of the information they need.'

Hugo nodded. 'Thank you for your assistance, Captain.' They stood and watched as the solider left, then the doctor started to slowly pick up the bedding from the floor. Hélène went to help him, then mopped up the blood, her heart sinking. Tomas. What the hell was she going to do now?

CHAPTER 63

When they were done, Hélène focused on her breath while Hugo patted her back and kept repeating that it would be all right. She didn't know how it could be, for of course the boy would denounce them to save his own life. She watched bleakly from the window as the SS dragged two old men away, one the grandfather of Emile, who had been a hero of the Great War and now lived only for his grandsons. It was too awful.

The moment the square emptied of soldiers, Hugo told her to leave for home. She gathered her belongings, kissed him on the cheek, and then hastened along the now silent cobbled streets. Her breathing was rapid, shallow, as she snaked through the walnut grove avoiding the geese, then ran down the track until she reached her own gate. She didn't go through the front door but stole around to the side from where she spotted Florence lower down the garden. From the set of her shoulders,

Hélène saw her sister was feeling uncommunicative. She approached carefully.

'Florence, I need to talk to you.'

Florence turned, eyes unblinking, her face inscrutable. 'What is it?'

'They are bringing Tomas to the village so he can denounce the people who hid him.'

Florence gasped and grabbed Hélène's arm. 'What are we going to do?'

'You and Élise must go to the little tucked-away house. The place I showed you, do you remember?'

'The Red Riding Hood house?'

'Yes. And stay there until the coast is clear.'

'What are you going to do?'

'I'll think of something. At least we had warning it would be today. Pack a few things in a bag and go now, okay?'

Florence looked terrified. 'I don't know where Élise is.'

'Nor me. I'll keep a lookout for her. Take some food and a warm shawl. I hope I can bring you more later but be quick now.' She didn't want to spell out that it was possible she might be arrested by then.

'It's my fault. If I hadn't insisted on putting him in the attic.'

'Never mind. Just go.'

Florence raced through the house and within minutes, her bag ready, she was kissing Hélène on the cheeks. 'I'm so sorry, Hélène,' she said.

'Forget it. We'll talk later.'

After Florence had struck out for the safe house, Hélène

threw together a bag for Élise, just in case, and then tried to work out what to do. She would stay in her nurse's uniform and hope to get away with some excuse. But if it was true Tomas had already told them something, then what? Maybe she could say she had treated him medically and then advised him to give himself up. It didn't seem much of a plan. Perhaps, before she had a chance to let the Milice know about him, he had scarpered? Not much better.

She wandered the house in a state of anxiety and then, feeling claustrophobic at being indoors, she went outside. It was a still day, with not even a blade of grass moving, nor the leaves of the chestnut tree, nor the few clouds in the sky. Everything remained motionless. Waiting. She felt her own heart pumping the blood through the veins. Felt her pulse beating in her neck – too fast. Her stomach tensed. Her jaw locked. The whole world contracting around her, closing her in. And the silence. The ghastly silence. She felt a tremor in her hands and clasped them together, digging her nails into the soft flesh.

Then, all at once, the silence was shattered by Élise. 'You know then?' she said.

The spell broken, Hélène spun round as Élise came bounding towards her. 'Keep your voice down. You mean about Tomas?'

'Yes. We got the confirmation from Hugo. I've brought Henri with me. Don't worry, he's out of sight.'

Hélène glanced around. 'Because?'

'He's the only one who can take Tomas out with a single shot.'

Hélène gulped. How insane it was. The chateau owner was now an assassin, and they were planning to kill the same boy they had previously tried to save.

'What if he misses?'

'It's a calculated risk,' Élise said, looking as steadfast as ever. 'Don't worry. Henri is in the abandoned barn near the start of our track. We have two lookouts ready to spot which direction the Germans or the Milice come from. We think from the village, but we don't know for sure.'

'And Henri will fix his sights only on Tomas?'

'Absolutely. We daren't risk anyone else being killed. Henri is by far the best shot we have.'

'So, he *has* been working for the Resistance?'

She smiled. 'Naturally. We kept it quiet though.'

'I'm glad.'

'There will be repercussions, but we want them to think it's just some reckless Maquis sniping at any old passing German soldiers. A follow-up to the derailment.'

'But surely they'll guess?'

'Maybe, but we've organised similar action elsewhere. Lots of action, but mainly shooting out tyres or radiators so we don't set in motion too many more reprisals.'

'So they'll think it's part of that.'

Élise shrugged. 'I hope so. Now listen, if Henri doesn't manage to dispatch Tomas, you will hear a shrill whistle. Stay here in the garden all day – but if you hear the whistle, you need to run and hide until you can get to the safe house.'

The sisters gazed at each other darkly. Hélène felt fearful, certain something would go wrong, but Élise clasped her hand and squeezed it. 'Come on. You can do this. I reckon after your experiences in Bordeaux you can do anything.'

Hélène gave her a wan smile. 'How did you organise all this so quickly?'

'Suzanne was listening in at the castle last night, so we had time. Now we don't know when the guards accompanying Tomas will come, but we think they'll be questioning the villagers first, so we'll get some warning. Suzanne said they don't believe Tomas was hidden in the village itself, but in a barn or farmhouse nearby.'

'A place just like ours.'

'Well yes. But don't forget there are others dotted about.'

'What if he told them there were three women? Won't that stand out?'

'He was terrified, delirious, you sedated him, and then he was blindfolded. His memory is probably pretty shaky.'

'What about when you tried to get him to safety, you and Victor?'

'Tomas was blindfolded some of the time and I was dressed as a man with a cloth cap hiding my hair.' She reached out for Hélène's hand again. 'Don't overthink this, Hélène. Relax. All you need do is listen out for the shot. If it's followed by a whistle, run, if not stay put until I come.'

'Where will you be?'

'I'll be within earshot. Now enough with the questions. We've got this.'

Élise slipped inside the house and came out a few minutes

later looking almost unrecognisable as a farmhand. Hélène raised an eyebrow at her. 'You won't be able to get away with that when you're six months pregnant.'

'I'm hoping I won't have to.'

Hélène gave her a smile. Élise had always enjoyed surprising people, not like the girls who opted to train as shorthand typists only to catch one of the bosses and then settle down in a lovely little house, with two lovely children. Lovely was not a word to use about Élise – beautiful, yes. Fierce as well. And Hélène realised how much she admired her for it.

CHAPTER 64

Florence

Florence ran through the woods, stumbling over twisting roots and fallen branches, losing her balance now and then, reaching out and only just saving herself from falling. More than once she skidded on wet leaves and went flying, managing to break her fall by clutching at the rough bark of the nearest tree trunk. She smelt the damp earth, the wildflowers, heard the birdsong and the dead branches cracking underfoot. From somewhere close came the sound of running water, frogs croaking, and the drumming of a woodpecker. Tap, tap, tap. She spotted a red squirrel as it darted up a tree, but today she wanted to get past the trees quickly. The woods were gloomy, eerie and for once not comforting at all. She only paused to glance up at the green canopy twice, and waving away the flying insects from her face, ran on. When she reached the meadows leading to the safe house, she bent double, breathless from the effort, holding her sides and panting until the cramp passed.

She circled the meadows from the shade of the oaks lining the track, watching all the time for signs of soldiers. The long grass rustled in the breeze and the meadows themselves were a riot of colour. She longed to stop and enjoy the day but knew she could not. Before long she came to the trees concealing the little house. She slipped through a gap and ran along the overgrown path but stopped short when she spotted a partially covered motorcycle. Was Élise here already? She knew her sister sometimes used the bike that had been Victor's. She approached cautiously and, reaching the door, saw it was already unlocked and had been left ajar. She pushed it open and softly called her sister's name. No reply.

At the sound of footsteps, she shrank back, her heart skittering as she glanced around the kitchen hoping for a hiding place. Save for one door, the place was bare. Memories of the BNA attack assaulted her, and the fear ripped through her. The larder! She had to hide in the larder. She ran to what she thought was its door, pulling and twisting the handle. Panicking she tried again but the door would not budge.

'Merde!' she muttered as the footsteps drew closer and her heart began to beat even faster.

'Well, that's no language for a well-brought-up French girl.'

Recognising his voice, she spun round. 'What are you doing here?'

'I was about to ask you the same question,' he said.

'Oh Jack, Hélène is in terrible danger and it's all my fault.' She hung her head, feeling miserable and scared.

'Come here.'

His voice was kind and gentle, so she went to him and he held her by the arms and looked into her eyes. 'Tell me everything.'

She explained what was happening and told him Élise hadn't turned up, at least she hadn't when she, Florence, left, and Hélène was going to have to face the German soldiers and Tomas on her own. As soon as he heard that, he sprang into action, spinning round and grabbing the keys for the bike from the table where they had lain. Florence knew Hélène was very fond of him and since Bordeaux there had been a new light in her eyes. But she hadn't realised how much Jack cared for her, too. Had something happened between them in Bordeaux? She didn't know. He certainly looked worried about Hélène now as he made for the door, then glanced back at her.

'Lock up after me, close the shutters and stay upstairs. Don't let anyone in. Only Élise, Hélène, or me. I'll be back as soon as I can.'

After he'd gone, Florence closed the shutters and locked the door, then went up to lie down on one of the beds, although first she swept away the dust and grit fallen from the ceiling beams and that now formed a thin film over the covers. When she did finally lie down, she gazed at cracks in the walls, stretching from floor to ceiling and visible even in the dim light. Judging by the debris on the bed, the wooden rafters must be full of woodworm, maybe the floorboards too. She wondered about the family who had lived here, the husband dead, and the wife and child gone. She wasn't surprised the wife hadn't wanted to stay on without her husband. It would have been so lonely, and Florence thought she could feel the sadness that still haunted the house.

She didn't want to lie in semi-darkness all on her own but did not dare disobey Jack. There was something so masculine, so definite in him, she felt safe just thinking about him. Her champion. His was an easy-going leadership, she thought, but then as she pictured him, she experienced an unexpected feeling, a yielding almost, or a need maybe. A need to surrender. It surprised her. But it grew. She felt she would give him whatever he wanted, do anything he asked of her. Hand over her life to him. Yes, that was it. How odd. Was surrender the same as submission? What did it mean? She didn't understand herself.

For the first time she recognised her feelings for Jack were complicated. Unlike the sweet gentleness of Anton, Jack's strength of character was intoxicating and since those innocent days when she had gone for walks with Anton, she had changed. Nothing was simple anymore. Life had changed her and what she wanted had changed too. Now she felt drawn to Jack despite herself. She pictured his face, his green eyes, his broad smile and felt herself smiling back. For a moment she hesitated, then she placed a palm flat on her belly, more to distract herself than anything else, but feeling a surge of longing, she imagined it was Jack's strong hands on her tummy. On her breasts, her legs, her neck. And his lips on her mouth.

She traced the soft flesh on the inside of her lips with a fingertip. Felt her nipples harden and pressure begin to build, so much so the sensation between her legs became intense. She squirmed in pleasure, breathing rapidly, giving in to the growing feelings. Surrendering. She would let him do anything he wanted to her. Take her any way he wanted. And now she'd gone so far, she couldn't access her self-control, even if she'd wanted to, and she did not want to. Instead, still feeling it was Jack touching her, she widened her legs and her knees fell open. The emotional and physical need overwhelmed her. She touched herself more and more urgently, the yielding, the allowing, driving her until the waves began. It took only moments and briefly, as her breathing gradually slowed, she basked in a burst of unexpected joy. Maybe she wasn't as damaged by the violation as she had thought. Maybe there might be hope for her after all.

But now, as Hélène's face came to mind, the disloyalty of her behaviour sank in. Hélène loved Jack. Horrified at what she had done, she scolded herself. She absolutely must not allow herself to think of Jack that way and she could never ever do it again, even if only in her imagination. He was not hers, never would be. How would she be able to look at him knowing what she had wanted, how she had thought of him? How would she be able to look at Hélène? She felt dirty, soiled by her own stupid desire. It was despicable. She was despicable. It had never been fairy tales that frightened her but her own wild thoughts, her own self-destructive instincts, and her own powerful imagination.

She swung her legs out of bed and got up. Then she paced back and forth as she worried about what was happening at home. What a terrible person she must be to have forgotten, even for a moment, the danger Hélène was in. Hélène who had looked after her for years, who had mothered her, and never put herself first. 'Hélène,' she whispered. 'I'm so sorry.'

CHAPTER 65

Hélène

As afternoon sunlight filled the kitchen, Hélène made herself a coffee and stirred it slowly. Then she went outside again, put it on the ground and promptly forgot to drink it, something her mother often used to do. Their father had complained bitterly about the cups of tea abandoned all over the house, full, cold, unwanted. Much as she and Élise had felt. Well, the cold, unwanted part. It had been an unlikely habit for someone as controlled as Claudette, but Hélène was more aware of the cracks in her mother's mask now; the places where a different mother lived inside her. Hidden, possibly not quite dead. Take the red silk dress. It had been her mother's, but how inconceivable that Claudette could be so passionate, so infuriated, that she ripped the skirt to shreds in a drunken rage.

Hélène felt as if she'd been waiting in the garden for

hours but when she checked her watch, she saw it had only been a little over an hour. The waiting was intolerable, and she itched to go inside, find something useful to do with her hands, but Élise had insisted she stay outside to hear the whistle, if it came. If. Such a small word. She glanced back at the shutters of their house, the paint flaking. They needed repainting. She'd do it, as soon as this was over. She exhaled in a long heartfelt sigh. So much needed doing and she couldn't bear to be twiddling her thumbs like this and feeling such overwhelming trepidation.

In the garden she prowled catlike, searching out her prey, only this time it might be she who was likely to be the prey. She raised one hand to her brow and wiped the sweat away. Surely it couldn't be much longer.

And then, suddenly . . . was that Jack emerging from between the trees, then disappearing only to reappear again a little closer? She screwed up her eyes to see more clearly, shading them from the sun with her hand. Yes, surely it was him, standing in the gloom of the trees, only just visible. She stared again. Surprised. Delighted. Aghast. Still thinking she might be imagining it. Would the light change and she'd see it wasn't him after all? But as she walked closer, she saw the unmistakable smile on his face.

'You can't be here,' she hissed.

'I thought you could do with some help.'

'It's all in hand. You mustn't let them see you. Please, Jack.'

For a moment she almost forgot her own name as she

studied his face, thinner than before, but the green eyes still shining and bright.

'How did you know?'

'I saw Florence.'

'At the house?'

He nodded.

'I hate this, Jack,' she said, and gulped back tears. 'But you *must* go now.'

He wiped her tears away with his fingers.

'I'm not crying.'

'Of course you're not.' He held up his hands in mock surrender then picked something out of her hair.

'A ladybird,' he said and let it fly.

It had been a gesture of affection, a recognition perhaps of this thing between them, whatever this thing between them was.

'You stay safe, Hélène. But I'll be nearby. Just in case.'

His confidence soothed her and after he had gone, she sat on the little cast iron bench feeling a tiny bit less anxious than before. She thought back to when she'd first seen Jack and his smiling eyes so full of warmth. He was a good man. An honourable man. She longed to hear him talk about his hopes and dreams. But could they ever include her? Maybe. Just maybe. She hoped he would stay well out of the way if the Germans came for her. There'd be no point both of them being arrested. She focused on listening but felt as if the whole world had instantly turned into a cacophony of sound. Sheep, cows, goats, chickens, birds, insects, trees, grass. Everything that could make a noise *was* making a noise. The breeze had got up as if from nowhere and now everything was moving too. How would she ever hear a whistle? And how had she, who had always been so cautious, how had she come to be in this position? Should they have all stayed in England, found a way to do it rather than simply obeying Claudette's commands? Her father came to mind when he had been teaching her how to ride. '*Sometimes you have to fall so you can learn how to get up and stay up*,' he'd said. '*Don't cling on so hard, Hélène*.'

But she wanted to cling on and never let go. To her life, to her sisters and to what had been their safe home. She ran her fingers along the rough wood of the gate and glanced up the track wishing something would happen, yet at the same time wishing it would not. What were the chances of this working? What were the chances Henri would be successful at targeting only Tomas before the guards had to time to return fire? Fifty per cent. Less? More? She blew out her cheeks in frustration and could not allow herself to think of the poor German boy who would be killed to save them. She pictured Henri, his finger on the trigger, keeping the boy in sight. All it would take was one bullet and a direct hit to the chest and it would be over. In her mind's eye she saw Tomas screaming in pain and clutching the wound before he took his final breath. Another poor mother's child. It was too dreadful to contemplate.

Her mind was spinning, and she couldn't prevent her thoughts flitting from one thing to another. But thinking was the only way she could stay sane, the only way she could try to sit this out, whatever the outcome might be.

She forced herself not to dwell on the worst possible outcome, the terrifyingly bleak thought that if Tomas identified her and the house, it would be the end. She would be tortured and executed; her sisters would have to flee. Her sisters. Oh God. Her sisters. Florence at least was safe at the house. But where was Élise?

Was she safe? Was she in the woods?

Hélène walked down to the bottom of the garden, from where she glanced back at the honeyed stone of their home. Then she gazed into the woods, hoping to see if she could spot Élise or Jack hiding there, but there was no sign of either of them. Which was good. Best if they were well out of sight. But she felt terribly lonely, waiting there with no one to talk to. Oh God! This was unbearable. In the presence of a tension she had rarely felt before, she turned to go back up to her favourite bench and heard the repetitive *coo coooo coo cu cu* of a wood pigeon.

And then, suddenly, a shot rang through the air.

CHAPTER 66

Moments after the first shot Hélène heard another. Then almost at the same time came a whistle. That was it. If the shot was followed by a whistle she had to run. Even as the sound of the shots had barely faded, she bolted through the garden, crossed the track and ran into the woods so fast her chest constricted, and she was forced to pause for breath. She clutched the bag hanging across her body. Yes, she had her papers, money too. Was this it now – would she have to flee for her life? She heard shouting but had no idea where it came from. She glanced back. Could it be Jack or Élise? Were they there? Following her? But neither Élise nor Jack would be shouting. She slipped between two ancient oak trees, more cautious now, intent on keeping silent, and before long she reached their picnic area. Instinct had brought her this far, but fear was dulling her mind. She began to run again, following the too-narrow earthen path twisting through the woods, winding round the trees and bushes this way and that. She hardly dared think where she was headed. And then she was tripping over tangled roots, clutching at tree trunks to break her fall, panting with the effort. Every few minutes she stopped, looked, and listened. Nothing appeared to be familiar. And all she could hear was the sound of her own heartbeat and the blood whooshing in her head. Even the birds were silent.

As the light began to fade, the trees closed in. She smelt the rich loamy earth, the animal scents, the sickly-sweet stink of something decomposing. She trod on twigs and small dry branches, crunching them underfoot. Was that a different noise? Footsteps? With a scudding, leaping heart she felt a rush of panic, hating the looming darkness. The woods were alive now, the sound coming from all around. A whistling, hissing, other-worldly noise carried on the air. Where was Jack? He said he'd be watching out, didn't he? She glanced around assessing the threat.

There had been a hut somewhere here. A hut Florence used to love, but which way was it? She swivelled her head from side to side. The darkness grew heavier, the night air thicker, the path impossible to identify. She set off again, picking her way carefully but then she fell, winding herself, gasping for air, crying out in frustration and fear. Once she was back on her feet and breathing properly, she launched herself into the darkness again. If she could just reach the hut, she could rest until dawn and then find the safe house where Florence would be waiting and worrying.

But now it was black in the woods and she couldn't continue blind. She needed to keep a clear head, but the forest had become her enemy. Darkness completely engulfed her. The trees towered over her, the canopy vast, unrelenting, holding her in, pressing her down. With her back against the trunk of an oak, she slid to the ground feeling small. She heard an animal moving, coming closer. Were there wolves? Surely not, they hadn't been seen for at least fifteen years. But in the darkness her imagination was ballooning out of control and then she saw it. The wolf. Saw its eyes, its terrible yellow eyes. Saw it bare its teeth as it padded towards her. Hungry. Desperate. Her insides turned to liquid and she let out a little whimper of fear. The wolf was going to eat her alive. She cringed, trying to make herself even smaller. And then she heard a voice. Jack's voice.

'Hélène?'

'Over here,' she called out softly, choking on her words, almost sobbing.

'Stay where you are. I have a torch. I'll find you.'

Relief flooded through her. She listened for him but when his footsteps grew quieter, she lost her nerve again. Sounds travelled strangely in the woods and she felt terrified the wolf was going to claim her after all. With one snap she'd be gone. Her mind unravelled. Had it really been Jack's voice she'd heard? Or someone else? Or had she completely imagined him? She felt as if she couldn't be sure of anything. Only one thing was clear – it wasn't just the Nazis she had to fear, it was also her own mind. 'Please let it have been Jack. I'll do anything but please let it be him . . .' She whispered the words over and over and then, at last, she saw the light from a torch.

'Hélène?'

'Yes.'

But all she could see was the bright light of the torch. He lowered it and came to her.

He sat beside her on the ground and held her quaking body until she calmed.

'I've found a hut. We need to go there now. Can you do it?'

'I wanted to reach the hut, but I didn't bring a torch and I don't know where I am now.'

'It's not far, but if you sit here too long, you'll be eaten alive by ants.'

'I thought you were a wolf. I thought I was about to be eaten alive by a wolf.'

He helped her up. 'No wolves here, Hélène. But an awful lot of ants.'

'What happened? I heard two shots and a whistle. How did it all go wrong?'

'It's okay. Henri got Tomas but only with the second shot.'

'But why the whistle?

'A mistake. Because of the two shots.'

'A mistake?' She felt her heart still pounding from the adrenaline of running and the wild brutal fear that had overcome her. Everything seemed to blur, and she blinked rapidly to clear her vision. Gradually his face came into focus – she had not needed to run.

'You okay?' he asked and held her by the arms. 'You're trembling.'

She took several long slow breaths. 'Where are the soldiers now – in the village?'

'No, they took Tomas's body and left.'

'Will they come back?'

'We don't believe so. But we can't be sure yet. Now come on.'

He held her hand as she trailed behind him, clinging on, until they reached the hut. He pushed the door open and flashed the torch around. An old blanket lay bundled up in the corner. He let go of her hand and spread it on the bare floorboards. Then they sat with their knees drawn up to their chests and leant against each other. She felt reassured his warmth, by the musky smell of his skin, by the sound of his breathing.

'We often seem to land in situations like this, don't we?' he said.

'Yes.'

She wanted him to kiss her, and instead of waiting for him, she turned and kissed him on the lips. He responded and she felt the energy coursing through her body. Overwhelmingly, she wanted to make love, but he stroked her cheek and gently said, 'This isn't the right place, Hélène. Or time. You know, right?'

'But why?'

'Look at this place.'

'Is that all?' Her voice faltered but she added, 'The place?'

He paused. 'There are things . . .'

'Things?'

'Things I can't talk about.'

'Oh Jack, I wish,' she said and her voice broke.

'I know.'

He was right, of course, it was a ludicrous idea, but still it felt like a rejection and her heart plummeted.

CHAPTER 67

Hélène was first to wake, not that she'd slept much. She scrambled up feeling stiff and sore, then she tapped Jack on the shoulder. He didn't stir so she shook him gently.

'Jack,' she murmured.

He was instantly on his feet, eyes fully alert as he glanced about. She got the impression that, under duress, he would always wake like this. 'Everything all right?' he asked.

She smiled brightly, wanting to keep her feelings under control. 'It's all right. Everything is fine. I'm fine.'

'Good.'

She took a step towards the door and twisted round to dart a look at him. 'But I want to go home now. Is it safe, do you think?'

'I reckon so. In any case, I'll come with you.'

'No. Could you go to the safe house and bring Florence back instead? She's been there all this time and I don't know if Élise made it there or not.'

'Sure. Will you find your way home?'

She opened the hut door and looked around, then glanced back over her shoulder. 'Why don't you point me in the direction of the picnic area? I'll know my way from there. I know these woods quite well. I can't understand how I got so lost.'

'Fear and the dark will do it every time.'

'I was bloody terrified, to be honest,' she said as she brushed dead leaves from her clothes.

'You have twigs in your hair. Here let me.' He stood behind her and gently picked out several stems, a few shoots and a couple of leaves, stretching his hand over her head to show them before letting them drop to the ground. Then he turned her around to examine her face and kissed the tip of her nose. 'I think you'll do.'

They both went outside. He pointed to a gap between two large oak trees. 'Go through there and then it's pretty direct. Just follow your nose.'

'And you'll bring Florence straight back?'

'Of course.'

He came across and hugged her for a moment before leaving.

Hélène walked in the direction he'd indicated, soon found the picnic area and carried on. There was little wind now and the woods felt harmless, full of life and light. The air smelt aromatic and she savoured it, filling her lungs with its sweetness. How good it felt to be alive. Then she glanced up at the canopy where the leaves, lit by the early sun, glittered and whispered. She stepped over tree roots, possibly the same ones that had tripped her up the night before, and felt ashamed of how terrified she'd been. But alongside the shame, a feeling of reprieve was taking hold. She had worried so much about it and, of course, it was truly appalling that he'd had to die, but they need have no fear of Tomas identifying them any more.

As she opened their gate and walked up to the house, the relief at being home and being safe almost took her breath away. She felt dizzy and light-headed and leant against the door until she could breathe properly. After a few minutes she opened it and went inside. All she needed was Florence to be home and it would be over. She realised her stomach was growling and she was absolutely starving, so put the water on for a tisane and then found the biscuits Florence had made a couple of days before.

She opened the tin then laid several biscuits on a blue patterned plate, one of Florence's favourites. There were enough biscuits for three of them. Herself, Florence, and Jack. She knew not to worry too much about Élise just now. These days her sister was here, there and everywhere, living a different life, and could not account for all her movements. Hélène could only pray she would come to no harm.

She went into the laundry room to wash and then nipped upstairs for clean clothes. It was a warm day, so she chose a pretty polka-dot dress in shades of blue. As she brushed her hair, she told herself she was just thankful to be home and it was nothing to do with hoping Jack might stay for breakfast. She picked a pair of silver earrings from a small velvet-lined box in her top drawer and held them up against her ears. They were shell-shaped with a tiny diamond at the heart, but still quite discreet. She shook her head and put them away again. Too obvious, she thought. Jack might not notice but Florence would and might well say something. She paused. 'Oh, to hell with it,' she muttered, fed up with being so careful and always trying to second-guess the outcome. What had happened to the artist in her, dormant for too long? Why not wear the damn earrings? It was time she did more of what *she* wanted. She took the earrings out again and slipped the hooks through her lobes, and turning her head from side to side to admire them in her dressing table mirror, she felt good. 'From now on,' she declared, but hearing footsteps on the stairs she paused. Moments later, Florence rushed in, bent over, and flung her arms about her.

After a moment Florence drew back and Hélène saw something flit across her face. Awkwardness? Guilt? Her sister rarely looked like that.

But now Florence was speaking all in a rush. 'Thank God you're all right, Hélène. I was alone all night and didn't know what had happened. It was awful.' She glanced around. 'Who were you talking to?'

'Myself, darling. I was just talking to myself.'

'I saw you laid the table for breakfast. I could eat a horse.'

'Were you scared in that house?'

'The darkness was the worst thing. And you know how your imagination can go crazy in the night when you can't sleep.'

Hélène got to her feet and reached out her hand to her sister. 'I most certainly do.'

'I was worried when you didn't come. I thought you'd been arrested. Where were you?'

'In the woods.'

'All night?'

Hélène nodded.

'On your own.'

'At first. But then Jack found me, thank goodness.'

Florence gave her a look that Hélène couldn't decipher.

'Did he stay with you all night?' her sister asked.

'In the hut. Yes. Is he downstairs now?'

'No. He had to go. Sorry.'

'That's a pity,' Hélène said, hiding her disappointment and glad her voice sounded steadier than she had expected. 'I wanted to thank him. But never mind, let's go down.'

They went down to the kitchen where Florence immediately sat and devoured two biscuits while Hélène, who had felt so hungry before, just stared at them. 'They got Tomas you know. He is dead.'

Florence gulped but then tears began to roll down her face and Hélène stared at the table, giving her sister space. After a few minutes Florence wiped her eyes with her sleeve and sniffed. 'I so wanted to save him.'

'I know. I feel dreadful about it too.'

'It's such a relief he can't identify us now, but I'm sad too and I feel guilty.'

'You did your best to help him.'

Florence shook her head. 'I shouldn't have. I was naive

back then, but now I realise how stupid I was. I put us all in danger and I'd never have forgiven myself if . . .'

'Wait,' Hélène interjected. 'It didn't come to that and we're all fine. And remember Tomas would have been executed as a deserter anyway.'

'I know he was German, but . . .' She looked up at Hélène with unfathomable eyes. 'So am I . . . now.'

Hélène gazed back at her and her eyes tingled with unshed tears. It had been staring her in the face and she'd known, of course she'd known, but she hadn't wanted to focus on what it was going to mean for them all. Now, all at once, she confronted the reality of how impossible it would be for Florence to go on living there.

CHAPTER 68

Élise

On the morning of 8 June, it was blisteringly hot and dusty. Élise was with Leo at the police station going over their plans to keep everyone safe – identifying where they could hide and so on – when he received a phone call. He spoke little but nodded a few times, his eyes anxious.

'What?' she asked as he put down the phone.

He drew in a long breath and then let it out in a rush. 'The Das Reich set off this morning at dawn.'

'Oh my God. They're on their way. The fucking SS Division is actually on its way.'

'It's a good 700 kilometres to Normandy.'

'All the more time for us to stop them then.'

Élise was aware that, although it was still early, many of the maquisards were already prepared for the multiple ambushes they hoped would delay the Germans.

'Apparently they've taken the D940 towards Tulle,' Leo said.

She let out a huge sigh of relief. 'They won't be coming through Sainte-Cécile then. We are safe.'

'Some people have already headed for the forests, just in case.'

The phone rang again, and Leo answered it. She stared at him, on tenterhooks as she waited.

'Right,' he said. 'Worse than we thought, then. Thank you for letting us know.'

He ended the call and, with his finger and thumb, he pinched the skin at the bridge of his nose.

'What? Tell me.'

'They're shooting civilians. A farmer driving his oxen in the fields and some women who foolishly decided to watch. And they've set fire to farmhouses.'

'Putains! The bastards.'

'Sparing no one.'

Élise stared at Leo as they both comprehended it was likely to be a *ratissage* – a final cruel attempt at the elimination of resistance.

'They want to make it seem like they still have control over us.'

'But they don't, not if we get our way.'

'Blood is going to flow, Élise. More than 15,000 men and over 1,400 vehicles are on the move.

'Your contact said that?'

He looked at her dismally. 'How can we ever hope to stop them?'

Élise froze as she heard a motorcycle arriving and then

pulling up just outside. A maquisard slipped in – thankfully not a German – and Élise recognised Mathius, the man who'd been Victor's friend.

He spoke rapidly. 'One battalion has turned west at Gourdon, which means they are heading towards Sainte-Cécile after all.'

'*Merde!*' Élise squeezed her eyes shut at the thought. 'I'll have to warn everyone to keep as far away from the square as they can.'

'Hurry,' he said. 'There's not much time.'

As Élise left the police station, she heard the screech of his motorbike as he pulled away and, systematically, she began knocking on doors while listening for the sound of engines. How long did she have? Five minutes? Ten? First, she hurried to Clément's house, and he answered the door holding his ancient gun tight against his chest. 'I'll have them covered from my upstairs window,' he said in a gruff voice. 'Don't you worry.'

'No,' she insisted. 'You have to hide, Clément. Go out to your shed.'

He sucked in his breath. 'Can't leave my wife.'

'Stay upstairs with her, then. But don't show your face. And don't shoot. Understand?'

He acquiesced reluctantly and she carried on knocking on doors. Maurice, the blacksmith, stood outside his front door clasping a revolver and argued when she told him to keep out of sight.

'I will face them like a man,' he said.

'Think about it. If you do anything so stupid, they'll take their revenge on the whole village.'

She tried to gauge his resolve and hoped to lead him away by the arm, but he resisted.

'Maurice, they're a massive modern army. A terrifying army. Leave the fighting to the Resistance.'

But he stood firm and in the end, she had to leave without convincing him.

She carried on to the hotel, to Lucille's aunt's house and to Arlo's place. They all looked petrified and promised to keep well out of sight. Several others did not answer their doors, which was doubtless a good thing. Either they were already gone, or already hidden.

Suddenly a sickening shriek of engines ripped through the air. Her heart lurched at the thought of the SS advance motorcyclists and their tremendous speed. Was there still time to get to Hugo's? She was now on the opposite side of the village, and in one of the furthest streets. If she ran it would mean cutting it fine and she might run straight into them. But it was either that or duck into an alley and hope not to be spotted and that wouldn't be safe either, especially if they fanned out through the village. She felt the sharp bite of her own fear in her throat, in her chest. But her fingers turned themselves into fists and, galvanised into action, she raced through the streets, tripping on the cobbles, straightening up and then propelling herself back across the square. Hugo stood there holding the door open for her. 'Make haste,' he called. 'Hurry.'

She ran faster still and with only seconds to spare, she slipped into Hugo's house, bolting the door behind her, heart pounding and gasping for breath.

He grabbed hold of her hand. 'Thank God! Upstairs. Quickly!'

She managed to catch her breath and he pushed her up the stairs. From the landing he led her into a small front bedroom where they could watch from behind the gauze curtains of an open window. She could hear her heart pulsing in her ears, in her head, so loud she felt he must hear it too.

He pulled the curtains aside just a little.

'For God's sake, don't let them see you, Hugo,' she whispered.

'Christ,' he muttered. 'The motorcyclists *and* the first armoured cars are here.' Then he drew back and stepped away.

She moved slightly to peer through the chink in the curtain herself and gasped at the sight of the massive Nazi vehicles clanging and clattering across the square. Please don't let anybody be in sight, she whispered. Please let them pass through without terrorising the village.

'Gun-mounted half-tracks,' Hugo said in an undertone. 'Monstrous. With capacity of a tank and the handling of a car.'

She stole another look and froze when she saw they were fitted with mortars and flamethrowers, utterly primed for warfare; the sight of them enough to scare anyone half to death.

Élise anticipated gunfire and prayed the blacksmith had heeded her warning. She held a hand over her lips and chin to stop the trembling and waited as images of death and destruction in her own village raced through her head.

But she'd heard no shots so far, only the commotion of a colossal army on the move and the awful smell of oil, petrol, dust. The noise went on and on and then gradually began to fade. She let her breath out slowly.

'Is that it?' she whispered. 'Have they gone?'

Then she gazed at Hugo as they heard a new mechanical boom, boom, boom. 'What?' she said raising her eyebrows.

'It's the trucks,' Hugo muttered and they both waited in silence as the entire unit passed slowly through and then headed towards Sarlat.

'Why Sarlat?' she whispered.

'God only knows.'

'I'm going to go out and check if everyone is all right.'

'Is it wise? There may be more coming along behind.'

'I have to be sure nobody has been hurt.'

Outside, a few villagers had crept out from their homes and were in the square, cautiously congratulating themselves on their luck; the convoy had passed through and nobody had been hurt. The air was thick with dust which spiralled around them in the sunshine as they spoke in whispers. Élise walked over to Lucille, who hugged her; then the girl also hugged Leo, who turned bright red. Élise made sure Clément and his wife were safe, and Madame Deschamps too, but as she was heading back over to Hugo's, she heard the thundering noise of the convoy grinding its way towards the village.

Élise gasped. 'Oh dear heaven!' Hugo had been right. There were more coming. But no, she realised, it wasn't that. These were the ones who'd just passed through and they were heading back towards them.

Lucille screamed. Leo grabbed her and together they ran for cover in the police station. A few other villagers seemed transfixed. Élise yelled at them to move and then she ran herself, making it to Hugo's and, only just in time, raced upstairs to join him.

As the advance motorcycles swept in, she didn't know if everyone had managed to reach safety. And now, from the window, she could see the whole of the German unit returning.

As she stared out, she saw Maurice Fabron had not gone home after all. He was running from the smithy into the square, his parents calling after him to come back. But he was yelling now and shooting wildly. He managed to hit one of the motorcycles. It swerved but the rider got off unhurt. Élise held her breath. This would not be the end of it. Within an instant, several battle-hardened German soldiers leapt out of a half-track, swiftly trapping Maurice. He was no match for the Das Reich. Her breath stuttered as she watched him stand firm, point his revolver at the Germans and then crumple to the ground as they discharged a barrage of automatic fire at him. The motorcyclist and his bike were hauled into a truck. Then she reeled in horror as the SS dragged Maurice's parents from outside the smithy where they stood weeping, and in the centre of the square, shot them both in the head, leaving the bodies where they fell. After that they set fire to the smithy and it began to fill the village with the acrid sulphurous smell of smoke.

Her heart ached when she saw the Germans were now firing cannons at the hotel and blasting the windows of the bakery. The flamethrower disgorged a burst of orange fire as if from an enraged dragon. Madame Deschamps, wandered into the street weeping, her nightdress soiled and her face smeared with soot. Élise yelled at her to get back. Thank God the woman heard and escaped a final burst of gunfire by quickly squatting in the alley.

But then another shot rang out and another. Élise and Hugo jumped for their lives as a bullet flew through the window and hit the opposite wall. They stared at each other in shock.

At that point the Germans turned and took the riverside road towards the east leaving the smell of burning, petrol and oil hanging in the dusty air.

It was over.

CHAPTER 69

Thank goodness the sun was strong, Élise thought, at least the wet streets would dry up quickly. She and Hélène had joined with others to help clean up the village after Leo, Arlo and two maquisards had removed the bodies. The smoke got into their hair, their noses, their throats, and washing away the viscous blood that had blackened in the heat was stomach-churning. The sweet metallic scent of it as it had flowed over the sun-bleached cobbles and into the drains. Some of it was on their clothes now. Their hearts had stalled as they attempted to soothe the terrified old people who trembled and shook and clutched their rosary beads. Clément had appeared and sat in the doorway of his house with his accordion although he was not playing it; he just sat there in silence, looking broken. Élise went to the fountain, as they all did, to rinse their sticky blood-stained hands and as she watched the water turned pink, she shuddered.

Slicked with sweat, she, Hélène, Leo and Arlo were sitting in the café now, wiping their brows, exhausted from both the sheer horror of it all and the effort of trying to put things right. Arlo had boarded up the bakery windows but there wasn't much anyone could do about the hotel. That would take builders. In the café Élise handed round the ersatz coffees as they talked quietly, relieved it was over but terribly sad about the loss of Maurice and his innocent parents.

'What was Maurice thinking?' Arlo said, staring at his hands twisting in his lap as if they had a life of their own. 'I just don't get it.'

Élise shook her head. 'He thought he was doing the right thing.'

'He sacrificed himself,' Leo said.

'But for what?' Arlo sighed. 'All I can see is the way he crumpled to the ground and then his parents being shot. Not to mention what happened to the hotel and the bakery.'

'He was brave.'

'No. He was foolish.'

'I don't really understand either,' Élise said. 'But it doesn't help to keep going over it.'

'You're right,' Leo said. 'And at least it's over now. We must remember that, and we have to look to the future.'

Arlo looked at him with sad, doubtful eyes. 'Do we?'

'Come on, Arlo,' Leo said. 'It's not like you to be so

gloomy. I know what happened is terrible, but we can rebuild, heal, make the village whole again.'

Arlo nodded slowly. 'Yes, you're right. It's not easy, but for the sake of everyone who died, we must look to the future. But do you think it really will be over? The war has gone on for so long. I can't imagine . . .'

Leo gave him a gentle smile and Élise said, 'Absolutely, it will be over. You'll see. Before long we'll have our country back and our old lives too. The markets, the celebrations, the weddings, the long Sunday lunches, all the food we can eat. And happiness. Think of that!'

'And best of all, the damn Nazis will be gone!' Arlo said, at last picking up on their nascent optimism.

'That's better,' Leo said and patted him on the back.

'Well, I must be getting back to Justine,' Arlo said and began to rise

Just then there was a knock at the door and Élise opened it to Jack. He glanced around at them. 'I have news.'

Arlo sat down, and Hélène stood up. 'Nothing to do with Florence?'

Jack shook his head and pulled up a chair next to hers.

Élise watched her sister sit down again. She looked relieved. Hélène hadn't taken part in the conversation the rest of them had been having, maybe because she felt too numb, but now Jack was here she looked a little livelier.

But Jack seemed unwilling to speak. He opened his mouth but still no words came out. Hélène placed her hand over his.

'Tell us,' Élise pleaded.

'It was,' he paused and screwed up his eyes. 'It was . . . utterly barbaric.'

'What happened?' Leo asked gravely.

'Revenge. Terrible revenge.'

'Where?'

'In Tulle.'

'Why?' Élise asked.

He took his hand away from Hélène's, pulled a piece of crumpled paper from his pocket and smoothed it flat on the table. 'This is one of several posters pasted on walls all over Tulle.' He read it out loud:

Citizens

Forty German soldiers have been brutally murdered by the communist Maquis.

As a result, there will be punishment by hanging for these terrorists. For each German soldier killed, three will be taken. Therefore, one hundred and twenty men will be hanged, and their bodies will be cast into the river.

As a gesture of kindness, we will not burn the town to the ground.

He stopped reading and there was silence in the room. After a moment Hélène spoke in a halting voice, with a shaking hand half covering her mouth. 'Are you telling us this is what happened? The SS were so enraged they did this?'

He stared down at the table. 'To teach everyone a lesson, yes, but it wasn't Maquis they killed. The SS hunted men in their homes, in the streets, workplaces, lodging houses, cafés. They declared it was an identity check.'

'Dear God!' Leo exclaimed. 'Did people believe them?'

Jack shook his head. 'I doubt it. Some went willingly. Others not so much. They arrested hundreds of men aged between sixteen and sixty, herded them together, then whittled the number down.'

'Oh my God,' Élise said, picturing the anguish of the women as their brothers, fathers, husbands, sons were dragged away.

'They took anyone, even the local barber and his greengrocer brother, a teacher, a bartender, a street cleaner who was hanged just because his shoes weren't clean. Then those with influence in the town or with connections were freed.'

'So, who were the men they did kill?' Leo asked.

'Not Maquis. They'd headed for the forest. In the end it was mainly loners or the feeble-minded, men who had no one to speak up for them. They were lined up, hands tied behind their backs, and the young men of the village were ordered to collect ladders and ropes.'

Hélène and Élise stared at each other, eyes wide, Élise biting the inside of her cheek until she tasted blood.

'First they used the lampposts with a ladder either side, one for the prisoner, the other for the executioner. Some men wept, some screamed, some kicked and some . . . well, they twitched at the end of the rope and had to be shot.'

Someone in the room gasped, Élise wasn't sure who. She stared at the floor, willing herself not to cry.

'When there were no more lampposts left, they tied nooses from first-floor balconies, next to baskets of red and pink flowering geraniums.' He paused, swallowed visibly, clearly fighting for control of his feelings. 'The killing took more than three hours, and the entire town was made to watch.'

Hélène gasped. 'Including children?'

He didn't reply.

'They hanged all one hundred and twenty?' Élise asked, just about finding her voice.

'No. They ran out of rope at ninety-nine. Then the young men were ordered to cut them down. For sanitary reasons, instead of throwing them in the river, they took them on trucks and dumped them on the rubbish tip outside the town.' He bowed his head.

There was a chilling silence in the room.

Only Leo tried to speak. 'I . . . I . . .' But then he gave up.

'The spectacle was designed to terrorise the population,' said Jack. 'And as a final insult, a group of SS officers watched all the hangings while knocking back bottles of fine wine on the terrace of the Café Tivoli.'

No one else spoke. Élise could hear Hélène's rapid breathing, panting almost, as if she were fighting to remain in control. Élise reached out a hand but Hélène shook her head and groaned as if her heart might break. And now tears ran down Élise's cheeks and she could not stop them, while Arlo and Leo looked numb with shock.

The dreadful silence continued.

In the end Jack spoke again. 'Nothing can make what happened in Tulle better, but at least it's over for Sainte-Cécile. We have to be thankful for that. And the Germans are, at last, in the process of leaving the chateau.'

CHAPTER 70

Hélène

Hugo had convinced Hélène to take the next day off, and so she had, although she would much rather have been at work. Now, still in her nightdress, she was cleaning the kitchen. It was the only thing she could think of to do, the only way to take back command of her life and her emotions. As she cleaned and tidied, the house felt a little lighter and she had hoped she would feel lighter too. It hadn't worked. She had already scrubbed the table and bleached the stains in the sink but couldn't shift the gloom that had enveloped her.

Florence came downstairs and stood in the doorway watching her. 'Do you remember cinnamon buns?' she said.

Hélène straightened up and sniffed the air.

'They are the first thing I'm going to bake the moment I get my hands on some decent flour.'

'Then what?'

'Then the stickiest, sweetest, gooiest almond croissants you can imagine.'

Hélène's mouth watered.

'We were lucky to escape the worst,' Florence said. 'What happened in Tulle is unspeakable, but our village got off lightly.'

Hélène knew that was true, but couldn't feel so positive.

'Maybe we'll be able to get back to something like normal life before too long,' Florence added.

Hélène held back her feelings of dismay. Her sister was right, but at what a terrible cost, and in the meantime, she had to go on cleaning or nothing good would happen. With increased vigour, she swept the floor, filled a bucket, and then began mopping.

'Stop it, Hélène,' Florence said. 'We should try to do something nice today. Something positive. To make us feel better.'

'Cleaning makes me feel better,' Hélène said, but broke off from mopping. 'Did you have something in mind?'

'No. I just need to do something. Anything.' She gazed at Hélène. 'Is it awful to feel kind of relieved it was Tulle and not us. Is that too terrible to admit?'

Hélène shook her head. 'No. I feel it too.'

'And then I feel guilty for feeling relieved.'

'Me too.'

The evening before, after Hélène had told Florence what had happened in Tulle, her sister had lit candles and insisted they hold a vigil for everyone who had died, and they'd both stayed up half the night. Now, despite being bone-tired, Hélène felt she had to keep going.

'We can't go out, you know. It's best to stay home.'

'But they've gone now, haven't they? The Nazis.'

Hélène shook her head and started mopping again. 'Maybe. But it's safer to stay put for now.'

'Aren't you tired of always doing the safe thing?'

Hélène paused and thought about it. 'Well yes,' she said. 'I am. When all this is over, I want to do something more with my life.'

'Like what?'

Hélène shook her head. 'I don't know yet.'

'I feel like that too.'

'Like you don't know?'

'Well yes,' Florence said. 'But I meant I want to do something different. Something that counts. Maybe I'll become a dancer or an explorer or a detective.'

'That's a funny old mix of things,' Hélène said and laughed.

'Yes, but you get my point.'

'I do.'

'And we'll have plenty of time to do all sorts of wonderful things soon.'

Hélène straightened up. 'Yes. You're right. I do believe that. For a moment there I'd forgotten it. We must have faith. *And* I'm hoping for us the worst is over too. Just as you said. Thank you.'

Florence grinned. 'Well, in the meantime, I'll make us a nice lunch, shall I?'

Hélène smiled. 'Now that, my dear girl, is a great idea.'

'At least we have eggs. I can make us an *omelette aux fines herbes.*' She glanced around the kitchen. 'I've got chives, tarragon, chervil and parsley. Perfect. Are you hungry now?'

Hélène considered it. She hadn't eaten for twenty-four hours and she realised she was absolutely ravenous. 'I could eat a horse,' she said.

'Well I can't offer you that, but it will be a mighty delicious omelette. Leave the floor now. You can help with lunch. Honestly, you and your cleaning!'

'And you and your cooking.'

'What about Élise?' Florence said.

'Well, Élise and her . . .'

'Risk-taking,' they said together and laughed.

Hélène put away her mop and bucket and Florence collected her tools and ingredients and for now it did feel as if normal life might resume.

'Chop those herbs and combine them in that bowl, okay?' Florence said and pushed a blue and white bowl across to Hélène. 'Is Élise here too?'

'No.'

'Where is she then?'

Hélène shook her head and blew out her cheeks. 'You know Élise.'

After choosing four of the six eggs she had laid in a shallow bowl, Florence broke the shells against her chopping board, then slid the eggs into a white bowl. She whisked them, adding the herbs, salt and pepper with her usual flair, then heated a knob of butter in a cast iron pan until it was foaming.

How confident Florence was, Hélène thought. Like a master chef. She had become stronger, more determined, but still Hélène couldn't shake her concern over how her sister would fare after the war.

Once the foam died down, Florence poured in half the egg mixture and shook the omelette pan. Once it began to bubble, she spun the egg, keeping it moving to draw the cooked egg into the centre in order to heat the uncooked egg at the edges.

'Ta dah!' she said after a few minutes, looking pleased with herself. 'Here's yours.' When she shook the pan, the edges rolled together perfectly. She turned the omelette onto a plate and passed it to Hélène. Then Florence moved back to the stove to cook the second omelette.

As Hélène lifted a forkful to her mouth, they heard a motorbike and listened for footsteps. *What can it be now?* she thought. *I need my lunch.* A moment later the door burst open and Élise rushed in. 'Quick. Hélène, you have to come to the chateau.'

'Now? Why?'

'I'll explain on the way. Hurry!'

'I'm not dressed.'

'For Christ's sake, Hélène. Just put a coat over your nightie.'

'No. I'll throw something on. You'll have to wait.'

'There's no time. You have to come now! It's Violette.'

Élise went into the hall and grabbed a thin summer jacket. 'Here,' she said as she came back in. 'Put it on. Let's go.'

'What about me?' Florence said.

'I can't get three on the bike.' She glanced at the table. 'You stay and eat your omelette.'

Hélène threw the jacket over her shoulders and slipped on a pair of sandals. They ran outside, climbed onto the bike, Élise gunned the engine and then accelerated at speed. She took the rough country route, yelling at Hélène to hold on tight. She tried to explain what was happening at the chateau, but the engine noise and the wind in her ears made it impossible for Hélène to hear.

Hélène felt anxious as Élise took the bike at breakneck speed, but she was also worrying about what might have happened to Violette that demanded such urgency. As they drew nearer, she was expecting Élise to take the back route to the chateau, but instead she took the main tree-lined driveway which, of course, was much quicker.

'The Germans have gone,' Élise shouted.

'What?'

She turned her head and swerved. 'The Germans have gone. From the chateau. All of them. I've been there.'

This time Hélène heard her, shouted out 'Hurrah,' and then, 'Keep your eyes on the road, for goodness' sake.'

Élise pulled up outside the huge front door which had been left wide open, and then she shut off the engine. They got down and hurried into the main hall.

'Where?' Hélène asked, glancing round.

'Follow me.'

Élise led her towards the dining room and Hélène immediately saw a body lying just inside the doorway. She stooped to look, gasping when she recognised Captain

Meyer, his blue eyes blank and a red stain in the middle of his chest.

'Oh, no,' she whispered, appalled. 'He was a good man. He helped us. Who did this?'

'Violette. But this isn't the worst of it.'

'Violette? Dear God. Why?'

'I can't explain . . . It's too terrible, you'll have to see for yourself. Quickly. come on.'

Hélène followed Élise through another room and towards an enclosed courtyard, a real suntrap Suzanne liked to use in the spring. She heard someone groaning. A terrible vulpine howl, worse than a groan, more anguished, more desperate and then when she entered the courtyard, she saw Suzanne sitting with her back against the wall, Henri lying injured and Violette keening over the body of her little boy.

Hélène walked towards her and stopped when Violette raised a pistol to her. Shocked, Hélène did not understand. What had happened? She took a faltering step towards Violette.

'Not any closer, Hélène,' Violette warned.

She looked crazy, her hair usually so tidy in complete disarray, her clothes dirty. And her eyes. Hélène had never seen such a haunted look before. Not ever.

'What happened to Jean-Louis?' she asked.

Violette began to visibly tremble. 'They shot him in the back. They were holding us here separately. Then, just before they left, they let him run to me and they shot him in the back, right in front of my eyes. My little boy.' Tears streamed down her cheeks.

Hélène wanted to comfort her but realized she could not.

'What happened to Captain Meyer?' she asked.

'I killed him.'

'Violette, why?'

'Because of Jean-Louis.'

'But surely he didn't shoot your boy?'

'No.'

'There's more,' Hélène heard Suzanne say. 'Tell her, Violette.'

Hélène gazed at her friend, unable to comprehend anything of this. 'Why did you kill him?'

'Because . . .' And she groaned again. 'Because he threatened to tell Suzanne and Henri everything.'

'I don't understand. Tell them what?'

Violette didn't reply.

Hélène turned to Suzanne. 'Is Henri all right?'

'I'm fine,' he said. 'It's only a minor leg injury. A graze.'

'I'd better take a look.'

But Violette raised her pistol again. 'No. It can wait.'

Helen held her gaze. 'So, you are really going to shoot me if I disobey? I thought we were friends.'

'I have no friends.' Violette gave a bitter laugh but did not lower the gun. 'Sit.'

Hélène sighed in despair but squatted down.

Suzanne began to speak but Violette narrowed her eyes and her face tautened into a mask of anger and rage. 'You are all so stupid, with your friendship and your trust. There can be no forgiveness.'

'What do you mean?' Hélène said. 'You're not making sense.'

The moments passed. Nobody said a word.

Then Violette spoke, her voice cracking with pain, 'It was me, don't you see?'

Hélène shook her head.

'Jean-Louis has Jewish blood on his father's side. They found out.'

Another silence.

'I thought I'd got away with it. But they threatened to deport him if . . .'

Hélène's throat hurt and her mouth went dry. 'If?'

'If I didn't give them what they wanted.'

'You mean the SS officers weren't only coming to you for hats? Were they coming for sex, too?'

Violette doubled over for a moment then twisted to look up at Hélène, her eyes unblinking. 'If only it was just that.'

'What else?'

Violette raised her other hand as if to ward her off.

'What else?' Hélène asked, a feeling of ice running through her now.

'Information. But I didn't tell them everything I knew. I promise. Only the things I hoped wouldn't hurt you.' She hung her head. 'Except for Tomas.'

Hélène felt stunned. 'You told them we had concealed Tomas?'

'No. No. Not that. I told them I'd heard rumours that someone in the village had sheltered him. They had brought us here and were going to kill Jean-Louis if I refused to give them something. He was only five years old.'

Hélène heard her sister groan, a sob of horror as she realised. 'Victor?' Élise asked. 'It was you who told them about the rescue attempt?'

Violette nodded.

Élise's voice was hoarse, almost at breaking point. 'Four people were executed. They killed the father of my baby because of you.'

'What would you have done? Let them take your only child? Let them kill him?' She laughed, a harsh bitter sound. 'They did that anyway, didn't they?'

Hélène opened and closed her mouth, too shocked to speak.

Violette began to shiver, grabbing fistfuls of her own hair and staring wildly. Nobody else moved.

'Come on, Violette,' Hélène said, finding her voice. 'Please put down the gun. We can find a way through this.'

'There is no way through, not for me,' Violette said in a tremulous voice.

And now Hélène had a terrible feeling she knew what Violette intended to do. The dread crept up her spine as she did her best to stall her friend. 'Why did you leave Paris? You never said.'

'I thought you might have guessed.'

'Not at all.'

'Pierre was not Pierre. He was Gustav Peter, a German officer. He was not my boy's father, but once I realised I was already pregnant, he abandoned me, and the local Resistance knew about us so . . .'

No wonder she felt she had no choice, Hélène thought.

'Please, Violette,' she said. 'I don't blame you for what you've done. You can get away from here. Start again somewhere.'

Violette shook her head. 'You know it's not possible, Hélène. I am so sorry. I realise I can't expect any mercy.'

Again, nobody spoke. Nobody agreed. Nobody disagreed.

Hélène felt tears burning the back of her lids and struggled not to cry. 'Give me the gun, Violette,' she said as if speaking to a child. 'Come on. Please. We'll find a way.'

And then, right in front of them, Violette shook her head and pointed the gun upwards into her own throat.

'No!' Hélène screamed and leapt to her feet, but in that instant Violette pulled the trigger.

Hélène stood with a hand over her mouth, unable to take in Violette's beautiful face half blown away – the bone, the blood, the flesh – the horror of it something she could never forget. For a few minutes the shock was so great Hélène felt completely hollow. She could neither breathe, nor speak, nor look away as Violette lay dead, her body now shielding her little boy. Hélène sank to the ground and began to moan. Élise came to her, holding her until her body stopped shaking.

CHAPTER 71

Hélène sat with Florence on the bench in the garden, with a heavy knot of grief lodged inside her. She pressed her crossed arms tight against her stomach as if to hold herself in by the elbows.

'I thought what happened in the village was awful,' she said and let out a ragged breath. 'And it was bad, really bad, but this was even worse. I don't know if I'll ever get it out of my head.'

Florence wrapped an arm around her shoulder. 'This was more personal. She was your best friend.'

'But how could they kill a child like that? How could they do it?'

'I don't know.'

'He was so little.'

Hélène shook her head and gazed out across the garden. Despite the flowery, honey-scented air, an endless blue sky, and the beautiful spirit of this place, she felt completely undone and saw none of it. Her world was splintering, falling to pieces around her. She felt wounded, her heart beating erratically every time she thought of a grown man cruelly shooting a young child in the back. She stood abruptly then walked back and forth in front of the bench.

Florence didn't speak either.

Hélène made a fist with her right hand and thumped it into the palm of her left hand and shook it. 'I feel like I want to smash something. I want to rage against what happened, but the anger feels stuck . . .' She uncurled her fist, screwed up her eyes, raised her hand and pressed her palm hard into her chest. 'Here. Inside me.'

'Oh Hélène,' Florence said. 'I'm so sorry.'

She sat down again and, bending forward, hunched up. 'I'm frightened of feeling so out of control. How can I stop it?'

'You can't. But it will get a bit better.'

Feeling tears prickling, she closed her eyes and pressed three fingers into each eyelid to stop them. 'I don't know what the point is any more.'

Florence sighed. 'Things happen. Things we don't ask for, and we must find a way to live with them. There isn't a point, Hélène.'

'I don't want to live with this,' she said tearfully.

'I know.'

'It's not just Violette I can't forgive. I will never forgive *them* for what they did to *her*. How do we know we wouldn't have done the same? I can't bear to think of what she must have been going through.'

Eventually Florence rose to her feet. 'Come on. We

can't just sit here. For now, we need to do something, something good, or it will only get worse and worse. If there's one thing I've learnt, it's that you can't let them win.'

Hélène glanced at her. 'Because of what happened to you?'

Florence gazed at her. 'At first, you're blown apart by emotions you don't understand and that can go on for ages but, eventually . . . things change. There's a moment when you get to choose how you want to feel. How you want to be. I could have gone on feeling angry and small and ashamed for the whole of my life. I chose not to. I choose not to every single day, even now.'

Hélène gazed at her. 'You've never said this before.'

'No.'

'I don't feel I'll ever be able to do anything ever again.'

'You will. But for now, let's go inside, do something together. The heat out here is draining. Come on.'

Hélène nodded.

'I know,' Florence said, and her eyes lit up. 'We'll paint.'

'Paint what?'

'A mural. We'll paint a mural. Why not?'

Hélène wiped her eyes. 'Really? I don't think . . .'

But Florence was smiling at her and reaching out a hand. 'We'll paint beautiful sunflowers on the kitchen walls. You've still got paints, haven't you?'

Hélène told her she had.

'We always said we'd do it, so let's do it.'

And so for the next few hours they painted sunflowers, until their hands were covered in paint, their fingernails were dirty, and their arms ached. Florence had been right to suggest this and Hélène's mind did calm a little. She still experienced a terrible sickening feeling whenever she thought of Violette, but with each flower head she painted she felt a little better.

'You have to stop thinking,' Florence commanded. 'Focus on the flowers.'

Hélène dabbed her brush in the bright yellow paint and carried on, the flowers blooming on the wall, delicate and pretty. Her hand moved instinctively, almost as if she wasn't thinking about how to paint. She'd forgotten this, but it felt so much better than cleaning. And the flowers and the act of creating them was healing, the sunny yellow flowers becoming symbols of hope. When had her little sister turned so wise? The only sound was the swish of their brushes against the wall and the flies buzzing at the windowpanes. Hélène felt as if time itself was suspended, allowing her an interlude of peace, a respite from the pain of what had happened at the chateau. At least for the moment. It couldn't last, but for now she was grateful.

She gazed at her sister. 'You have yellow paint on your cheek.'

'Have I?'

'Rather a lot.'

'Perhaps we'll take a break. Are you hungry?'

Hélène was surprised to feel she was.

'I'll just wash my hands and face and then rustle something up. Okay? You can use the sink in here.'

After Florence had gone into the laundry room, Hélène went over to the sink, but she didn't turn on the taps.

Instead she gazed out of the window until she heard a tap on the door. As it opened, she turned and saw Jack walking in. Hélène was not a fainter, but she felt suddenly terribly light-headed and nauseous and then, in a flash, everything went black.

She came back to life to find Jack carrying her upstairs.

'What?' she said.

'You passed out. I'm putting you to bed.'

'I feel sick.'

'I know.'

'Did Élise tell you what happened?'

'Yes. It's grim. I went to the chateau to help. I'm not surprised you fainted.'

He pushed open her bedroom door and laid her on the bed.

She began to shiver. 'I feel cold. Terribly cold.'

'Under the covers with you then. I'll ask Florence to bring you something hot and then I'll stay with you.'

He left the room and she heard him talking to Florence.

The monstrous images bloomed in her mind again; full colour, every detail replaying, punching her in the stomach over and over. So much blood. She began to cry, the huge silent sobs wracking her body as he came back in. He handed her a box of tissues and his kindness made her cry even more.

He lay on the bed beside her, holding her and stroking her hair. 'Oh my dear, dear girl. You have been so strong, so brave.'

'I'm sorry,' she gulped.

'Let it out, Hélène. You can't hold on to something like this.'

And she did let it out. She cried for Victor, for little Jean-Louis, for Captain Meyer, and for her friend, Violette. She cried for France and all the people whose lives had been turned inside out. She cried for those who had died, and for those who had been taken away. She cried for herself and for her sisters. For Florence and for Élise, whose child would be born without a father. She cried for her failure to keep her sisters safe in the way she had wanted to. She cried until her eyes were stinging, until her head felt as if it would explode and until she could no longer breathe properly, her body shaking and trembling as if it might never still. But after she had blown her nose again and again, he wiped away her tears and she finally did lie still. Then he kissed her forehead and sang softly until she fell asleep.

She woke in the night to find him still there, under the covers now, in just his underwear.

'Make love to me, Jack,' she whispered, and in the darkness, the moonlight slid across his face. She saw his gently spreading smile and didn't think what she would do if he didn't reciprocate.

For a moment he did hesitate. Then he kissed her, and her heart turned over. She helped him peel off her clothes and then his own. He traced a finger around her forehead, along the side of her cheek and then down her neck to her breasts. He kissed her neck and her lips and then he stroked her body. She felt every touch so intensely it was almost impossible to contain the sensations. This was the moment his heart finally opened to hers and when they made love, gently, slowly, deeply, it was the most tender experience of her life. She cried again afterwards, but these were different tears, not tears of sorrow now, but of love and hope. She listened to the quiet night-time world outside her open window. And then the house sank back into the safety of silence too, and she fell into a deep peaceful sleep.

CHAPTER 72

The next morning Hélène woke before Jack. The sun was already up, dancing patterns through the branches of the chestnut tree. She went over to the window and leant out to breathe sparkling fresh air. Birds were flitting from tree to tree and singing in the branches. There was a breeze and the whole garden seemed to be moving, the air alive with the buzz of flying insects. It was going to be a hot day. For that one moment the world seemed new and she felt not exactly happy, but perhaps a little comforted. When she glanced back to look at Jack, she saw he was watching her with sombre eyes. It wasn't that she'd forgotten what had happened at the chateau; it was just for those few moments it had seemed far away. And she had felt untouchable. There had only been Jack and herself and her bedroom but now she wondered how he felt and hoped he didn't regret their night together.

But he gave her a gentle smile and held out his hand.

She went over and perched on the edge of the bed. He squeezed her hand in silent acknowledgement, she felt, before he spoke.

'Been awake long?' he asked.

She shook her head.

'Any chance of breakfast?' He glanced at the clock on the bedside table. 'I'm going to have to get a move on.'

'Oh,' she said. 'I thought . . .'

'I'm really sorry.'

She had hoped they might spend the day together and now she didn't know how she was going to get through the hours ahead, nor how she would keep the dreadful images of what had happened at bay. She glanced at the window again. The garden, the woods beyond, now seemed too hard-edged, overly bright, and she longed for everything to blur and soften.

His eyes searched hers . . . waiting for her, but she was at a loss for words.

'Hélène, are you all right?'

She smiled too enthusiastically and he gave her a funny look. 'Florence makes wonderful crêpes,' she said, unwilling to have to beg him to stay. 'I'll see if she's up. Just come down when you're ready.'

She pulled her robe from the hook on the door, wrapped it around her and left the room.

Downstairs she found Florence already up, with her blue apron tied on over her white nightdress. Her sister looked beautiful with her blonde curls framing her face and her complexion so pink and clear. She seemed sad but not defeated and Hélène recognised how much older she had become. For a moment she contemplated what the revelation about Florence's father would mean for them all.

'Did Jack stay?' Florence asked and Hélène pushed the unwelcome thoughts away.

'He'll be down in a minute. Are you making crêpes?'

'Yes. There'll be just enough flour, I think.'

Florence put a pan on the stove and began mixing the batter while Hélène dealt with the table. 'I'm thinking Claudette's best crockery,' she said.

Florence looked surprised. 'For Jack?'

'For us. I think we deserve it, don't you?' She went to retrieve the crockery from a cupboard in the drawing room. Delicately decorated with silvery grey flowers in the Art Nouveau style and made in Lunéville, Claudette had explained it was the Marguerite pattern.

Hélène went back through the hall as Jack came down the stairs. They gave each other a half smile. 'Can I carry that box for—'

She interrupted awkwardly. 'I'm fine. It's not heavy.'

When he followed her into the kitchen he glanced around. 'Good morning, Florence,' he said in a sober tone.

'Morning,' she replied, but barely turned to look at him.

'Your sunflowers look . . . well, they look like . . .'

'Sunflowers?' Hélène said and raised her eyebrows.

He nodded but she thought the cheerful yellow flowers looked rather too bright today and seemed to mock them.

He pulled out a chair and sat at the table but then just stared out of the window as if he wasn't fully there.

'What about Élise?' Florence said. 'Will you wake her?'

'Let her sleep,' Hélène replied, then laid out the crockery

and the cutlery. 'Coffee?' she asked and brought across a jug of the ersatz brew and placed it on the table next to Jack.

He blinked as if coming back from wherever his thoughts had taken him. 'Yes. Sorry.'

'You were miles away.'

'I have some tasks to see to today.'

The room went uncomfortably quiet. Hélène listened to the kitchen clock – quieter than the one in the hall – and the kitchen was normally too noisy to even hear it. Today was different, the ticking in the otherwise brooding silence seemed intrusive. She heard her own voice in her head, uttering half-formed thoughts, and she willed her lips to move, say something, say anything in fact. But the silence only grew even deeper and even on this warm morning she shivered.

Florence turned back to her batter, made the first crêpe and slipped it onto a plate for Jack. 'Lemon and honey . . . on the table? Hélène?'

She snapped out of it. 'Sorry. I wasn't thinking. I'll get them.'

Florence carried on making the pancakes but although they were delicious, Hélène's stomach was in knots and she could only manage one. She had a headache and part of her wanted only to retreat to her bedroom and close the shutters on the world.

'Have we any cucumbers?' she asked Florence.

'For breakfast?'

'No, for my eyes. They're stinging and my head hurts.'

Jack leant across and placed a hand over hers. The action was comforting, and she gave him a half smile.

'You're thinking of Violette, aren't you?' he said.

She nodded. 'Yes, I was. But not only of Violette.'

'Oh?'

'There's something I've been avoiding.' She looked from one to the other and then back to Florence, before she spoke again.

'I think we have to talk about your safety if you continue to live here,' she eventually said, feeling miserable to have to do this.

Florence gazed at her. 'I've been thinking about it too, but what else can I do?'

'Well,' Hélène said. 'We need to look at the options.'

'Maybe, we could just keep it quiet. People don't have to know about my father.'

'You already told Lucille.'

Florence frowned. 'I don't think she'd say anything.'

'You can't be sure.'

'Well I hope she wouldn't. She's my friend.'

'It's still a risk we can't take.'

Florence didn't speak but sat staring at her hands, deep in thought.

'You'd be so much safer in England,' Hélène said, not daring to look at her sister's face.

And now the words were out they hung there, heavy and uncomfortable in the silence. Hélène felt a chill, her heart ready to break.

'Jack, what do you think?' Florence eventually said.

He sighed. 'It might be all right here, at least for a while, but there'll always be a worry hanging over you. None of you would be able to relax. And we don't know what's coming. I hate to say it, but I think your sister is right.'

'I could stay at home until everything blows over,' Florence replied in a pleading voice.

Hélène shook her head. 'You'd hate it. You would feel imprisoned. And who's to say retribution won't go on for years.'

Florence screwed up her eyes but remained silent.

'Look. Nobody is going to force you to go. But if you stay with Claudette for a while, we can wait and then later see how things are here.'

'And perhaps I could come back?'

'You may not want to once you get used to being in England again.'

Florence was about to refute this, but Hélène carried on speaking and glanced at Jack. 'The thing is, I'm wondering if Jack might be able to take you to England. Nobody there will ever know you're half-German. It's not on your birth certificate.'

'They can't prove it here, either,' Florence said.

'I think when the liberation comes there'll be a savage backlash, not just against the collaborators, but against anybody they believe might be German. For a while we'll be living in the wilderness.'

'Hélène's right,' Jack said, nodding in agreement. 'It's about perception. You're already known to have a German father. No one will care about looking for proof.'

Florence tried to hide it, but Hélène saw her lip quiver.

'You'd always be looking over your shoulder. So would Hélène and Élise. No one can live like that for long.'

'I really don't want to go,' Florence said, blinking away the tears and gazing at Hélène. 'I'll miss you too much.'

For a little while, nobody spoke. This was the end of an era and they all knew it. Yes, the war would be over, but a parting like this was going to be a terrible blow for all of them.

'Anyway, if I go, what will you eat?' Florence continued.

'We'll manage,' Hélène said.

'And what about my garden?'

'We'll manage that too.'

'And what about when the baby is born?'

Hélène smiled. 'I think Élise and I can cope with one small baby.'

'Would you visit me in England?' Florence said with tears in her eyes.

'Of course. Just as soon as we can.'

Hélène gazed at her sister, her eyes burning too. Then Florence burst into tears and left the room.

'How soon will she have to go?' Hélène asked him.

'Tomorrow before dawn,' he said with a sigh.

She stared at him aghast. 'So soon?'

'I already have my orders to leave.'

She felt shocked by that too. 'You mean you were leaving anyway. You didn't say.'

'I couldn't bear to mention it last night. This is the first chance I've had to say.'

'You weren't going to say goodbye?'

'Of course I was.'

There was an uneasy silence.

'So, what do you think about Florence?' Hélène said, holding his gaze.

'We'll get her out across the mountains to Spain.'

'Oh. I wasn't expecting that. Can't you arrange an airlift?'

He shook his head. 'Too much going on for anyone to worry about how I get back home. The country will still be crawling with Germans, especially around Bordeaux, so the mountains will be the only way for me, and for Florence.'

'Will she cope with it?'

'It won't be easy. Even with some of the Germans moving north, we're still at war. I have my motorcycle to get us to the mountains, although petrol may a bit of an issue.'

'Élise will help with that.'

Hélène thought about it. She had looked after Florence, mothered her for seven years, but now, suddenly, she was going to have to let her go.

'You will take care of her, Jack?' she said.

'Of course. The very best care.'

Then, feeling her heart truly breaking now, and her headache intensifying, she pushed back her chair and walked out of the room, into the garden and then into the woods. It hurt. It hurt so much. She loved her sister and couldn't bear for her not be in her life. She would miss her more than she could say and it was inconceivable that after everything else, this should be happening.

She reached the picnic area and lay on the ground looking up through the canopy, listening to the birds and thinking of the seven years they had spent together here, how they had grown and changed and developed. All the fun they'd shared and all the sorrow. How strong they had become and how strong their bond was. But it wasn't the end. It couldn't be.

When Hélène arrived home an hour or so later, she bumped into Élise who was on her way out.

'You've heard, then?'

'Florence told me. It is for the best – you're right. Don't feel too bad.'

She reached out a hand and Hélène squeezed it.

'Look I'm sorry, but I have to go out. Shouldn't be too long.'

Hélène went inside and climbed the stairs with a heavy heart and found Florence in her room with all her clothes laid out on her bed. From the door Hélène could see she had made small piles of different items. Dresses in one pile, underwear in another and so on. She looked up as Hélène entered the room and then stretched.

'Argh! I don't know what to take,' she said, and Hélène could see how valiantly she was trying to be cheerful.

'You won't be able to take all that, I'm afraid.'

'Are you sure?'

Hélène sucked in the air through her teeth and nodded.

'By the way, Jack has gone out. He said we have to leave early even before the sun comes up . . .' Her voice broke. 'It's tomorrow, Hélène, tomorrow.'

Hélène nodded then watched as Florence took a sharp breath in and pulled herself together.

'He wants to make sure Claude has everything he needs.

He says there may be a few more battles here, but eventually the Germans will give up and completely withdraw from the Dordogne.'

'Do you know where Élise was going? I saw her but she didn't say.'

'She went to commiserate with families who lost someone to the Das Reich.'

'Fair enough,' Hélène said and turned away to hide her face.

She had hoped to spend some time with Jack on what would be his last day there, but then she comforted herself with the thought of the night. And, of course, she was incredibly glad to be able to spend the day with Florence. Her heart lurched at the thought of her leaving. How could this be her last day with her little sister?

Florence was standing still and when Hélène turned back, she smiled at her. 'You like Jack, don't you?' she said.

Hélène smiled.

'And you spent the night together.'

'Yes.'

'Well, I'm happy for you.'

Florence bent over the bed and began humming as she started moving clothes around haphazardly.

Hélène stopped her. 'Come on, we need to make proper decisions.'

Then she then got to work choosing suitable clothes for a trek across the mountains and for the remainder of an English summer. Florence looked on in dismay as Hélène removed all the pretty skirts and dresses and put them in a separate 'not to go' pile.

'But I'll need dresses.'

'You won't have room for them in your bag.'

'Please, Hélène.'

Hélène sighed and gave in. 'Okay, you can have one. You've got to be practical and it will be chilly in the mountains at night. Maybe I'll be able to send more of your clothes on later.'

Florence seemed to accept the situation. It seemed her unworldly sister really had gained a grain of common sense as well as wisdom.

Hélène neatly folded the few items she deemed necessary: one dress, a pair of shorts, a blouse, and a change of underwear. She dug out her old duffle bag and began slipping the clothes into it. Then she went to fetch a small towel, a bar of soap, a toothbrush, and a hairbrush.

'Now what are you going to wear for the journey?'

Florence blinked rapidly, looking stricken, as if it had finally hit home.

'Darling, I'm so sorry.'

Florence gulped and held up a favourite blue and red spotted dress.

'You've already got a dress in the bag,' Hélène said gently. 'Maybe you ought to wear trousers.'

'Please?'

Hélène took the clothes out of the bag and replaced the shorts with a pair of navy trousers. 'Okay? At least you'll have some with you.'

A tear slid down Florence's cheek and she brushed it away. 'What am I going to say to Maman? I'll have to tell her about Friedrich coming here.'

'Yes. You will.'

'She'll be so angry. She won't like us knowing the truth.'

Hélène thought about it. It was possible her mother might be relieved, or she might be embarrassed. She might even deny it or invent a half-truth. After all, she'd fed them lie after lie and forced herself into a life that didn't fit for so long.

'What are you thinking?' Florence said.

'That it won't be easy for her.'

'If you don't reveal something important that affects other people, is that still a lie, do you think?'

'A lie by omission. Yes. But to give her the benefit of the doubt, she may have thought it was for the best. Remember, the truth can hurt.'

'And how do you feel about it, Hélène? After all, you were there when she ripped up the red dress.'

'I feel confused, sad, sometimes a bit angry, especially because it now means . . .' She paused.

'Because it means me leaving.'

'Yes.'

They gazed at each other.

'Don't feel bad about it, Hélène. It is the right thing to do. I've realised that. And you know, while I'm with Maman, I might ask about her sister Rosalie. She never talks about what happened.'

'Family secrets, eh?'

'Exactly. When I get married, I want to always be honest.'

'I think it's even more important to make the right choices, including who you marry.'

'Trouble is we don't always know what the right choices

are. My head will tell me one thing, my heart another. So, which do you listen to?'

Hélène wondered. Which did *she* listen to? She'd found that being honest with herself was brutally difficult. Being her sisters' 'mother' by proxy had been a major part of her identity, and as she was letting that go a little, she felt an ache inside her. It was the beginning of freedom for them all, but when you didn't know who you were anymore, freedom could feel a little frightening.

'Hélène?' Florence was saying. 'Heart or head?'

'Well, my sensible self says you have to listen to both.'

'I think I'll always go with my heart.'

Hélène tilted her head to one side and gazed at her sister. 'I just want you to know that none of what has happened makes any difference to how I feel about you.'

'I know. Thank you.'

Hélène took a long slow breath and regained control. 'Now, come on, let's finish this.'

They had forgotten to add a cardigan or jumper, so Florence opened a drawer and held up a yellow cardigan.

Then they had lunch together, lentil soup followed by a small green salad and afterwards Florence explained the garden to Hélène. She showed her which crops were doing well and which not to bother with next time. She showed her the seedlings and the mature plants, told her how to deal with pests, and explained how the secret outdoor larder worked.

'I'll miss my goats and hens,' she said, looking teary. 'Oh Hélène, I don't want to go.'

'I know, darling.'

'This is my home.'

Hélène closed her eyes. There was nothing she could say to make it any better. And then, with a sob, Florence slipped upstairs to her room saying she was going to write everything down so they wouldn't forget what to do.

Élise came back in time for supper, which Hélène had insisted she would cook herself. Just a simple vegetable and butter bean stew but she didn't have Florence's magic touch and, although it was edible, nobody had much of an appetite.

They passed the time watching the sun setting, blazing scarlet, orange and purple, then they relaxed, or tried to, in the sitting room. Hélène sensed they were all avoiding the moment when the evening had to end. She fiddled with her hair, glanced at her sisters from time to time, picked up her novel, read a few words then put it down again. The unease wrapped itself around the room, and around them. But Florence lay back on the sofa with her feet up on Élise's lap, doing her best to look as if nothing was wrong. Hélène studied their faces in repose. Despite what had happened to Florence, and perhaps not in the naive way of old, her sister still believed people were essentially good. Élise was changing too, the pregnancy softening her features. But then she felt the ache inside her deepen as she watched Florence get up and stretch. This loss felt more than she could take.

'I need to sleep,' Florence said. 'It's going to be an early start. You know me. Hopeless if I don't get enough sleep.'

Then she glanced around the room with a forlorn expression, as if to imprint every detail on her memory.

Élise set her alarm clock for 4 a.m. and handed it to Florence. They were all close to tears as Florence hugged both her sisters.

'It will be all right,' she said. 'We'll see each other again.'

Hélène couldn't speak.

Élise smiled. 'Of course we will.'

But Hélène was filled with a sense of misgiving she couldn't identify. She tried to smile but failed miserably.

'Hey,' Florence said, noticing. 'Everything will be fine.'

'You will take care in the mountains?' Hélène said.

'Of course, and I'll have Jack, won't I?'

'I'll turn in too,' Élise said and patted her tummy. 'This little one is stealing my energy. Please write to us when you get to England and let us know about Marie too.'

'I'll wait up for Jack,' Hélène said, and when her sisters had gone upstairs she curled up on the sofa and tried to read but her eyes were heavy and the words would not remain still on the page. By midnight, when Jack had not returned, she hid the back door key where she knew he would find it and took herself upstairs. When she got into bed the pillow still smelt of him. She breathed him in, then hugged the pillow to her chest, not wanting to let him go.

She awoke a few hours later to find Jack by her bedside. He held a torch in one hand and his canvas bag was over his shoulder.

'I just came to say goodbye,' he said, and his fingers brushed her hair.

No,' she said and felt her heart thud. She stared at him as he touched her on the cheek. 'I'm sorry I couldn't get back last night,' he added.

She couldn't speak but got out of bed and hugged him, feeling his heart beating against her own.

'Florence is ready, waiting by the kitchen door.'

'Will you come back?' she asked, but he looked her in the eyes and she read something desolate there.

'Thank you for everything,' was all he said. 'I will never forget you.'

Oh God, this was it. He was going. But worse, Florence was going. Hélène grabbed her robe, threw it on and ran down the stairs. She went into the kitchen and wrapped herself around her sister. She had promised herself she would not cry but felt the tears burning anyway.

'Oh darling,' she said in a broken voice. 'I love you so much.'

Élise came down and put her arms around them both. They held on to each other so tightly it felt as if they simply would not, could not, let Florence go. This couldn't be happening, and yet it was, and Hélène felt as if a limb was being torn from her body. She felt the pain of it coming and going in waves and would have given anything to stop Florence having to go. They had been everything to each other for more than seven years, shared each other's joys, each other's sorrows. It was impossible to accept it was over.

'Love you too,' Florence said, kissing her and then Élise.

She was being so brave it only made things worse and now Hélène could not stop the tears from brimming though not yet falling. Florence held out her hand and Hélène squeezed it. Florence noticed her tears and with her own handkerchief wiped them away. Then she took a step back.

'Well, I suppose this is it,' she said.

Hélène could not speak for the constriction in her throat.

Élise rubbed her eyes. 'I guess it is.'

Hélène gave up resisting and now the tears poured down her cheeks and although she swiped them away with her palm, they kept on coming.

'I'm so sorry,' she managed to say through her sobs, trying desperately to blink them away. 'I promised myself I wouldn't cry. Be safe, little sister, be safe.'

'I will.' Florence pressed her lips together and screwed up her eyes as if summoning some inner strength. After a moment she opened them, gulped and then with a look of determination said, 'Look after each other.'

And now Élise was crying too.

Florence turned away and, head held high, she walked outside to where Jack was standing beside his motorcycle. Hélène and Élise went out too, shivering in the gloomy darkness. There was just a hint of dawn on the horizon. But Hélène flicked a switch, and the back door light came on and, with their arms around each other, she and Élise watched in silence. Hélène heard an owl hooting, a fox crying, something rustling in the undergrowth and she felt more forlorn than she'd ever felt before.

Jack and then Florence climbed onto the bike and he revved the engine. Then, as they took off, Florence glanced behind her, waved bravely and flashed them an unforgettable smile. That was it. She was gone. Leaving Hélène and Élise bereft.

CHAPTER 73

Hélène went to work later that morning, walking numbly through the village, past the damage and the broken windows. Hugo asked her to sit with Madame Deschamps in the surgery. He had been looking after her, and the poor old woman, obviously senile, knew enough to be able to say she couldn't find her daughter. Maybe she didn't realise the men had been looking for Amelie since the day after the clean-up when it became known she was missing. Although the villagers had put the fire out quite quickly, one side of the hotel was in ruins. This was where they were focusing the search.

Madame insisted on going back to see for herself and while they were there, Arlo indicated they had found someone trapped beneath the fallen masonry. Hélène shepherded the old woman away from the hotel and persuaded her to sit in the square to wait. A little while later Hélène's heart sank when Arlo came across shaking his head. Amelie was dead.

Doctor Hugo made all the necessary arrangements for the body and then he told Hélène to go.

'You need to go home. You look exhausted.'

'But what about Madame Deschamps?' she said. 'Who is going to look after her?'

'She isn't your problem. I will sort something out. Don't worry.'

Hélène trudged home. It was terribly hot, and she felt sick.

For the rest of the day she lay in bed, unable to move, as if she had been felled like a tree in the woods. Florence was gone, Jack was gone and hadn't said anything about coming back, and Violette and her darling little boy were dead. She closed her eyes, but the bedroom walls pressed in, the colours pulsing, and she could not rest. When she did snatch some sleep, a bad dream woke her. Slippery with sweat, all she wanted was for it to all go away. The pain. The loss. Everything. A gust of wind blew one of her shutters open. It banged noisily, hitting the outside wall again and again. Thump, thump, thump. She knew she should get up to close it but could not.

Élise came and went, trying to tempt her with food and drink, but Hélène was unable to touch a thing.

'You can't just turn your face to the wall,' her sister said.

'Why not?' Hélène muttered.

'This isn't you, Hélène.'

Hélène didn't reply. Her entire world had disintegrated

and there was nothing to get up for. Could people die from grief? She could never stop loving Florence and Jack, even Violette, but her heart felt shattered and it hurt so much that all she could do was withdraw still further. Jack had taken root in her heart and in doing so had broken it. That night, when she finally felt herself sinking into a place she need never come back from, her febrile, feverish dreams woke her and she lay staring at the ceiling in a melancholy no man's land.

The next morning, she felt light-headed, dizzy, as if she might float off into the light. She closed her eyes and saw lush groves and silvery lakes, smelt the sweetness of flowers in the air, heard the lilting notes of wind instruments. So, this was how it was going to end, she thought. Then she heard the waves of the ocean, gently slipping in and out, and she could see herself picking up a shell lying crushed on the seashore. She felt the ocean breeze, the salt, the foamy spray on her skin and she longed to walk into the sea.

She woke again, this time surprised to hear Élise's voice, sharper than before, insisting she get up and have a bath. Her sister marched over, slid the curtains apart and threw open the window. 'Jesus! It stinks in here.'

Hélène buried her head under the pillow.

'No you don't,' Élise said, and grabbed it from her and then pulled off her bedclothes.

'Leave me alone.'

'Absolutely not. Get up. This self-pity has to stop.'

'Leave me alone!' Hélène shrieked at her again. 'Go away!'

Élise stood her ground, her eyes fierce. 'I will not.'

So Hélène swung her legs over the side of the bed but then bent forward with her head in her hands. What was happening to her? Élise sat beside her and wrapped an arm around her waist.

'I know you loved him, Hélène, but sometimes things just don't work out. You can't let yourself be beaten by this.'

'This isn't about Jack.' She sucked in her breath and then the words came out in a rush. 'Well maybe a bit. It's Florence. I feel so dreadful about sending her away.'

'You did the right thing. *We* did the right thing. I'd have said if I didn't agree.'

'And I don't know how to feel about Violette. One minute I still love her, the next I hate her.' She glanced at Élise. 'I'm sorry. I know she's the reason Victor had to die.'

Élise closed her eyes for a few seconds. 'Listen, I've been working on an idea. There's something we're going to do. First you need to wash, get dressed and eat. Okay?'

After Hélène had done exactly as Élise suggested, she did feel a bit better. She selected a faded summer dress which brought out the colour of her eyes and brushed her hair until it shone. Then she glanced in the mirror. God, she looked so pale.

'Don't worry,' Élise said. 'We're going for a walk later. It'll put colour back in your cheeks. And you need to go outside for a bit. That'll help.'

Hélène obeyed and sat on a bench in the garden, raising her face to the sun. There was no point arguing with Élise once she had an idea fixed in her head. So, while Élise busied herself about the house, Hélène continued to feel the sun warming her skin. Had Jack loved her at all? She'd certainly felt the depth of his care but perhaps the love itself had never been as strong for him as it had been for her. She watched the bees hovering and then landing on the zinnias and Queen Anne's lace. She watched the leaves of the shrubs fluttering in the breeze and she knew life had to go on. She would find a way, maybe a different way, but she was not going to live her life wallowing in regret. Maybe *her* moment to choose had arrived, just as Florence had said it would. And this beautiful garden would always be a reminder of her little sister's vision and her incredible determination to overcome what those men did to her.

Later in the afternoon Élise came outside with a pair of secateurs and began to cut several stems of white roses.

'What are you going to do with those?' Hélène asked. Her sister wasn't usually one for flowers.

'I know I said we'd go for a walk but it's still too hot. There's enough petrol to go on the bike instead.'

'Where?'

Élise tapped the side of her nose. 'You'll see. Come on.'

Élise stashed the roses and a bottle of water in a bag attached to the back of the bike. They climbed on and Élise instructed her to hold tight as they'd be taking the cross-country route. Hélène felt mystified until she began to recognise the way they were going. They flew past trees at breakneck speed, narrowly avoiding colliding with the trunks. Hélène's windblown hair whipped around into face, making her eyes sting. She felt a sudden and unexpected thrill, almost happy to be alive.

But then, as they reached the long tree-lined drive leading to the chateau, she shuddered. What was Élise thinking, bringing her here? She never wanted to see that courtyard again.

But Élise did not pull up at the chateau door. Instead she took a track that wound behind the house to a small flat area backed by trees and overlooking the glittering river which looked as if it was made of silver and stars. There she pulled up and switched off the engine. Hélène climbed down and went over to a small fire set in a circle of stones, just behind where the earth had recently been dug. She saw Suzanne and Henri appear from between the trees. Suzanne held a basket and despite his limp, Henri was carrying a spade and some plants.

Hélène stood staring at the earth, her heart juddering.

'They are buried here?' she asked.

Élise nodded as she joined her.

Hélène dropped to her knees. 'Where is Violette?'

'On your left with Jean-Louis in the middle. Captain Meyer on the right. Henri has brought rose bushes for them all.'

Henri gave Hélène a comforting tap on the shoulder. 'Hello, Hélène. Are you feeling better?'

She twisted round to look up at him and said she was.

'Would you like to make a start?'

He handed her the spade, a pair of gardening gloves, and the first plant. She rose to her feet and dug a small hole over Violette's grave, then she placed the plant in the hole and filled in the earth.

Suzanne took a bottle of water from her basket and

drizzled some over the dry earth. 'For Violette,' she said. 'A pink rose.'

Then Hélène dug a hole for Captain Meyer. Suzanne handed her the tiny rose bush and said, 'A red rose for his bravery.'

Again she filled in the earth, patting it down. And they all bowed their heads.

'And this is a white rose for little Jean-Louis,' she continued, picking up the final one and handing it to Élise. 'For his innocence.'

Hélène's stomach was in knots as she handed her sister the spade. She pictured the sweet curly-haired boy jumping up on her lap and screwed up her eyes to stop the tears.

But by the time Élise had planted the rose for the child, they all had tears in their eyes. Hélène gently placed the white roses they'd brought with them on top of his grave and patted the earth in the way she might have patted the child himself. 'Sweet boy,' she softly said. 'Sweet, sweet boy.'

Suzanne lit three lanterns Hélène had only just spotted and marked the head of each grave with one. Henri opened the first bottle of wine and handed them each a glass where they now sat on the grass.

'What shall we toast?' he asked.

There was a moment or two of silence, then Hélène stood up and held out her glass. She thought of her friend and the good times they'd once had. Then she thought of what the Nazis had put her through, the torment she must have been in and the terrible pressure she must have felt. She thought of her being forced to betray her friends to save her son's young life. She blinked away her tears and took a deep breath. The others were all watching her, waiting. Élise was watching her too. Could she do it? She paused. Then something switched inside her and she knew she had to. For if she didn't, how would she ever be able to live again?

'To forgiveness,' she eventually said, in a breaking voice, not knowing if any of the others would follow suit.

She held her breath. No one moved.

But then, after a further few moments' hesitation, Suzanne and Henri both rose to their feet, and each held out their glass. 'To forgiveness,' they said, together.

The minutes passed.

Hélène could not look at her sister. Could not think of a thing to say. She could only hear her own pounding heart.

The silence went on stretching, further and further, until Hélène felt so vulnerable, she thought she might cry out. She glanced at her sister, but Élise looked preoccupied as if she were struggling with herself and Hélène didn't know what to do.

But then, after a little longer, Élise slowly stood up and managed to smile at Hélène. 'To forgiveness,' she said. 'To our love and to our sorrow.'

Through tears of relief spilling down Hélène's cheeks, she silently thanked her sister – and Élise was right of course. If you opened your heart to love you opened it to loss too.

Then Élise took out a folded piece of paper and began to read.

'Do not stand at my grave and weep,
I am not there; I do not sleep.
Do not stand at my grave and weep,
I am not there, I do not sleep.'

Once again Hélène only heard the first words. Her heart swelled as memories of her father and of his funeral flooded her mind. She wished she could turn back the clock, go back to when they were small and her father would hold her on his lap and laugh at silly little things. She felt sure Élise must be thinking of Victor, who did not even have a funeral; nobody knew where his body had been taken. She watched Élise, how calm she was, how controlled, and she felt so proud of her. Then she thought of Violette and said a silent prayer for her friend. Once again, she heard the final line of the poem and it meant even more this time.

Do not stand at my grave and cry.
I am not there; I did not die!

And Hélène felt her father was with her. In her heart and in her soul, he could never die. Violette and Jean-Louis too. Even Captain Meyer. She went across to her sister and they stood arm in arm, gazing at the view over the river and the opposite hills. And Hélène knew, much as she loved this place, it was time to do something different with her life. Her sisters had grown up. And with those sunflowers they'd worked on together, Florence had reawakened her passion for painting. Hélène was not going to let it go again.

'It's all going to come right,' Élise said, 'you'll see.' But then she gasped as if in astonishment.

'What?' Hélène asked. 'Are you okay?'

Élise had a hand on her belly and her eyes shone in amazement. 'The baby moved. He moved. I felt him flutter for the first time.'

Hélène grinned. 'He?'

'Of course. His name is Victor.'

'And if he is actually a *she*?'

'Then . . . I shall call her Victoria!' Élise punched the air, her eyes blazing with joy.

The light of this day was fading, but a door to the future had opened just a crack, and through it Hélène glimpsed the light of a life free from war. Shining, brilliant, incandescent. When the time was right, they would throw that door wide open and they would dance in the streets. But now, as the evening approached, they watched the river shimmering in shades of gold and pink. Their beautiful world would recover. They would recover. They raised a toast to baby Victor, or Victoria. To Jack and Florence too, and to all the villagers of Sainte-Cécile.

Hélène wondered if there was a chance she might even be able to forgive her mother or, if not, at least be able to talk to her. And, as she breathed in air that smelt of hope, anything seemed possible in this new world, this better world.

She held her sister close and finally said. 'To all our futures, because now, no matter how long it takes, we *are* going to have a future.'

ACKNOWLEDGEMENTS

I'm so grateful to my agent, Caroline Hardman, for her constant good humour, her unstinting support, and for her all-round brilliance. I'd also like to thank my new editors at HarperCollins, Lynne Drew and Sophie Burks, for their superb work, and my eagle-eyed copyeditor, Cari Rosen too. I've been constantly impressed by the enthusiasm with which the entire team at HarperCollins have welcomed me and the energy they've shown for this book as it makes its way into the world. You've all been a dream to work with.

As we all know, the pandemic changed all our lives and how! So I want to say a big thank you to Gill Paul for keeping our spirits up by organising virtual Zoom 'cocktail parties' for a group of us historical fiction writers. Hazel Gaynor, Liz Trenow, Jenny Ashcroft, Eve Chase, Tracy Rees, Heather Webb – it has been a pleasure getting to know you and I'm looking forward to raising a glass in the real world. A grateful thank you to the Gloucestershire writers for being there. I have missed our lunches.

I want to thank my brother-in-law, Ian, for his advice about Devonshire birds in the 1940s and the bloggers who work so tirelessly to bring our books to the attention of readers. And finally, I want to say a huge 'thank you' to all my readers everywhere. Isabel Wolff, a wise author friend of mine, once said, 'Reading is an act of empathy.' So, from me to you, I thank you for your empathy. I do hope you enjoy this new book, the first in my HarperCollins trilogy.

AUTHOR NOTE

I was fortunate to be able to work from home. Even without a pandemic, writers usually spend most of their time in isolation, so I braved the first lockdown by throwing myself into writing the first draft of *Daughters of War*. I loved losing myself in the world of my three fictional sisters and forgetting, at least for a few hours every day, what was going on in the world outside my door. Of course, I worried for my family, my friends, my neighbours. But I also worried as I saw my research trips to France cancelled, one by one, and increasingly I was forced to rely on distant memories of the Dordogne and the recollections of friends.

More than ever, I turned to the internet, to YouTube, and to films and television for the vital information and imagery I needed to bring the book alive.

Three television series that inspired me:

Resistance – The awe inspiring French TV series about France's young heroes who risked their lives to save their country.

The Sorrow and the Pity – A heart-breaking 1981 French TV documentary by Marcel Ophuls about a French town under German occupation.

Auschwitz, The Nazis & The Final Solution – Laurence Rees's eye-opening history. BBC 2005

A few of the many books I found helpful:

Walking in the Dordogne by Janette Norton, Cicerone 2018

Fighters in the Shadows by Robert Gildea, Faber & Faber 2015

Das Reich by Max Hastings, Pan Books 2000

Defying Vichy by Robert Pike, The History Press 2018

Sisters in the Resistance by Margaret Collins Weitz, John Wiley & Sons 1995

Maquis by George Millar, The Dovecote Press 2013

Blue Guide, Southwest France by Delia Gray-Durant, Somerset Books 2006

Vichy France and Everyday Life edited by Lindsey Dodd & David Lees, Bloomsbury Academic 2018

IF YOU'VE ENJOYED *DAUGHTERS OF WAR*, READ ON FOR AN EXCLUSIVE PREVIEW OF THE NEXT NOVEL IN THE SISTERS' STORY, *THE HIDDEN PALACE*, COMING AUTUMN 2022 AND AVAILABLE FOR PRE-ORDER NOW.

PROLOGUE

The woman on the deck glanced up as a dozen bad-tempered seabirds yelled and hooted. *Fool! You fool. Fool,* they cackled as they hurtled towards her. She ducked, raised a hand to ward them off, but it was the wind snatching at her hair, not the birds. She swallowed, tasted the tang of salt on her tongue with a hint of seaweed. Was she even safe? It had been a leap of faith to board this ship in Syracuse, and the further she leapt, the further away was safety. She gazed at the shifting ocean. This was what she'd wanted, wasn't it?

The sun began to set, and the ship edged towards land. She gripped the railings, leaning over as far as she dared, mesmerised by something moving in the violet water.

She closed her eyes, felt the breeze cooling her burning cheeks.

The seabirds shrieked again, and she raised her head, opened her eyes, straightened up. How long had she been clutching the railings listening to the voices in the sea? Because now, as the sun finally sank into the ocean, the sky was darkening to a deep velvety indigo, with such a sweep of stars it stole her breath. And right before her eyes, as the ship slid closer to the island, a glittering scene unfolded, as if a curtain really had been raised upon a fairy world. Spellbound by the sight of the water in Valletta's Grand Harbour dancing with the reflected lights of hundreds of illuminated vessels, she hugged herself. Then turned to her companion.

'It's going to be all right,' she whispered. '*I'm* going to be all right.'

CHAPTER 1

ENGLAND

LATE AUGUST 1944

Florence

Jack cursed under his breath, wincing in pain as he attempted to force the window shut, and Florence coughed, her throat dry and sore. Completely jammed, the window resisted, and the acrid black smoke continued to billow in.

'There's no point,' she said. 'Save your strength.'

'It'll disperse when we're out of this damn tunnel,' he said.

She nodded, leant back against the carriage wall, and slid to the floor where she rested her forehead on drawn-up knees and wrapped her arms around her shins. Anything to escape the engine smoke, the sour odour of unwashed bodies, and the cheap tobacco that hung in blue-grey clouds throughout the train. Sitting in the corridor like this, crumpled and dirty, trying not to breathe, Florence felt exhausted and not quite able to relinquish the fear in the pit of her stomach that had been her constant companion for the past weeks.

They'd been stuck in the dim light of the tunnel for more than three quarters of an hour.

Eventually there was a bone shaking jolt.

Florence lifted her head and caught Jack's eye. He nodded as they heard a shrill whistle and, from the weary passengers, a muted cheer as the wheels turned, clanking and rattling as the train awoke. A thin, uniformed guard approached, climbing over three or four servicemen lying half asleep on the floor by the door, their heaps of kit blocking the corridor.

'Westbury,' he yelled. 'All change for Exeter.'

Just as well he had such a loud voice. You could let off steam that way. Plus, all the station signs had been removed, so unless you were a local, you had no idea where you were.

Jack scowled. 'Typical,' he said, as he scrambled up from where he'd joined Florence. 'If I'd known we were this bloody close to the station, we could have just got out and walked.'

'Don't think I'll walk anywhere ever again,' she said, and meant it.

He gave her a commiserating smile. It wasn't easy for him either. When, as they made their escape across the Pyrenees mountains, she'd tripped and fallen, Jack had reached out to save her. He'd hurt himself and seriously aggravated his old injury. Her legs felt like jelly; he was a one-armed man. Fine pair they were.

As the train drew in, people pushed and shoved, desperate to exit the hot carriage and get to wherever they were going. Fatigued soldiers longing to see their families again, no matter how briefly, had perked up, but the worn-out nurses still in their uniforms gazed about with glazed eyes. Everyone was grey and drawn.

'Platform for Exeter?' Jack asked a red-faced platform guard and was told which way to go.

As the crowd shuffled across to the waiting Exeter train, Florence caught two men behind her speaking what sounded like German. She froze and Jack, noticing her distress, was forced to take her elbow and propel her forward.

She could never reveal her secret, not back home in the Dordogne, nor in the Pyrenees as they dodged Nazi patrols, and not in Franco's Spain either. Slowly, oh so slowly, they had avoided capture as they made their way under a burning sun from the north to the south of Spain. In Gibraltar they boarded *The Stirling Castle* which, before the war, had been an ocean liner, and was now a troop ship sailing back and forth between Gibraltar and Southampton.

'It's all right,' Jack said, now linking arms with her. 'Only Polish servicemen. Come on, we don't want to miss the train.'

This dreary worn-out England wasn't the England she remembered. But it would have been unthinkable to stay in France. Unthinkable. Irrevocably altered by what had happened to her, she prayed that surely, *surely* she'd be safe here.

Once in the carriage and settled into her seat, she leant her head back in relief. She would survive this, she told herself. She had survived much worse. Through the window she could see a poster with a head and shoulder image of the British Prime Minister, Sir Winston Churchill, and a quote from him too. *Let us go forward together*, it proclaimed. Yes, she thought. We all need to go forward, and she would just have to find a way to stop herself from looking back.

Jack woke her as the train pulled into Exeter station. She felt lightheaded as she and Jack straightened up, then stood to stretch their legs and smooth down their crumpled clothes. Tired, hungry, filthy dirty, they were here at last.

* * *

Forty minutes later as Jack's father, Lionel, drove them down the long bumpy track, she caught her first glimpse of the Devonshire cottage Jack's grandmother had left him. Thatched and tucked into a cosy space between green hills, it had surely grown out of the meadow, the sun beginning to dip and lengthen the shadows of the trees all around. A fairytale cottage. And, except for the scuttling pheasants, it was completely silent. There could be no greater contrast between what they had been though than this, and just the sight of it revived her.

'A place to restore the heart and soul,' Lionel said with a knowing look back at Jack. 'Glad to see you safely back in Blighty, son.' He was tall and solidly built, a bear of a man, with a full head of grizzly salt-and-pepper hair and ruddy cheeks.

'Like a sanctuary,' Florence said, breathing properly for the first time in days. 'And the hills standing guard.'

'Hope it will be a sanctuary for you, my dear,' Lionel said and coughed awkwardly, as if that might have been a bit too personal for a first meeting.

Florence smiled at him.

'Can't drive across the brook in winter, mind,' he added. 'Should be fine now though. Had a go at mowing the lawn myself, but the grass was too long and too thick. Needs a scythe, Jack.'

'I don't think I've seen a more romantic place in my whole life,' Florence said, glancing at the teeming wildflowers, the tangled rose bushes, and the climbers cascading over the front of the cottage. 'Look at that clematis.'

'Like to garden, do you, my dear?' Jack's father asked.

She did her best to resist the image of her garden at home in France as it flashed in her mind and almost stopped her breath. She swallowed. 'I adore it,' she managed to say.

'She's something of an expert, Dad,' Jack added.

Lionel drove over the shallow book and pulled up outside the cobbled pathway to the house near a massive horse chestnut tree. 'Well,' he said. 'Welcome to Meadowbrook. But for the farmer's wife, you won't see another soul.'

'I love it,' Florence said. 'Thank you so much for driving us. Sorry we're so filthy.'

'Not at all. The house has been well aired and there are a few basic supplies. Bread, milk, bacon, and so on. Make yourselves some supper.'

'Thanks Dad,' Jack said and clapped his father on the back. 'I don't know about Florence, but more than anything I need to sleep.'

Florence glanced down at the ingrained dirt in her nails. 'Me too. And tomorrow a bath.'

Jack gave her a weary smile. 'I think that can be arranged. Come on. Ready to go inside?'

CHAPTER 2

How could she be the person she was before? She couldn't. But dead? No. All night Florence had hoped for a garden. But it wasn't a garden she found; in her dream it was a cemetery with her name carved on a headstone, torn paper roses strewn before it. Was she back in France? Or still crossing those awful mountains? Her mind felt fuzzy but then relief flooded her body because now, in that hazy state before the day opened properly, she recognised the sound of the brook outside her bedroom window. England – the early morning light here fragile, diffused. She heard water running over stones. And tapping. Someone tapping on her door. Barely able to remember the dream now, she heard Jack and rubbed the sleep from her eyes just as he poked his head around the door.

'Sorry to disturb. You all right?'

She pulled the sheets up to her chin, acutely aware she wasn't wearing a nightdress. The previous night, he'd dug out a long-sleeved winceyette one that had once belonged to his grandmother. She didn't like to say how much she hated the horrible itchy thing and had taken it straight off again.

Jack ran his fingers through his hair, leaving it tousled, and didn't quite meet her eyes.

'You didn't disturb me,' she said. 'I was half awake.'

'Good. I thought you might be hungry.'

'Might be? I'm famished!'

'There's eggs and sausages from the farm next door and a fresh loaf.'

She grinned. 'Give me fifteen minutes. No, ten.'

'Scrambled? Fried? Poached?'

'Up to you.'

'Good. Truth is I can only really do fried.'

She laughed and he left the room. She splashed her face and then gave herself a quick flannel wash with water from the china jug and bowl on the marble-topped washstand.

Then she pulled on a jumper and crumpled skirt and brushed her tangled blonde hair, tying it back in a low ponytail, unfamiliar relief at being safe bubbling inside her. She glanced in the small wall mirror, smiling at her own gunmetal grey-blue eyes, the ingrained dirt on her heart-shaped face and the annoying red spot on her chin. Too bad. She would have to do. As she opened her bedroom door, she smelt the sausages frying in the kitchen. Mmmm. De . . . li . . . cious.

She hurried down the narrow stairs. There was a brick-built, outdoor bathroom, complete with a lavatory, a huge Belfast sink, and an old bath, but no electricity. At night you had to use a torch or a candle. You reached it via the scullery, so at least you didn't have to go outside, and she dashed through before going to the kitchen.

'Smells wonderful,' she said as she joined Jack. 'I missed a good old British banger when I was in France.

He pulled a wry face. 'Sorry. Burnt them a bit.'

'The only way sausages are meant to be eaten.'

'You like them?'

'And how.'

Dark-blonde hair framed his strong face, clean shaven now for the first time, with even his sandy moustache gone. This man who had come into their life so suddenly, who had been a friend to her sisters as well as to the Resistance, had been her way out of France, her means of escape. He smiled at her, his green eyes bright with life. 'Better?'

She nodded, her mouth full of sausage, then glanced around the oak-beamed kitchen. It was small but immaculate with a cream-coloured Aga, which Jack filled from a store of anthracite in one of the sheds. She'd take over that task when he was gone.

When he was gone.

She didn't dwell on what else she might do when he was gone. Jack had brought her here so she had somewhere quiet to regroup and recover while she contacted her mother. He hadn't told her where he would be going, and she didn't want to think about him leaving, but he was still an SOE operative as far as she knew, albeit with one injured arm.

In the kitchen there was also a built-in wooden dresser, latticed cupboards with wire netting on the inside, hooks hanging from beams, another Belfast sink, and four oil lamps but also a fragile electricity supply. The deep window seat, on one side of the pine table, overlooked the water meadow in front of the house. From another window at the back all you could see was the green slope of the hill behind the house where he told her the pheasants ran about like lunatics at the merest hint of anything heading their way. Even a shadow in the window was enough to set them off. A massive, open fire-place with an oak mantel and a bread oven at the side took up almost one wall, and a heavy chopping block lay on a smaller table in the middle of the kitchen.

'It's lovely to be here,' she said.

'Can't swing a cat,' he replied.

'It's cosy, and anyway you haven't got a cat.'

'Would you like one? Gladys has kittens up at the farm.'

'Maybe,' she said. 'But I can't see my mother letting me take a kitten to her cottage.'

'Fair point. When Dad brings his dog over, do you fancy taking him for a walk?'

'Just as long as I can have a bath first.'

She could already feel the Devonshire landscape calling her. She loved the feel of the countryside - the animals she'd seen on the nearby farm, the stream, the water meadow, the wildlife. And from the moment she arrived the evening before, she'd loved the earthy green smell of it too. It helped revive her spirits and lessened the exhaustion, the homesickness, and the loneliness when she thought of her sisters, Hélène and Élise, still in France. It had been more than two months since she'd seen them or been in contact. After the success of D-Day, Germany had surrendered Paris on 25 August, but parts of France were still under occupation, England was still at war, and Hitler was still wreaking destruction, not to mention the terrible fighting going on in the Pacific.

Occasionally she caught Jack's eyes on her, glittering, intense, and she felt he was about to speak, but when she smiled to encourage him, he frowned and looked away.

Later, after Florence had finished her bath and had scrubbed her skin until it was pink and glowing, Lionel turned up, bright and jolly, waving aside offers of tea and saying he needed to get going. He left them with Justin, a young, lolloping, black Labrador with heart-melting chocolate eyes, and a huge amount of energy. There were hats, boots, jackets, waterproofs, and wellingtons in the cottage, accumulated over the years, Jack said, and she could always find something to wear.

It felt strange to be here suddenly, not endlessly on the move, and Florence found it helped to have the dog. The lolloping creature weaving around them eased the edge between them and they laughed as he jumped up and bounded off to bark at pheasants and imaginary rabbits.

They were walking along the gravelled track that led up from the cottage, with a valley on the left where the brook meandered, and beyond that a bank of beech, elm, and oak trees that marched up another steep hill. Jack strode on ahead and, as she watched him, she couldn't help thinking about what they'd been through.

'Do you think about Biarritz?' she called out.

He twisted back to look at her and frowned.

'Oh God, I was so frightened,' she said, as she caught up with him.

'I try not to think of it, Florence, and I wish you wouldn't. But I have to admit I thought we'd never find a *passeur*.'

'I can't help going over it in my head. What could have gone wrong.'

He nodded. 'I know.'

She remembered blindly following the man into the darkness and the narrow passes of the foothills of the Pyrenees with Jack coming up behind. She'd stumbled and tripped and cried out in fear, her heart pounding.

'It'll be all right. The Boche won't find us here,' Jack had said when they spent the first night in an abandoned shepherd's hut listening to gunfire. After everything that had happened, it was hard to even recall the girl she had been a year ago.

Now, as he tramped on, calling to the Labrador, she picked up speed too.

'What's up?' Jack asked.

'Oh, I don't know.'

He ruffled her hair and smiled. 'What a funny one you are, Florence Baudin.' And though he sometimes treated her like a kid sister, she liked it.

That night, after she closed the curtains at the three casement windows, she sat on the sofa, feet tucked beneath her. Larger than the kitchen, the beamed sitting room was rectangular, with a comforting smell of old books. Jack had decided to light a fire and she watched as he layered the twisted paper, kindling, and smaller pieces of wood, and tried to work out what he was feeling. But his face, as usual, was unfathomable.

She knew she needed to write to her mother and get a message to her sisters too, to let them know she and Jack were safe in England. Hélène would be sick with worry. She tasted something acidic on her tongue and then smelt something too. Guilt maybe? Could you smell or taste guilt?

But they had already lost so much of their lives to war. Didn't you just have to grasp each day and live it?

She shook the images away as she realised Jack had been asking her something, wishing she didn't keep going over these dark thoughts. But no one else could understand, no one else had been with them on those wild mountains with the constant risk of death. Just her and Jack. And then Hélène came into her mind again and a feeling of shame inflamed her cheeks as her sister's face danced in the firelight.

⋆ ⋆ ⋆

You can pre-order *The Hidden Palace* now – and coming in 2023, the third book in the sisters' series, *Night Train to Marrakech*. For more information, follow Dinah on Facebook, @DinahJefferiesBooks, or visit her website, www.dinahjefferies.com